DANCING
—IN THE DARK—

DANCING
IN THE DARK

MARY JANE CLARK

ST. MARTIN'S PRESS ❦ NEW YORK

DANCING IN THE DARK. Copyright © 2005 by Mary Jane Clark. All rights reserved. Printed in the United States of America. No part of this book may be used or reproduced in any manner whatsoever without written permission except in the case of brief quotations embodied in critical articles or reviews. For information, address St. Martin's Press, 175 Fifth Avenue, New York, N.Y. 10010.

www.stmartins.com

Library of Congress Cataloging-in-Publication Data

Clark, Mary Jane Behrends.
    Dancing in the dark / Mary Jane Clark.—1st ed.
      p. cm.
    ISBN 0-312-32315-8
    EAN 978-0-312-32315-8
    1. Women journalists—Fiction. 2. Young women—Crimes against—Fiction. 3. Ocean Grove (N.J.)—Fiction. 4. Seaside resorts—Fiction. 5. Serial murders—Fiction. I. Title.

PS3553.L2873D36 2005
813'.54—dc22

                                                      2005042899

First Edition: July 2005

10 9 8 7 6 5 4 3 2 1

Once again, for Elizabeth and David.

And for all those who struggle with mental impairment
as a treatment or a cure for Fragile X Syndrome draws closer.

DANCING
—— IN THE DARK ——

PROLOGUE

Thursday Evening, August 18

Now that she was deprived of sight, her other senses were intensified. She stood in the darkness, seeing nothing but hearing the persistent roar of the Atlantic Ocean in the distance and the soft flapping of wings right above her. Her nostrils flared at the smell of must and decay. The ground was damp and cold beneath her bare feet, her toes curling in the wet, sandy dirt. She felt something brush against her ankle and prayed it was only a mouse and not a rat.

Three days in this dank chamber were enough. If she had to stay any longer, she would surely lose her mind. Still, when they found her, as she fantasized they would, the police would want to know everything. To survive this, she'd have to be able to recount every detail of what had happened.

She would tell the police how he'd leave her alone for what seemed like hours at a time. She would tell them how he'd gagged her when he left so nobody would hear her screams and how he would lower the gag only to press his mouth against hers when he returned.

The police would want to know what he'd said to her, but she would have to tell them that she had stopped asking him questions after the second day of captivity because he never answered. He'd expressed what he wanted by touch. She'd be sure to tell them how he'd caressed her and lifted her up, how he'd maneuvered his body against hers, how she had known she must follow his lead.

As she continued to mentally organize the information the police would surely need from her, she felt a familiar rumble from her stomach. She had eaten sparsely of the meager provisions, but that didn't really bother her. Hunger was a familiar friend. She knew the ability to survive with minimal sustenance was one of her most impressive strengths, though, of course, her parents didn't see it that way. Nor did her former friends or teachers or the health care professionals who had worked so hard to steer her away from the path she had taken. They didn't see what to her was only obvious. Not eating was the ultimate control.

As she listened to a pigeon cooing from the eaves above her, she thought more about her parents. They must be frantic with worry. She imagined her mother crying, and her father pacing and cracking his knuckles, over and over, his annoying habit whenever he was upset. Was everyone in town out looking for her? She prayed they were. She hoped that anyone who had ever wronged her, anyone who had ever snubbed her, anyone who had ever hurt her was worried about her now.

The low rumble of the waves rolled in and out, and she began to rock to the rhythm, trying to soothe herself. It was all going to work out. It had to. She would tell the police what had happened, how he'd silently pulled her to her feet. Without words, he'd shown her what he wanted her to do by the way he moved his body next to hers. She had danced in the dark for him. Danced again and again, trying desperately to please him. Dancing for her life.

Four Hours Later, Ocean Grove, New Jersey

The security guard raised his arm and pointed the flashlight at his wrist. Still an hour to go before his shift was over. Time for one last patrol.

Strolling along the empty paths, George Croft pulled his handkerchief from his uniform pocket, wiping his forehead and the back of his neck. Except for the excessive heat, it was a night like many others in the quiet oceanside town. An occasional throaty snore emanated from the dwellings he passed. The association rules permitted no loud talking after 10:00, and most lights were off by 11:00 P.M. The combination of sun, heat, and salt air had left the summer occupants ready for a good night's sleep.

Finishing up on Mt. Carmel Way, the guard cut across the grass and stopped to check the doors of Bishop Jane's Tabernacle and the Great Auditorium one last time. The massive Victorian-style wooden structures were locked up tight as drums. The illuminated cross that shone from the top of the auditorium, serving as a landmark for passing ships, beamed into the night, signaling that all was well.

He was satisfied that everything was in order, but he still had another fifteen minutes before he was officially off duty. God forbid something happened before 2:00 A.M. and he wasn't on the grounds. He'd lose his job over that. And, although she didn't live in his patrol area, that young woman was still missing. If some sick nut was intent on abducting another Ocean Grove girl, the guard wasn't going to have it happen on his watch.

Lord, it was hot. Longing for a drink of cool water, George turned his flashlight in the direction of the wooden gazebo that protected the Beersheba Well. He knew the first well driven in Ocean Grove had been named for a well in the Old Testament. Beersheba's waters had been good enough for the Israelites back then, and good enough for his town's founding fathers, but he preferred the bottled stuff. Still, the gazebo was as good a place as any to wait it out until his shift was over.

With no breeze blowing in from the ocean, the night air

was especially still. He trained the yellow light on the lawn in front of him and walked slowly, trying to kill time. Noticing one of his shoes was undone, he put the flashlight down in the grass and stooped to tie the lace. It was then that he heard the scratching sound.

The fine hairs tingled on the back of his clammy neck, and George spun the flashlight in the direction of the noise. He squinted, trying to identify what he was seeing. A dark mound, motionless, at least as far as he could see, lay at the base of the gazebo.

George stepped a little closer. Just when he heard the scratching again, he detected slight movement coming from the form. Slowly, slowly, he approached until, finally, the glare of the flashlight reflected off the pale skin of a female face, blindfolded and gagged.

FRIDAY
AUGUST 19

CHAPTER

1

Diane could feel the heat from the sidewalk seeping through the soles of her shoes as she hurried down Columbus Avenue. Beads of perspiration slipped down her sides, and she wiped the dampness accumulating at her brow line with one swoop, negating the twenty minutes she had spent in front of the bathroom mirror with her hair dryer, round brush, and styling mousse. Her freshly laundered cotton blouse stuck to her back, and the starched collar was beginning to droop. The day hadn't even begun and already she was a wilted mess.

She was anxious, as usual, about being late, and she wished she had not promised herself to walk to work. The twenty-block trek was the only dependable exercise she got these days, and she needed it. She had let her gym membership lapse since she found she wasn't using it on any routine basis. There just wasn't time anymore—not if she was going to spend the time she felt she should with the kids right now.

Sniffing the sickening smell of garbage already baking in the morning sun as it waited to be picked up from the curb, Diane felt relief that her two-week vacation was about to begin. It would be great to get out of the city, away from the oppressive heat, away from the noise and the hustle and the pressure. These last months had been tough on all of them, brutal really. Sometimes, it didn't feel like any of it could have happened. Yet the reality was all too clear when she spotted Michelle biting her nails or watched Anthony's shoulders slump when she caught him staring at his father's framed picture on the piano—or when she reached out in the middle of the night to the empty place in her queen-size bed.

She cut across the courtyard at Lincoln Center, stopping for just a moment at the wide fountain, hoping to catch a bit of fine spray. But there was absolutely no breeze to propel the mist her way.

Adjusting her shoulder bag, Diane continued walking. No matter. Soon she and the kids would be someplace where the air didn't stink and the water flowed cool and clear. Maybe they weren't going the way they had originally planned, maybe it wasn't the way they would have wanted it, but it was the way things were. They were going on this vacation. They deserved it. They needed it after all they had been through.

Life, even without Philip, had to go on.

Pushing through the heavy revolving door into the lobby, Diane welcomed the blast of cool air. She smiled at the uniformed security guards as she fumbled in her bag for the beaded metal necklace that threaded through the opening on her identification pass. Finding it, she swept the card against the electronic device that beeped to signal she was cleared to enter the KEY News Broadcast Center. She knew many of the other correspondents found it annoying to produce their IDs. They thought their well-known faces should be enough for entry, but Diane didn't mind. Security had an increasingly tough job, and it was easy enough for her to pull out her card. She did draw the line, however, at wearing the thing around her neck all day. That wasn't a fashion statement she cared to make.

She purchased a cup of tea and a banana at the coffee trolley, then walked up the long, wide ramp to the elevators, passing the large, lighted pictures of the KEY News anchors and correspondents, grouped according to their broadcasts. Eliza Blake beamed from the *KEY Evening Headlines* poster. Constance Young and Harry Granger grinned beneath the *KEY to America* morning show logo. The *Hourglass* photo, taken over a year before, showed Cassie Sheridan surrounded by the newsmagazine's contributing reporters. Diane didn't stop to study her own face, with its blue-gray eyes and nose she wished was just a little bit straighter, smiling from the wall with her colleagues. She needed no reminder. The worry and aggravation of the past few months were showing. The fine lines at the corners of her eyes had deepened, and new ones had formed around her mouth, vestiges of unconscious frowning. Lately, Diane noticed she was forced to apply concealer several times a day to camouflage the dark circles that had developed beneath her eyes.

Another good reason for a vacation, she thought as she pressed the elevator button. If she could just get away and relax

for a bit, her appearance would benefit. All of the female correspondents were acutely aware that the way they looked played
into their success. It was just a fact of broadcast news life. The
guys paid attention to their appearance too, of course. But they
could let their hair go gray, sport some wrinkles, gain a few
pounds and get away with it. The women couldn't. They
groused about it with their friends, but it wasn't going to
change and they knew it. For the on-air journalists, experience
counted, but youth and beauty were idolized.

The elevator bell pinged, and the doors slid open. Walking
directly across the sixth-floor hallway, Diane slipped into the
ladies' room. She pulled paper towels from the wall dispenser
and patted at her face, trying not to wipe off her makeup as she
dabbed at the mascara that had run at the corners of her eyes.
As she worked to re-create some semblance of a hairstyle, she
heard the click of a lock opening in one of the stalls behind her.

"Hi, Susannah," Diane said as the young woman limped toward the sink next to hers and pumped out some liquid soap.

"Hey, Diane. Hot enough for you?" Facing the mirror, Susannah smiled her crooked smile, which reflected its way back
to Diane.

Diane was about to start complaining about her flattened
hair and her sweaty walk to work, but she stopped herself,
knowing how insensitive that would be. Susannah would probably give just about anything to be able to take the walk that
Diane took for granted.

"Thank God for air-conditioning," Diane answered, pulling strands of ash-blond hair from her brush before putting it back into her shoulder bag. She rifled through the satchel and pulled out a small can of hair spray. "And tomorrow I leave for a vacation with my kids. It may be hot at the Grand Canyon, but it won't be as muggy as it is here."

"That sounds fabulous," Susannah answered with enthusiasm. "Do you have all the information you need before you go? I could get a little research package together for you."

That was one of the great things about Susannah, thought Diane, shaking the can and taking the lid off. She was always so upbeat and eager to help. God knew, Susannah had plenty to be down about. But she didn't play the victim. Maybe she knew that a poor-me attitude wore thin with folks after a while.

"Oh, you're a doll, Susannah, but I don't need a thing. I'm going to just sit back and let the tour guides do their jobs. I'm looking forward to a vacation where I don't have to read any maps or make any decisions or be responsible for anything more than which pair of shorts to pull on in the morning. I just want to relax with my kids for two weeks and let someone else worry about what we're going to do every day."

Diane waited until the researcher made her way to the restroom exit before pushing the button to release the hair spray. The smell of the aerosol fumes was just reaching her nostrils when Susannah called back from the doorway.

"I guess I should give you a heads-up, Diane. Joel is looking for you."

"Any idea why?" Diane asked as she recapped the hair spray can. But Susannah was already gone.

CHAPTER

2

The detective stood at the foot of the hospital bed in the small examining room, his face impassive as he took detailed notes on Leslie Patterson's answers.

"How many times do I have to tell you?" the young woman's voice rose in frustration. "I never saw his face. I'm telling you the truth. I never saw him."

She watched the detective for a reaction, but his expression gave nothing away. It was the way he was rephrasing the same questions over and over that tipped her off: he didn't believe her.

"Let's go over it again, Miss Patterson. You were on the boardwalk taking a stroll at midnight?" The detective stressed the last word of his question, signaling his skepticism. "Do you usually go out alone late at night like that?" he asked.

"I told you. I had a fight with my boyfriend and I wanted to be alone to think about things. I thought a walk would clear my head and maybe tire me out so I could fall asleep."

"Your boyfriend would be Shawn Ostrander, correct?"

"Yes. I told you that too." She picked up a spoon from the breakfast tray and threw it back down again. Some nurse had thought she was doing Leslie a favor by bringing in the tray as she waited to be released. *As if I would eat this,* Leslie thought. She sighed as she pushed back the rolling table that held her untouched food.

"And Shawn said he didn't want to see you anymore, is that right, Leslie?" The detective used a gentle tone as he led her onward.

"Yes. And that he'd met someone else." Leslie studied the red marks the plastic handcuffs had left on her wrists and then pulled the cover up higher.

Beneath the hospital blanket, where the detective couldn't see, she pinched the top of her thigh. Without a safety pin or razor blade, a manually inflicted wound would have to do. A hard, mean twist intended to make her feel better. As the pain pulsed, the expression on her face never flinched.

"That must have hurt," said the detective.

Leslie blinked, for a moment thinking the man somehow knew she was pinching herself before realizing he was referring to the hurt of knowing that Shawn had found someone else.

"Yes. It did. I love Shawn." Leslie grabbed again at her hidden flesh and pressed tight. This time, tears welled in her eyes. Not because of the physical pain but because she couldn't stand the thought of losing Shawn. Didn't he realize that no one was ever going to love him the way she did?

"Did you want Shawn to worry about you, Leslie? Did you hope he would reconsider his decision to break up if he realized how much he missed you? Did you hope that disappearing for a couple of days would make Shawn come around?"

Leslie considered her answer. Yes, she did want Shawn to worry about her, and yes, as she'd lain in that dark, damp place for three days and nights, she'd been sustained by the hope that Shawn was missing her. She'd hoped that the horror she was going through would all be worth it because, when faced with the thought of losing her forever, Shawn would realize he loved her as much as she loved him.

But if she told the detective that, it might help confirm what Leslie knew he already suspected. That she had staged a three-day disappearance to get attention. She didn't want him to think that.

"Look, Detective, someone abducted me, blindfolded, gagged, and tied me up, and left me somewhere for three days. I feel like you're accusing me when you should be out there searching for a real criminal."

"We are, Leslie, believe me, we are. I'm not the only man working on this case. The better part of the Neptune Police Department is involved. We will get to the bottom of this. You can count on that." Something in the detective's tone made the words feel more like a threat than a reassurance.

The hospital room door opened, and the doctor who had examined her in the emergency room walked in and stood beside the bed. He looked at his clipboard before speaking. He looked at the cop too. As part of a crime investigation, the police as well as the patient had a right to know these test results.

"The rape kit came back negative. So we have that to be grateful for, Leslie. Even though you didn't claim to be raped, it was good to have done the test. You can never be too sure in a situation like this one. You could have been drugged or knocked unconscious and not even known it." The doctor smiled reassuringly and put his hand on her shoulder. "So, physically, you check out fine. Those scrapes on your wrists and legs will heal in few days. So will the cuts at the corners of your mouth. You can go home, Leslie. You are going to have to talk to someone, though, get your feelings out. Do you need a reference for a therapist? We have some excellent ones on staff."

"Thanks, but I already have a therapist." Leslie nodded, knowing that it made no sense to protest. Sure, she'd go back to therapy, and she'd fool Dr. Messinger the same way she was fooling the emergency room doctor right now. He had no idea that she was pinching herself, over and over again, beneath the white hospital sheet.

CHAPTER

3

In August, other television news executive producers might be out playing golf in the Hamptons or relaxing in the south of France, but Joel Malcolm was at his desk, clicking the remote control at the half dozen television monitors mounted on his office wall when Diane knocked on the back of the open door.

"Ah, good. You're here," he said, waving her in. Joel nodded toward one of the TV sets. The identifying tag at the bottom of the screen read OCEAN GROVE, NEW JERSEY. A reporter was doing a stand-up report from a beach, the ocean in the background. His face was flushed, his shirt collar was open, and his hair didn't move. If there was no breeze to ruffle this guy's hair, Diane thought, it must be brutally hot, even at the seashore.

"You know about this girl that's been missing from the Jersey Shore?" Joel pointed at the television.

"I haven't been paying that much attention to the story," Diane said, taking a seat on the leather sofa, "but I bet you're going to tell me all about her."

If Joel detected any sarcasm, he ignored it. "Well, she'd been missing for the last three days, but she turned up last night. Matthew got it, off the record, from the local police that they think this girl is making it all up—that she faked her own abduction. Apparently, she's a real head case."

Diane felt her pulse quicken. *Here it comes,* she thought. With *Hourglass* segment correspondents already working on two stories similar to this one, Joel had been rooting for just one more. In Michigan, a college student had disappeared for six days, afterward telling police she had been abducted at knifepoint. In Oregon, two teenage sisters were reported missing after their mother found blood-covered sheets and a broken window in their bedroom. Frenzied searches had been launched for all of them. But police were convinced that the young women hadn't been kidnapped at all—that they'd staged everything.

It was perverse, but Diane was certain Joel coveted another misguided soul, one with her own twisted tale. Someone new and something timely to kick off the show's season opener in September.

"This is perfect for us, Diane. It's a third girl who's cried wolf. I want you to do the story."

"I'm going on vacation tomorrow, Joel," she said, crossing her legs, trying to stay calm, and hoping he had merely forgotten that she had the next two weeks off. Yet she already knew he hadn't. Joel didn't forget a thing.

"This is important, Diane. Your vacation can wait, can't it?"

"No, it can't wait, Joel. This trip has been planned for months."

"You got travel insurance?"

Diane was tempted to lie but thought better of it. One lie always led to another, and usually the truth came out, sooner or later. Lies were what had gotten Philip in so much trouble.

"As a matter of fact, I do," she said. "But I bought it in case one of the kids got sick or something. I didn't buy it to cancel our trip out west so I could work more."

Joel frowned the frown that had intimidated countless other reporters and producers before Diane. The creator and executive producer of the award-winning newsmagazine program was a television legend. With forty years of broadcast journalism experience under his trim belt, he'd gotten to this point by virtue of his quick mind, keen visual sense, and refusal to give in or give up, ever. From his earliest days in the business, when film, not videotape, was the news production medium; even in the days when news lagged hours and, sometimes, days in getting to the public because airline schedules dictated the arrival of newsreel footage in New York before it could be broadcast around the country; in those simpler days before satellites and cell phones and computers on every desk in the Broadcast Center—even when there had been so much less to control, Joel had been a control freak. Throughout his career he'd wanted everything his way, and he was accustomed to getting what he wanted.

"Changing the subject for a second, Diane . . ." He picked up a pen and began doodling on the yellow legal pad on his desk. "Your contract is up for renewal in a few months, isn't it?"

"In January," she replied, her lips tightening. *The conniving cheat.* This wasn't playing fair. Joel knew her situation and was using it to his advantage. Everyone at KEY News was aware of what had happened to Philip. It had been in all the New York newspapers, it had been on the Internet, it had even been on their own network television and radio news. That Joel was using Diane's misfortune to get what he wanted shouldn't have surprised her; still, she found herself dumbfounded at his audacity.

Joel knew that she was the head of household now. He knew that her salary kept her family fed, clothed, and housed. With Philip gone, she had no other income to fall back on. Though Joel wasn't coming out and saying it, he was clearly trying to tie the certitude of her contract renewal, and therefore the financial security of her family, to her acceptance of this assignment. She resented him for it, deeply.

"Well, you know how these things go, Diane. The front row will come to me. They'll want my opinion before they get back to that agent of yours, who undoubtedly will be lobbying for a hefty pay increase for his star client."

Joel tossed the pen on top of the legal pad. "Of course, I'll want to tell them how valuable you are to KEY News, how important it is to *Hourglass* ratings to have that great-looking face of yours on the screen, to have you delivering our stories. I'll want them to know one of the reasons we have to keep you is that you are such a team player."

Diane leaned forward on the sofa. "Listen, Joel. Can't you please understand? You know my children and I have been through a lot these past months. We all need to get away."

For a moment, she thought the executive producer was actually considering her plea as he leaned back in his chair and stared at the office ceiling. "I'll tell you what," he said. "If you want to bring your kids along with you, that's all right with me. In fact, I'll even find a way to pay for it from our budget."

"You've got to be kidding, Joel. Michelle and Anthony are counting on this vacation. It's the only thing they've shown any enthusiasm for since everything happened. And going to Ocean Grove won't be a vacation, not for me anyway. I'll be working and worrying about getting back to the kids all the time."

Joel tilted his head downward and stared directly at her. "No. I'm not kidding, Diane. This is my final offer. I can make it only because *Hourglass* did so well last season and the finance department isn't about to give me any flak about booking some extra rooms. As for you, I'm sure the quality of your work won't suffer. You're a pro. You can straddle both worlds. That is, if you want to."

She knew Joel was fully aware of the fact that she didn't want to, and she also knew he didn't care. He just wanted what he wanted . . . a ratings winner. Another edition of *Hourglass* that attracted the audience share that determined the advertising rates the network could charge. That was what it was all about for him. His ego demanded that his broadcast remain the nation's premiere newsmagazine show. To feed that ego, he was not beyond bullying when he felt the occasion called for it.

Diane rose from the sofa, knowing she'd lost. She pushed away the thought of breaking the news to her children. They were just going to have to accept the inevitable. She wished they didn't have to learn the hard facts of life so soon, but it was unavoidable, just as the other rough lessons they'd learned lately were. Canceling their vacation out west was another blow, but in the larger scheme of things, it was nothing.

She had read somewhere that children who had tumultuous childhoods could just as easily grow into healthy adults, stronger for their experiences, as develop into maladjusted misfits. Diane prayed every night that was true. Prayed that Michelle and Anthony would benefit from learning early that life goes on despite disappointments. Prayed they'd be resilient and learn to make the best of things. Prayed they'd get a valuable lesson from the example of a mother who was trying to hold everything together and doing what she had to do to support the family.

She had no other choice. With their father in jail, she was all they had.

CHAPTER

4

Helen Richey stood on the front porch, sweeping away the sand from the wooden planks. She found the swishing sound of the broom comforting. It reminded her of the summers of her childhood, when her parents would bring her and her three sisters to spend their vacation here in Ocean Grove. From the weekend after school got out until Labor Day, Helen and her family had lived in one of the tents on the grounds of the Ocean Grove Camp Meeting Association.

Each structure was made up of a wooden porch, an eleven-by-fourteen-foot tent, and a roofed cottage at the rear. Each tent came with electricity, running water, a tiny but complete kitchen, a toilet, and a shower. It was up to the "tenters" to supply everything else: furniture, carpeting, linens, dinnerware, wall hangings, even air conditioners. Some residents brought radios and television sets. Helen's parents hadn't, though. They'd insisted their girls get away from the boob tube, as her father called it, for the summer.

After children's Bible study class in the morning and an

early lunch in their tent, the days continued by walking the two blocks to the Atlantic Ocean with their towels and plastic beach toys in tow. Mom would set up a sand chair, attach a portable umbrella to its aluminum arm, and settle in to read her magazines and paperback novels in between shouting cautionary directions to her daughters as they played in the surf. Some days there were lots of waves; some days it was relatively calm. Always there was the fun of digging in the sand, building castles and moats, and choosing a Creamsicle or Dixie cup from the ice cream man.

That was the kind of summer Helen wanted for Sarah and Hannah. Simple, idyllic weeks spent reveling in the sunshine, fresh air, and the glory of the Atlantic Ocean, along with learning some lessons about God and what it meant to be a caring member of a community. She believed childhood summers as part of the Ocean Grove Camp Meeting were time well spent. They helped lay a firm foundation for the adult years. She wished she could make Jonathan understand that.

Her husband couldn't stand Ocean Grove—or "Ocean Grave," as he called it—because if you were looking for excitement, you had to go elsewhere. But Helen knew the town wasn't what Jonathan really detested. It was tent living. He said the primitive and claustrophobic conditions made his skin crawl. He dreamed of a house or condo in another part of town, a place not associated with the religious "tent community."

All summer long he'd managed to come down from their home in Paramus only on weekends. But today Jonathan was going to leave work early and brave the Friday traffic of the Garden State Parkway to spend a full week with his wife and two children in their tent on Bath Avenue. As much as Helen was looking forward to all of them being together, she was apprehensive as well.

The tents were so close together that sometimes, if a resident of one of them sneezed, a neighbor answered "God bless you." The tents had ears. If Jonathan lost his temper and voiced his opinions in any but the softest voice, the other tenters would know all about his discontent. More than once Helen and Jonathan had been forced to retreat to their car to air their disagreements.

Finished with her sweeping, Helen walked off the porch to inspect the flowers she had carefully planted when the kids and she had arrived in June. Red geraniums, white impatiens, and purple ageratum formed a patriotic border around the base of the tent platform. They complemented the American flag that hung from the wooden post supporting the striped canvas awning covering the porch. The heat was doing a real job on the impatiens, and the little white flowers were wilting and closed. As Helen was about to go fill her watering can at the kitchen sink, she heard the creaking screen door of the neighboring tent.

"Hello, dear," said the frail old woman who stood just feet away.

"Good morning, Mrs. Wilcox. How are you today?"

"Oh, pretty good." Her high-pitched voice cracked. "A little stiff, but other than that, I'm fine."

"Did you sleep well?" Helen asked, gathering her honey-colored hair and twisting it up off her neck.

"Not really. It was too hot."

"When are you going to get an air conditioner, Mrs. Wilcox?" Helen didn't wait for a reply. "Jonathan is coming down later. He could pick one up and install it for you this weekend." The moment she made the offer, she worried about how her husband would react.

"I don't know, dear. I've always disapproved of having air-conditioning down here. The ocean breeze has always been good enough for Herbert and me. But this year is different. In the thirty-nine years we've been coming down, this summer is the hottest I can ever remember." She nodded back toward the tent. "In fact, Herbert's inside now, trying to take a little nap. He couldn't sleep either, so he got up early and walked over to Main Avenue to get the paper. Herbert said everyone at Nagle's was talking about the Patterson girl."

At the old woman's words, Helen had a sinking feeling in her chest. Fearing the worst, she managed to ask, "Has she turned up? Is she all right?"

Mrs. Wilcox shook her silver head. "She's turned up all right. But the police think she wasn't kidnapped at all. They think she staged the whole thing to get attention."

"Oh, that's terrible, Mrs. Wilcox. Terrible and so very sad."

Everyone in town had been following the story of the missing young woman, an Ocean Grove native who lived in the community all year round. Leslie Patterson lived with her parents over on Webb Avenue, and just last night Helen had walked with the children to light a candle in front of their pretty Victorian house. After they added their votive to the scores of others on the sidewalk, Helen had used the opportunity to remind the children about the dangers of talking to strangers.

Despite the suffocating heat, Helen felt a momentary chill on her bare arms. Even though she had had the benefit of being raised in a town Helen considered to be just about heaven on earth, Leslie Patterson was one troubled girl. The idea scared Helen as she thought about her five- and six-year-old daughters, who were probably singing "Jesus Wants Me for a Rainbow" in children's Bible study class about now. No matter how carefully you raised your children, no matter how you tried to take care of them and shield them from danger, sometimes they just didn't grow up right.

CHAPTER

5

Trying to keep her face expressionless, Diane held her head high as she left the executive producer's office, but inside she was seething. She resented feeling she had no choice but to take the assignment in Ocean Grove, resented the fact that Joel had the power to decide her fate. Another correspondent might have told the executive producer to go to hell, but she wasn't that brave, just as she wasn't that stupid.

She needed to have her contract renewed. In a tough economy and an industry that was becoming ever more technologically advanced, jobs at every level were getting harder to come by. Fewer people were needed to get a broadcast on the air. Gone were the days when an experienced television news correspondent could write his or her own ticket, hopping from one network to another.

It would be nice to have the economic security she'd once had. With a husband bringing home a major salary, Diane's slightly lower income had been icing on the cake. The Mayfield family had enjoyed their lives. The spacious co-op in Manhattan, the smaller but well-located cottage in Amagansett, the private schools for the kids. But that was before Philip was indicted. That was before their world fell apart.

Sometimes it still didn't seem possible how quickly things had changed. It had been just four years since Philip landed his dream job as chief financial officer for BeamStar, knowing of the plans to take the cutting-edge telecommunications company public. Diane still seethed at Philip's stupidity, but she was heartbroken at his dishonesty. He had overstated BeamStar's profitability in the papers filed in connection with the public offering. The fact that her husband had done it at the urging of his bosses only angered her more.

When BeamStar tanked, its investors were crazed. The government investigated, and Philip was taken down along with his greedy bosses. Though he cooperated with the investigation, he was sentenced to a year and a day in prison. But with good behavior, he could be out in October.

In the months since Philip had gone to serve his sentence at the federal correctional institution at Fort Dix, Diane had signed the closing papers on their mortgaged beach cottage and taken the profits to pay off some of the fines that had accompanied her husband's prison sentence. She could manage the co-op payments and school tuitions, but there was precious little left over. It constantly amazed her how quickly living in Manhattan ate up what most people in the rest of the country would consider a major-league salary.

As Diane walked into her own office, it occurred to her that maybe she should look on the bright side. Perhaps it was for the best that she was being forced to cancel the trip out west. It cost more than they could afford now, but Philip had insisted they go without him. He felt strongly that she and the kids should take the family trip they had been talking about for years to celebrate Anthony's tenth birthday. Diane had held out for a while but finally reluctantly agreed when her younger sister, Emily, announced she wanted to stay with them for the summer after she graduated from Providence College. Having her sister along as they took in the sights would somehow make it less sad. Even though Emily was closer in age to Michelle and Anthony than she was to Diane, she was a good companion and another adult to fill the void where Philip should have been.

Diane reached for the phone on her desk. She would get her sister on her side before breaking the news to the kids. She might even ask Emily to tell them. Diane didn't want to relay the news to them over the phone, and it was going to be hours before she got home. Instead of packing hiking boots and backpacks, they needed to pack bathing suits and beach towels, and fast. Joel wanted her in Ocean Grove in the morning.

"Knock. Knock."

Matthew Voigt towered in the doorway.

"I can't believe this," Diane groaned. "Come on in and shut the door, will you?"

Matthew took a few steps into the office, closing the door

behind him. "So I gather you talked to Joel?" Intense brown eyes sparkled mischievously beneath his dark eyebrows.

"Yeah. He told me."

"I'm sorry about your vacation, Diane," he said as he took a seat in the chair across from her desk.

"It's not your fault. Our fearless leader is a ruthless tyrant."

"Still, it's a bitter pill, huh?"

"I've swallowed worse."

Matthew's mouth formed a wry smile. "Yeah, I guess you have."

Diane sighed heavily, accepting the inevitable and turning to the task at hand. "At least I have you as my producer. That's one good thing."

"Thank you, ma'am." Matthew bowed his head and raised his hand to his forehead as if tipping a hat.

Diane pulled a Sharpie from the cup on her desk. "What do you know so far?" she asked, poising the pen above a reporter's notebook.

Matthew reached out and passed a piece of paper to her. "This write-through gives most of the details up to this point. I've talked to the Neptune police. Apparently, this girl has a psychiatric history, and she pulled a runaway stunt when she was in high school. Turned out she was hiding in a storeroom off the school gymnasium. With this rash of fake kidnappings across the country, the police think the girl's just copycatting."

Matthew waited while Diane sat back in her chair and read the information. Leslie Patterson was twenty-two years old. Her parents had reported her missing when they found her bed unslept in Tuesday morning. Police and Ocean Grove residents had combed the town for three days. Finally, three nights after her disappearance, a security guard found her, blindfolded, bound, and gagged, on the grounds of the Ocean Grove Camp Meeting Association.

"What's the Ocean Grove Camp Meeting Association?" Diane asked, continuing to train her eyes on the wire copy.

"It's some sort of religious retreat. I did a little web research, and it seems the Methodists founded it after the Civil War as a seaside place for worship. Today you don't have to be Methodist to belong, but you do have to uphold the association rules. And get this. The people live in tents."

Diane looked up. "As in canvas?"

"Yep. There are a hundred and fourteen of them. There's a waiting list of a decade or more to get one, and rental rights can be passed down from generation to generation."

"Does Leslie live in a tent?" Diane asked, biting the end of her pen.

"No. A house. She's a year-round resident. The tent people are only there in the summertime."

Diane finished reading the Associated Press account. An unnamed police source had told the AP reporter the investigation uncovered that Leslie had been treated off and on for anorexia, "cutting," and other impulsive behavior. The source said the police were convinced that she'd faked her own abduction as a cry for help.

"Poor kid, huh?" Matthew remarked as she lay down the paper.

"Poor parents, too." Diane shrugged her shoulders and exaggerated a shiver. "Anorexia *and* cutting. Two of a parent's worst nightmares."

"Yeah," Matthew agreed. "But horrible or not, it's perfect for *Hourglass.*"

CHAPTER

6

As soon as Matthew left her office, Diane picked up the telephone and dialed her home number.

Her sister picked up on the fourth ring. "Hello?" Emily sounded out of breath.

"Hey. It's me. What are you doing?"

"My abs."

"Good girl." Diane had the mental image of her sister standing barefoot in her shorts and cropped T-shirt as she talked on the kitchen phone. Her short brown hair would be tousled. The ever-present water bottle would be in her hand.

"What's up?"

"I've got bad news, Em."

"And that would be . . . ?"

"We're not going on our trip. I have to work."

"You have *got* to be kidding. The kids are going to freak."

"I wish I were, Em." Diane recounted her conversation with Joel Malcolm and his suggestion that Michelle and Anthony come with her to Ocean Grove while she worked on her *Hourglass* story. "But it really wasn't a suggestion, Em. It was more like an order."

"God, Diane, the kids are going to be so disappointed."

"Tell me something I don't know. I'm dreading telling them."

"Want me to do it?" Emily offered.

"I was hoping you might suggest that."

"All right. I'll tell them when they get up."

Diane glanced at her watch. It was after eleven o'clock. She envied her children's ability to sleep so soundly for so long. It would be such a relief not to wake up in the middle of the night and stare at the darkness in her bedroom, to have hours of deep sleep with no tossing and turning. Perhaps nature had planned it that way, knowing that, since the waking hours of adolescence and the teenage years could be so difficult, it would be necessary for kids to have long rests to regroup. Too bad adults hadn't gotten the same pass.

"Thanks, Em. You don't know how much I appreciate it."

"I've got a vague idea."

Diane could sense a knowing smile on her sister's face. Emily had been born an old soul, their mother used to say. Even as a little child, Emily had seemed older than her years. Diane thought there was something fey about the baby sister seventeen years her junior. From the time she began to talk, Emily could figure out people and situations in an uncanny manner. Maybe it was because, as a child, she spent so much time in an adult world.

The sisters talked for another few minutes about what needed to be done. The call to the travel agent to cancel the flight and tour reservations, decisions about what needed to be packed for the new vacation venue. As she hung up, Diane took solace in the thought that Emily would be with her in Ocean Grove. She would be able to work with at least some level of comfort, knowing that her children were not being neglected. Truth be told, she knew Michelle and Anthony had more fun with their aunt than they did with their mother these days.

CHAPTER

7

In Nagle's Apothecary Café, Shawn Ostrander sat on a swivel chair at the Formica counter and asked the cheerful waitress for two cups of coffee to go. The ceiling fans whirred quietly, creating turn-of-the-century atmosphere while moving the air within the old pharmacy turned ice cream parlor and sandwich shop. Though the air-conditioning was cranked up inside, the excessive heat outside blasted through each time the front door opened.

As he waited for his order, Shawn stared at the black ceramic rosettes on the white tile floor, his mind trying to focus on the task at hand. No matter what Leslie had been through, he had work to do this morning. He had to concentrate on his research. But first, Shawn wanted to see if Carly Neath would meet him tonight at his bartending job in Asbury Park.

As the waitress affixed plastic lids to the paper coffee cups, Shawn made his pitch. "It's Guitarbecue at the Stone Pony tonight, Carly. Guitar and barbecue. Wanna come?"

Carly slid the coffee containers into a paper sack and handed it to him. "That sounds like fun, but I have to babysit tonight."

"For who?" Shawn asked.

"The Richeys. Tent people."

"What time will they be home?"

"Not too late." Carly shrugged. "Elevenish, I guess."

"You could come after that," he offered.

Carly looked down at the counter. "I'm kind of surprised you even want to be seen with someone tonight, Shawn," she said in a low voice.

"You mean . . . because of Leslie?"

Carly's blond ponytail bounced as she nodded.

"Look, Carly," he began slowly. "I feel bad about Leslie. I really do. But I can't help her anymore. I have to get on with my life. And I can't worry about what people might think, either."

Carly felt sorry for Shawn as she watched the dejected expression on his face. He'd told her a little about his former girlfriend, and she didn't sound all that stable. But if Leslie had faked her own kidnapping to get his attention, as the gossips were yakking about this morning, Carly felt some responsibility. She knew Shawn had told Leslie that he wanted to see someone else right before she disappeared.

"Okay," she said. "I guess I could meet you there." She felt better as she saw Shawn's face brighten.

"Great, Carly." He grinned. "I'll see you tonight, then, at the Stone Pony. I'm off now to track down Arthur."

Carly looked at her watch. "Oh, I wish I could come with you, but I still have a couple hours to go here."

"Don't worry. I'll tell Arthur you were asking for him."

Carly smiled. "I really enjoyed meeting Arthur the other day, Shawn. I admire you for wanting to help him."

Shawn brushed off the compliment. "It's no big deal, and sometimes, I think I get more out of it than he does."

He paid for the coffee and exited the restaurant, turning left on Main Avenue. Squinting in the glaring sun, he peered out toward the Atlantic Ocean as he walked the two long blocks to the boardwalk.

As he trudged on through the heat, irrepressible thoughts of Leslie clouded his mind. Shawn felt guilty about having broken up with her when she was so needy. He felt ashamed he hadn't joined the search party that had scoured the town looking for her. He was sorry he really didn't care anymore about what had happened to her and was feeling such relief that he was finally done with her.

If anyone had told him the day he met Leslie, when he went to Surfside Realty to find out about a new apartment, that the rail-thin young woman behind the reception desk was going to be so much trouble, Shawn probably would have ignored the warning anyway. He found himself immediately attracted to Leslie Patterson. She was not particularly pretty, not like Carly;

but her dark brown eyes pulled him in like magnets. There was a wistfulness to her, as if she was waiting for someone to come riding in to save the day for her.

As he reached Ocean Avenue, Shawn stopped to let the cars pass before crossing over to the boardwalk, telling himself that Leslie was not his problem anymore. Out of pity and a sense of responsibility, he had stayed with her way too long. He'd thought he could help her, cure her, fix her. He'd thought that he could *will* her to get better, that patience and attention and affection would nurse her to health.

What colossal ego he'd had.

Finally, Shawn had come to understand that neither he nor anyone else could make Leslie Patterson well. Her problems went too deep. Much deeper than the cuts she made with safety pins and broken glass behind her knees and into the flesh of her inner thighs.

CHAPTER

8

His conversation with the police had been deeply troubling. Owen Messinger breathed a heavy sigh as he replaced the phone receiver in its cradle.

All the hours of therapy over the last years hadn't made Leslie Patterson healthy. The police believed she had staged her own abduction, an obvious cry for help. Leslie was still a very sick young woman.

Owen got up from his desk and went over to the bookcase, where he pulled out the bright yellow binder from the shelf. Yellow was Leslie's color. The green, red, blue, orange, and purple binders contained the files of the other young women he was treating for eating disorders, self-inflicted wounding, and other impulsive behaviors. Each book contained pages of the therapist's progress notes on both the illness and therapy for his patients.

Taking a seat on the couch that Leslie had sat upon so many times, Owen opened the yellow binder and began flipping through the pages. The entries went back eight years. Leslie had been a high school sophomore when her mother first noticed the razor marks on her daughter's legs. Not the minor nicks inflicted by an inexperienced adolescent shaving her legs but angry slits executed with the sharp edge of the blade.

In his unique brand of shorthand, Owen had scribbled down his impressions:

— *L.P.'S EATING DISORDER = EXTREME WEIGHT LOSS.*
— *L.P. TALKS OF EATING 3× A DAY. CLOSER ANALYSIS SHOWS AMOUNT OF FOOD ACTUALLY CONSUMED VERY LIMITED.*
— *L.P. HAS ENGAGED IN EXCESSIVE STRENUOUS EXERCISE AS A WEIGHT CONTROL MEASURE.*
— *L.P. HAS PERSISTENT PREOCCUPATION WITH BODY IMAGE. SEES HERSELF AS OVERWEIGHT.*
— *L.P. DENIES SEEING HERSELF AS EMACIATED THOUGH SHE IS SEVERELY UNDER RECOMMENDED WEIGHT LEVELS.*
— *L.P. IS TRYING TO RELIEVE STRESS BY CUTTING. UNEXPRESSED OR UNRESOLVED ANGER.*

Owen realized that the notes he had made back then weren't all that different from what he would write about his patient today. Only now he knew for certain that Leslie had expanded her arsenal of cutting tools from razor blades to safety pins and shards of broken glass. And that she wasn't responding at all to the new therapy.

The intercom buzzed, and his assistant's voice came over the speaker.

"Anna Caprie is here, Dr. Messinger."

"All right, Christine. I'll be just a minute."

He closed the yellow binder and slid it back into its place on the shelf. As he pulled out Anna Caprie's green book, he hesitated for a moment, wondering if he should continue with his innovative therapy. But he quickly dismissed the thought as he went back to his desk and pulled a package of razor blades from the drawer.

CHAPTER

9

"I'm not hungry." Leslie shook her head as her mother rested the plate on the coffee table. "Why are you always forcing me to eat when I don't want to?"

"I'm not forcing you, Leslie. I'm offering you some lunch. You have to eat something, honey."

Audrey Patterson tried to keep the frustration out of her voice. For the past three days she had made bargains with God. If her daughter was returned to them, if Leslie came home, healthy and in one piece, then she would be more patient with her daughter. She would not nag; she would try harder to be a better mother and friend to her only child. But the initial relief over having Leslie back safe and sound was ebbing away as Audrey felt the familiar pattern reestablishing itself. Three days spent away, God only knew where, hadn't changed things. Leslie was right back to her old behavior.

"Look, sweetheart." Audrey pulled back the edge of the whole grain bread. "It's turkey. The white meat. Nice and lean."

"Please, Mom. Just leave it there, will you? I'll have some later." Leslie pointed the remote control at the television set. With trepidation, Audrey took a seat on the couch beside her daughter as the WCBS noon news broadcast began. The anchorwoman Cindy Hsu welcomed viewers and launched into the top story. A record heat wave was gripping the Northeast. Hospitals were reporting an increasing number of cases of heat-related maladies. People were fainting in the New York City subway. Macadam was melting on city streets. Officials warned of power outages if consumers kept their air conditioners cranked up, and the fire department cautioned that there would be a catastrophe when a fire emergency arose if hydrants continued to be opened by those seeking relief from the oppressive heat.

Audrey watched from the corner of her eye as her daughter tucked the crocheted afghan around her thin legs. Though it was scorching hot outside, the temperature was pleasant in the house. There was certainly no need for a blanket. But Leslie was always cold. It was no wonder, thought her mother. There wasn't any flesh on those bones.

As Audrey had feared, the story after the first commercial break was about her daughter, the girl who authorities claimed had faked her own abduction and forced the entire shore town into a frenzied three-day search.

Leslie whispered at the TV screen, "It wasn't the entire town. Shawn Ostrander didn't bother to look for me at all."

Audrey went to take her daughter's hand, but Leslie pulled away. "Don't bother, Mom. You can't make it all right. Just leave me alone."

Together, they watched the rest of the local news in silence. As the news anchors were thanking their audience and saying good-bye, the phone rang. Audrey's brow wrinkled with concern as she looked over at her daughter.

"It's probably another one of those reporters." Audrey sighed. "Why can't they leave us alone?"

"I'll get it," Leslie said and began to get up from the couch. A bit too eagerly, thought Audrey.

"No," she said quickly, gently pulling her daughter back. "It's better if I handle it." Picking up the receiver, Audrey heard a female voice.

"Hello. This is Diane Mayfield from KEY News. Am I speaking with Mrs. Patterson?"

"Yes." Audrey held back from executing her original plan to shut down immediately any request for comment. This wasn't some local news reporter. This was the national news calling. Audrey was a regular *Hourglass* viewer and admired Diane Mayfield. Diane had a nice way about her, getting the information she wanted by coaxing her subjects to open up, not hammering at them. Not like some reporters. The ones who were sharks going in for the kill.

CHAPTER

1 0

Matthew Voigt sat in Diane's office, listening to her side of the phone conversation and occasionally mouthing suggestions. As Diane put down the receiver, he leaned forward. "Well? What did she say?"

Diane shrugged. "At least she didn't say no. She said she'd think about it."

"And?"

"She's seen me on *Hourglass* and says she admires my work."

"Good. That should help us." Matthew sat back. "You can bet we aren't the only ones who want to interview Leslie Patterson. If her mother likes you, it increases our chances of getting a shot with her daughter."

"Okay," said Diane as she stood up and walked to the front of her desk. "That's about all we can do from here. When are you leaving for Ocean Grove?"

"I'm stopping home to pack a bag, and then I'll head right down," Matthew said. "I'll be there later this afternoon and try to get some elements lined up. I'll see you there in the morning."

Diane nodded. "Who's our crew?" she asked.

"Gates and Bing."

Diane rolled her eyes. "Great. Just great."

"Believe me, I'm sorry too, Diane. I tried for Cohen and Doyle, but they're on vacation. We're stuck with Sammy."

"God, Matthew. The last time Sammy Gates shot my stand-up, I looked like a hag. He didn't bother telling me that my hair was sticking up in the back, and it was as if he was actually trying to enlarge the dark circles under my eyes. The guy doesn't even make an effort to set up the lighting gear properly."

Matthew nodded. "I know. But I promise, I'll be all over him, Diane. I'll make sure Sammy makes you look good."

She knew Matthew would be true to his word. Of all the talented *Hourglass* segment producers, Matthew was her favorite. He was meticulous in his researching and planning, yet able to fly by his wits when the situation called for it. There was no such thing as a predictable shoot, and Matthew Voigt was skilled at understanding what needed to be done in a changing situation. Each of the *Hourglass* correspondents had a list of which producers they preferred to work with. Matthew was on everyone's roster.

"Okay, if you say so. I'll be counting on you." Diane glanced at her watch. "So, I'm going to go downstairs, grab something to eat at my desk, and finish some paperwork I had planned to get done before leaving for the vacation I'm not taking. Then I'll go home to pack and face the firing squad."

CHAPTER

11

Shawn started to pull out his sunglasses but thought better of it. He knew from experience that Arthur didn't trust anyone who covered his eyes.

His bartending job at the Stone Pony paid the bills, but the release of the mentally ill into the community had been Shawn's true focus all summer. He was working on his master's thesis, and Ocean Grove provided a good location for research, since at one point, the town had become a dumping ground for people released from downsizing New Jersey psychiatric hospitals. The town's old wooden hotels and boardinghouses were convenient places to deposit the mentally ill. Ocean Grove became known not only for having a large concentration of Victorian homes but for having one of the largest concentrations of discharged psychiatric patients in the United States.

Shawn had grown up watching the poor souls aimlessly walking the boardwalk, smoking cigarettes, and drinking coffee. Everyone complained that the state had made few provisions for their care once they were living in the outside world. No outpatient clinic was opened, no activity center or vocational training program was offered. Little effort was made to assure that the patients took their medication.

The state had given scant thought to the discharged people and none to the quality of life of the citizens who lived around them. Though Ocean Grove had a long tradition of tolerance and caring for the less fortunate, residents were beside themselves as incidents of shoplifting and indecent exposure infested their lovely seaside enclave. Owners of hotels and bed-and-breakfast inns saw their businesses decline, and Ocean Grove property values sharply decreased.

Finally, the townspeople organized and got legislation passed that limited the number of boardinghouses for discharged psychiatric patients. Residents were relocated in other communities around New Jersey with vows that, this time, more outpatient services and rehabilitation would be provided.

As he looked for Arthur, Shawn recalled the day that had influenced the rest of his life, the day he had watched a former mental patient commit suicide by jumping from the roof of a hotel in the center of town. For a ten-year-old boy, the sight had been scarring, fascinating, and formative. It had led an impressionable child to wonder about things he had never really considered before. Why were some people deranged and others weren't? Wasn't there something that could be done to help the ones who had been so unfairly afflicted? Wasn't it his responsibility to try?

His father hadn't been thrilled when Shawn told his parents he wanted to become a social worker, but his mother said she was proud she had raised a son who wanted to help others and contribute to making the world a better place. As an undergraduate at Monmouth University, Shawn had majored in social work. Next month he would go back to the New Brunswick campus of Rutgers University to continue working on his master's thesis. Today he was looking for Arthur Tomkins, released from the VA hospital, tormented by his memories of the Gulf War, and living in Ocean Grove.

Shawn scanned the boardwalk to the north, actually seeing waves of heat hovering over the planks. The pathway along the edge of the beach stretched all the way to the town limits, where Asbury Park's old, eerily beautiful Casino, a cavernous art deco building, stood in virtual ruins. The Casino, once the site of an ice-skating palace and carousel with hand-carved, gaily painted horses, now stood only as a reminder of the faded grandeur of Ocean Grove's next-door neighbor.

Arthur was nowhere to be seen. Shawn started walking toward the Casino, unable to keep from gazing at the ocean. The dark blue water teased him, tempting him to forget his research and run into the refreshing surf. His conscience made him keep going.

Shawn knew that Arthur had come to enjoy the time the two of them spent together. But when Shawn had brought Leslie along with him, and the other day, when he'd introduced Carly to Arthur, the poor guy had seemed to alternate between enthusiasm and sadness. Shawn could tell Arthur enjoyed meeting the young women, but there were times during the conversations when Arthur would shut down and stare out to the ocean. Shawn knew enough about Arthur's past to suspect that he was thinking about his old girlfriend who'd dumped him while he was in the service.

Just when he was ready to give up, Shawn spotted Arthur in his military fatigues coming around the side of the Casino, heading for the nearest boardwalk bench and circling it three times before sitting down.

Shawn picked up his pace, went directly to the bench, and took a seat beside Arthur. He noticed the man needed a shave and could use a haircut too.

"Hey, buddy. Where you been?" Shawn asked.

"Oh, you know, Shawn. Here and there."

"Been taking your meds, Arthur?" Shawn put his hand on Arthur's shoulder.

"Sure, Shawn." Arthur nodded three times. "You know I always do what you tell me to do."

CHAPTER

1 2

As he brought the couple and their baby back to their car, Larry Belcaro couldn't help but feel sorry for them. How were young people supposed to afford a place at the beach? The prices had gone through the roof. Though that was good for Surfside Realty and therefore good for him, Larry believed it wasn't all that good for the area in general. The Jersey Shore was meant to be a place where families could come to enjoy the ocean and one another. To his mind, those simple pleasures should be available to everyone, not only to those with hefty incomes.

As he was steering his beige sedan onto Webb Avenue, a memory flashed, uninvited, through Larry's mind. A little girl with dark, curly hair sitting under a brilliant blue sky, digging in the sand. A tiny nose and soft, white shoulders turning pink in the bright summer sun. A contented smile spreading across the face of his angel as she called to him to look at her castle.

Larry pulled to a stop in front of the salmon-colored turreted Victorian and shook his head, trying to clear the visions from his mind's eye. He never got used to them. Sometimes the memories came flooding back, catching him totally off guard, like now, after he'd been with a happy young family, a family just as his had once been. Sometimes the recollections were predictable in their arrival. They'd come when he'd hear someone talk of a kid's college graduation. They'd come at a wedding when the father of the bride danced with his daughter. They'd come at a niece's or nephew's christening party. Whenever a life event signaled something Larry had never had a chance to experience with Jenna, the memories haunted him.

How had it all gone so desperately wrong?

As he forced himself to get out of the car, Larry wondered why he even bothered asking himself that question anymore. It had been almost two years since Jenna had passed and a year since her mother had followed her. Larry had played and replayed it all in his mind, day after painful day, night after sleepless night. He always came up with the same answer. It was his fault.

He should have done more for Jenna, found better help for her. He shouldn't have been so trusting of that despicable charlatan who called himself a therapist. He should have insisted that Jenna stop seeing the quack when not only didn't they see any improvement but she actually seemed to be getting worse. But Jenna had begged to be able to keep going to her sessions with Owen Messinger. She was convinced that she needed him to get well. Finally, both her parents had given up, not knowing what else to do.

That was no excuse, Larry realized now. Sure, they had been

desperate to have someone help Jenna, but they should have acted on their instincts. Deep inside they sensed that Owen Messinger was hurting, not helping, their daughter. They should have moved heaven and earth to make him stop. They could have quit paying his bills or moved away or even locked Jenna up for her own good. Anything to protect her from that evil man.

Instead, they'd been accomplices in her death. Twice a week Larry and his wife had driven their daughter to the appointments. He would never forgive himself for that. Jenna's mother was consumed by guilt too, and that, along with her broken heart, had led her to take her own life—in effect, anyway. Marie had been drinking way too much in the months after Jenna slit her wrists. Finally, one night in her inebriated state, she crashed her car into a telephone pole.

Now, it was just him.

Noticing the pink and white geraniums brimming from the flower boxes strapped to the railing that circled the front porch, Larry was fully aware there wasn't anything he could do to change all that had happened. But he was determined to do something that would help other people in the same tortured boat as his family had been. Around Easter time, he had taken the first step, when he'd followed a thin young woman as she came out of Owen Messinger's office, tailing her right to the house he stood in front of now.

For weeks, he'd repeatedly driven by the house, catching sight of Leslie from time to time as she entered or, better yet, when she exited. He'd tailed her, and when the time was right, he'd seen her going into Lavender & Lace. He'd followed her inside and acted like a customer. He'd struck up a conversation with Leslie and her mother and mentioned that he was looking for help at his office. Now, Leslie worked for him and he could watch out for her.

Audrey Patterson answered the door. "It's so good of you to come, Larry. You've been a wonderful boss to Leslie, and a good friend as well."

After leading Larry into the living room to see her daughter, Audrey went to the kitchen to fix some lemonade. Larry turned to the young woman and spoke gently.

"I'm so glad you're all right, Leslie," he said, sincerity in his eyes as well as his voice.

"But no one believes me, Larry," Leslie said. "Someone took me and held me against my will. Why doesn't anyone believe me?"

"It doesn't matter what they think, Leslie. It only matters that you take care of yourself and get well. Nothing is more important than that."

As tears welled in Leslie's brown eyes, Larry was reminded again of his own daughter. He was fiercely determined to make amends.

"Do you believe me, Larry?" Leslie sniffed. "Please, tell me you believe me."

"I believe you have been through a terrible ordeal, Leslie. I also believe that probably the very best thing you could do for yourself is get back to work. Get your mind off everything. Take the weekend to rest. But I want you to know, your job is waiting for you. Please come back to the office on Monday morning, Leslie. It's always been my experience that work is the best therapy."

CHAPTER

13

What should have taken him just over an hour had taken him two and a half in the late Friday afternoon traffic on the Garden State Parkway. When he finally reached Ocean Grove, Jonathan had to spend another half hour looking for a parking space. By the time he found one, unloaded his gear, and walked the six hot blocks to their tent, he was smoldering, physically and mentally.

When he opened the screen door, there was no one inside

the tent. Jonathan wasn't sure if he was annoyed or relieved. Was it too much to ask that after he'd sat in that miserable traffic for so long his family be there to greet him? With disgust he walked the few feet back into the cabin portion of their tiny summer home and tossed his duffel bag down on the meticulously made-up double bed.

On the other hand, it was nice to have some time to himself, because for the next week, he knew he would have virtually no privacy at all. He and Helen and the kids would be tripping all over one another. And he should probably forget about having any intimate time alone with his wife. Helen would be worried that the children or the neighbors would hear any sound they might make. That was another reason Jonathan hated tent living.

But Helen loved it, and the girls always seemed so happy and healthy down here. What kind of a husband and father would he be if he deprived his family of storybook summers like these?

Another few steps took him into the minuscule kitchen area. He went to the junior-size refrigerator, took out a can of Coke, and guzzled it down. It wasn't the icy beer he craved, but it would have to do. Alcoholic beverages were not sold in Ocean Grove. Jonathan knew better than to bring a case down with him. Helen wouldn't hear of having it in the tent. That was just the way it was.

At least he had gotten her to agree to hire a babysitter and get out tonight. Last year they'd found a dance place that served drinks in Bradley Beach. Their tenth anniversary was coming up soon, and it would be great for them to get out alone together for the evening. They needed to reconnect, and he needed to blow off some steam. There were too many pretty girls with lean, young bodies working in his office, and he'd been finding himself admiring them a bit too much this summer.

CHAPTER

14

Table conversation at the Mayfield home was a mix of Diane and Emily's trying to paint a bright face on the changed vacation plans, Anthony's vociferously expressing his displeasure, and Michelle's sitting in sullen silence as she pushed around the spaghetti on her dinner plate.

"Look. It's not like you guys are being asked to go to boot camp or something," Diane said. "Do you have any idea how many kids would do anything to have a vacation at the beach?"

"Ah, Mom, give it up, will you?" Anthony shook his head. "Going to the beach is okay, but we've gone to Amagansett lots of other summers. Been there, done that. I told my friends I was going to the Grand Canyon, and now I'll seem like such a dork. If you ask me, the Jersey Shore doesn't even come close to the Grand Canyon."

Diane's patience was wearing thin. "You know what, Anthony? I am sorry we aren't going on the trip we were planning on. I really am, honey. But if I want to keep my job at KEY News, I have to take this assignment. That's all there is to it. You just have to understand." She paused, concerned that what she was tempted to say next would wound her son. But she decided to go ahead. Father in jail or not, her son needed to get it straight. "And to tell you the truth, Anthony, you sound like a spoiled brat."

Now Anthony joined his sister, staring at his plate in silence.

"More garlic bread, anybody?" Emily asked, trying to break the heavy mood. As the bread basket went around the table, Diane noted that her daughter passed on it while the three others at the table each took another piece.

"Michelle, Emily's garlic bread is delicious." Diane held the basket out again to her daughter. "Why don't you have some, sweetheart?"

"Because I've already had two pieces, Mom." Michelle didn't bother keeping the exasperation out of her voice.

Diane was ready to put her daughter in her place for the snippy response, but she knew that if she came down too hard, Michelle would only storm off and leave the rest of her dinner uneaten. Lately it seemed the fourteen-year-old was almost looking for a reason to get angry. Diane had been chalking it up as a reaction to the stress and embarrassment caused by knowing that her father was in jail along with a predictable case of teenage rebellion. But despite the many conversations she had had with her daughter, things were not getting better.

Deciding to ignore Michelle's comment, Diane plowed ahead, describing the advantages of their new trip. "Look. There's the beach every day. We can go to the movies or play miniature golf at night. There must be rides on the boardwalk somewhere nearby, so we can do that. Maybe there will be a concert you guys would want to see. Anthony, after dinner, why don't you see what you can find out on the Internet?"

At that, Anthony lifted his digital camera, held it steady with both hands, framed his mother in the light display, and pressed down on the shutter release. The camera's flash blinded Diane.

"Anthony!" Diane yelled, exasperated. "I've told you a million times not to bring that thing to the table. Daddy and I wanted you to have the camera as a positive influence, but you're getting to be so annoying with it. If you bring it to the table one more time, you can take a picture of me killing you!"

The rest of the dinner conversation consisted of Diane and Emily talking over what still needed to be done before the family left for Ocean Grove in the morning.

"May I be excused, please?" asked Michelle, and Diane felt a moment of relief. All traces of politeness were not entirely gone. There was hope.

"Yes. Go ahead."

"Me too?"

"Yes, Anthony. You too."

Both siblings took their plates into the kitchen. Michelle scraped hers into the trash can, and Anthony left his on the counter next to the sink.

"You did the cooking, Em. I'll clean up," Diane volunteered.

"No argument from me." Emily grinned. "I'm going to run out to the drugstore and get some sunscreen and lip balm. Want anything?"

"A large bottle of Advil would probably be a good idea."

"Done."

Diane heard the front door of the apartment click closed as she took Anthony's plate and napkin from the countertop and pushed her foot down on the trash can pedal. She was about to scrape the pasta left on the plate into the garbage when her eyes fell on the contents already in the can. Two pieces of untouched garlic bread lay on top of Michelle's paper napkin.

CHAPTER

1 5

"Diane Mayfield from KEY News called today, Lou. She wants to interview Leslie."

Leslie stood near the door, with her back against the dining room wall, straining to hear her parents' low conversation on the other side. Audrey and Lou Patterson were at the kitchen table, sipping decaffeinated tea and trying to decide what to do to unravel their daughter's mess.

"I don't think we should commit to anything, Audrey—not until we have an attorney who can tell us what Leslie will be facing if the police decide they can prove she faked the whole thing." It was her father's deep voice. "I've gotten a few names. One's local, and the other two are big shots from Hudson County. Which way do you think we should go, Aud? Go with the guy who knows the area and the Neptune police, or go for the best representation money can buy?"

"I want both." It was her mother's voice. "Can't we have both?"

"You mean hire the local lawyer as well as one from up

north?" Leslie surmised that her mother must have nodded her assent, because her father spoke again. "Not unless we suddenly win the lottery, Aud. We don't have that kind of money. You know that, honey."

As she heard her mother start to cry, Leslie could picture her father reaching out to take hold of his wife's arm, trying to reassure her. "It's gonna be all right, Aud. I promise."

"No. It's not going to be all right, Lou." Her mother's voice grew louder now. "It hasn't been all right for years, and it's not suddenly going to be all right now. All I know is I am not going to have my only child punished because she isn't well. That's really what this amounts to. Leslie is mentally unstable, and that's why she pulled this stunt. Any defense lawyer worth his salt should be able to prove that. We can show that she's been in one kind of therapy or another for years."

"I'm afraid the police don't consider this a mere stunt, Audrey. And people around town don't either. Some folks may feel sorry for Leslie, but they don't want to set a precedent by letting her off with a slap on the wrist. It cost a bundle to have all that searching done, and people don't appreciate having their time and tax dollars wasted. They don't want to get stuck footing the bill for the next girl who decides to cry wolf to get some attention. They'll want to set an example with our daughter."

Leslie could feel her pulse race as her cheeks grew hot. She had sensed the police didn't believe her story, but it hadn't occurred to her that her parents didn't believe her either, or that she could possibly go to jail. She had heard lots of stories about what happened in prison, and the idea terrified her. Leslie couldn't control the deep sob that forced its way up through her throat.

"Leslie? Is that you, honey?" Audrey got up from the table and went through the door, finding her daughter crouched and hugging herself in the darkened dining room.

"Oh, Leslie. Come here, sweetheart." Audrey wrapped her arms around the young woman and urged her to stand up. "It will be all right, Leslie, you'll see. Come in with Daddy and me and we'll talk."

"I don't want to talk," Leslie wailed. "I don't want to go to jail. I didn't do anything wrong, Mom. I swear I didn't."

"Shh, Leslie. It's all right. You aren't going to jail, honey." Audrey held her sobbing daughter as Lou came into the dining room and turned on the light. "Tell Leslie it's going to be all right, Lou."

"We're going to get the best lawyer, Leslie. Don't you worry," her father answered, unable to attest to something he wasn't sure was true. "He'll know how to handle this. He'll be able to straighten everything out."

Leslie could not be consoled. She continued sobbing, not only at the idea of the punishment she could face but also letting out the tension and hurt she had been feeling all day. It was bad enough Shawn hadn't looked for her when she was missing; he hadn't even bothered coming to see her today to tell her he was glad she was alive.

CHAPTER

16

Thank God, Helen had agreed to get out of Ocean Grove and drive south to Bradley Beach, where they could let loose a little bit. A nice lobster dinner and a couple of beers made Jonathan feel much better. Afterward, as he and Helen danced to the strains of the Motown music, he found himself actually having a good time. This was the way it should be. This was normal adult life at the beach. A few drinks and some loud music and some fun. Not tee-totaling and mind-numbing quiet after 10:00 P.M., or reading Bible passages before lights out, with nothing to look forward to but more of the same the next day.

But Jonathan's pleasure faded as he saw his wife look at her watch. "Come on, Helen. It's early," he groaned.

"It's almost ten-thirty. By the time we get home it'll be eleven."

"You've got to be kidding."

"The kids will be up early in the morning, Jonathan."

"So what? They can watch cartoons while we sleep a little more."

"We don't have television down here, remember?"

Jonathan smiled slyly. "I brought a portable with me. It's in the trunk."

She knew better than to fight with him. Helen had learned to pick her battles and ultimately win the war. She agreed to a few more dances, knowing full well that a television set would come into their tent over her dead body.

CHAPTER

17

As she walked down the hallway to get ready for bed, Diane heard the shower running. Michelle had left the door to her bedroom ajar, and Diane walked inside. A duffel bag lay on the floor, stuffed with enough clothes for an entire summer. The miniature DVD player Michelle had begged for as a Christmas present along with a stack of movies were piled next to the bag. Another canvas bag was filled with a boom box, Walkman, and CDs.

Demanding that her teenage daughter pack more economically wasn't worth the effort. Diane knew that. The other mothers she traded notes with reported exactly the same thing. The day would come when Michelle would want to simplify and carry as little as possible on a trip, but that day wasn't going to be for a while. Now her daughter felt it was necessary to bring everything she might possibly need or want with her.

Picking up the teen magazine that lay open on Michelle's bed, Diane began flipping through it. Between the articles on boyfriends and acne were pages of advertisements for jeans and shoes and handbags and makeup. As the shoes were danced in and the jeans swaggered in, there was no ignoring it. Every single one of the female models that the companies used to sell their products was thin. In some cases, almost impossibly thin.

Diane looked up to see her daughter standing in the doorway. There was a white towel twisted around her head and a larger, longer one wrapped around her body. Was she imagining it, or did Michelle's shoulders look bonier than the last time she had seen them? Diane tried to think back. They hadn't been at the beach or at a pool together all summer. When Diane came home from work in the evenings, Michelle usually had on a cotton T-shirt. Come to think of it, she'd been wearing ones with long sleeves, always complaining that the apartment air-conditioning was too cold. Diane hadn't thought anything of it, until now.

CHAPTER

18

It was a real drag that the Richeys didn't have a television set. But since this wasn't the first time Carly had babysat for them, she had known enough to bring her Walkman and some magazines. Hannah and Sarah had been worn out from the heat and a long day at the beach and had conked out only an hour after their parents left. They were sound asleep now in their bunk beds pushed against the canvas wall.

Carly got up from the wicker chair and wandered into the kitchen, stopping to adjust the air conditioner. There was no way she would have taken this job tonight if the Richeys hadn't had air-conditioning. She could live without TV for a couple of hours, but she wasn't into sweating. But even cranked up as high it could go, the air conditioner was fighting a losing battle against a heat wave that just wouldn't quit.

Carly pulled open the fridge and rifled through the contents. She spied some ice pops wedged on top of the ice cube tray in the tiny freezer section and selected an orange one. *Lots of bang for the caloric buck,* she thought as she pulled off the paper wrapper. And all water, nothing to bloat her. Carly patted her stomach to make sure it was still as flat as it had been the last time she checked, about an hour ago.

She wanted to look great for Shawn when she met him at the Stone Pony later. He wasn't the best looking guy she had ever dated, but there was something about him that really appealed to her. Shawn had the sweetest way about him. He actually listened when she talked—not like other guys, who were more concerned with what *they* had to say than what was on her mind. Carly really liked Shawn, and she could tell he felt the same about her.

Another thing she appreciated about Shawn was the fact that he didn't make her uncomfortable. He didn't leer at her, making her feel so uneasy. Not the way Mr. Richey had when she'd arrived tonight.

The only thing that bothered her about Shawn was the fact that he hadn't looked for Leslie Patterson. Just because they'd broken up didn't mean he shouldn't be concerned about what happened to his old girlfriend.

Going back to the front of the tent, Carly curled up in the wicker chair and opened the new issue of *InStyle.* She was engrossed in the pictures of Cameron Diaz's lean legs when she heard the screen door creak.

"It's me, Carly." Helen Richey whispered the announcement as she tiptoed into the tent. "We're home."

The mother went directly to look at her sleeping girls. "How were they?" she asked softly as she gently pulled the thumb from her younger child's mouth.

"Fine. They were great, Mrs. Richey. We played a couple of rounds of Candy Land, and then they actually asked to go to bed." Carly looked at the screen door again. "Where's Mr. Richey?"

"He's looking for a parking space. He dropped me off." Helen continued tucking in the cotton blankets on the bunk beds.

Carly began to gather up her paraphernalia. "Okay, Mrs. Richey. I guess I'll be going then. Call me again whenever you need me."

"Oh no, Carly." Helen straightened up from her bent position and went to open her purse. "You have to wait for Jonathan. I want him to walk you home." She pressed the folded bills into Carly's hand. "Thank you so much," she said.

The thought of walking alone with Mr. Richey creeped Carly out. "That's okay, Mrs. Richey. Really. It's such a short walk. I'm fine going by myself."

Before Helen Richey could utter another word, the babysitter bolted out of the tent.

Jonathan found a place to park right around the corner from the tent, but he took his time getting out of the car. He was in no rush. The thought of going back to the tent made him claustrophobic.

He stared out the windshield trying to summon up his resolve. He was going to break the news to Helen tomorrow. This would absolutely be the last summer vacation he would spend in the tent. If his wife wanted all of them to be together next year, they should spend this week looking for a real house down here.

He opened the car door and got out but decided not to go to the trunk and get the portable TV. There would be time enough tomorrow to have a fight. No sense having one tonight—not that they could have anyway, considering how everyone lived cheek by jowl in these damned tents.

As he was about to come to the corner to make the turn onto Bath Avenue, he saw a figure sprint across the street in the moonlight. It was Carly, her blond hair flowing behind her. He had forgotten he was supposed to walk her home. It would have been nice to have a little harmless fantasy, getting to spend a few minutes alone with her.

Jonathan was about to call out to her but thought better of it. Instead he just followed her.

CHAPTER

19

The bath didn't help. Neither did the cup of herbal tea. Diane just couldn't fall asleep. She lay alone in the darkness and wished that tonight, more than any night since he'd gone, Philip was lying beside her.

She turned over and pulled the pillow from his side of the bed, holding it close.

Visions spun through Diane's mind, things she hadn't thought much of when she noticed them. Michelle's recent preoccupation with exercise, her insistence that she get her run in every day, along with making sure she followed the instructions on that exercise video she always seemed to be playing. Diane had written it off as simply a teenage girl becoming more aware of her figure.

The container of ice cream that had been sitting, unopened, in the freezer for months. Ben & Jerry's Chunky Monkey, Michelle's favorite. For years Michelle had requested it every time Diane went for groceries. Again, she hadn't been concerned, knowing that what a kid loved wasn't always what a teenager preferred.

Diane hugged the pillow closer as she thought of Michelle's garlic bread in the trash and tried to recall her daughter's eating habits of late. There hadn't been enough family meals since Philip went to prison. Many evenings she'd gotten home from work and Emily and the kids said they'd already eaten. Truth be known, Diane guiltily admitted to herself, she'd been relieved on lots of those nights. It was easier to pour a bowl of cereal or scramble a couple of eggs for herself and eat in solitude with a magazine, not having to expend the energy to engage in conversation. The stress of having her husband away in such disgrace along with the pressures at the office left Diane wrung out at night.

Though she had been making it a point to avoid speaking engagements, dinner plans, and anything else that would keep her from being at home with the kids in the evening, Diane mentally berated herself. Being there physically didn't mean she'd always been there emotionally. She realized now that perhaps she had been so wrapped up in her own heartache and worry, she hadn't been paying enough attention to her daughter's.

But she had damn well better start paying attention now. Diane punched the pillow resolutely. If this was the start of an eating disorder, it had to be dealt with immediately and decisively. It would affect Michelle's health and could lead to even more destructive behaviors. Look at Leslie Patterson. How ironic that just this morning she had been feeling sorry for the Patterson family when Diane could be facing the same problem herself.

Thank God, Michelle wasn't cutting herself too, or at least Diane didn't think she was. Her heart beat faster at the thought. She wondered what had come first for Leslie Patterson. Did the cutting follow the eating disorder or vice versa? Did the two destructive behaviors go hand in hand? Diane squeezed her eyes shut tighter and concentrated.

Dear Lord, please help me nip this in the bud.

She felt a bit of ease as she silently prayed, but in the back of her mind, she knew that asking for God's help was only part of the solution. Diane was going to have to stay on top of this.

CHAPTER

20

Carly searched the dimly lit room until she spotted Shawn behind the bar. The slender blonde maneuvered her way through the crowd and slid onto an empty stool. Shawn's face lit up when he saw her.

"I thought you'd never get here." He leaned over the bar and spoke loudly into her ear to be heard over the band.

"Me, neither," Carly shouted back.

"What'll you have?" he asked.

"A Coke, I guess," she answered glumly. "Unless you feel like surprising me."

Shawn made no comment. He knew Carly wasn't of legal drinking age. She was old enough to drive a car and vote and even serve in the armed forces. But she wasn't legally allowed to have an alcoholic drink in New Jersey. It didn't make much sense.

He partially filled her glass with Coke and quickly splashed in some rum. If the boss found out he was mixing a drink for someone underage, he would be out of a job so fast it would make his head spin. But the boss wasn't around right now, and it wouldn't hurt Carly to have a drink or two.

"Do you think you should take it a little bit easier, Carly?" Shawn asked as he watched her suck the contents of a second drink through a straw. "At least just take sips."

"Don't worry about me, Shawn," she said with a smile. "I can hold my liquor. Hey, do you ever get a break? Do you think we can get in a dance?"

Even in the crowded room, she stands out. She's pretty and an-
imated and looks happy. And what a dancer! She gyrates to
the beat of the music as though she's been doing it all her life.
She's so obviously enjoying herself.

It's good that she's so petite. It'll make things much easier.

The music stopped. Carly and Shawn went back to the bar
while the band took a break.

"How was the babysitting?" he asked in an even voice, now
that they didn't have to yell to each other to be heard.

"Oh, fine. The kids are really cute, and Mrs. Richey pays
well. But that Mr. Richey . . ."

"What?" Shawn encouraged her to continue.

"I don't know. He doesn't exactly fit the 'tent' mold. I mean,
I don't think he's too happy about being there." Carly decided
not to mention the way Mr. Richey looked at her. She wasn't
sure yet if Shawn was the jealous type. She decided to change
the subject. "Have you heard anything more about Leslie?" she
asked.

"Oh, God, Carly. Let's not ruin the night talking about
Leslie." He groaned.

"I'd have thought you would care more about her, Shawn.
You went out with her for a long time." Carly tried to stifle a
hiccup.

"Look, Carly. It's over with Leslie. That's it. *Finito.* I don't want to talk about it. I thought you got that."

The liquor was working its wonders on her now. Carly didn't like the impatient tone of Shawn's voice, and she wasn't going to let things lie. "Well, I'd hope that someday, if we've been going out for a long time and I disappeared, you would give a damn," she sulked.

"Well, *I* would hope that you wouldn't be crazy enough to run away and hide and pretend you were kidnapped," Shawn shot back. He turned to fill an order called from the other end of the bar.

Trouble in paradise. She doesn't look so happy anymore.

Just an hour ago, who knew how things would turn out? Such a simple plan: find a girl to dance with—and keep hidden until she's served her purpose. Now that she's leaving, heading for the exit, plans need to change.

Carly heard the low roar of the ocean as she crossed the street. She turned right, heading south toward Ocean Grove. She could walk home from the Stone Pony in less than ten minutes.

The night air was warm but fresh and salty, and it sobered her somewhat. How had everything gone wrong so quickly with Shawn just now? Had she overreacted? Was he really a jerk and not the nice guy she had thought him to be?

She walked along the curb, watching out for pieces of glass that could cut through the thin soles of her sandals. The streets in Asbury Park weren't as clean as Ocean Grove's. Nothing about Asbury Park was the same as Ocean Grove. Fronting the Atlantic Ocean was the only thing they shared.

As she approached the border between the two towns, she could see the old brick Casino silhouetted against the night sky. The once grand building had been deserted for years. In the light cast by a solitary streetlamp, Carly could make out the DANGER: KEEP OUT sign.

She paused for a minute as she decided how to proceed. She could walk all the way around Wesley Lake or just follow the narrow pathway that edged around the Casino, then cut across the few yards of sand that led to the beginning of the Ocean Grove boardwalk. Her house was just a couple of blocks from there.

Though it was dark and she was a bit wobbly on her feet, she opted for the familiar pathway, the one she had played on so many times as a kid. She kept her left arm extended, her hand touching the Casino's outer wall as she followed the rounded contour of the building. It was just as she was about to jump down from the pathway to the sand that a gloved hand slammed an old brick down on her head.

SATURDAY
AUGUST 20

CHAPTER

21

The promise of the sun's arrival was signaled on the ocean's horizon. The light was changing, ever so slowly, the inky black sky fading to dark gray. As he stepped onto the boardwalk, Arthur knew the grayness would gradually get lighter and lighter until the sun's orange and yellow rays took over and finally lit up the azure sky over the dark blue sea.

It was basically the same every day. Arthur knew because he never slept well. He was usually out on the boardwalk by 4:00 A.M. It was his favorite time of day, before the joggers came or the fishermen arrived to cast their lines in the water. At this precious hour he had the boardwalk to himself.

Since he came to live in Ocean Grove after he'd been released from the VA hospital, there wasn't a morning gone by, a stroll down the boardwalk taken, that Arthur hadn't thought of Bonnie. The first time he saw the water every day, heard a seagull's early cry, and listened to the never-ending rumble of the ocean, he thought of her. Today was no different.

A welcome breeze swept in from the ocean, blowing

Arthur's partially unbuttoned three-color desert camouflage shirt open. A rare gift of late, the gust felt good against his face and chest. Arthur enjoyed it, dreading the unremitting heat that was coming again later today.

A blue-and-white Dodge Durango stopped at the curb alongside his spot on the boardwalk. "How ya doin', Art?" the overnight police officer called over the strip of grass that separated the two men.

"I'm doing all right. How 'bout yourself?" Arthur said amiably, concealing his disappointment that no matter how many times he asked the cops to call him Arthur, they continued to address him as Art.

"Fine, Art. Thanks for asking," said the cop. "Been out here long, Art?"

"No. I just got here."

"See anything out of the ordinary?" the policeman asked.

"Like what?"

"We got a call from the parents of one of the local girls saying she hasn't come home since she left for a babysitting job last night."

Arthur felt himself growing anxious. "Well, I didn't see any girl," he answered quickly, before coughing three times.

"Nobody's saying you did, Art. But if you do see anything, let us know, will you? We're looking for a blond girl, about five-foot-one, thin, pretty. In fact, she's a waitress at Nagle's. Carly Neath. Know her?"

Filled with trepidation, Arthur tried to decide how to answer. Yes, he knew her. Shawn had brought Carly with him one time when he came out on the boardwalk to talk. But Arthur was afraid to tell the cop about that. If the police thought he knew Carly, they might think he had something to do with her not coming home last night. People like him were always among the first suspected when anything went wrong.

"Nope. Don't know her."

Arthur kept walking on the boards that hovered over the beach as the police car followed slowly alongside for a while and then pulled away. Arthur thought about the pretty girl who had smiled so brightly when Shawn had introduced her that day. She'd reminded him a lot of Bonnie.

When he reached his favorite bench, he circled it three times before taking a seat. Uncontrollably, Arthur's mind segued from thoughts of Shawn's girlfriend to Bonnie, calling up the memories, still surprisingly clear, despite the time gone by and the medication designed to take the edge off his pain. The medicine, when he took it, did the job, somewhat. Though Arthur didn't get as agitated as he used to when he thought of Bonnie, nothing could eradicate her from his mind. And though he still harbored some anger toward her for what she'd done to him, to them, that didn't mean he would ever want to forget her.

She had been his first love and his only love. Arthur knew he could never love someone again the way he'd loved Bonnie. He also knew that someone like Bonnie was never going to love him. Not the way he was now. Who was going to love a man without a job, a guy living on the government dole? Who was going to love a man who spent his nights on a lumpy mattress in a boardinghouse and his days drinking coffee and wandering around town?

Arthur pulled a package from his breast pocket and shook out a cigarette. Striking a match, he lit up and inhaled deeply, peering down to the end of the boardwalk, where the old Casino was framed against the now dove-gray sky. He let out a long stream of smoke through his nostrils and let his mind wander farther down the torture trail.

What great times they'd had together. He pictured her petite figure swirling around on the dance floor, her pretty face beaming up at him. He remembered the way they'd laughed at the comedy clubs she loved to go to, the way they'd cheered and hugged each other at those Yankees games. He still remembered the fun they'd had picking out names for the children they were going to have someday, after they got married, after he finished his stint with the Army.

Arthur rose from the bench and, with an angry flick, threw his cigarette out onto the beach. Bonnie had promised that she would be waiting for him when he got back from Desert Storm. Bonnie had lied.

CHAPTER

22

"Mom," Anthony whined as they stood in the small lobby of the Dancing Dunes Inn. "You have *got* to be kidding."

Diane had a sinking feeling as she scanned the space. A sleeping cat lay curled up on a spindle-legged bench, the only piece of furniture in the room. The wallpaper featured seagulls and sandpipers, faded, she suspected, from blue at one time to almost white now. The beige cotton curtains at the windows had been washed many times, to the point that they were almost sheers. The gray paint on the wooden floor was scuffed bare in spots. The lobby was devoid of color, but at least, Diane consoled herself, it seemed clean.

"All right, so it's not the Ritz," she whispered to her son. "But quit complaining right now. I mean it, Anthony."

Diane stole a look at Emily, who rolled her eyes at her older sister.

"May I help you?" A good-looking Latino man had taken his place behind the tiny registration desk. He wore a pale green oxford shirt with the sleeves carefully rolled up, exposing tanned and toned forearms. Diane judged him to be in his early thirties.

"Yes, thank you. I'm Diane Mayfield. We have some rooms reserved?"

"Ah yes, of course." The man smiled, exposing a set of even, dazzling white teeth. "You are with KEY News, right?"

Diane nodded.

"I'm sorry I wasn't right out here to meet you. I was in the back working at my computer on brochures for the inn. And I hope you can excuse the decor—or lack thereof," he apologized, gesturing outward as Diane noticed the gold band on his left hand. "My partner and I have just bought this place. We have big plans for it. But the renovations won't begin down here until after the summer season."

Diane searched for something tactful to say as she looked around the plain lobby. "Well, I'm sure it will be beautiful."

"I know it's not what you must be used to, Ms. Mayfield, but if there is anything we can do to make you and your family's stay here more comfortable, believe me, we will be all too happy to oblige. My name is Carlos. Carlos Hernandez." He reached out across the desk to shake Diane's hand.

"Nice to meet you, Carlos. This is my sister, Emily Abbott, and this is my son, Anthony. My daughter, Michelle, is getting her things from the car."

Carlos acknowledged his guests and then turned to the Peg-Board behind the desk. "Three rooms, right?" he asked as he reached for the keys that hung from the hooks.

"Actually, there should be four."

Carlos frowned as he checked his registry. "Well, we do have four rooms booked for KEY News here, but one has already been taken by Mr. Gates."

"Sammy Gates?" Diane asked.

"Yes. Samuel Gates."

"Is Matthew Voigt registered?"

Carlos consulted his book again. "No. Just Mr. Gates."

Diane shrugged. "Well, that still doesn't explain why we don't have a fourth room for ourselves."

"Gee, I'm sorry, Ms. Mayfield. I wish we had another room for you, but we don't. Everything is booked solid at this time of year. As it is, we've reopened the top floor to accommodate you. We had been working up there to have some really nice rooms ready for the fall."

Diane looked at him with alarm.

"Don't worry," he reassured her. "It's not a disaster area up there. Kip and I worked all night getting things ready for you. We really are hoping to draw in people from the city, and we consider this a big opportunity. We want you to be satisfied."

As they entered the first room, Diane was charmed. The walls were painted a pale lemon yellow with bright white gloss on the baseboard and window trim. Twin brass beds were well polished and covered with clean, white, hand-crocheted spreads. A blue knotted rug decorated with garlands of yellow and white summer flowers covered the middle of the waxed pine floor. A series of botanical prints matted in blue and framed in white had been artfully hung. There were candles on the Victorian-style oak dresser, and a small pile of books and magazines were stacked on the bottom shelf of the night table between the beds.

"I call this room."

Diane turned to see Michelle in the doorway. She tried to keep her eyes trained on her daughter's face rather than on her body.

"Somebody's going to have to double up, honey."

"Not me. C'mon, Mom. I want my own room." Michelle walked over to the window and pulled back the eyelet curtain. "Look. This one has a great view of the beach." There was more enthusiasm in her daughter's voice than Diane had heard in a long while.

Diane looked at Emily while figuring out the arrangements in her head. Anthony should have a room to himself. That left two rooms for the three females. But would it be better if Michelle wasn't left alone?

"What do you think, Em?"

"I don't mind sharing, if you don't."

"All right," Diane decided. "We won't be in the rooms that much anyway. You can have this one, Michelle."

Carlos beckoned to them to follow him across the hall. "Well, then, that decides who will get the other rooms. There's a double bed in the Nautical Room and twin beds in the Shell Room. So, Anthony, this is your room."

Again, Diane was pleased. Pale blue walls, white trim, a fresh navy bedspread on the knobbed pine bed. The prints on these walls displayed sailing vessels, and a sisal rug covered the floor.

Anthony nodded, grudging but approving as he tried out the mattress. "Not bad."

"Okay then. On to the Shell Room." Carlos led them down the hallway, stopping at a small doorway. "Here's the bathroom."

"*The* bathroom? As in the *only* bathroom?" Michelle asked with alarm. Carlos nodded.

"It's not the end of the world, Michelle, if we have to share a bathroom," Diane said, trying to keep the annoyance from her tone.

"I'm sorry there's only one bathroom up here," Carlos apologized. "We plan to put in another one, but for now there are plenty of clean towels, and we will collect and replace them every day."

"It's no problem at all, Carlos," Diane said, refraining from giving Michelle the withering glance she felt her daughter deserved. "This will be just fine."

A few minutes later, Diane and Emily were dividing up the drawers and unpacking their things. "Smell this sachet," Diane said as she held up the silk pouch she had pulled from the dresser drawer. "They've thought of everything, haven't they?"

Emily laughed. "What do you expect, Di?"

"What do you mean?"

"Duh. Carlos and his partner are gay."

Diane shrugged her shoulders as she replaced the sachet in the drawer. "Well, they sure know how to put the charm into a hotel."

CHAPTER

23

Helen had finished making up the beds and was in the kitchen stacking the breakfast dishes in the sink when she heard three raps on the front door frame. She pulled a tea towel from the rack, wiping her hands and wondering if Jonathan and the girls were back so soon from their walk into town to buy a newspaper. Why didn't they just come in? Opening the wooden door, she was greeted by a blast of hot air and two uniformed police officers, who stood on the narrow porch.

"Mrs. Richey?"

"Yes. Is something wrong?"

"We'd like to ask you a few questions, ma'am."

Helen noticed the sheen perspiration on the foreheads of both policemen. "Would you like to come inside, where it's cooler?" she asked.

"Thank you, ma'am. We would."

One man was a good five or six inches taller than the other, but both were broad-shouldered and solidly built. Their looming presence crowded the small front room of the tent.

"Please, sit down." Helen indicated the wicker chairs. "Would you like something to drink? I have lemonade all made."

"No thank you, ma'am," said the taller one.

Helen took a seat on the edge of the bottom bunk bed and looked across the room at the policemen. "All right then. What can I help you with?"

"Mrs. Richey, did you have a babysitter here last night?" the shorter one asked as his partner took a notebook from his shirt pocket.

"Yes. Carly. Carly Neath. Why?"

They ignored her question and continued with their own. "Carly's mother says her daughter has worked for you before. Is that right?"

"Yes, Carly's been here several times this summer. My girls are crazy about her."

"What time was she here?"

"She came at seven o'clock and stayed until we got home

around eleven. Actually, it was just about eleven-thirty." Helen absentmindedly fingered the fringe of the kitchen towel as the front door opened and her husband and daughters entered the tent. Jonathan stopped short when he saw the policemen but quickly introduced himself and shook hands with the officers.

"Why don't you girls go outside and water the flowers while Mommy and I talk to these nice policemen?" he suggested.

As soon as the girls were out of earshot, Helen explained what had been going on. "The police want to know about Carly. I was just telling them that we got home around eleven-thirty."

"So you got home about eleven-thirty," the officer taking the notes pondered out loud. "And then what happened?"

"I wanted to walk her home, but Carly insisted on going alone. We paid her, and she ran out the door before we could stop her," Jonathan answered.

Helen bit her lower lip and didn't contradict her husband. "Please, tell me. Has something happened to Carly?" she asked.

The officers rose from their chairs. "We hope not, ma'am. But her parents say Carly didn't come home last night. That's not necessarily something to get riled up about. Kids pull this kind of stunt all the time, and normally, we'd wait to see if she turned up later today or tomorrow. But with what happened earlier this week with the Patterson girl, we're getting involved right away."

"I thought Leslie Patterson faked her own abduction. That's what I heard anyway," Helen said.

"We can't comment on an ongoing investigation, ma'am."

"No, of course not. I understand that. But if something has happened to Carly—if she was kidnapped or something—maybe there really is some sort of lunatic out there."

The policeman didn't respond. But Jonathan put his arm around his wife's shoulder. "Don't worry, honey," he said.

As Helen watched the officers walk down the steps, she replayed the events of the night before in her mind. The babysitter had rushed out before Jonathan had gotten back from parking the car. In fact, it had been a good thirty minutes after Carly left before Jonathan had returned to the tent. Helen had just assumed that her husband had had a hard time finding a parking spot. If she were honest with herself, she had been hoping it would take him as long as possible. Helen was determined to avoid doing her wifely duty. She didn't want to fight with him about it.

Helen dreaded marital intimacy in the close confines of the tent. The girls were sleeping so nearby, and the neighbors were able to hear the slightest noise. She'd pretended she was already asleep when she heard the screen door creak open, knowing that Jonathan would soon be nudging at her. But he hadn't. Her husband had undressed, slipped between the cotton sheets, and fallen asleep without even touching her.

Last night, she had been relieved. This morning the half

hour that had led to her reprieve was time unaccounted for, time she wasn't sure where her husband had been. And just now, Jonathan had deliberately misled the police, indicating he had been here in the tent all along.

She waited until Sarah and Hannah were getting their bathing suits on and then beckoned to Jonathan to follow her to the kitchen.

"Why did you tell them that *you* wanted to walk Carly home? That *we* paid her? You weren't even here, Jonathan. Why did you lie?" Helen's clean, scrubbed face appeared solemn and worried as she whispered.

"Would it have been better for me to say I wasn't here, Helen?" he countered. "I heard about Carly going missing in town just now. I don't want the cops looking at me as a suspect. Do *you*?"

CHAPTER

24

"Hi. It's Matthew. I'm in the lobby."

"Okay. I'll be right down."

Diane flipped her cell phone closed. Turning to her sister, she said, "I'm sorry, Em, but I have to get going. Please tell me again that you're all right with this."

Emily slid her emptied suitcase under her twin bed and stood up. "Will you stop worrying, Diane? We're going to be fine. The kids and I will find plenty to do. The first thing on the agenda is getting our suits on and hitting the beach."

"What would I do without you, Em?"

"Don't worry, you can pay me back when I have kids—if you aren't too old to handle it by then."

"Funny, Emily. Very funny."

Diane grabbed a bottle of sunscreen and threw her sunglasses and cell phone in her canvas tote bag. Pulling out her wallet, she counted off several twenty-dollar bills and handed them to Emily. After making hurried stops in Michelle's and Anthony's rooms to say good-bye, she rushed down the wooden staircase.

Matthew stood at the foot of the stairs, dressed in a red KEY News T-shirt, khaki Bermuda shorts, and brown sandals.

"You lucky dog. I wish I could be wearing what you are."

"That's why it's great to work behind the camera." Matthew smiled as he gestured toward the door at the side of the lobby. "Want to go in there and sit down? We can get organized before we head out."

No one was in the old parlor, but a pitcher of iced tea and sparkling glasses were arranged on a gleaming silver tray on the refectory table at the side of the room. A basket packed with daisies sat on the mantel. They were nice touches in an otherwise tired space. Diane looked around, noticing the intricate molding along the edges of the high ceiling, the carved stone that framed the fireplace, the dulled bronze chandelier. The room had been neglected for years, but it had good bones. With some attention and good taste, it could be a Victorian showplace.

They poured themselves some iced tea and took seats on either end of the sofa. Matthew began to outline his game plan. "First and foremost, of course, we need to get Leslie Patterson. Our story cries for an interview with her."

Diane nodded. "That's my job. I'm going to call her mother again as soon as we finish here."

Matthew took a small spiral notebook from his knapsack and flipped back a few pages. "You could do that. But maybe it would be a better approach to go see her in person."

Diane wasn't enthusiastic about this suggestion. "You mean

just go over to her house and knock on the door? I hate doing that."

"Actually, I was thinking that you could go to her store." He consulted his notes. "The mom runs a gift shop called Lavender & Lace. The Pattersons used it as a headquarters for the volunteers who searched for Leslie."

"I guess I could do that," Diane mused as she took a sip of tea. "But I'll go alone, without you or the crew. I don't want the poor woman to feel like she's being ambushed. Are you sure she'll even be there?"

"Well, she's supposed to be. I stopped over there when I got down here late yesterday afternoon, and a letter was taped to the front door. It thanked the community for their concern about Leslie and said that the store would reopen for business this weekend."

Diane jotted down the Main Avenue address in her own notebook. "What else?" she asked.

"The police have scheduled a noon press conference."

"About charges being pressed against Leslie?"

"I doubt it. That will probably come from the D.A.'s office. No, I'm not sure what the cops want to say. But I'll go over and cover it with the crew."

"That reminds me," said Diane. "What's with Sammy Gates using one of my rooms here?"

"Oh, God." Matthew groaned. "I'm sorry, Diane, but when Sammy saw his room in our motel, he threatened to go back to

New York. I had to appease him. I just wish it wasn't at your expense."

Diane was skeptical. "You mean the place you're staying at is worse than this?"

Matthew uttered a low laugh. "The hole we're staying in makes the Dancing Dunes Inn look like a palace. These accommodations were the best I could do on such short notice. The shore places are booked months in advance."

"So, you and Gary Bing are stuck in a fleabag. I'm sorry, Matthew."

"Ah, it's no big deal. We won't be there much." Matthew glanced at his watch. "I better get going. I told Gates and Bing I'd meet them at the police station. Want me to drop you at Audrey Patterson's store?"

"Yeah, thanks. Let me get that over with."

CHAPTER

25

A bell tinkled as Diane opened the front door to Lavender &
Lace. The shop's cool air was filled with the aromas of potpourri
and scented candles. Embroidered linens, fine lace, and hand-
milled soaps were displayed on white shelves that lined the
lavender walls. Antique hat pins stood in tall porcelain holders,
while boxes of ornate stationery and greeting cards crowded
the counters. There were gaily colored parasols in umbrella
stands, a display case full of fanciful gloves and feathered fans,
and dozens of beaded evening bags hung from tiny hooks
throughout the store. As she surveyed the room, Diane wondered how a search headquarters could possible have existed in
this place. There wasn't enough room for one more stickpin, let
alone a small army of volunteers.

She paused to look at the collection of stuffed teddy bears
that were arrayed on the steps of an old wooden ladder. Each
was dressed in a lavender taffeta skirt, wore a matching wide-
brimmed bonnet with lace trim, had a strand of faux pearls

draped around its neck, and held a feathered fan in one of its paws.

A trim, middle-aged woman came out from behind the beaded curtain that covered a door at the back of the shop. She managed a wan smile as she navigated her way down the narrow aisle toward Diane.

"May I help you?" the woman asked automatically, pushing strands of gray-streaked hair behind her ear.

"These are delightful," said Diane, picking up one of the bears.

"Thank you. I've been carrying them for years, ever since my daughter fell in love with hers."

Diane put the bear back on the ladder step. "Are you Mrs. Patterson?"

"Yes." There was caution in the woman's voice.

Diane took off her sunglasses and extended her hand. "I'm Diane Mayfield."

"Oh." Audrey Patterson was flustered. "Forgive me. I didn't recognize you. I'm so sorry. I guess I have too much on my mind."

"Please. There's absolutely nothing to apologize for. I shouldn't have left my sunglasses on."

Diane could feel Audrey studying her face. *She's looking for every line and wrinkle,* she thought—just like most people do when they meet someone they've seen only on television. She'll want to tell her friends that the KEY News personality looked prettier, homelier, thinner, fatter, older, younger in real life than she does on the screen.

"I was hoping that we might be able to talk some more," she said, getting to the point.

"About Leslie being on your show, right?"

"About interviewing her. Yes."

The bell at the front of the shop rang as a pair of older women walked inside.

"Let's go to the back," Audrey suggested.

"I can wait, if you need to help your customers," offered Diane.

"No, come on." Audrey lowered her voice to a whisper. "Those two are in here all the time. They're browsers, not buyers."

They went through the beaded curtain into a large storage room. Cardboard shipping cartons had been stacked high against the walls to make room for trestle tables that were littered with used paper coffee cups and empty donut boxes. A map of Ocean Grove and the surrounding towns was mounted on a giant easel. Grids had been drawn in red crayon across the map, organizing search areas.

"Would you like to sit down?" Audrey indicated a metal folding chair.

"Thank you."

Audrey leaned against the corner of the table. "I talked about it with my husband last night, and he says we have to wait until we hire a lawyer and see if he thinks it's all right for you to talk to Leslie."

"When do you think that will be, Mrs. Patterson?"

"Lou is making more phone calls today. But you know, Leslie hasn't been officially charged with anything yet."

"Let's hope she isn't," Diane said with sincerity. "It would be a terrible ordeal for a young woman to go through. I have a daughter of my own, and I can imagine how worried you must be."

Tears welled up in Audrey's dark eyes. "How old is your daughter?"

"Fourteen."

"Fourteen," Audrey repeated. "That was the year Leslie started to have problems."

Diane felt a pang of anxiety as she thought of Michelle. The idea of her own daughter following Leslie Patterson's path was beyond distressing. But the journalist in her recognized an opportunity. Audrey Patterson was opening up, and Diane had to encourage her to keep going.

"What kinds of problems?" she asked gently.

"Eating problems." Audrey cast her head downward, as if ashamed. "She got thinner and thinner. She was exercising more and more. At first, I didn't think too much of it. I'll always blame myself for that. By the time I realized anything was really wrong and got her to a doctor, he diagnosed her as having anorexia."

"Was he able to help her?" Diane felt herself rooting hard for an affirmative answer.

"God knows, he's tried." Audrey shook her head. "Owen Messinger is a saint as far as I'm concerned. He's treated Leslie for all these years, and he's been unfailingly patient with her when I . . ." Audrey's voice trailed off, and a tear rolled down her cheek.

"Why is it that mothers always blame themselves?" Diane asked gently. But the real question she wanted to ask was, If Owen Messinger was such a good therapist, eight years later why wasn't Leslie well?

CHAPTER

26

Matthew and the crew staked out their positions in front of the yellow concrete building on Central Avenue. Gary Bing attached a microphone to the wooden podium set up by the entry to the Ocean Grove substation of the Neptune Township Police Department. Sammy Gates picked out an advantageous spot to set up his camera.

Finding a tree to stand under as protection from the blazing sun, Matthew relaxed as he scanned the competition and waited for the news conference to begin. There was no other national network news presence, though New Jersey Network was represented. So was WCBS. A couple of print reporters, notebooks poised, stood at the curb. All in all, less media representation than might have been expected. Yet Matthew wasn't all that surprised. Given ever-decreasing attention spans and limited coverage resources, assignment editors had chosen not to send any of the few camera crews they had on the weekends to follow up on the Leslie Patterson story . . . a story that could be considered old in a twenty-four-hour news cycle. Leslie Patterson went missing, Leslie Patterson had been found, and police thought Leslie Patterson had staged the whole thing. The television editors were making an educated guess: there wasn't going to be anything announced at this news conference that couldn't just as easily be told in twenty seconds by the anchor on the evening news. As long as an Associated Press reporter was there, the broadcast outlets were covered. They could get the information they needed from the wire service. The only reason KEY News had a crew here was that Joel Malcolm had a bee in his bonnet for this story for *Hourglass.*

The door of the station house opened. A police officer emerged and took his place at the podium.

"Can everyone hear me?" he asked. The broadcast technicians checked their meters.

"Go ahead," one of them yelled.

"I'm Chief Jared Albert of the Neptune Township Police Department."

"Spell it," the AP reporter shouted.

"J-A-R-E-D. A-L-B-E-R-T."

The officer paused before reading his prepared statement, waiting until the print reporters looked up from their notebooks.

"Early this morning, the Neptune Township Police Department was notified by the parents of a twenty-year-old female Ocean Grove resident that their daughter had not returned home after a babysitting job last night. Because it comes on the heels of the disappearance of another Ocean Grove resident earlier this week, the Neptune Township Police Department is investigating this situation immediately and is appealing to the public and the press for help."

Matthew straightened from his slumped position beneath the shady branches of the tree and edged closer to the podium, where Chief Albert was holding up a photograph of a youthful, smiling face. The pretty blond wasn't Leslie Patterson. What was going on?

"This is Carly Rachel Neath. She is five feet, one inch tall and weighs approximately one hundred pounds. She is blond, blue-eyed, and has a birthmark on the inside of her left wrist. She was last seen wearing a pair of white hip-hugger slacks, a blue-and-white-striped halter-type shirt, and white leather sandals. Anyone with any information that might help in finding Carly Neath should notify the Neptune Township Police immediately."

Matthew snapped his gaze in the direction of Sammy

Gates. The cameraman had his video lens trained on the glossy picture. As Chief Albert finished his statement, Matthew shouted out the first questions. "What about Leslie Patterson? Does this mean that you no longer think she staged her own abduction, that the same person who kidnapped Leslie has now kidnapped Carly Neath? Are charges still going to be filed against Leslie?"

The police officer wiped the perspiration off his brow with the back of his hand before answering. "We are investigating all possibilities. At this time, no charges are being filed against Leslie Patterson."

CHAPTER

27

Carly opened her eyes but could see nothing. She realized that she was blindfolded. Her head throbbed so painfully that she was almost grateful for the darkness. Where was she?

The soft but persistent sound of dripping water felt closer than the roar of the ocean she could hear in the distance. Was that ruffling noise birds' wings above her? Was that cooing sound coming from a pigeon or a dove?

Shivering with fear, Carly lay on the damp ground and tried to recall what had happened. She'd been walking home, that was it. She'd left Shawn and was walking home from the Stone Pony. Now she remembered. She'd gotten mad at him and stalked out.

And then what? Carly concentrated despite the headache that made her pray for the relief of sleep. Gradually, the memory began to come back to her. She'd come out of the club and crossed the street. Then she'd had to decide which way she was taking back home. She'd chosen the shortcut around the old Casino when she was hit from behind and must have been knocked unconscious.

Was the pounding in her head from what hit her or was it one of her old migraines come back? Whatever its source, it was the worst pain she'd ever felt.

She had to get out of here. Carly struggled to get up, falling back again as she realized that her hands and feet were bound. The gag cut into the sides of her mouth as she tried to scream for help.

CHAPTER

2 8

After leaving Lavender & Lace, Diane found a bench beneath a tree on Main Avenue, sat down, and pulled out her cell phone to call information for the listing for Dr. Owen Messinger. Knowing that it was a long shot to reach him in his office on Saturday, she was about to try his number anyway when her phone rang. She glanced at the tiny identification screen before placing the device next to her ear.

"Hi, Matthew."

"Diane." There was urgency in his voice. "There's another girl missing."

"What?"

"Another young woman. Carly Neath. Just about the same age as Leslie Patterson. She never came home from her babysitting gig last night."

"And the police think there's a connection?" Diane asked.

"They didn't go so far as to say that, but they are pursuing it earlier than they would have at another time. And they say they aren't filing charges against Leslie."

"Wait till Joel hears. He'll be apoplectic," Diane predicted, thinking her boss could be agitated about this newest development. If another young woman was missing, was Leslie Patterson telling the truth? If Leslie hadn't cried wolf, would that leave her out as a subject for the *Hourglass* broadcast? But whether Joel decided to include Leslie Patterson or not, the fact that another young woman had been kidnapped was newsworthy on a national level. Matthew's next words didn't surprise Diane.

"*Weekend Evening Headlines* wants a piece on this tonight," he said.

"Let me guess. I'm the correspondent."

"Yes. The assignment desk doesn't have anyone in the Northeast Bureau to send down here. With the exception of the correspondent at the Broadcast Center who's there on bulletin duty, everyone is on vacation."

"Just like *we* should be," Diane said before switching into planning mode. "I'm starving. Let's get a little lunch and figure out where we're going. Oh, and Matthew? I haven't gotten the green light to interview Leslie Patterson yet. I don't know if Joel will even care anymore for *Hourglass*, but I'd love to get her reaction to Carly Neath's disappearance for the *Evening Headlines* piece."

Ten minutes later Diane and Matthew were escorted to a table in the open-air courtyard of the Starving Artist.

"You don't have a table inside by any chance, do you?" Matthew asked the host.

"Sorry. Everything inside is taken. Everybody wants the air-conditioning."

They ordered two iced teas right away and scanned the restaurant offerings.

"There are lots of things I love on this menu, but I'm too hot to eat them," Diane said. "I guess I'll go with the tuna salad platter."

"It's a double Italian-style hot dog and fries for me." Matthew closed the menu. "I'm never too hot to eat."

After placing their orders, he laid out what they had so far. "Okay, we've got the police presser and a picture of the second missing girl. We also have pictures of Leslie Patterson and the search for her earlier this week."

"Where did you get those?" Diane asked. "We weren't here."

"Well, I don't actually have them in my hands, but I called the WKEY local desk, and they are going to dub off what they have and bring it over to the *Weekend Evening Headlines* studio. Since we didn't bring editing gear with us, we'll feed our material back to the Broadcast Center, and they'll edit the piece up there."

"When will the satellite truck get here?" Diane asked.

"About four o'clock. We'll want to feed at five."

She looked at her watch. "Okay, so we've got about four hours to see what other elements we can gather and then write the piece." She continued, "Of course, one of the best things we could get is still an interview with Leslie Peterson."

"Her mother wasn't biting, huh?"

"No. But that was before Carly Neath was declared missing. That changes the landscape considerably. Now it looks like Leslie Patterson could be telling the truth."

CHAPTER

29

Shawn walked into Nagle's and took his usual place at the counter. It was too late for breakfast, so he ordered a close approximation as his first food of the day.

"Egg salad on toasted rye and a cup of coffee," he instructed the thin, brown-haired waitress behind the counter. Shawn knew Anna because he and Carly had given her a ride to a doctor's appointment one night last week when Anna's old car was in the shop. She was staring at him now as if she had something she wanted to say. Shawn looked across the counter at her expectantly.

"Have you heard about Carly?"

"Heard what?" asked Shawn.

"Carly didn't come home last night. Her parents are frantic, and the police are out looking for her." Anna looked at him with some compassion. "She was supposed to come home after her babysitting job, but she didn't. No one knows where she is. I'm going to have to do a double shift to cover for her."

Shawn slid off the counter stool. "Cancel my order, will you, Anna?"

He escaped outdoors but didn't feel the scorching rays of the sun or the hot, still air. Shawn's mind raced. He should go talk to the police before the police came to talk to him. It was just a matter of time before they found out that he had been with Carly last night at the Stone Pony. If the Nagle's waitress recognized him as Carly's boyfriend, there were others who would as well.

If he told the police the truth, it was going to look bad. He had fought with Carly, just as he had fought with Leslie right before she disappeared. He was the obvious common denominator between the two women.

Shawn knew from the questioning he'd gone through when Leslie disappeared that the police had looked at him as a prime suspect. He knew from the course he'd taken on family violence that women were most often attacked not by strangers but by people they knew—disgruntled boyfriends or husbands leading the pack.

Closing his eyes and running his nail-bitten fingers back through his hair in desperation, Shawn knew that he had to think of something. The police were going to think he was responsible for Carly's disappearance, and they'd go back and try to pin Leslie's on him, too.

CHAPTER

30

"Do you believe me now?"

Audrey jumped as her daughter spoke from behind her.

"Don't sneak up on me like that, Leslie. You scared me to death." She turned around but continued sorting through a box of scented candles. "I didn't hear the bell at the front door ring when you came in. I guess my mind is on other things."

Seeing the look of resignation on her mother's face, Leslie asked, "You haven't heard yet, have you?"

"What?"

"There's another girl missing." Leslie's brown eyes were bright with excitement.

Audrey put the box of candles on the counter and leaned against the edge.

"Mom? Did you hear me? There's another girl missing. The police will believe me now. Everyone will believe me."

"Leslie!" Audrey hissed. "Lower your voice, will you please?"

Leslie's thin face darkened. "Well, I thought you might be happy for me, Mom. Don't you see? This proves I was telling the truth."

"Of course I'm relieved that you will be vindicated, dear." Audrey reached out to stroke her daughter's fine brown hair, noticing it had lost some of its sheen. "But, honestly, it's hard to be happy at some other poor girl's expense. Who is she? Do I know her?"

"I doubt it. But she's a waitress at Nagle's, and she's the one Shawn's been going out with."

"Dear God," Audrey exclaimed. "Another girlfriend of Shawn's disappeared? The police *must* be looking into that. Well, God help her, and God help her family," Audrey said softly, thinking about what she and her husband had just been through. "I think we should do something to help them, Leslie. Maybe we should volunteer our storeroom again as a community search headquarters."

Audrey could almost see the wheels spinning in her

daughter's mind before she answered. "Yeah, I guess that would be okay. And I'll come in to help. I want everyone who doubted me to have a chance to tell me how wrong they were."

CHAPTER

31

Trudging up Main Avenue, Sammy Gates grumbled as he carried his heavy camera gear over his shoulder. "Jesus, it's hot. Remind me again why we're doing this."

"Because if we can't get Leslie Patterson, at least we might get some reaction from her mother." Diane tried to sound patient, but inwardly she was in no mood for Sammy's complaints. This was his job, for God's sake. "If she agrees, and we're ready to shoot right then, she won't have time to change her mind."

"Sounds half-baked to me." Sammy sneered as he turned to his partner. "What do you think, Gary?"

"It makes no difference." Gary shrugged. "I'm on the clock, and whatever they want while they're paying the freight is fine by me." Gary Bing was as sweet and agreeable as Sammy Gates was ornery and argumentative. Diane thought Gary was a saint for working with Sammy. While most KEY News staffers avoided Sammy as much as possible, poor Gary was stuck with the curmudgeon day after day.

Sammy didn't take the cue his partner offered. Instead, he continued with his litany of complaints. "And the accommodations here leave a lot to be desired. I like a television set in my room, and I'm not into hooked rugs and sharing a bathroom at the end of the hall."

"Matthew told me the Dancing Dunes Inn is much nicer than the place you were originally going to stay in," said Diane, still a bit resentful that her family had been forced to give up one of their rooms to make Sammy happy. "It's tired, but it's clean and really charming in places."

"Charming, schmarming. It's a dump too. Give me a Marriott any day. Room service and a minibar, that's for me."

Diane held her hand up, cutting Sammy's complaints short. "Look. I think that's Leslie Patterson."

Across the street, a very thin figure was stepping from the curb in front of Lavender & Lace. "Get ready, you guys," she ordered as she scooted between cars cruising on the main street. "Leslie? Leslie Patterson?" she called to the young female, who backed up again onto the sidewalk.

As Diane got closer, she took a deep breath. Though she knew that Leslie was eight years older than her own daughter, the young woman didn't look it. It was almost as if she was stuck in adolescence. The legs that poked out from her denim shorts had none of the feminine curves associated with a little meat on one's bones, and she had hardly any chest at all.

"I know who you are," Leslie said proudly. "You're Diane Mayfield from KEY News."

Diane held out her hand. "Nice to meet you, Leslie."

"My mother told me you called yesterday about interviewing me."

"That's right," Diane said. "And I can certainly understand why she didn't agree to it yesterday, or even this morning when I went to see her. But now, with the other girl's disappearance, I was hoping you and your mother might reconsider."

"I don't need my mother's permission, Diane," Leslie said. "I'm an adult."

"That's true enough," agreed Diane. "But under the circumstances, it might be best to consult her." She knew it was the mother in her offering the counsel. She hoped if, God forbid, Michelle were ever in a situation like Leslie's, her daughter would turn to her for maternal advice.

"I don't have to talk to my mother about it," Leslie said as she looked over Diane's shoulder and eyed the camera crew.

What was she going to do? Insist that Leslie get her mother's approval? Leslie was legally an adult. If the young woman agreed to the interview, Diane would be a fool not to ask the questions.

"All right," she said, turning to Gary. "Mike her up, will you? We can do it right here on the sidewalk."

Leslie was one step ahead of her and, Diane realized at that moment, extremely media savvy. "Why don't we go over to the Beersheba Well, where the security guard found me? It's just a couple of blocks from here. We could do the interview there."

Sammy set up his tripod. Gary clipped a little microphone to the collar of Leslie's sleeveless blouse and handed her a small black battery pack. "Here. Slide the wire from the mike under your shirt, and clip the power pack to the back of your shorts."

Leslie obeyed. "Don't I get a makeup woman or something?"

Diane smiled. "Sorry. If we were in the studio in New York, yes. But out here in the field, it's every woman for herself." She pulled out a makeup case and hand mirror from her bag. "Would you like a little blush?"

Leslie nodded.

Diane selected the most youthful colors from the collection of cosmetics she kept with her virtually all the time. A peachy lipstick and blush and a dark brown mascara would work best with Leslie's coloring.

While reapplying her own lipstick, powdering her face, brushing her hair, and hitting it with some hair spray, Diane made small talk, asking Leslie what she was planning to do now that she was free again.

"I'm going back to work on Monday, but this whole thing

has made me realize I want to do more with my life. I hope I can go a bit further than the office job I have at Surfside Realty."

"What are your duties now?" Diane asked politely.

"You know . . . answering phones and sending faxes, going through the mail, ordering things for the office."

Diane saw the crew had finished setting up. "Leslie, why don't you and I stand over here beside the gazebo?" she suggested.

Leslie tentatively took her place beside Diane. "It's strange being back here now, when it was just two nights ago that they found me here."

Diane reached out to pat Leslie's arm. "Don't worry. It's going to be all right." She turned to the crew. "All set, you guys?"

"Go," Sammy ordered.

"All set, Leslie?" Diane asked.

"Uh-huh."

Diane turned to her and began. "We're here, sitting together on the spot where you were found very early Friday morning after having been missing for three days. Tell me what happened to you, Leslie."

Leslie sighed heavily before answering. "I was walking on the boardwalk late Monday night when someone came up behind me and knocked me out. When I came to, I was blindfolded and bound, and there was some sort of rag tied around my mouth so I couldn't call for help. I didn't know where I was." She rubbed her bare arms, as if trying to get warm.

"That must have been terrifying."

Leslie nodded but said nothing.

"What happened then?" Diane urged.

"Well, he—I'm guessing it was 'he' because whoever it was never spoke to me—he just left me lying there, wherever 'there' was. He would come back once in a while to bring me something to eat, but I ate very little. And each time he came back, he would pull me up and want me to dance with him."

"Dance with him? I don't understand," said Diane.

"There was no music or anything, but I think you'd call it dancing. He'd pull me up and press his body against me, rocking back and forth, almost in rhythm with the waves flowing in. We must have been near the ocean. I could hear it."

With every word Leslie spoke, Diane was more certain that the piece she would be offering on *Weekend Evening Headlines* in a few hours would be mesmerizing.

"It was horrible. So horrible. The only way I could get through it was thinking of dancing with my boyfriend Shawn." Leslie's voice rose plaintively. "But the worst part is that I don't think anyone believed me."

"Another young woman is missing, Leslie. Do you think people will believe you now?"

"I hope so," Leslie answered softly as tears welled up in her brown eyes. "And I feel sorry for her."

CHAPTER

3 2

Though Carly Neath's father said neither he nor his wife would have anything to say to the press, Matthew thought it was a good idea to go over to their house anyway. People could easily say no on the phone, but when actually face-to-face with another human being, they sometimes changed their minds. Without the intimidation of a camera crew, Matthew felt he might have a better chance of getting the Neaths to talk with him.

He found the house in the middle of the block on Surf Avenue. There were no shutters or window boxes on the aluminum-sided colonial. Though it was a bland dwelling now, Matthew suspected that beneath the worn white siding there were the wooden boards and elaborate moldings of the original Victorian structure. Someone's idea of progress had left the house totally without charm.

He knocked on the front door, waited, and then knocked again. Matthew couldn't be sure if the Neaths were inside or not. He pressed his cupped hands against the window and tried to see through the glass.

"They're in there all right."

Matthew spun around in the direction of the voice. A very elderly man stood on the porch of the house next door.

"I know they're in there in case that daughter of theirs calls. They don't want to miss out if the police call with news, neither."

Matthew walked away from Neaths' front door, sensing that this old guy, with his bony shoulders and arms sticking out of his sleeveless undershirt, might be a good source of information. He went next door and struck up a conversation.

"So, I guess you know Carly?"

"Yep. I've known her since she was a little kid. Always gettin' into everything, that one. It looks like she got into something bad this time."

"Have any theories on what might have happened to her?" Matthew asked.

The old man shrugged his shoulders. "I have my suspicions."

Matthew waited for the man to continue.

"You know, it's tough gettin' old. You don't even think about that now, do you, sonny?"

"Not much," Matthew said, noticing the flaking skin at the man's temples. There were a couple of teeth missing from the old guy's bottom gums, and a vague odor of decay reached Matthew's nostrils.

"I didn't think about it when I was your age either. But it comes before you know it. And it brings with it all sorts of miserable things. For me, the worst is not sleepin'. Can't tell you when the last time I slept through the night was."

"That's too bad," said Matthew, wishing the old codger would get to the point. The man took a seat in the rocking chair on his porch.

"It was so hot last night. Lord, was it hot. I don't have air-conditionin'. Don't usually need it here, even in the summertime. And it costs money to run those things, and that's something I don't have enough of."

Matthew was growing impatient. He had to keep himself from tapping his foot on the porch floor. Instead, he nodded in agreement, as if he understood the old man's problems.

"So I came out here to sit in my rocker because I thought it would be cooler. But it wasn't. I expect it was just about as hot as inside."

Matthew anticipated where this was going and wanted to move things along. "So you saw something from here on your porch last night?"

The man rocked. "Yep."

"What did you see?" The old guy seemed to be enjoying stringing this out.

"I could see Carly walkin' up the street. That yellow hair of hers was catchin' the moonlight."

"What time was that?" Matthew asked.

"About eleven-thirty, quarter to twelve."

"Did you say anything to her, or did she say anything to you?"

"She didn't even see me, and I didn't have nothin' to say to her."

The elderly man paused, enjoying his power. After rocking for a minute, he continued. "Well, I might as well tell you what I told the police when they were here today askin' all their questions. I wasn't a bit surprised when I saw it. You know these kids today, comin' and goin' at all hours of the day and night. Even the girls. In my day, no self-respectin' girl would be out by herself alone at night like that. Even here in Ocean Grove."

"What did you see?" Matthew pressed him.

"I seen her walk right by her own house and keep on goin'." The old man shook his head. "Yep. She just kept on walkin'. Toward the ocean. Late at night like that. It's a disgrace what young girls do today."

"So, you said you had your suspicions about what happened to Carly." Matthew tried diverting the man's attention from the mores of today's youth. "What do you think happened?" He leaned forward to hear.

"Like I told the police. I think that guy got her."

"Guy? What guy?"

"The one that was following along behind her. She didn't see him, but he sure was makin' a beeline for her."

CHAPTER

33

A small, curious crowd gathered on the grass surrounding the red gazebo that covered the Beersheba Well to watch the news team shooting the interview. Diane was used to the gawks and stares, but Leslie was not. It wasn't that she didn't enjoy attention, but Leslie was uncomfortable about exposing herself in front of people she didn't know. Somehow, anonymous television viewers didn't unnerve her nearly as much as the real human beings straining to hear what she was telling Diane Mayfield.

"I think that's all I have to say right now." Leslie pulled at her microphone.

Diane knew better than to push. She would want another opportunity to interview Leslie at greater length for the *Hourglass* segment if Joel decided to go ahead with it. For now, she had more than enough for the relatively short piece for *Evening Headlines*. And, on a more personal level, Diane didn't want to force anyone else's daughter to do something against her will.

"What time will this be on?" Leslie asked as she stood up.

"I'm not sure where the story will be scheduled in the show, but the broadcast begins at six-thirty," Diane answered. "Thank you so much for doing this, Leslie. We really appreciate it."

Diane watched the young woman make her way through the onlookers, cut across the lawn, and head back toward the heart of town. As Sammy and Gary packed up their gear, Diane sat back down on the well's step and took a notebook from her bag. She was beginning to rough out a script when her cell phone rang.

"This call is from a federal prison," announced the recorded voice.

Diane knew the drill. When prompted, she pressed five to accept the call.

"It's me."

In spite of everything, his voice never failed to thrill her. Since the first time he had spoken to her, back in that psychology class in senior year in college, she'd been a sucker for his soft West Virginia drawl. Diane got up, turned her back, and walked away from the camera crew.

"Hi, it's me," she answered softly.

"Well? How is it? How was the flight? Have you hooked up with the tour yet?" His questions were rapid-fire.

Diane bit the inside of her mouth.

"Diane? Are you there?"

"Yes, Philip. I'm here."

"Well? How's it going? Are the kids all excited? Tell me what's going on." There was such enthusiasm in his voice, Diane hated to disappoint him. She knew he was craving some happy news; he needed to have something to think about after lights out, when sleep would not come.

"Actually, Philip, there's been a change in plans."

"This call is from a federal prison." The recorded voice again, interrupting and reminding them of something they never forgot.

"What kind of change of plans?" There was wariness in Philip's voice. "Has something happened? Is something wrong? Are the kids sick?" Now there was panic in his tone.

"No, Michelle and Anthony are fine," she quickly reassured him. There was no way Diane was going to discuss her fears about Michelle and a possible eating disorder now. Philip couldn't do a thing about it, and there was no point in giving him more to worry about.

"Are you okay, honey?" he asked.

At the term of endearment, Diane felt a tug in her chest. For richer, for poorer, in sickness and in health . . . Despite her disappointment at what he had done professionally and her anger at what his actions had done to their family, Diane still hoped that, with time, she would be able to forgive her husband. What they'd had together once had been so good. Even though Philip had made a terrible mistake, she hadn't stopped—couldn't stop—loving him. They had too much history. They shared two children. And their emotional and physical chemistry had always been strong.

How she ached to be with Philip again. Not in some large room with theater-style seating, with prison guards and security cameras watching. Knowing that, when the visit ended, he would be forced to go through the indignity of a strip search. Dear God, she wanted their old life back, with all the privacy they had taken so much for granted.

"I'm fine, Philip. Really. But I had to cancel the vacation. Joel Malcolm insisted I cover a story."

"Ah, Di, you're kidding." The disappointment in his voice was palpable.

"I wish I were, believe me, but I'm not. Instead I'm in Ocean Grove, New Jersey, doing a story on missing girls."

"And where are the kids? They must have been so bummed out."

"That's an understatement, especially Anthony. But Joel said I could bring them with me. They're probably with Emily at the beach right now."

"This call is from a federal prison." Again, the damned recording.

"I have to get back to my room for the four o'clock count, Di." His voice sounded heavy.

The thought of Philip standing up and being counted as a criminal by prison officers sickened her. In fact, everything she knew about what Philip was forced to endure at the federal prison sickened her. What she didn't know, the things she suspected he didn't tell her, truly terrified her.

But he had committed a crime, and if there was any chance he or they could go forward and live an honest life, Philip had to pay for what he had done.

CHAPTER

34

The KEY News satellite truck operator parked his rig at the designated meeting place, the cul-de-sac at the end of Ocean Avenue. Leaving the motor running, Scott Huffman sat back to wait for Diane Mayfield and Matthew Voigt and whichever their crew was for this *Weekend Evening Headlines* assignment. The view out the window was a reminder that it was a summer weekend and he was working yet again. People in shorts and bathing suits strolled on the boardwalk. Some were filing into a large wood-frame structure that backed up to the beach. Others were lined up in front at a take-out window.

Scott's stomach rumbled, recalling that it hadn't been fed anything since the cheese Danish and coffee early in the morning. When he opened the door of the truck, the hot blast of air that pushed inside tempted him to stay put in the nice, cool cab. But hunger trumped comfort. He got out of the van, locked it up, and joined the others waiting in line.

Scott paid for two hot dogs with the works, fries, and a root beer. He didn't want to stink up the truck, so he carried the cardboard tray with his order to a bench farther down the boardwalk. He wolfed down the late lunch, gazing out at the ocean between bites.

As he chewed, he thought about himself. He had to get a life. Sure, the overtime was great, but he hadn't spent a full weekend at home the whole summer. Last month he'd been away for over a week when *KEY to America* had broadcast from Newport, Rhode Island. It wasn't fair to his wife and kids, and it wasn't fair to himself. He didn't want to become one of those guys who missed the important things just to have a bigger cushion in the bank. He had to start saying no to the weekend assignments. There were other guys who could run the satellite rig and feed the audio and video back to the Broadcast Center. Let *them* get the overtime.

Scott tossed the trash from his lunch into a garbage can and headed back up the boardwalk, passing a guy who might have been about his own age going in the other direction. Despite the oppressive heat, the man was wearing pants and a long-sleeved military camouflage shirt. He was muttering to him-self. Scott couldn't help staring at the guy. It was clear some-thing wasn't quite right with him.

There's a troubled soul who really got screwed in the lot-tery of life, he thought. But as he spotted Diane Mayfield wav-ing beside the satellite truck, the pathetic stranger was quickly forgotten.

CHAPTER

3 5

Diane was in the satellite truck, putting the finishing touches on her script, when her cell phone sounded. She listened as Matthew filled her in on what Carly Neath's neighbor said he had seen the night before.

"Wow," said Diane. "Think we should add something about Carly's being followed to the script?"

"I'd feel better about it if we had the police comment on it," Matthew replied, "but nobody is returning my calls."

"I wish you'd had the crew with you, Matthew. Think your witness would say it all again for the camera? If we had him on tape saying that he saw someone following Carly, the piece would be stronger."

"It's worth a shot. Send Sammy and Gary over, and I'll see if I can get the old guy to say it again."

"And guess what?" Diane asked after jotting down the address. "Leslie Patterson talked to us."

"You're kidding. That's great! Good stuff?"

"Enough. I think we're in good shape for tonight's story. But I'll want to get her later for the *Hourglass* segment. Once we see what happens with Carly Neath, we'll need more reaction from Leslie."

After instructing the camera crew to go to Surf Avenue, Diane looked at her script again and made the adjustments necessary to include a sound bite from Carly's neighbor. She also wrote an alternate line of track, explaining what the witness had seen, in case Matthew was unsuccessful in securing another interview. The extra narration could be edited in at the last minute if necessary.

Satisfied it was set to be read by the executive producer at the Broadcast Center, Diane clicked the SEND icon on the computer and sat back to wait for script approval.

CHAPTER

36

It wasn't long into the police questioning that Shawn realized he should have brought an attorney with him. So he waited for another two hours until the public defender arrived at the station house. The guy was dressed in a golf shirt and Bermuda shorts, as if he'd been called away from a round of golf or a family barbecue. After getting up to speed on Shawn's version of what had happened so far, the lawyer signaled that the officers could come back into the small interrogation area.

"My client came in here of his own free will," the attorney began. "He's told you that he was with Carly Neath last night, that she walked out on him at the Stone Pony, and that that was the last he saw of her. Unless you have something to book him on, we're outta here."

"So it's just a coincidence that the young woman who was abducted earlier this week happened to be a girlfriend of his as well?" one detective asked.

"That's sure the way it looks," the lawyer said, keeping his face expressionless.

The other detective shook his head, knowing that, for now anyway, their hands were tied. They needed to get some solid evidence on the guy. "All right, Ostrander," he snarled. "Get out of here. But don't go anywhere we can't reach you."

CHAPTER

37

"The old guy won't talk again, Diane. We're not going have his sound bite for the piece."

"All right. We'll go with Plan B. Thanks, Matthew."

Diane flipped the phone closed and picked up the lip mike. Holding it close to her mouth, she began recording the approved track.

"For the second time in less than a week, a young woman has gone missing in an idyllic New Jersey shore town. Twenty-year-old Carly Neath did not return home last night after finishing her babysitting job in the quiet, picturesque town of Ocean Grove."

She paused to give the instructions on inserting a sound bite from the police news conference. "Use the bite we'll feed you after the track. It's Chief Jared Albert, J-A-R-E-D A-L-

B-E-R-T, Neptune Township Police Department. The sound bite is: 'Coming on the heels of the disappearance of another Ocean Grove resident earlier this week, the Neptune Township Police Department is investigating this situation immediately and is appealing to the public and the press for help.'"

Diane cleared her throat. "Track two: Police and volunteers are scouring the town known as 'God's Little Acre,' a square-mile community an hour from New York City, as they did just days ago for twenty-two-year-old Leslie Patterson. After a three-day search, she was found, bound and gagged, on the grounds of the Ocean Grove Camp Meeting Association. There was speculation that Leslie might have staged her own abduction to get attention. But this latest disappearance changes things. Leslie spoke exclusively to KEY News today at the site where she was discovered early Friday morning."

Diane stopped to consult her notes on Leslie's interview. "Okay. The sound bite is: 'I was walking on the boardwalk late Monday night when someone came up behind me and knocked me out. When I came to, I was blindfolded and bound, and there was some sort of rag tied around my mouth so I couldn't call for help. I didn't know where I was.'"

Going back to the script, Diane continued. "Track three. To-night, the search goes on for Carly Neath.

"Sound bite, Chief Albert again. 'She is five feet, one inch tall and weighs approximately one hundred pounds. She is blond, blue-eyed, and has a birthmark on the inside of her left wrist. She was last seen wearing a pair of white hip-hugger slacks, a blue-and-white-striped halter-type shirt, and white leather sandals. Anyone with any information that might help in finding Carly Neath should notify the Neptune Township Police immediately.' "

Here was the spot she would have liked to include a sound bite from Carly's neighbor. Instead, Diane recorded the alternate lines she had written. "KEY News has learned that a witness has come forward with information that may provide a clue. A man was seen following Carly last night as she walked near her home. Whether that man had anything to do with Carly Neath's disappearance is unclear. But Leslie Patterson says she feels sorry for Carly and what she might be facing.

"Okay, pick up Leslie's sound bite in the middle of her sentence. Start with: 'whoever it was never spoke to me,' and then just continue on. 'Left me lying there, wherever "there" was. He would come back once in a while to bring me something to eat, but I ate very little. And each time he came back, he would pull me up and want me to dance with him.'

"Last track. Dancing a sick dance that family and friends pray Carly Neath is not performing now. Diane Mayfield, KEY News, Ocean Grove, New Jersey."

CHAPTER

38

The minute he walked through the door, Larry loosened his tie and kicked off his shoes. It had been a long day, but it had been worth it. Today was no different from every other Saturday this summer. He'd made a sale. Knock wood. Larry knew from painful experience that it was never truly a sale until the closing. When all the documents were signed and all the money had changed hands, then, and only then, did the real estate agent get paid his commission.

But Larry had a hunch this deal was money in the bank. The buyers were prequalified for their mortgage, and they had already lost two other houses in the heated market. They weren't going to make waves about anything that came up in the physical inspection of the property. They just wanted to secure their own place at the shore.

Larry popped open a beer, shuffled across the living room to switch on the television set, and settled back on the couch. He wished he had someone who would talk about his day and celebrate his success. This was when he missed his wife and daughter most. Going off to work in the morning from an empty house was bad enough, but coming home at night to face another dinner by himself was worse. Sitting alone, evening after evening, watching the boob tube, gave him too much time to think.

Propping his feet up on the coffee table, he aimed the remote control at the set and clicked. Golf was just wrapping up on KEY, and the network news was about to begin.

The first story was about the war in Iraq, the second about the president's day. Larry got up and went to the refrigerator again. As he uncapped another beer, he heard the words "Ocean Grove" and hurried back to the living room.

He watched the piece with its pretty pictures of Ocean Grove and a smiling Carly Neath, and listened to Diane Mayfield's narration. But he was especially interested in what Leslie had to say.

"He would come back once in a while to bring me something to eat, but I ate very little."

For Larry, those words, and the sight of Leslie's sharp jawline and thin arms, brought back the pain that never went away. The memories of Jenna and all the times he'd tried so unsuccessfully to get her to nourish herself. Larry had spent countless hours trying to think of and procure any morsel that might tempt his daughter. But nothing had worked. Jenna went from thin to skinny to gaunt to emaciated.

Leslie was his chance to make up, in some way, for his mistakes with his own daughter. He had to help Leslie, make her see that while her eating disorder was extremely serious, it was solvable, and the solution lay within her. Not with that quack therapist. Owen Messinger had ruined Jenna, and now he was having his way with Leslie as well.

Burping as he switched off the set, Larry wondered why Leslie couldn't see what she was doing to herself. She had to learn that there were much bigger problems out there, problems that people could truly do nothing about. Being held against one's will was certainly a good example. If that didn't scare a kid straight, what would?

Larry held out the hope that Leslie had learned something from her terrifying experience and that it would lead to a real change in her self-destructive behavior and outlook on life. He was looking forward to Monday. Leslie would be back at work, and he could keep an eye on her again.

CHAPTER

39

Owen Messinger stared at the television set long after the KEY *Weekend Evening Headlines* concluded. He had been stunned to see Leslie Patterson speaking in the report. Her mother had told him only yesterday that Leslie didn't want to go out of the house.

But with Carly Neath's disappearance, Owen supposed Leslie felt vindicated and wanted to say so. Perhaps all this ugliness would end up being a good thing for Leslie. It might, in some bizarre way, make her feel better about herself. If the community saw that they had misjudged her and that she had been telling the truth, sympathy would flow her way and Leslie would get positive attention. She could use that.

God knew, he wasn't getting anywhere with her. All these years and Leslie was still anguished about food and still cutting herself. His therapy wasn't working at all with her on the cutting score. He was worried about that.

Owen went to the bar in his dining room and poured himself a double Scotch. He studied the amber liquid in the glass, unsure what he should do next. He had been working on his innovative approach to treatment with enough success that he was almost ready to publish. But Leslie was the fly in the ointment. His results with her negatively skewed the predicted outcomes of his study.

"Here, Cleo," he called out. "Where are you, baby?" Owen walked over to his desk while he waited to see if the cat would appear. He sat down, determined to do something about the stack of mail that had been accumulating all week. First he sorted out all the catalogs and tossed them in the wastepaper basket. That act alone made him feel he'd made a nice dent. Next he separated out the bills. That left a couple magazines and just one envelope.

The black-and-white feline jumped into Owen's lap as he took the letter opener and sliced open the envelope. He stroked the cat's fur as he read the message inside.

YOU ARE A CHARLATAN.

THAT THERAPY OF YOURS HAS HAD TOO MANY VICTIMS.

IF THE POLICE OR THE MEDICAL COMMUNITY WERE TO FIND OUT WHAT YOU DO TO THESE POOR WOMEN, YOU WOULD LOSE YOUR LICENSE. BUT, IF YOU DECIDE TO GO TO THE AUTHORITIES, HERE'S MY CARD. I CAN'T WAIT TO TELL THE POLICE ALL ABOUT YOU.

OR, IF YOU WANT A PIECE OF ME, I'D BE GLAD TO TAKE YOU ON DIRECTLY. COME ON OVER.

LET THIS BE A WARNING TO YOU. CEASE AND DESIST BEFORE
YOU DESTROY ANOTHER LIFE.

Owen picked up the white business card that had fluttered
to the carpet. It read "Surfside Realty" and had Larry Belcaro's
name emblazoned on it.

CHAPTER

40

When Diane got back to the Dancing Dunes, she found Anthony and Emily playing Scrabble in the parlor.

"I can see what you guys did today." She laughed. Both her
son's and her sister's faces reflected the time spent out in the
sun. "Does it hurt?"

"Quit worrying, Mom, will ya? We put on sunscreen."

"Where's Michelle?" Diane asked as she looked around the
room and through the entry to the dining room.

"She's upstairs." Emily didn't take her eyes off the Scrabble
board. "Queen. Q-U-E-E-N, and the Q is a triple-letter score,"
she said triumphantly.

Anthony's face fell, acknowledging the gap between him-

self and his aunt was almost insurmountable now. "I'm starving," he said. "When are we going to eat?"

"What are you in the mood for?" Diane asked, although the
last thing in the world she wanted to do after the long, hot day
she'd had was go out to dinner. A nice cool bath and long stretch
on the bed in her air-conditioned room sounded infinitely more
appealing. But this was their first night here, and she knew the
kids and Em had been waiting for her.

"Pizza?" Anthony suggested.

"Em?"

"Fine with me."

"Great," said Diane, grateful that they wouldn't have to sit
through a two-hour dinner service somewhere. "Anthony, run
up and get your sister, will you?"

While she waited for her children to come downstairs,
Diane pulled out her cell phone and finally left the message
at Dr. Owen Messinger's office that she would like to interview him about women's health issues for the *Hourglass*
piece.

"Please call me at your earliest convenience," she said into
the mouthpiece. "Of course, I understand you can't speak
specifically about Leslie Patterson, but I do have some general
questions our viewers would be interested in."

When asked for his suggestion, Carlos said they should drive over to Asbury Park to his favorite pizza parlor. "It's not long on atmosphere, but the pies are the best I've ever had."

Fifteen minutes later they were seated in the storefront restaurant. They ordered two pies, one just tomato and cheese, the other topped with pepperoni. Anthony dug right in, polishing off four slices in rapid succession. Emily and Diane both berated themselves for going for thirds. But Michelle took only one, nibbling at it and leaving all of the crust on her plate.

Diane hated the fact that she was keeping track now, watching every morsel of food that went into her daughter's mouth.

CHAPTER

41

Now that it was dark, it was as safe as it was ever going to be. The moonlight made going to the Casino risky, but there was nothing that could change that. It had to be done tonight.

Keeping close to the gently rounded outer wall of the Casino lessened the chance of being spotted. Around the curve, a breeze finally came in from the ocean, blowing at the giant copper sea horse that hung by metal threads, ready to snap from the roof of the neglected art deco building. A rickety fence blocked the entrance. Iridescent letters spelled DANGER: KEEP OUT. PRIVATE PROPERTY. NO TRESPASSING.

There was no difficulty slipping through the opening in the fence. Once inside, it was safe to turn on the flashlight. The yellow beam shot out over a wet cement floor strewn with bird droppings, broken shells, and seagull feathers. Bits of broken glass crunched underfoot.

Beneath the old sign that proclaimed the cavernous auditorium as the Casino Skating Palace, there was a hole in the wall, smaller than the one in the fence outside. It hadn't been easy dragging the dead weight of Carly's body through the hole last night, but traveling alone now, it was a snap to get in. There were more animal droppings and water damage on the wooden planks strewn around the neglected floor. Dominating the room was an abandoned stage, where in Asbury Park's heyday, so many popular acts had performed. It was now overgrown with brambles and littered with tar sheeting. Moss covered the long benches where fans once sat and cheered the summertime entertainment.

Rusted metal wagon-wheel-style chandeliers hung from the iron rafters. A thin shaft of light sifted through a hole in the roof. Strange. It almost seemed to point the way to the old refreshment counter, the place that was now Carly's hellhole.

It was essential that everything be done just so. Carly must go through the routine. It had been almost twenty-four hours since she'd been abducted and imprisoned. Now it was time to cut the plastic flex cuffs that bound Carly's ankles. It was time for her first dance.

CHAPTER

42

Carly couldn't see a thing, but she could hear just fine. Too well. She listened as the creature approached, shuffling through the debris. As the sounds grew closer, Carly couldn't tell if they were made by an animal or a man. She wasn't sure which would be worse.

She could feel her heart beating through her chest wall, reacting to the adrenaline shooting through her body. Her head was still throbbing, her wrists were sore and raw from whatever bound them. She tried to concentrate on her breathing, only able to take air in through her nose because the gag covered her mouth.

The footsteps stopped right beside her. A sliver of brightness slipped in through the thin opening at the bottom of Carly's blindfold. It must be a human being, who'd turned on the lights.

Carly felt tugging at her ankles and could feel the bonds slip off. Then her arm was gently grabbed and pulled upward. Maybe he was going to let her go.

She worked at getting to her feet, feeling dizzy and struggling to maintain her balance. Unable to make a sound, and not knowing what else to do, Carly stood and waited for what was coming next.

Hope was replaced with terror as the caressing began.

She wasn't sure how long it went on. A minute? Ten? Half an hour? It seemed like an eternity. Something smooth brushed back and forth across her cheeks and up and down her bare arms. Was it leather? A gloved hand?

And then a body pressed itself against hers and nudged her to move. Carly's hands were still bound, but she felt the fabric-covered arms wrap around her bare ones. She could hear soft swishing. Was that the sound of nylon rubbing against nylon? The sound ski pants made when they rubbed together as you walked through the snow?

As her tormentor's body started to rock to the rhythm of the tide, pulsing in and pulsing out, Carly's body automatically followed the lead. But she let her mind go to another place, trying to recall what it had been like to go sledding and make snowmen.

SUNDAY
AUGUST 21

CHAPTER

43

She opened her eyes and reached out for her watch on the table next to the bed. Diane was stunned to see it was almost ten o'clock and to realize that she'd slept soundly through the night.

She and Matthew had agreed that he would check with the police in the morning and then call her around noon to make their plans for the day. If there was anything to shoot earlier than that, Matthew and the crew would cover it. That left her two hours to spend with the kids.

Turning over, Diane watched her sister, still asleep in the twin bed beside her. She thanked God again that she had Em with them this week.

Trying to make as little noise as possible, Diane got out of the bed and pulled on her thin summer robe. Rummaging through her suitcase, she found the pair of terry-cloth slippers and put them on. Treading softly, she crossed the room and opened the door to the hallway. On her way to the bathroom, she noticed that the door to Michelle's room was ajar.

She knocked softly and poked her head through the doorway. "Michelle?" she called gently.

The room was empty, but it looked liked a tornado had swept through it. A suitcase lay open, its contents spilling over the sides. Clothes were strewn across the floor and unmade bed. Michelle's bottles of shampoos, conditioners, and creams were spread out over the dresser, and her CDs and DVDs lay in a jumbled mess on the night table. Diane shook her head and sighed. How had her daughter managed to wreak such havoc in such a short time?

And where was she?

Hoping that she wouldn't run into anyone but driven to go anyway, Diane started down the stairs. No one was in the lobby, or in the parlor. But Carlos and another man were in the dining room, arranging food and flowers on the buffet table.

"Excuse me," Diane said.

The men turned. Carlos smiled broadly. "Good morning, Ms. Mayfield."

"Diane. Please."

"Okay, Diane." Carlos turned in the direction of the other man. "Diane, this is my partner, Kip."

"Nice to meet you," Diane said as she pulled her robe closer around herself. "I'm not usually out prowling around a public place in my bathrobe, but I'm looking for my daughter."

"I haven't seen her yet this morning," said Carlos.

"Is she about thirteen or fourteen, brown hair, very thin?" asked Kip.

Diane nodded, wincing inwardly at the last description.

"Then I saw her leave about a half hour ago. She had shorts and sneakers on and had a Walkman with her. I just assumed that she was going for a run."

By the time Diane went back upstairs, showered, brushed her teeth, and returned to the room to dress, Emily was awake.

"Good morning, sleepyhead."

Her sister stretched out in the bed and sighed. "Oh, that felt good. If this is any indication of how the sleeping is going to be down here, I'm glad I came."

Diane pulled a black Donna Karan T-shirt over her head. "Want to come downstairs with me for some breakfast? I smelled something good cooking."

"Are the kids awake already?" Emily showed no signs of rising.

"Anthony is still sleeping, but Michelle's up and out already. I think she went for a run." Zipping up her white slacks, she added, "Em, can I ask you something?"

"What?"

"It's about Michelle." Diane swallowed. "Do you think she could have an eating disorder?"

Emily shifted her pillows and propped herself up. "God, Diane. I hadn't really thought about it."

Diane recounted her observations. The uneaten garlic bread, the barely touched pizza, the loss of interest in what were once her favorite foods. "She's been exercising like crazy, too, and it looks to me like she's lost some weight."

Emily was silent for a moment as she considered her sister's words. When she finally answered, Diane felt a bit better.

"Yeah, all that might be true," Emily said. "But do you remember when you were that age? All the competition to be the prettiest and have the best figure? Heck, that never changes. I think Michelle could just be responding to the pressures of being a female in our society. Does that mean she has an eating disorder? I doubt it, Diane."

"God, I hope you're right, Em. I hope you're right."

CHAPTER

44

Wanting to get the local version of what was happening, Matthew stopped at Ocean Grove Stationery on Main Avenue to buy a copy of the *Asbury Park Press*. He especially needed to find out where Carly Neath had been babysitting the night she disappeared. That was an element they hadn't had time to pay attention to for the piece last night but something they'd definitely need for the *Hourglass* segment. The police had refused to provide that information at their news conference, but local reporters had their own sources—sources that a journalist just coming into town couldn't possibly match. Matthew was hoping that the *Asbury Park Press* reporter had done some of his work for him.

He stood on the sidewalk in front of the candy store and read the front-page article. Sure enough, it revealed that Carly had been babysitting for the Richey family, summer residents who lived in one of the tents on Bath Avenue. The information excited Matthew, because he knew that not only were the tents visually attractive but their story would be an interesting sidebar.

He continued to read, discovering that Carly also worked as a waitress at Nagle's Apothecary Café. That was the place on the corner of Main, not so far from the beach. He'd noticed it yesterday on his way back to the motel. It was within walking distance now. It was worth trying to see if he could talk with anyone who knew Carly.

A few minutes later, Matthew reached the café. There were small tables set up on the sidewalk, but he opted for the interior's air-conditioning. Scanning the room, he saw that all the tables were filled, but there was one seat open at the end of the counter. He slid onto the stool, next to a balding, middle-aged man.

"What'll it be?" asked the waitress.

"Some coffee, for starters, Anna," Matthew said, reading her name tag. "Black, no sugar. Then I'd like a couple of eggs, over easy, and whole wheat toast."

"Bacon?"

"Why not? Life is short."

The middle-aged man turned to look at him, leaving Matthew with the feeling he had said something wrong. Matthew smiled uncertainly.

"How ya doin?" he asked the man.

"Fine." The man took a drink of orange juice. "You here on vacation?"

"No, but I wish I were. It's beautiful around here."

The man nodded as he reached into his pocket, pulled out a

white business card, and handed it to Matthew. "I'm Larry Belcaro, Surfside Realty. If you're ever looking for a place in Ocean Grove or Asbury Park, I'm your man."

"Thanks, Larry," said Matthew, slipping the card in his pocket and seizing the opportunity to talk to a local. "So I guess you live around here?"

"Yep. Been in Ocean Grove for over twenty years."

"Family?"

Larry looked down at the counter, and Matthew was immediately sorry that he'd asked. "Not anymore," the man answered quietly.

Matthew's bacon and eggs arrived, relieving the awkwardness of the moment. He took a bite of his toast, folded his newspaper, and positioned it on a clear section of the counter. "This is some story, isn't it?" he asked, motioning with his fork in the direction of the newsprint.

Larry nodded. "Yeah, it's hard to believe that all this has been happening in our little town. It's usually so nice and quiet around here. You shouldn't think we have a high crime rate or anything."

Matthew shook his head, realizing that the salesman wanted Ocean Grove to be seen in the best possible light. "No, I wasn't thinking that at all."

The waitress came back, refilled their coffee cups, and left both checks on the counter. As Larry picked his up, Matthew spoke. "It says in the article the missing girl works here. Do you know her?"

Larry nodded. "She was a pretty little thing. Always bright and chipper when she waited on me. But I used to tease her that she should eat something herself. She was too thin if you ask me, just like Anna here." Larry nodded in the direction of their waitress as he laid her tip on the counter and maneuvered himself off the stool. "Well, gotta go. But remember, if you're ever in the market for some real estate, call me."

"Will do." Matthew smiled and watched Larry walk out the front door, noting that he had referred to Carly Neath entirely in the past tense.

CHAPTER

45

As Diane was going down the stairs, she met Michelle coming up. Her daughter's face was bright red, and brown strands had escaped the covered elastic band that pulled her hair back in a ponytail.

"Have a good run?"

"Yeah, it was fine."

"Where'd you go?"

"Up and down the boardwalk a couple of times."

Diane nodded. "I'm going down to the dining room to get something to eat. Want to come with me?"

"No, thanks. I want to go up and take a shower."

Diane's face fell.

"What now, Mom?"

"Listen, honey. I want to be able to spend some time with you. I have to go to work in about an hour, and I don't know when I'll be back. I just was hoping we could sit down together for a little while."

Michelle sighed heavily. "All right." Diane ignored the grudging tone in her daughter's voice.

When they entered the dining room, Diane noticed Sammy Gates sitting at a table by the window. At another time she would have forced herself to invite him to join them, but this morning she just waved, called a greeting, and led the way to a table in the corner on the opposite side of the room. Carlos came over right away, took their drink orders, and pointed to the buffet.

"Help yourself to as much as you want," he said. "If you want toast, just let me know and I'll make it in the back. But you must try the sticky buns. Kip bakes them, and they're absolutely divine."

"Shall we?" Diane asked her daughter.

The buffet table was laden with silver chafing dishes containing scrambled eggs, sausage, and home-fried potatoes. A napkin-lined wicker basket held blueberry muffins and mini bagels. There was a big crystal bowl full of granola ready to be scooped into flowered bowls and a pretty pitcher full of milk. The special sticky buns were displayed on a large round tray. Their aroma was intoxicating.

"Wow, this looks delicious," Diane said. Not knowing when she would get another chance to eat, she began helping herself to a bit of almost everything.

"Is that all you're going to have?" she asked, staring at the dollop of scrambled eggs and the lone bagel on Michelle's plate.

"That's all I want right now, Mom."

"Oh, come on, honey. You have to eat more than that," Diane urged.

"No, Mom, this is all I want."

They went back to their table, and Carlos brought Michelle's Diet Coke and Diane's iced tea.

"It's not good to drink soda so early in the day, honey."

Michelle rolled her eyes. "Stop nagging me, will you, Mom?"

Diane salted her eggs. "I'm not nagging you. I'm just a little worried about you, sweetheart, that's all."

Michelle took a sip of soda before answering. "You don't have to worry about me. I'm fine."

"Are you, Michelle? Are you really fine?" Diane searched her daughter's face.

"You mean about Daddy?"

"Partly," Diane said softly.

"What's the other part?"

Diane took a deep breath and then blurted it out. "I'm worried about the way you've been eating, Michelle. I've noticed that you barely pick at your food, and I think you've lost some weight."

Michelle's face brightened. "You think I look thinner? Great."

"Honey, you didn't need to lose an ounce. You look wonderful."

"You're my mother. Of course you're going to say that."

Diane put down her fork. "No, I mean it, Michelle. You look just fine, in fact I think you could stand to gain a few pounds."

"No way." Michelle frowned.

"I'm not saying you have to put the weight you've lost back on, but I really think you shouldn't be trying to lose any more."

"You don't get it, Mom."

"Oh yes, I do. But I know that how thin we are isn't the thing we should be focusing on. It's not the most important thing."

Michelle sat back in her chair. "What, are you kidding me, Mom? I've seen you studying yourself in the full-length mirror in your bedroom. I've heard you worry about your weight all the time."

Diane felt slapped. Had she contributed to her daughter's obsession? "The reason I do is because the television camera makes you look heavier than you are. If I didn't have to be on

TV all the time, I can assure you I wouldn't pay so much attention to my appearance."

"Sure, right." Michelle smiled smugly. "Do you mean to tell me that if you weren't on television, you wouldn't color your hair blond, or have your nails done, or buy nice clothes?"

"I don't follow you."

"You do all those things because you want to be attractive, Mom. It has nothing to do with being on television. You want to look good."

Diane thought about what her daughter was saying. "Yes, but I have to look good to make my living."

"And I have to be thin to be popular at school, to be in the A group, to make guys like me. You brought it up, so I'm telling you, Mom. That's just the way it is." Michelle folded her arms across her chest.

Diane wasn't going to let those be the last words. She reached across the table and took hold of her daughter's arm. "Oh, Michelle, honey. Don't you see? It's not what's on the outside that counts most. Sure, it's nice to be physically attractive. There's absolutely nothing wrong with that. But it's not healthy to be obsessed with your weight and how you look. There are so many more important things in life. Your character is what counts, the content of your mind and the goodness of your heart. Not the external things."

Michelle's eyes glazed over. Diane could tell her daughter wasn't buying it.

CHAPTER

46

Arthur had no shadow as he stood at the end of the boardwalk. The sun was directly above his head, beating down mercilessly. He looked out at all the people baking on the sand, blistering and risking heatstroke. And they called *him* crazy.

He jumped down onto the sand and trudged toward the water, fully aware of the stares. People were always looking at him, thinking him odd, grateful they weren't him. Arthur had gotten used to it.

Turning north, he left the more crowded beach of Ocean Grove behind in favor of the neglected sands of Asbury Park. No barrier separated one beach from the other, but the empty beer bottles, soda cans, and paper debris littering the Asbury Park beach distinguished it from the well-tended Ocean Grove sand just yards away.

The screeches and laughter of the children playing in the rolling surf grew fainter as Arthur distanced himself from the sun worshipers. He turned around to look back at them. They weren't paying attention to him anymore.

He tried to appear aimless as he plodded across the sand toward the old Casino, knowing that when he did it, he had to do it like lightning, in a flash. Just where the Casino jutted out farthest toward the ocean, there was about two feet of space between the sand and the giant concrete slab upon which the building stood. He cut gradually across the scorching sand, and then he dropped down on all fours and slithered forward on his belly into the darkness beneath the giant concrete slab.

It took all of three seconds. Arthur was confident that no one had seen him. No one ever did. It was dim and cool inside, a relief from the blinding brightness and heat of the beach. As he'd been taught for combat in Desert Storm, Arthur scurried, like a sand crab, deeper into the darkness.

CHAPTER

47

The camera crew waited on the sidewalk in front of Lavender & Lace while Diane and Matthew went into the shop to ask for permission to shoot the activity at the makeshift search headquarters. Once the consent was given, Sammy and Gary carried their gear inside, careful not to knock into the merchandise that crowded the store.

The storeroom was abuzz with activity. People were clustered around a giant map of the area, sipping coffee as they got their instructions on where to search. The copy machine whirred as it printed out flyers with Carly Neath's smiling face. At a long trestle table, a middle-aged man held a telephone receiver to his ear.

"That was the police," the man said as he hung up. "They say they're bringing in search dogs. That's more than they did for Leslie."

Audrey Patterson held her finger to her lip and shook her head. "Don't, Lou. This isn't the time."

Diane overheard the exchange and realized the man must be Leslie's father. She was about to introduce herself when the man rose from his chair and strode over to the doorway, coming face-to-face with a younger man who'd just arrived.

"Hello, Mr. Patterson," the younger man said in a low voice.

"What are you doing here?" Leslie's father demanded.

"I came to see what I could do to help."

"Oh, I see. You never showed up to search for Leslie, but you want to look for Carly. That's nice, Shawn. Haven't you done enough already?"

"Please, Mr. Patterson. Please understand. I'm sorry about Leslie. I just couldn't come."

"Couldn't come or wouldn't come?" Lou Patterson didn't

wait for the answer. "You have a hell of a nerve showing your face around here, kid. First you dump my daughter, and when she disappears you're nowhere to be found. Now all of a sudden you want to help find another girl who had the misfortune to get involved with you. I know the cops are looking at you, Shawn. And you're here as the concerned boyfriend? What a joke."

"That's not true, Mr. Patterson."

"Don't tell me it's not true." Leslie's father's face reddened. "I can see right through you, and so can the police. I only wish Leslie could have seen through you too. Now get the hell out of here."

CHAPTER

48

The smell invaded the air, wafting up through Arthur's nostrils. It was a recognizable, distinctive smell. The odor that resulted from sickness, revulsion, or fear. He had known all of these.

Arthur wasn't sure if he wanted to investigate further. He

had just come in to escape for a while, to get away to somewhere dark and cool and peaceful. He sat on the old bleacher, looked up at the hole in the auditorium ceiling, and tried to decide what to do. He could ignore it and leave, or he could follow the smell and see where it led.

He got up, thinking that it would be best to leave. Glass and pebbles crunched beneath his high-top sneakers as he walked across the bleachers, heading for the passageway back out to the beach. But as the smell grew stronger, Arthur found himself compelled to follow it. He stepped down to the auditorium floor and went toward the old refreshment stand. The odor pulled him closer.

Arthur poked his head behind the counter. In the dim illumination from the hole in the ceiling, he could see a human form lying there. He stopped and waited to see if it moved. It didn't.

Nervously clearing his throat three times, Arthur inched forward. Spying the long, light hair, he forgot his reticence. He bent over the figure and rolled it over. Pulling off the blindfold that covered the eyes, he gasped. It was that pretty Carly Neath, Shawn's friend. As Arthur began to untie the gag around her mouth, he realized the smell was coming from the vomit soaking the cloth and covering Carly's cheeks.

She wasn't moving. Arthur shook her shoulders. He tried to clear her mouth and perform the resuscitation he had learned so long ago. But he couldn't get her to breathe on her own.

He had to get her out of here. He had to get her some help. Frantically, Arthur pulled at the sturdy plastic strips that bound Carly's ankles and held her wrists together. He felt at the birthmark on the inside of her limp wrist, searching in vain for a pulse.

CHAPTER

49

While Matthew and the crew stayed behind, capturing the images and sounds of the volunteers' search headquarters, Diane followed the young man who had been ordered out of the Lavender & Lace storeroom by Leslie Patterson's father.

"Shawn. Shawn," she called after him.

He turned around and looked at her with bloodshot eyes. "Yes?" he said warily.

"Shawn, I'm Diane Mayfield with KEY News." She put out her right hand. As he automatically reached out to shake it, she added, "Would you be willing to talk with me?"

Shawn pulled his hand back and ran it through his auburn hair. Diane noticed that his nails were bitten to the quick.

"I don't think that would be a very good idea," he said. "Not in here, anyway." He looked uncomfortably around the store's display area. "Maybe we should go outside."

On the sidewalk, Diane spoke first. "That was pretty rough for you in there, wasn't it?"

Shawn nodded, squinting in the bright sun. "Yeah. I shouldn't expect Mr. Patterson to understand how terrible I feel about what happened to Leslie. But I couldn't get involved in the search for her. I just couldn't."

"Why not?" Diane asked gently.

"Look, I really shouldn't be talking to you. The police think I have something to do with Leslie's and Carly's disappearances. They don't think it's a coincidence that I happened to be dating both of them."

"It doesn't look good," Diane agreed. "Maybe it would be a good idea to get your side of the story out there, Shawn."

"No," he said, shaking his head. "I don't think I should say anything on camera—at least not until I talk to my lawyer." He put the tip of his index finger to his mouth and tore at the ragged nail.

"All right, I understand," said Diane. "But how would it be if we talked off the record? You can tell me your side of things. To tell this story fairly, I need to know where you're coming from."

" 'Off the record' means you can't tell anyone what I say?"

"Not unless you decide to give me your permission."

Diane could see he was still uncertain. "Look, let's just start with some simple things. Like spelling your last name for me."

He complied, and she wrote it down in her notebook.

"And what do you do, Shawn?"

"I'm a graduate student, and I tend bar some nights at the Stone Pony to make money."

"What are you studying?"

"I'm working on my MSW."

"Social work?"

Shawn nodded.

"Admirable," Diane said. "And what do you want to do after you finish school?"

"Work with the mentally ill."

The wheels in Diane's mind sped. "Was that why you were attracted to Leslie Patterson, Shawn? Because she was troubled?"

He looked down at the sidewalk. "Maybe," he muttered. "I guess I didn't even realize it at first."

"Leslie was pretty needy, huh?"

"That's the understatement of the year." Shawn sighed heavily. "No matter how much attention I gave her, it was never enough. I thought I could help her, but I couldn't. I thought that if I made her feel secure, she would feel better about herself and start eating right. You'd think, with all the studying I've done, I'd have known better. I couldn't make Leslie well. She had to do that for herself."

"I thought she was in therapy," Diane said.

"She was. But I don't know what good it was doing. That

therapist of hers had a helluva job, though. Anorexia wasn't Leslie's only problem."

Diane waited.

"Leslie was cutting herself. When I found that out, I couldn't take it anymore."

"So you broke up with her?" Diane asked.

"Yeah, I'm not proud of it, but I did. I had to get out of the relationship. It wasn't healthy. But I felt guilty about breaking up with her, believe me. And when Leslie disappeared, I didn't think she had been kidnapped at all. I thought she was hiding somewhere, just to get attention. My attention. That's why I didn't join the search. I didn't want to feed into her sickness."

"So what do you think now, Shawn? Now that Carly Neath is missing too?" Diane's eyes searched his face. "Do you still think Leslie was faking it?"

Shawn stopped to consider the question. "No. I guess I don't. Carly is one of the most well-adjusted, happy girls I've ever met. I'm sure Carly isn't faking this, so maybe Leslie wasn't either."

CHAPTER

50

He was as angry with God as he was with himself, so Larry didn't bother going to church anymore. But that didn't mean he had no Sunday ritual. Every single week, after breakfast at Nagle's, he drove the five miles to St. Anne's Cemetery.

Larry parked the car, got out, and walked across the parched, brown grass, careful not to step where he estimated the bodies to be lying beneath the ground. Weathered granite headstones marked the final resting places of hundreds, all somebody's loved ones. Husbands, wives, sons, daughters. Acres and acres of sadness and heartache.

Jenna's and his wife's markers stood out from the others around them, still fresh and bright, the years of exposure to the elements yet to take place. Though Larry took some small comfort from the thought that the two people he loved were lying down there, side by side, the rage he felt at the injustice of their deaths trumped all other emotions.

He knelt on one knee and instinctively crossed himself,

knowing as he did it was wrong to cloak himself in religious ritual while he had so much anger in his heart. He knew he should let go of his hatred of Owen Messinger, but he just couldn't do it and he shouldn't be expected to. That man had ruined all their lives.

Larry rubbed his hand over the granite gravestone, then traced Jenna's carved name with his finger as he whispered, "I promise you, honey. I swear. I'll make sure that Owen Messinger can't do to other girls what he did to you. I've warned him now, and if he doesn't stop on his own, I'm going to stop him."

CHAPTER

51

Leslie spent her morning doing her sit-ups and leg lifts, washing her hair, taking a shower, and dressing, killing time before leaving for Lavender & Lace. When she got to search headquarters, she was going to do whatever was asked of her to help find Carly Neath, even though Carly had stolen Shawn away.

She pulled on a pair of cotton capri pants, noticing that they were a little looser than the last time she'd worn them. It seemed like so long ago now, but it was only the week before last. Shawn had taken her to play miniature golf, and she'd thought they were having so much fun. But when they went out to get something to eat after the game, they'd gotten into another fight. Shawn had insisted that she eat; Leslie didn't want to. The next time they went out, Shawn told her he didn't want to see her anymore.

Even though she was devastated Shawn had broken things off, Leslie almost felt sorry for him now. Last night she had overheard her parents talking about him and how the police must be looking at him as a suspect in both her and Carly's disappearances. Her father had been especially angry, declaring Shawn a no-good SOB. Her mother had quieted her husband, saying that he should just be relieved to know their daughter had been telling the truth all along.

Leslie went downstairs and stopped in the kitchen, opening the refrigerator and taking out a couple of celery stalks. She was looking for her other flip-flop when the telephone rang.

"Leslie? It's Dr. Messinger. How are you?"

Leslie closed her eyes. "I'm fine."

There was a pause on the line. The kind of pause Leslie was used to in their sessions. The pause that meant Dr. Messinger was waiting for her to continue talking. Well, she wasn't going to fall for it this time.

Messinger gave in. "I just wanted to remind you about group tomorrow."

"I don't think I'm going to be able to make it this time, Dr. Messinger. You know, I'm just going back to work tomorrow and everything. I think it's better if I skip it this time."

"I don't think that's wise." His voice was calm and patient. "It's important that you come. You've just been through a very traumatic time. Come and let the group congratulate you on your survival."

"To tell you the truth, Dr. Messinger, I'm sick of therapy. I don't think it's doing me any good. I want to try things on my own."

"We can talk about that when you come, Leslie. Four o'clock tomorrow. And remember, bring your stuffed animal."

"All right," said Leslie, already hating herself for giving in. "But this is the last time I'm coming."

It was as if the gods didn't want her to get to Lavender & Lace to help with the search for Carly. Leslie was standing on the porch locking the door when a police car pulled up at the curb. Chief Jared Albert himself, accompanied by another officer, got out of the vehicle and strode up the sidewalk. Leslie was pleased to see him take off his cap as a sign of respect when he reached her.

"Leslie, we have some questions to ask you," he said. "Your answers might help us find Carly Neath."

"Would you like to go in the house?" she asked. "It's so hot out here."

Chief Albert looked at the front door. "Are your parents home?" he asked.

"No, they're at the store with the search volunteers."

"It's just as well we talk out here on the porch then," he said. He might believe Leslie Patterson's story now that Carly Neath had gone missing too, but he still wasn't sure how stable she was. He didn't need to take any chances with a young woman who could falsely accuse the police of improper behavior. No, it was better to stay right here on the porch for everyone to see.

Leslie took her place in the rocker, while Albert and the younger officer sat side by side on the wicker sofa.

"We need more details about what happened during your abduction, Leslie," said the chief.

"I already told everything I remember when I was in the hospital," she replied. "What else do you want to know?"

"We'd like to know more about the dancing you described. There was no music playing?"

"No, just the sound of the ocean."

"You said you were blindfolded. But could you feel anything?"

She closed her eyes and tried to get a mental image. "I felt the man was wearing a nylon jacket of some kind. I could hear it swishing as his arms moved."

"Anything else?"

"I'm pretty sure he was wearing gloves too."

"Do you think they were latex, the kind a dentist wears?" asked Chief Albert.

"No, I think they were leather. I could smell the leather."

"Thank you for your cooperation with this, Leslie."

"That's okay," she answered. "I want to do anything I can to help. I'm on my way to the volunteer search headquarters now."

"Can we drop you off?" offered Chief Albert.

"No thanks. I'll walk." As she stood on the porch and watched the officers get back into their car, Leslie let out a sigh of relief. The police finally believed her.

CHAPTER

5 2

They decided to go back to the Starving Artist for lunch. After a ten-minute wait, they were seated at a table for four. Diane, Matthew, and Gary ordered club sandwiches, while Sammy, ever happy to take advantage of the KEY News expense account, ordered the more expensive crab cakes, a side of beer-battered onion rings, and a slice of cheesecake.

"What are you, begging for a heart attack?" said Matthew.

"Don't worry about me. I've got good genes," Sammy boasted. "No heart disease in my family."

"Ever hear of not tempting fate?" Matthew asked, to which Sammy only smiled smugly.

While they waited for their food, Diane recounted her conversation with Shawn Ostrander, giving his explanation of his relationship with Leslie Patterson and why he'd had to break up with her.

"I don't know," she said, stirring her iced tea. "I just can't picture this guy abducting women. He seems so earnest and sincere."

"Those are the ones you have to watch out for." Sammy sneered.

Diane ignored the remark.

"What about Carly?" asked Matthew. "Shawn must know that it looks bad for him that both of the missing women have been his girlfriends."

Usually quiet, Gary spoke up. "I sure wouldn't want to be in *his* shoes."

"Me neither," Sammy agreed.

After they'd finished eating and were waiting for Sammy to wolf down his dessert, Matthew pulled out the newspaper and showed Diane the section about Carly's babysitting for a tent family named Richey on Bath Avenue. "I think we should head over there next," he said. "Get pictures of the tent, see if someone will talk to us."

"Each one of these is cuter than the next. They're all so charming," said Diane as they walked down Bath Avenue. The tents, with their colorful striped awnings and hanging baskets full of summer flowers, created a scene from another world. A simpler, safer world, where young women didn't have to think about being abducted in the dark of night.

Sammy and Gary went about shooting the street and the various tents, knowing it was important to give the video editor

as many choices as possible for when he or she put the piece together at the Broadcast Center. Meanwhile, Diane and Matthew
tried to find someone to tell them which was the Richeys' tent.
But the tent porches were empty, their usual residents driven
either inside or away by the afternoon heat.

"I guess we'll have to start knocking," said Diane.

There was no answer at the first two tents they tried. At the
next, a little blond girl opened the screen door.

"Hello. Is your mother or father home?" Diane asked.

"My daddy's out, but my mommy's here." The child stood
staring at Diane.

"Could I speak with your mother, please?"

The child let go of the screen door and turned away.
"Mommy," she yelled into the tent. "There's someone here."

"Who is it?"

"I don't know."

Diane was about to tell the child who she was when the
mother came to the door. Diane thought the woman flinched
slightly as she introduced Matthew and herself. "We're looking
for the Richey family's tent."

"This is it. I'm Helen Richey. May I help you?"

"Oh, great," said Diane. "I suppose you can guess why
we're here, Mrs. Richey. The article in the *Asbury Park Press*
said Carly Neath was working here the night she disappeared."

Helen Richey turned and called back into the tent. "Girls,
I'll be out on the porch." Closing the door behind her, she indi-

cated that Diane and Matthew could take seats in the wicker chairs. "I don't want the children to hear anything," she said.

"Of course not," said Diane.

"We were hoping you could tell us about what happened that night," said Matthew, looking over Helen's shoulder to see if he could spot the camera crew and signal them to come over.

"We've told the police everything," said Helen, twisting her slim gold wedding band as she decided to corroborate her husband's story. "Carly babysat for the girls for about four hours. We got home after eleven o'clock. We paid her, and she left. It was a night like so many others when she's worked for us."

"So Carly went home on her own?" asked Diane. "No one walked her?" She tried to keep her tone from sounding accusatory. But she could sense the tension in Helen Richey's voice when she answered.

"Carly lives just a few blocks away. She was insistent that she walk home on her own. My husband and I thought it would be safe enough." She bit her lower lip, and tears welled in her eyes. "We made a mistake in letting her walk home alone, and if something terrible has happened to Carly, we'll never forgive ourselves."

CHAPTER

53

The tops of his feet were red, Anthony noticed as he sloshed through the salty water lapping over the sand. He supposed he should go back and slather on more of the sunscreen in his aunt Emily's bag, but he didn't want to. He had no desire to hang out with his aunt and his sister. He wanted to be by himself. He was still bummed out over missing his chance to go to the Grand Canyon. This boring beach vacation wasn't cutting it.

He took a picture of a sand castle, deserted by its architects, before he kicked the structure over. Then he bent down to pick up a piece of sea glass and continued his walk up the beach. Anthony watched the kids on boogie boards surfing in the waves, deciding that he was going to get his mother to buy him one of his own. Over the ocean, a windsurfer, tethered to a motorboat in the water below, glided through the air. Maybe he could get his mother to let him give that a try too.

She owed him. Big time. Even though he knew, deep down, his mother was doing everything she could to make him and Michelle happy, and he knew he should appreciate it and stop giving her a hard time, he was ticked off. He had bragged to all his friends about the cool trip he'd be taking this summer. Now, when school started and they found out he hadn't gone, they'd say he'd been full of crap. Coming on top of his father's going to jail, Anthony couldn't afford one more thing to make him look bad.

Maybe he could figure out a way to put a different spin on things. But what could possibly happen in Ocean Grove that would impress his friends? His mother would kill him if he tried to get involved in the search for that girl. But it would be neat if he could find her. That would be so cool. He'd probably be on the news.

"Anthony. Annnnthoneeee."

He turned around. Emily was standing down the beach, waving her arms, calling him like he was a little kid. Resigned, he started to trudge back through the water. He hadn't gone far when he saw the man dressed in army fatigues slip from beneath the concrete that surrounded the big round brick building. Anthony stared as the man planted himself in the sand and curled up in a fetal position. He snapped a picture before he hurried down the beach.

CHAPTER

54

God forgive her. She'd made it sound as if Jonathan had been with her when Carly was paid for babysitting that night—that he was in the tent with his wife when Carly insisted on walking home by herself. Helen had misled Diane Mayfield and the KEY News producer just now, as she had stood by when Jonathan lied to the police yesterday. She prayed that God would forgive her.

In order to be forgiven, Helen knew she had to be truly repentant. God could see into her heart, so He would know that she was truly sorry. But He must also see that she didn't know what else to do. Jonathan was her husband, the father of her children, and there was no way she was going to point a finger at him.

Helen went back into the tent and admired her children's artwork as they colored at the kitchen table. "That's beautiful, Hannah. I think we should hang that one up. Yours too, Sarah."

She taped the crayoned seascapes onto the refrigerator,

knowing that Jonathan would be back soon from his run on the beach. Fueled by suspicion and fear, she went to the bedroom dresser to find her husband's wallet. Inside the leather billfold there was a couple hundred dollars in cash to get them through the week, a Visa and MasterCard, a new high-tech New Jersey driver's license, and a white business card. "Surfside Realty" was stamped across it in blue block letters. Helen turned the card over and read the handwritten notation. "Thursday, August 18. 4:00."

It didn't make sense. Jonathan couldn't have had an appointment to look at real estate on Thursday afternoon. He hadn't even been here on Thursday. Jonathan hadn't come down to the shore until Friday.

CHAPTER

55

"I'm always going to love this town," said Carlos, taking his partner's hand as they and their real estate agent walked along the near-empty boardwalk. "Asbury Park issued us our marriage license."

"Well, you and Kip would be very smart to buy something here as soon as you can," said Larry, pulling off his tie in the heat. "The prices have already escalated dramatically, and now that the billion-dollar development project has the green light, you can be sure things are only going to get more expensive."

"Yeah," Kip agreed. "Once they pour that money into developing all this empty space on the waterfront, Asbury Park should really return to life."

"I hope to God they don't ruin things by tearing down all the interesting and historic places." Carlos frowned. "I'm still sick about the Palace. Who'd have thought a wrecker's ball would demolish the nation's oldest indoor amusement park? It was on the National Register of Historic Places and everything. I'll never understand what passes for progress."

They slowed as they reached the decaying old Casino, with its wind-scarred copper filigree work. "You haven't heard that they're going to tear this place down, have you, Larry?" Kip asked. "I'd die if they destroyed this place. It's my favorite building in Asbury Park."

"Well, I know there's a few preservation groups who say they'll never let it be torn down," said Larry. "But I guess you can never say never."

The three men stood looking out toward the ocean and discussed the fact that gays and lesbians had found a tolerant community in Asbury Park, a town grateful for the help these newcomers were giving to its revival.

"Asbury Park is what South Beach, Florida, was twenty years ago," said Carlos. "We want to get in on the turnaround."

Kip agreed. "Yes. We love the way we have been welcomed in Ocean Grove, and we're thrilled with our inn. We already have reservations for next season. But by the end of the year, we'll be finished with our renovations on the Dancing Dunes. We'll be ready to take on another project."

"Well, should we start looking at what's available now?" asked Larry. "Even though you don't think you're ready to buy quite yet, you can start educating yourself on the Asbury Park market. I have a couple of listings right now that, with some tender loving care, could be fabulous bed-and-breakfast places."

"Sounds good," said Kip. "And, Larry? Before I forget. Can I have a few of your business cards? I have some friends who are interested in finding something in Asbury Park as well."

As Larry took out his billfold and handed over the white cards, a police car skidded to a stop in front of the Casino.

CHAPTER

56

A small crowd gathered in front of the old Casino as the police led the man from the beach.

"It's going to be all right, pal," said one of the officers. "We're going to get you some help."

The man stumbled through the sand, flanked by two policemen, who struggled to keep him walking. His camouflage shirt was open, his hair mussed. He stared straight ahead, his eyes glassy. Arthur didn't utter a sound.

CHAPTER

57

They searched for as long as the light held out, knocking on doors, looking under the boardwalk and up and down the streets. Since it was church property, the Ocean Grove Camp Meeting Association gave permission for the volunteer search parties to look under every tent on its grounds. Tenters themselves readily opened their doors, sure that Carly Neath was not going to be found in their tiny canvas homes.

It was just after nine o'clock when everyone returned to Lavender & Lace and called off their search for the day, not knowing where they could possibly look tomorrow.

CHAPTER

5 8

When it had been dark for a few hours and it came time for the second dance, Carly's blindfold was off. Her gag was gone too, though her hands and feet were still bound.

Behind the deserted refreshment counter inside the Casino, the beam from the flashlight illuminated Carly's lifeless face. Her mouth hung open. Fine blue veins showed beneath the translucent skin of her eyelids. Her cheeks and beautiful golden hair were matted with vomit.

This wasn't the way it was supposed to happen. It was supposed to go off just like the last time.

The yellow beam searched the littered ground, finding the discarded blindfold and gag. The rags were tied back in place, just as they had been the last time. But now, it would be different. The young woman the guard found this time would be dead. There was no sense in holding her for the full three days. The police would likely be able to figure out that Carly had not survived even two days in captivity.

MONDAY
AUGUST 22

CHAPTER

59

Diane awoke to the sound of her ringing cell phone. She felt on the bedside table for her watch. In the early morning light, she was barely able to see that it was only six o'clock.

"Hello," she answered groggily.

"Diane. It's Matthew. You've got to get up."

"What?" She rubbed at her eyes.

"Meet me at the police station. A satellite truck is on its way down, and you have a seven-twenty live shot for *KEY to America.*"

Diane sat upright, trying to focus as Matthew continued talking.

"Carly Neath has been found, Diane. She's dead."

By the time Diane arrived at the police station, Matthew had written a script for her. Gary Bing recorded her narration and ran with the tape to the satellite truck that had just arrived from New York City. The narration was fed to the Broadcast Center to be edited with various video elements that had already been fed in for Diane's *Evening Headlines* piece along with video recorded yesterday at Lavender & Lace and some of the tent shots taken on Bath Avenue. Meantime, Sammy Gates set up the gear to record the police press conference and transmit Diane's live portion of the report.

"The police said they would have a presser at seven o'clock," said Matthew, looking at his watch. "It's seven-oh-five. We better figure out what you're going to say if they don't talk in time."

Diane looked down, appearing to study the ground as she tried to compose what she would say when Harry Granger tossed to her from the studio in New York. The minutes ticked away, and still no police spokesperson came out to address the hastily assembled media.

Gary returned from the satellite truck and outfitted Diane with a wireless microphone and a tiny plastic earpiece. Once she inserted the earpiece, she could hear directions from the control room and whatever Harry Granger would ask her from the *KEY to America* studio.

"Five minutes, Diane," the warning voice came.

She gave the thumbs-up signal to Sammy's camera lens, knowing her image was flowing to the receivers at the Broadcast Center. She switched her cell phone to vibrate so it couldn't ring during the live shot.

"Let's have a mike check, Diane, please."

"Testing. One, two, three, four, five. Five, four, three, two, one."

She turned to check the empty podium set up on the sidewalk in front of the police station.

"Two minutes, Diane."

She pulled a mirror out of her purse, reapplied her lipstick, and smoothed her hair.

"One minute."

She could hear the story before hers wrapping up. Next she heard Harry Granger's deep voice introducing her. Diane swallowed as she waited for the toss.

"KEY News Correspondent Diane Mayfield is in Ocean Grove, New Jersey, with the story. Diane?"

"Good morning, Harry," she began, her face somber. "Already in the grip of a record heat wave, this small beach community is now gripped by terror and fear—fear that there is a murderer on the loose. Early this morning, the body of twenty-year-old Carly Neath was discovered on the grounds of the Ocean Grove Camp Meeting Association—the same place where another young woman was found Friday morning after she had been missing for three days. Leslie Patterson was alive; Carly Neath, who never returned home after a babysitting job Friday night, wasn't as lucky."

At that point, the control room switched to the edited video package. For the next minute and a half, Diane listened through the earpiece to her own voice narrating the story that was being fed out to the entire KEY network. Matthew's script covered all the bases, leading with Carly's disappearance after babysitting at one of the tents, talking about the townwide search that had followed the search for Leslie Patterson just days before. The script said local police had suspected Leslie Patterson of faking her own abduction, but with the disappearance of a second victim, now found dead, the investigation had taken another turn.

Diane knew the package was almost over. The camera would be coming back to her. She listened for the last words she had recorded. "The outcue is: 'mortal danger that lurks in Ocean Grove,' " came the voice in her ear.

She heard the closing words, waited a beat, and began speaking into the camera. "A police spokesperson is expected to come out any moment, Harry, to give us more details on the situation. Authorities have their hands full here. This is the height of the vacation season, and this town has almost twice the population it has in the winter months. That's a lot of frightened folks, Harry, and they want to feel safe again."

"What about Leslie Patterson, the young woman who was thought to have cried wolf?" the anchor asked. "She must take some comfort that people believe her now."

"We talked with Leslie this weekend, Harry. Of course, that was before Carly Neath was found. But Leslie said that was the worst part of an ordeal which included being held against her will for three days and nights and forced to dance, blindfolded, with her abductor. Worse than anything she'd been through, she said, had been the fact that people thought she was lying about it all."

Within moments of her signing off, Diane's cell phone vibrated.

"Nice piece."

She recognized the voice and winced.

"Just make sure you get exclusives for us. I don't want the day-of-air broadcasts to rob *Hourglass* of its thunder."

"Don't worry, Joel. There's plenty of misery to go around down here." Diane shook her head and rolled her eyes at Matthew. "Though this isn't the story we thought it was going to be, Joel. You sent me down here to cover a girl who cried wolf. Now it looks like we've got a young woman who was telling the truth and a killer on the loose."

"Not to worry." Joel's voice had a twisted lilt to it. "This could work out even better. Give our *Hourglass* broadcast another dimension."

"You mean . . ."

"I mean," Joel interrupted, "we already have the stories about the girls who really *did* cry wolf. Yours can focus on what it's like to be telling the truth and have no one believe you."

CHAPTER

60

Owen Messinger spooned cornflakes into his mouth as he watched Diane Mayfield on the television screen. He was going to have his work cut out for him with Leslie when she came for group therapy today—that is, *if* she came for group therapy.

If she had already seen herself as unfairly persecuted by everyone who hadn't believed her, her story getting national attention would only create further psychological issues for her to address. If Leslie had ever craved attention, she was certainly getting it now.

Stashing the cereal bowl in the kitchen sink, Owen took a can of cat food from the pantry and emptied its contents into the aluminum bowl on the floor. "Okay, Cleo, I'm leaving your food out, baby," he called. "Daddy's gonna be home late tonight."

He exited through the kitchen door, forgetting that he had left his cell phone recharging on the counter. He got into his black Volvo and adjusted the air-conditioning as high as it would go. Another scorcher was on the way.

It was a short drive to the office. When Owen pulled into

the parking lot, he noticed two police cruisers parked near the entrance of the professional building. He parked the car in his reserved space, went directly into the building, and took the elevator to the third floor.

The door to his office was wide open.

"What's going on here?" Owen asked as he surveyed the overturned furniture in the reception area.

"Oh, Dr. Messinger," said Christine with relief. "I've been trying to reach you, but there was no answer on your cell. This is what I found when I came in." His assistant made a sweeping gesture at the disarray.

Owen looked past her, through the doorway to his office. The police officers were taking stock of the chaos in the room. "Can you tell if anything's missing?" asked one of them.

Taking his key ring from his pocket, Owen unlocked his desk drawers and checked each one. "Nothing has been touched here, thank goodness," he said.

"How about anywhere else? Anything missing?"

Owen looked over at the bookcase and saw the gaping space where his patient binders used to be. All of his treatment notes were gone.

CHAPTER

6 1

"Leslie. If you're going to go to work today, you have to get up."

Hearing her mother's shrill voice call up the stairs, Leslie groaned and turned over in her bed. She was still tired and didn't want to get up.

"I'm not kidding, Leslie. If you don't hurry, you won't have time for breakfast."

That's fine by me, thought Leslie as she rubbed her eyes. She lay on her back, staring up at the ceiling and the glow-in-the-dark plastic stars she had affixed there a good ten years ago. No wonder she was depressed. This was a kid's room, not a woman's. But if she had any hope of getting away from her parents' nagging and treating her like a child, she had to have an income of her own.

She forced herself to get out of bed, her bare feet landing on one of the hooked rugs her mother was so proud of making. Pale pink rosettes sprinkled the cream-colored background. Leslie looked from the rug to the pink walls and the white furniture painted with clusters of tiny flowers and made a vow.

When she got a place of her own, there would be none of this frilly, girlie stuff.

She took off the T-shirt and gym shorts she'd slept in and stood before the mirror. As she turned from side to side, examining her body from different angles, Leslie promised herself she was going to eat as little as she possibly could today. That would be no small feat with her mother and Larry Belcaro watching her like hawks.

In the shower, the warm needles of water pounded against her tightly stretched skin. The towel felt rough against her back as she dried herself. Running the toothbrush around her mouth, she liked the way the white paste made her teeth look brighter.

She chose a short, brown cotton skirt and peach-colored blouse to wear for her first day back in the office, in part to please Larry. He always complimented her when she wore peach. He said it made her brown eyes look especially warm and pretty.

"Leslie. When are you going to get down here?"

"I'll be right there, Mom."

Spinning in front of the mirror again and sucking in her stomach and cheeks, Leslie wasn't satisfied with her appearance, but she couldn't do anything more than she already planned not to do.

Audrey Patterson scooped a large serving spoon of scrambled eggs onto her daughter's plate, followed by three strips of bacon and a buttered English muffin.

"Orange or pineapple juice, Leslie?"

"Orange, please."

As her mother turned her back to go to the refrigerator, Leslie ripped off a piece of her muffin, snatched a strip of bacon from her plate, and dropped them into the canvas tote bag she'd carefully lined with wax paper the night before and positioned on the floor next to her chair. As Audrey poured the juice into her daughter's glass, Leslie noticed her mother's eyes scanning her plate. Leslie slipped her fork under the scrambled eggs and put some in her mouth.

"Stop looking at me while I eat, will you, Mom? How many times have I told you how much I hate it when you do that?"

Audrey bit her lower lip. "I'm sorry, honey. I guess I don't even realize that I'm doing it. I just want to make sure you're eating."

"Well, you're only making things worse. It makes me nervous." Leslie put down her fork and sat back in her chair.

"All right. All right. I'll stop watching you."

Audrey went to the sink, squirted in some liquid detergent, and turned on the water. With her back to her daughter, she scoured the frying pan while Leslie deposited the rest of the bacon and half of the muffin in the tote bag. She knew well enough that if everything disappeared from her plate, her mother wouldn't believe she had eaten it all. By moving around the eggs and leaving a bit of muffin, she could get away from the table with her mother thinking she'd had enough for breakfast when in fact she'd consumed only a mouthful of egg and a few sips of orange juice.

"All right, I'm done." Leslie pushed back her plate. "I can't eat any more. I've got to get going."

Her mother turned from the sink, her eyes sweeping Leslie's plate and then searching her daughter's face. "Leslie, I have to tell you about something before you go."

"What?" Leslie asked cautiously.

"I had the news on before you came down for breakfast, honey, but I didn't want to tell you before you'd eaten."

"Tell me what?"

Audrey sat down across the table and reached out to take hold of her daughter's arm. "Carly Neath was found at the Beersheba Well early this morning."

"Good," said Leslie, her face brightening. "Now everyone will totally believe me."

Audrey looked down at her lap.

"I didn't mean that was the most important thing, Mom," Leslie added hastily. "I'm glad they found Carly."

Audrey looked up again. There were tears in her eyes.

"What, Mom? What is it?"

"Carly is dead, sweetheart."

Leslie was silent.

"Leslie, honey, are you all right?"

"Yeah, I'm fine. I just don't know what to say. . . . Except I guess that could have been me. I realize how lucky I am, Mom." She picked up her tote bag and started for the door but stopped. "I forgot Lee Lee," she said. "I need her for group today. Dr. Messinger wants us to bring in our favorite childhood stuffed animal."

She ran back upstairs to her room and pulled the tattered teddy bear from its spot on the bookcase. Then she carefully lifted the wax paper lining from her tote, wrapped up the remains of her breakfast, and put it back inside the bag to discard later. She placed her beloved Lee Lee on top.

CHAPTER

62

Why hadn't he gotten that lawyer's beeper number or something? Shawn's heart pounded, and he could feel the heat in his cheeks as he hung up the telephone. The news, all over national television, that Carly's body had been found left Shawn feeling panicked. Leslie had disappeared, but Carly was actually dead. Both were his girlfriends, and the police suspected him. Before it was for kidnapping; now it could be for murder.

He was also ashamed. The fear that the police were going to come and drag him away superseded any emotion he felt over Carly's death. At the end of the day, he was just like so many others, wasn't he? Concerned primarily with his own well-being.

Shawn paced back and forth in the small living room of his apartment. He had to calm down, had to try to think rationally. The public defender would return his call and tell him what to do.

The ringing of the telephone cut the air. Thank God, the lawyer was calling back already. Shawn sprang for the receiver.

"Hello?"

"Shawn Ostrander, please."

"Speaking." It must be a secretary or receptionist calling. The lawyer would surely be on the line in a second.

"This is Jersey Shore University Medical Center calling. We have a patient, an Arthur Tomkins, admitted here. He has your name in his wallet as the person to notify."

"Is Arthur all right?" Shawn asked automatically.

"He's in stable condition. But you'll have to speak with the doctor for more details."

Shawn's chest tightened. He didn't want to be bothered with Arthur right now. He needed to concentrate on what he was going to do to get himself out of this nightmare.

"Mr. Ostrander?"

What kind of person was he? If Arthur needed him, he had to go to the poor man. He had to do the right thing. Besides, the police would be watching him. He should go about his business as though there was nothing amiss. In an instant, Shawn committed himself.

"Please tell Mr. Tomkins I'll be there as soon as I can."

CHAPTER

63

Chief Albert came out to apologize and say the press conference would be postponed until ten o'clock. At 10:00, he came out to promise he'd have something for the media at 11:30. Finally, at noon, he emerged from the tiny police station and stood behind the wooden podium, ready to make the announcement. The KEY satellite truck fed the video and audio to the Broadcast Center for use on the local news noon broadcast.

"Due to the urgency of this situation, an autopsy has already been performed on the body of twenty-year-old Carly Neath. The county medical examiner's office has determined that Ms. Neath died of asphyxiation."

"She was suffocated?" Diane called out.

Chief Albert consulted his notes before answering. "She choked on her own vomit."

"So she wasn't murdered?" asked the *Asbury Park Press* reporter.

"We don't know that," answered the policeman. "This is an ongoing investigation. But I can say, under New Jersey law, when someone abducts another person and that person dies during the abduction, the kidnapper would be considered responsible."

"So that means you think there is someone else out there who is responsible for Carly's death?" another reporter pressed.

"I didn't say that." There was annoyance in the officer's voice. "I can tell you that we are looking at every possibility." Chief Albert glanced in Diane's direction again.

"Of course the police understand that the community is extremely anxious about this case, Chief." Diane spoke in a measured tone. "They're terrified there's a killer on the loose in Ocean Grove. What would you tell them to alleviate their fears?"

"I'd tell them that the police are on top of the situation. That's all I'm going to say at this point, though we might have something more for you later today." With that, Chief Albert spun around and went back inside the station.

CHAPTER

64

With the sun so harsh she couldn't let her girls outside, and with all the tension and anxiety in town, Helen Richey finally agreed to allow a television set into the tent. She asked Jonathan to go out and buy one, only to have him remind her he already had one in the trunk of the car. He happily set it up.

While her daughters sat at the kitchen table eating tuna sandwiches, Helen sat in the front room of the tent, watching the clips of the police news conference on the WKEY noon news, careful to keep the volume low so the girls wouldn't hear. She saw Diane Mayfield and listened to her question about what could be done to alleviate the town's fears. When Chief Albert responded that the police were on top of the situation and might have more information later in the day, Helen shivered despite the warm air in the tent.

Carly Neath, that sweet girl, was dead. What if Jonathan had something to do with it? What if her husband had followed the young woman as she walked home Friday night? And what if Jonathan had also been involved in Leslie Patterson's disappearance last week?

Helen switched off the television, sat back down on the wicker chair, and tried to concentrate. The Surfside Realty business card she'd found in Jonathan's wallet indicated he'd had an appointment in Ocean Grove last Thursday afternoon. If that was true, why hadn't he told her about it? And if Jonathan was in town on Thursday, that meant he could have been the one who left Leslie Patterson tied up at the Beersheba Well gazebo in the middle of the night.

Where was he now, she wondered, as she got up, walked over to the screen door, and opened it. Helen looked up the street to see if he was coming back from his walk to the hardware store. He was forever doing errands, and in her heart, Helen suspected her husband was looking for reasons to get out of the tent and away from her and the kids.

Her mind raced. What if, somehow, Jonathan had cracked under the pressure of her demands that they live in a way he detested? That would make her partly responsible for what had happened to Carly and Leslie Patterson. She couldn't live with that.

Helen went inside. "Finished with lunch, girls?" she called as she strode resolutely toward the back of the tent. As soon as Jonathan got back from town, she was going to encourage him to get out the big umbrella and take the kids to the beach. Then she would be free to do what she had to do.

CHAPTER

65

Larry insisted on switching the phones over to the answering service, locking up the office, and taking Leslie to lunch. He decided against Nagle's or the Starving Artist, knowing that the locals would be gossiping about the Carly Neath tragedy and staring at Leslie. Instead, he drove around Wesley Lake to Asbury Park and the Italian restaurant that had been Jenna's favorite before his daughter obsessed about every morsel she put in her mouth.

For Larry, it was a painful hour as he watched Leslie eat very little of her salad. He knew better than to comment. He had learned that much at least when they were dealing with Jenna's problem.

"I'm so glad that you've come back to work, Leslie," he said as they waited for the check. "That's right where you should be. It's good to keep busy."

Leslie nodded and spoke softly. "You know, Larry, those three days were very, very scary. I have never been so afraid in my life. But when I was tied up and there all by myself, I found myself thinking about how messed up my whole life is."

Larry leaned forward to listen more closely.

"Now that I have another chance, I've been thinking about getting my real estate license."

"That would be super, Leslie." His weathered face beamed. "You know I'll help you any way I can."

"I know you will," she said.

They drove back to the office, chatting about where Leslie could take the real estate licensing course and how difficult the state exam was. As Larry pulled into his parking space, they noticed that a woman was waiting at the front door. He hurried up to meet her, apologizing that she had been forced to wait outside in the heat.

"That's all right," said the honey-haired woman. "I just got here a little while ago."

"I'm Larry Belcaro." He extended his hand. "And this is my assistant, Leslie Patterson."

The woman shook Larry's hand, but her eyes stared at Leslie. "Helen Richey," she said.

Leslie took her seat at the desk near the door and picked up a magazine while Larry ushered the woman into his office.

"What is it you're looking for?" Larry asked. "Do you want to rent or buy?"

"Well, actually, neither," said the woman.

"Oh, you have a place to sell." He uncapped his pen. "Is it here in Ocean Grove?"

"No, it's not that either." Helen looked uncomfortable as she zipped open her purse and pulled out a small white card. "I'm trying to find out about this." She handed the card across the desk. "You see, I found it with my husband's things, and I wanted to ask if he had an appointment with you last week."

Larry looked at both sides of the card. "Let's see," he mused. "Last Thursday at four o'clock. I don't think so." He opened the appointment book on his desk. "No, that's right. I had a closing last Thursday. I didn't show any real estate that afternoon."

CHAPTER

66

"God, now *Evening Headlines* wants a piece for tonight." Matthew snapped his cell phone shut. "I tried to talk them into sending down one of their own producers and another correspondent, but they want you."

"I'd be flattered if I didn't know how short-staffed they are in August. It's me by default," Diane said. "Does Joel know?"

"Yep," Matthew replied. "Range Bullock talked to him, one executive producer to another."

Diane smiled. "I can just imagine that conversation, Joel reminding him again and again how much Range was going to owe him."

"Yeah, and we're the currency," Matthew declared, uncapping his pen and flipping open his notebook. "We might as well get to it. The only new video we have is the police presser this afternoon."

"And we can only hope they are going to say something else before airtime," Diane added.

"Range said he'd like us to try to give the flavor of the town, let the viewers see and feel Ocean Grove, get some reaction from people on the street. Do you want to go over to Nagle's, where Carly worked, and see if we can get reaction from people who knew her?" Matthew asked.

"Sounds like a plan," Diane agreed.

CHAPTER

67

He hated the smell of hospitals. Shawn tried not to inhale, listening to the squeak of his tennis shoes against the linoleum floor. *What a silly thing to focus on,* he thought as he walked down the long hallway. *You could be accused of kidnapping and murder—and you're wrinkling your nose at the scent of disinfectant.*

Shawn felt slightly better, though, since the public defender had called him back. The attorney said that the police would already have arrested Shawn if they'd had enough to connect him to Leslie's and Carly's abductions. The lawyer assured him that unless there was physical evidence or an eyewitness who tied him to the young women's disappearances, it was highly unlikely he could be convicted of anything. Just the fact that he had dated two women who had disappeared didn't make him a kidnapper or a killer. Shawn was holding on tight to those words.

The door to the hospital room was open. It was a double room, but the bed closer to the door was empty. Shawn treaded quietly toward the bed on the other side of the curtain.

"Arthur?" he whispered.

He opened his eyes and turned toward Shawn, his hair getting more disheveled as it rubbed against the pillow. Arthur's usually tanned skin looked almost ashen against the faded cotton hospital gown.

"How you doin', buddy?" Shawn asked.

Arthur didn't answer.

"What's wrong, Arthur? You can tell me, man," Shawn urged.

"He hasn't said a word since they brought him in here."

Shawn jumped at the woman's voice.

"Sorry, I didn't mean to startle you. I'm Dr. Varga," she said as she walked around the bed and reached for Arthur's wrist.

"I'm Shawn Ostrander."

"A relative?"

"No, a friend." There was no point in getting into the long story of how his association with the mentally ill man had started as a research project. Arthur had become more than that. "His relatives don't have anything to do with him anymore."

The doctor nodded.

"What's wrong with him?" Shawn asked.

"Nothing physically, but he's not talking. When the police brought him in, they filled us in on his mental status."

"Yeah, Arthur is pretty well known around town." Shawn smiled crookedly.

The doctor scribbled a notation on the chart. "Fortunately, he had his meds in his jacket pocket. We can't be sure if he was taking them before he got here, but he's getting them now."

"When will you let him go home?" Shawn asked.

"That depends," answered Dr. Varga. "But I would suspect there is no rush, is there?"

Shawn shook his head, thinking of the sad little room in the tired boardinghouse that Arthur called home. "No, there isn't any rush at all," he said.

The doctor patted Arthur's arm before leaving the room. Shawn sat down and held a one-sided conversation about the hot weather and how crowded Ocean Grove was with all the summer visitors. He didn't mention the extra people who were streaming into town to cover Carly's story.

"Okay, buddy," he said, rising from the chair he had pulled alongside the bed a half hour before. "I'm gonna get going for now. But I'll call the nurses' desk later to see how you're doing." He put his hand on Arthur's shoulder. "You just rest now, Arthur. Don't worry, guy. Everything is going to be all right. Just rest, you hear me?"

Arthur's watery eyes looked directly into Shawn's, and he uttered the only words he'd spoken since he'd been brought to the hospital. "Okay, Shawn. I always do what you tell me to do."

CHAPTER

68

Diane, Matthew, and the crew stood on the sidewalk and asked the lunch customers who came out of Nagle's what they thought about the state of affairs in Ocean Grove. There was no shortage of people willing to talk, and their sentiments were all largely the same.

"I think it's just awful. To think in a pretty little town like this, such a terrible thing could happen. God help that poor girl's parents."

"I'm scared to death. I have children, and I won't let them out of my sight. Plus, how do I explain something like this to them?"

"It's horrible. We're down here on vacation, but we're thinking of going home early. This isn't what we had in mind when we were looking for a peaceful week at the beach."

Within half an hour they had plenty of reaction sound bites for the *Evening Headlines* piece. Yet not one of the people said they had known Carly Neath.

"I think we should go inside and see if anyone who actually

worked with Carly will talk with us," Diane suggested. "Why don't I find out if there's anyone in there who will talk, and I'll see if we can get permission to shoot inside as well."

The air-conditioned restaurant was a welcome relief from the heat outside. Diane walked over to the counter and introduced herself to the man operating the cash register.

"We're doing a story on Carly Neath, and we'd like to talk to people who actually knew her. Would it be all right if our camera crew came inside?"

"I'd prefer not," said the man. "People are all stirred up as it is. They don't need to be reminded of this horror while they eat their lunch."

"Of course. I understand," said Diane, disappointed. "But would it be all right with you if I asked some of Carly's co-workers if they'd be willing to be interviewed? They could come outside for a few minutes, and we could do it out there."

"Oh, all right." The man sighed. "It's a free country."

"Let me start with you then, sir. Would you care to talk about Carly?"

"No. I would not," he answered shortly. Diane had long since learned not to take the response personally. If they didn't want to talk, they didn't want to talk. With rare exceptions, there was no use trying to pressure them into it.

She looked down the counter. "How about her?" she asked, indicating the young brunette pouring iced tea into a tall glass. "Did she know Carly?"

"They both work the breakfast and lunch shifts," he answered. "I mean worked."

"Think she'd be willing to talk with me?" Diane asked.

The man shrugged. "Ask her yourself."

The slight young woman came out to the sidewalk, pushing her lusterless brown hair behind her ears.

"Thank you for agreeing to do this," Diane said. "It will only take a few minutes."

"That's okay," the waitress said in a sweet voice. "My shift is really over now. The only thing I have to do is a doctor's appointment, but that isn't until later."

Diane smiled as Sammy signaled that the camera was rolling. "Okay. First of all, will you state your name and spell it for me?"

"Anna Caprie. A-N-N-A C-A-P-R-I-E."

"And where do you live, Anna?" Diane asked.

"Ocean Grove."

"And you work right here at Nagle's, the restaurant that Carly Neath worked at?"

Anna nodded. "Um-hmm. Carly and I worked together sometimes, but not always. Sometimes she would be on and I wasn't. Sometimes I would be scheduled and she wouldn't."

"When was the last time you saw Carly?" Diane asked.

"I saw her Friday morning. That was the last time."

"So that was the day she disappeared."

"Yes, that's right." Anna looked toward the ground.

"Did you talk much to Carly that day?" Diane asked.

"Not that much. The restaurant's pretty busy in the summer. There's not usually time to talk."

"Is there anything you remember about that day, Anna? Anything different or unusual?"

Anna looked up, and Diane couldn't be sure if the pink rising on her face was from the sun or a blush. Either way, it suited the young woman. Diane thought she was too pale. Too pale and too thin.

"Well . . ." Anna hesitated. "Not really. Carly's new boyfriend came in to talk to her, but he'd been by before."

"Shawn Ostrander?" asked Diane.

"Um-hmm. Carly told me she really liked him but . . ." Anna's voice trailed off.

"But what, Anna?" Diane urged gently.

"I don't know if I should be saying this, since Shawn was so nice to me last week when my car wasn't working. He and Carly dropped me off at my doctor's appointment, and they even waited to take me home afterward," said Anna, twisting a strand of her dull hair. "I don't want to say something that could hurt someone as nice as that."

"I understand, Anna. Of course I do. But this is a serious situation, and if you think you know something that might in some way help in finding out what happened to Carly, you have to say it. If not to me, then to the police."

Anna swallowed resolutely. "It's just that Carly didn't like it that Shawn hadn't looked for Leslie Patterson when she was missing. And she told me she was going to tell that to Shawn when she saw him that night."

CHAPTER

69

"Larry, I know it's my first day back and everything, but I'm going to leave early."

The real estate agent looked up from his desk to see Leslie standing in the doorway. It was always painful for him to look at her achingly thin frame. "That's all right, dear." He gently smiled at her. "You must be tired. Good work today."

"You are so good to me, Larry. I didn't do much work at all, and you know it."

"You did plenty. And there will be plenty more waiting for you tomorrow, don't you worry. Now just go home and eat a good dinner and get some rest."

Leslie walked back out to her desk and picked up the canvas

tote bag from the floor. She was searching for her car keys when Larry came out with a file in his hand.

"I was just going to leave this on your desk for tomorrow," he explained. His eyes caught the stuffed bear peeking out from the tote. "Leslie, you aren't going home, are you?"

"No," she admitted. "I'm not. I have a therapy appointment. I didn't want to tell you because I know how you feel about therapy."

Larry took off his glasses, rubbed his eyes, and let out a deep sigh. "Oh, Leslie, Leslie, Leslie. I don't know what to say anymore. It's not that I'm against therapy. That's not it at all. But I think you have to make sure you have the right person treating you."

CHAPTER

70

Diane was in the front seat of the satellite truck letting the cold air from the air-conditioning vents blow directly on her face. She was polishing her script when her cell phone rang. Owen Messinger's secretary was calling to say that the therapist could talk to her at five o'clock.

"Gee, that's going to be difficult for me to make," said Diane as she looked at her watch. "Could he fit me sometime tomorrow?"

"No, his schedule is completely booked for the next few days."

"All right," Diane reluctantly agreed. "We'll be there."

She turned to Matthew, who was screening the video they'd shot in front of Nagle's, taking time code on the sound bites Diane wanted to use for her piece. "We need this interview with Messinger for the *Hourglass* piece, and if we don't get it today we may not get it all. The *Evening Headlines* script is finished. Let's see if we can get an early approval from Range Bullock. I'll track and leave the narration here with you to feed to New

York while the crew and I go to Messinger's office. If he sees me right on time, I should be done by five-thirty and back here by about six. If anything breaks, I can update then for the six-thirty broadcast."

Matthew whistled. "Jesus, that's cutting it close, Diane. I hate to take a chance like that."

"Ah, come on, Matthew. You've cut it closer."

"All right," he grudgingly agreed. "We need Messinger's professional perspective, and if this is the only time we can get it, we don't have much choice."

CHAPTER

71

Every one of the young women who sat in a circle in the therapy room held a doll or a stuffed animal in her lap. Unsmiling and very thin, all six of them were cutters.

Dr. Messinger started the session. "Since we last met, some painful things have happened. Leslie was abducted and missing for three days, and then another young woman was abducted. Her body was found last night."

"I knew her," a childlike voice piped up. "Carly Neath. I worked with her."

Owen glanced quickly from Anna to Leslie, who was already issuing the response he could have predicted.

"Earth to Anna. You may have *known* Carly Neath, but I'm sitting here right in front of you. I think what I have to work out today is a little more important than what you have to say right now."

Anna shrank back in her chair and stroked her black stuffed rabbit, her face becoming as pink as the toy's nose.

"How do you think Anna is feeling right now after hearing that your experience is more important than hers?" Owen asked.

Chastened, Leslie plucked at her teddy bear's ear. "I guess she doesn't feel too good. I'm sorry, Anna."

"Do you want to talk about what happened to you, Leslie?"

Owen Messinger listened to Leslie's story and endeavored to watch his other patients' reactions to what was, by any estimation, a harrowing ordeal. He made sure that each of the young women felt free to ask Leslie questions and offer her support.

Anna Caprie confessed that, upon hearing about Leslie's disappearance, she'd locked herself in her bedroom. She'd wanted to join in on the town's search but felt too overwhelmed. "I took a straight pin from my mother's sewing kit and cut myself over and over."

This was a good opportunity for the therapist to do some patient education. Some of the girls had been in therapy for years, but none of the more "accepted" therapeutic techniques seemed to be having any salutary effect on them. They were still refusing to eat. And whenever they felt powerless or out of control, they'd find anything sharp enough to do the damage that, somehow, inexplicably, gave them relief. He felt that something more drastic, more dramatic would convince these young women that cutting themselves might bring short-term relief, but in the long run it was an unsuccessful and, ultimately, very dangerous coping mechanism.

As he had every week for the past three months, Owen handed out the razor blades. At the start of the summer, he had instructed the girls to run their fingers along the edges of the blades—without cutting themselves—and to talk openly about how the sharpness made them feel. As the weeks progressed, he tried to get them to "demystify" the razor blades, to divest them of any power to help them.

Now it was time for the biggest lesson of all.

"Anna, why don't you go first?" Owen suggested, gesturing toward the stuffed animal in her lap.

"I couldn't hurt Mr. Velvet. I just couldn't." Anna's eyes teared up.

"Why not, Anna?" Owen asked. "You've cut yourself. Why won't you cut some fabric and stuffing?"

"Because Mr. Velvet means everything to me. I could never hurt him," Anna whined.

"But you can hurt yourself so easily, Anna. Aren't you at least as important as your stuffed rabbit? Aren't you just as lovable?"

The tears were flowing freely down Anna's cheeks now.

"Aren't you?" he pressed.

"Anna doesn't think she is," Leslie called out. "She doesn't think she's important at all."

All eyes but the therapist's turned to look at Leslie. Owen's stare continued to bore into Anna.

"How does what Leslie just said make you feel, Anna?"

Anna didn't utter a word. Instead, she took the razor blade and slit Mr. Velvet's throat.

CHAPTER

72

The girls coming out of the professional building looked shell-shocked and exhausted. If therapy was supposed to make them feel better, shouldn't there have been a more lighthearted energy coming from them? If they had unburdened themselves, why did they look like they carried the weight of the world on their shoulders?

Larry slunk down in his seat so Leslie wouldn't spot him. He'd taken care to park next to another beige sedan at the far corner of the lot, hoping that his vehicle wouldn't stand out to her. He watched as she approached her own car, a dark expression on her face, the stuffed bear dangling by its arm as she held on to its paw.

He saw Leslie drive away but waited to get better looks at the others. The little one, Anna, the waitress from Nagle's, looked especially distraught as she got into the waiting car. Larry assumed that the middle-aged man at the wheel must be her father. The poor guy. He leaned over to give his daughter a kiss on the cheek, and Larry could imagine the words he was saying to her, inquiring how everything had gone, asking her if she felt better. Just as Larry had often asked his darling Jenna.

Larry felt the anger bubbling to the surface as he gripped the steering wheel, his knuckles whitening. He wanted to strangle that damned therapist.

Finally, all of the young women had been picked up or had driven themselves away. Larry went to turn the key in the ignition when he noticed a woman and two men carrying camera equipment walking toward the entrance of the professional building. He leaned forward to get a better look. He thought he recognized the woman. Yes, that was Diane Mayfield. She was in town with the rest of the press corps that had invaded.

On impulse, he opened the car door and got out.

"Hello there," he called.

All three heads turned in his direction.

"Miss Mayfield?"

"Yes?"

"Hello. My name is Larry Belcaro. I have a real estate agency in Ocean Grove."

Diane shook his extended hand. She was used to people coming up to her and introducing themselves. When you were on television, people felt like they knew you. She always made it a point to be pleasant. "Glad to meet you," she said. "But I'm afraid I'm going to have to keep right on going. I have a five o'clock appointment for an interview with a doctor, and he and I are on very tight schedules."

"It wouldn't happen to be Dr. Messinger, would it?" Larry asked.

Diane looked at him curiously. "As a matter of fact, it would."

"Talking to him about what's happening in Ocean Grove, I guess?"

"That's right."

"Well, the real story, the story that should be exposed, is the quackery that man practices. He should be in jail for all the havoc he has wreaked, all the lives he has ruined, including that of my daughter, Jenna."

"Mr. Belcaro, I wish I could really talk with you now, but I can't. Do you have a number where I can reach you and maybe we can talk more about this?"

Feeling he was getting the brush-off, Larry handed Diane his business card, his shoulders slumped. "I've written my private number on the back," he said, with little hope that she would actually call him.

CHAPTER

73

While his sister lay on a beach towel with her eyes closed and his aunt went for a walk down the beach, Anthony saw his opportunity to take off in the other direction. He grabbed his camera and headed north, toward Asbury Park and the old Casino.

Since he'd seen the man slip underneath the building yesterday, Anthony had thought of little else. The guy had disappeared—just like that. Where had he gone? What was in there?

He stopped to take a picture of the big brick structure, careful to center it in the viewfinder. As the Casino loomed closer, Anthony started to think better of his plan to explore inside. What if there was a bad-ass gang or something living in there? What if they were nasty and violent? What if they retaliated against him for trespassing on their territory? What if his mother found out he'd taken such a risk?

Wait a minute! What was he? A wuss?

He reached the base of the building and paused to look around. No one seemed to be paying any attention to him. Anthony counted to three, inhaled deeply, and ducked into the space between the concrete slab and the sand.

At first, the sun's bright rays seeped through, illuminating his path, but as Anthony went farther, the light faded. As his eyes adjusted to the dimness, he cautiously felt his way the last few yards. Then he climbed through an opening.

Once again the sun was his friend as it tried to light the space by way of a hole in the ceiling high above Anthony's head. He looked around, trying to figure out exactly what he was seeing. Moss-covered bleachers and an empty stage, rusted chandeliers and a deserted refreshment stand. He could imagine what the place had once been, filled with happy fans cheering for the acts onstage. It was awesome to think that now the auditorium was filled with their ghosts.

He clicked away, taking pictures of the secret world he had discovered. Then he stopped to look at the tiny screen on the back of the camera to see if the shots were coming out all right. The flash had done its job. The images were clear.

Picking his way over debris and broken glass, Anthony climbed the bleachers to get an aerial shot of the auditorium. From the elevated vantage point, he spotted something he couldn't identify sticking out from the corner of the refreshment stand. Carefully, he hopped back down to investigate.

Anthony peeked behind the stand. What he'd seen from above was the edge of a Styrofoam cooler. Beside it, a dirty yellow blanket was spread over the ground. *Somebody must be staying here,* he thought. Maybe the military guy he had seen yesterday.

On top of the blanket, next to a tattered magazine, lay a maroon-colored ski jacket. *Does it get really cold in here at night?* Anthony wondered, because why else would that jacket be here in the middle of this heat wave? He picked up the garment and stuck his hand in the pockets, finding only a small white card. Anthony's eyes, now accustomed to the dim light, made out "Surfside Realty" in dark lettering before sliding the card back into the pocket.

Anthony snapped pictures of the mini-campsite from a few angles. And then he got up the gumption to open the cooler. Inside were two cans of diet soda, an orange, and a box of saltine crackers in a plastic ziplock bag. There was also a package of some kind. He reached into the cooler, pulled it out, and tore it open, excited by the sturdy plastic strips that fell to the floor at his feet.

CHAPTER

74

While the microphones were clipped on and the lights set up, Diane chatted off camera with Owen Messinger.

"Thank you for fitting us in, Doctor," she said.

"I'm glad we could work things out." Owen smiled, a bit too toothy for Diane's taste. "The day started with a burglary here, and it's been nonstop since then."

"Oh, I'm sorry," said Diane. "I hope nothing too valuable was taken."

"Actually, I could never put a monetary value on the things that were taken." He nodded in the direction of the bookcase. "All the patient notes that I had been keeping for a clinical study I've been working on."

Diane groaned. "How miserable for you. Will you be able to reconstitute them?"

Owen frowned. "I'm not sure."

Segueing to the interview, Diane explained what they were going to be talking about. "As I told you in my phone message, Dr. Messinger, *Hourglass* is doing a story on 'girls who cry wolf'—women, that is, who disappear for a few days, only to show up falsely claiming that they'd been kidnapped. I was originally sent down here to cover the Leslie Patterson story, and though the abduction and death of Carly Neath changes the dynamic, we still want the same questions answered for our viewers."

"Okay," the doctor said, smoothing back his hair. "I'll do my best."

Diane glanced at her camera crew. "Ready, guys?"

"Rolling," Sammy confirmed.

Diane cleared her throat. "First of all, Dr. Messinger, research shows that while kidnappings themselves may be on the decline, falsified kidnappings are more common than anyone would suspect. More often than not, these kinds of hoaxes are perpetrated by females. What's going on?"

"You're right, Diane. Despite all the publicity and hysteria, abductions by strangers have actually been falling for years. Statistically, a child has a greater chance of dying of a heart attack than of being kidnapped and killed by a stranger."

"And what about the young women who are faking these things? Why would a woman do that?"

"Many times, it's a call for help. They crave attention. The woman may feel unloved and uncared for. Invisible, as it were." Owen reached for his glass of water and took a swallow before continuing. "Unfortunately, when a person makes a false report, it damages the credibility of real victims, not to mention wasting police funds. It also frightens the public."

Diane knew she already had some solid sound bites. She crossed her legs and continued. "Here in Ocean Grove, Leslie Patterson, the first young woman to disappear, was *suspected* of crying wolf until Carly Neath was abducted. What does it do to a person who is telling the truth when people don't believe her?"

"Well, I can't comment on Leslie's case specifically, but you can imagine how you would feel, can't you, Diane? Feelings of frustration and even anger would be pronounced. And there is also a sense of terrible isolation. You know you are proclaiming the truth, and yet no one believes you. You feel totally alone, and you want vindication."

At his last words, the doctor stared intensely into Diane's eyes, and she felt herself grow uncomfortable. Owen Messinger was a natural for television. His answers were succinct and interesting. Yet there was something she couldn't quite put her finger on that disturbed her. She thought of the middle-aged man who had pleaded for her attention as she and the crew had arrived downstairs. Larry Belcaro didn't think too highly of Dr. Messinger. Suddenly Diane wanted to know why.

"Dr. Messinger, when we were in the parking lot here, we couldn't help but notice the group of young women who had just left this building, Leslie Patterson among them. Were they all your patients?"

"I can't really say."

"Of course not," said Diane. "Well, let me put it another way. Do your patients usually leave weeping?"

"Therapy can be painful, Ms. Mayfield."

CHAPTER

75

"Anything new from the police?" Diane asked when she got back to the satellite truck.

Matthew let out a deep breath, relieved that she was back. He didn't like to admit it, but he worried about her, about everything. That was the producer's job. He'd been taking a chance in agreeing that she could run out and do the interview with that therapist. But he hadn't wanted to seem overly cautious. For the last hour he had been sitting with a knot in his stomach, praying that something else wouldn't break in the Carly Neath case before she got back. He'd done his share of "crash-and-burn" stories, the ones where the details came flying in up to the last minute, the ones where there was precious little time to get all your ducks in a row. He didn't enjoy the adrenaline rush anymore. That was why working on *Hourglass* suited him. He had time to plan and polish his stories, unlike the day-of-air pieces that were done under incredible deadline pressure.

He shook his head. "No, Diane. Now the cops are saying they won't be making any more announcements until tomorrow."

"Well, that makes it easier for us, doesn't it?" she observed. "With no new information, we won't have to update the piece. When are we slated to air?"

"After the first commercial break."

Diane looked at her watch. "Great. We've still got about twenty minutes." She pulled her makeup case out of her bag and began to apply fresh foundation. "Where are we going to do the stand-up for the end of the piece?" she asked.

Fifteen minutes later Diane was standing on the grass in front of the Beersheba Well. The protective gazebo was roped off with yellow police tape. She was not alone. Reporters from other media outlets thought this was the perfect place to do their on-camera closes too. Groups of curious onlookers had gathered.

Across the lawn, the Ocean Grove Camp Meeting Association's Ladies Auxiliary was holding a fish and chips dinner in the auditorium pavilion. Helen Richey smiled and made small talk as she helped serve the homemade fare. But her eyes kept searching the assemblage for Jonathan and the girls.

Since Larry Belcaro had told her that he hadn't had an appointment with Jonathan last Thursday afternoon, Helen was feeling a bit better. Maybe Jonathan hadn't been in a position to have deposited Leslie Patterson at the Beersheba Well after all.

But the question still nagged at her. What did the notation on the business card mean?

Jonathan swallowed the last piece of fish and wiped his mouth with a paper napkin. He hated eating this early when he was on vacation. He much preferred to have a couple of drinks or cold beers and then head out for something to eat around eight or nine o'clock. But he'd known enough not to make a fuss with his wife about going to the fish and chips dinner at five-thirty.

After nine years of marriage, and three years of dating before that, Jonathan knew in his gut when something was on Helen's mind. He could tell she was upset that he'd misled the police. Yet what else could he have done? If he had told them he followed Carly that night, they'd surely have tied him to her disappearance. By now they'd be trying to pin her death on him too.

He gathered up their paper plates and napkins and tossed them into the trash receptacle. "Come on, girls," he said. "Mommy still has to work for a while. Let's go take a walk."

"Can we get an ice cream cone, Daddy?" asked Sarah.

"Sure," said Jonathan. "That sounds like a good idea, honey."

Sarah and Hannah skipped in front of their father, certain of the direction they wanted to go. Their favorite spot was

Day's Ice Cream Parlor, just off the association grounds on the other side of the Beersheba Well.

"Girls," Jonathan called. "Get back here." There were too many people gathered around the well, and Helen was always reminding him how easy it would be for one of their daughters to get lost in a crowd or stolen by some stranger. He vividly remembered the time he had lost Hannah at the Paramus Park Mall. Those ten minutes searching the aisles at Sears had been some of the scariest of his life.

He held Sarah and Hannah firmly by their hands as they got closer to the well.

"What are they doing, Daddy?" Hannah asked, pointing to the people with the cameras and microphones.

"They're doing news reports, sweetie. For television," Jonathan explained. "Let's stop and watch for a while, want to?"

His daughters were content to watch for a few minutes, but the promise of chocolate or strawberry cones meant more to them than the explanations of anxiety in Ocean Grove coming from the grown-ups with microphones. They pulled their father by the arms, eager to get to the ice cream store. Jonathan had heard all he wanted to hear as well.

CHAPTER

76

After they were good-nighted from the studio in New York, Diane invited everyone out for dinner. But Sammy said he was tired, and Gary said he was going to ride up the Garden State Parkway to see his wife and kids for a few hours before driving back early in the morning.

"Make sure you're back by five," Matthew warned. "If something breaks and *KTA* wants a story in the morning, we'll need you."

"Don't worry, Matthew. I'll be back."

Diane and Matthew left the crew to pack up their gear. "Where do you want to go?" she asked as they turned onto Main Avenue. "We've had Italian two nights in a row, so something other than that."

"How 'bout the obvious?" Matthew said. "Seafood."

"Great," Diane agreed. "I'll go back to the inn to freshen up and get the kids and Emily. You pick a place, call me on my cell, and we'll meet you there."

Fried calamari, broiled scallops, baked stuffed shrimp, and fillet of sole were served up piping hot and devoured hungrily. Diane noticed that Michelle even finished most of what was on her plate.

"I was starving," said Anthony as he popped the last piece of buttered corn bread into his mouth.

"The sea air increases your appetite," Diane observed. "Or at least that's what they always say."

The adults ordered coffee. Michelle didn't want dessert. Anthony took a picture of the group and then suggested they play miniature golf and stop for ice cream afterward.

"I saw a mini-golf place near my motel," Matthew offered.

All five of them went out to the parking lot. "I want to drive with Matthew," Anthony announced. "I'm sick of being with girls all the time."

When they arrived at the course, Anthony suggested they split the group. "The guys go together and the girls go together," he said. "And the guys should go first. It's sexist that the girls always go in front."

Diane did her best to ignore the tug she felt in her heart. It was apparent that Anthony wanted to be with Matthew. These were important years in a boy's life, and Diane knew her son needed a male presence. She was sure Anthony missed his father desperately. Watching him tee off with Matthew, Diane ached for Philip to be there with them.

After the ninth hole, Matthew and Anthony sat on a bench waiting for the group in front of them to finish.

"So, you having a good time down here?" Matthew asked.

Anthony shrugged. "It's all right, I guess."

"But it's not the Grand Canyon, huh?"

"No way."

Matthew tossed his green golf ball up in the air and caught it again. "I know your mother felt really bad about having to cancel that trip. She couldn't help it, you know. Our boss made her do it."

"I know," Anthony said grudgingly. "It's just . . ."

"It's just what?"

"Nothing." Anthony got up from the bench and positioned his golf ball on the rubber mat.

Later, as they waited at the end of the course while the females finished playing, Anthony wanted to share something other than his feelings with Matthew. He pulled some plastic strips out of his pocket.

"Look what I have."

"Wow." Matthew took one of the strips from Anthony's outstretched palm. "Where did you get these?"

"They're flex cuffs. Plastic handcuffs. I saw the cops use them on television."

"I know what they are, Anthony. I asked where you got 'em."

Anthony paused, uncertain what to answer. Matthew was his mother's friend, and he might tell her. Anthony was sure his mother wouldn't want him prowling around in the dilapidated Casino. But the Casino was the best thing about this trip so far. He didn't want to give it up, and that was what he would have to do if his mother forbade him to go in there again.

"My friend's dad is a cop," Anthony lied. "He gave them to us."

TUESDAY
AUGUST 23

CHAPTER

77

OCEAN GROVE NOW OCEAN GRAVE

Every journalist camped out in front of police headquarters read the *Asbury Park Press* headline and accompanying story as they waited for the press briefing to begin. It was just after noon, in time for the local news broadcasts, when Chief Jared Albert came out to make his next announcement.

"Neptune police apprehended forty-year-old Arthur Roy Tomkins in connection with the death of Carly Neath. Mr. Tomkins resides at a boardinghouse here in Ocean Grove and is a Gulf War veteran. He is currently in police custody in Monmouth County Jail in Freehold. He will be arraigned tomorrow on charges of unlawful imprisonment, kidnapping, and depraved indifference murder. I'll take a few of your questions now."

When he heard the reference to a boardinghouse, the ears of the *Asbury Park Press* reporter perked up. "Would that be a boardinghouse for the mentally ill?" he asked.

"Yes. It would," Albert answered.

"So the suspect is mentally ill?"

"Mr. Tomkins has been treated for mental illness, yes."

"What evidence ties Tomkins to Carly Neath's death?" Diane asked.

"Fingerprints."

"Can you expound on that, Chief? Where were the fingerprints found?"

"No. That's all I'm willing to say about that evidence at this point." Chief Albert looked in another direction.

The next reporter spoke up. "Did Tomkins know Carly Neath? What was the connection between them?"

"We don't know. We're investigating that."

Diane called out the next question. "Do you think Tomkins was involved in Leslie Patterson's abduction as well?"

"There would seem to be a link between the two cases, but we can't prove that at this point. I will say this much," Albert declared. "The citizens of Ocean Grove and the vacationers who are visiting with us can feel much safer today."

litical forces of this country to concert themselves in order to bring into harmony what can be brought into harmony only by a broad majority.

The Great Coalition of Social Democrats and Christian Democrats—as a provisional alliance—applied itself even in its first year to more tasks, and more important ones, than other Federal administrations had done throughout entire legislative periods. If two such large parties join hands for practical work, they must take the path of reason, and sometimes the path of compromise. In our situation some desires are always unfulfilled. To see in an ad hoc alliance the danger of crippling parliamentary democracy would be shallow and unjustifiable.

It has been said that the Great Coalition is doomed to success. So it is, though not in the sense the critics have in mind when they say this. The whole of the German nation is doomed to success if it is to survive as a nation and secure its future. Our task is to strengthen the Federal Republic of Germany by a properly understood national policy. What I mean by strength here is not economic strength or even military strength. Economic strength is useful and can lend effective support to foreign policy, but that alone will not make policy. And the Federal army is not a factor of power that could be used by us in the sense of old-fashioned national politics. Even if it were, anyone who even toyed with this notion would belong in a lunatic asylum.

No, what I mean by the strength that must grow within us is the intellectual and moral strength we need in order to arouse confidence, understanding, and good will. If this goal is not to remain idle fancifulness, the interests of others must be understood as accurately as possible, the points of mutual interest must then be found, and thus the true interests of our own country will be promoted. Such a policy of accommodation and of renunciation of force has need of firm principles, of an integrity that can sometimes be brutal, of the same speech with all partners, and of the courage to be unpopular at home.

The United States possesses the potential for carrying on a war in Southeast Asia, for providing other peoples with material and technical aid, and at the same time for preparing to land people on the moon. The Soviet Union has become the second world power; it recently celebrated, with much self-awareness and immense pomp, the fiftieth anniversary of its revolutionary birth. In the competition for the conquest of outer space it is neck and neck with America. Both superpowers command an atomic potential for destruction that can scarcely be grasped by the human imagination, and the smaller powers with atomic combat capacity remain secondary in comparison. Very probably in the next decade China will step onto the world political stage as a third factor of global weight. Taking into account the conjunction of territorial extent, economic resources, technical dynamics, military ascendancy, and human reserves, no one with an ounce of common sense could regard the Federal Republic of Germany as an equal factor in world politics. Even a reunited Germany, even if it were to become master of its own decisions, would play merely a modest role in the future interaction of global forces. No European state in its present shape constitutes a world power. These are facts that cannot be changed by references to a historical past of the nation.

We know the ending of earlier attempts, begun under less hopeful premises, to secure Germany "world stature." Today we are carrying on policy for ourselves as a half of Germany and with a glance at the whole. We suffer from a division that has been forced on us by world politics but that must also be understood as a consequence of the Hitler war, one we cannot overcome through our own strength alone, however much we might wish to.

In any case, I shall hardly be contradicted if I make the statement that the center of gravity of our tasks lies in Europe. Although we lack the means and the possibilities of influencing world politics in a decisive way, we are not relieved of the responsibility of taking part in everything that is happening in the world even if we cannot stop much of what is happening there or bring about much that would seem to us desirable. These given circumstances are disregarded by a segment of our public, which often demands that the Federal Republic adopt a unilateral position, emit sharp condemnations, or even "take steps" when events occur somewhere in the world that run counter to the ideas of justice and humanity. No one is going to demand that we approve of something that is manifestly bad, but it would be foolish and presumptuous for us to understand our practical foreign policy as a moral seismograph for all world events. Nor, for that matter, is our moral position in the world of such a nature that we might venture to assume the role of ethical umpire.

Walter Rathenau once spoke of a counterweight to the mood of the people, in which a reasonable foreign policy might or sometimes would even have to be expressed. It is not only today, and not only in Germany, that common sense has a difficult time of it. In any case, I should like to say to the people of good will that it is unfortunately not enough to show even good will; it is not enough to know what ought to be or to imagine how it might work; it is too little merely to ascertain that things are not proceeding rapidly enough or broadly enough or clearly enough. An "ideal" foreign policy without a parliamentary majority and in contradiction to the consciousness of the population may be easy to devise, but it is worth nothing because it cannot be realized.

It happens that there are very many realities that one must see, realities that are pushing toward a change—and it would be prudent for our partners in the East and West to help them change. I shall avoid denying that our partners can be prudent. But it remains our affair not to overdraw our own account.

3

PEACE
FIRST
AND FOREMOST

The will to peace and to reconciliation is the primary idea and the foundation stone of our foreign policy. It is on this principle that I became Foreign Minister and Vice Chancellor, and I have kept to it, at home and abroad, at the conference table and in conversations with partners from East and West and from many parts of the world.

To be sure, all foreign policy must directly serve the interests of one's own people. For this reason the first thing I said in Paris in December 1966 was that our interests speak for intimate collaboration and in America two months later that we represent our own interests with awareness—but without arrogance. It is my conviction, however, that there is no longer any national interest that can be separated from the collective responsibility for peace and for the cooperation of nations. The interest of Germany is peace as it never was before in our history, for war would be the end of us.

In December 1966, when a new administration was formed for the Federal Republic of Germany, we thought it of the greatest importance to give vigorous emphasis to our readiness to organize a genuine peace, which is the criterion for our efforts on behalf of European unity and of the healthy development of the Western alliance, as well as for our efforts on behalf of a better relationship with our neighbors in the East and of a relaxation of the situation within Germany.

Before the organization of the new administration at the end of 1966, I, together with my political associates, had stated that what was at stake for our foreign policy was

To deflect the danger of isolation and to stabilize our disturbed relationship with Paris and Washington

To advance European collaboration and unification

To normalize our relations with the Eastern European states

To relax the situation in divided Germany

and, as the sum of these and of other efforts,

To put in high relief the German contribution to the consolidation of peace and of a European peace order.

The linking of German foreign policy to the common denominator of the consolidation of peace means making an active contribution to a secure peace order in Europe. Germany cannot have any interest in letting the conflict between East and West go on, to say nothing of heightening it. Germany has an interest in a détente—for general, European, and national reasons. Here we are in accord not only with our allies—with Washington and Paris, with London and Rome—but with almost everyone. Here we join with the nations and governments of the uncommitted world. Here interests we have in common with the Communist-governed states also come to light in spite of some polemics. This contribution to peace remains our criterion even when the advance is slow or when there are setbacks.

We wish to contribute to this détente—without illusions,

but with tenacity. What that means, in the concrete situation, is not only to promote the European community but at the same time to encourage the process that will allow Western and Eastern Europe to come together again. We quickly passed the initial stage of our new peace policy. The common denominator of our foreign policy has been discussed in the eyes of the world, largely heeded, widely greeted, though to be sure occasionally doubted or even opposed.

I should like to emphasize that not only the allies but also nearly all our partners in the uncommitted world have hailed the goals of our European peace policy and—though in various degrees—displayed a positive attitude toward the policy with respect to Germany that is included in it, as has been confirmed in numerous encounters. In Scandinavia and in Africa, in Tokyo and in Bucharest, from Latin America and from India, we have received many communications of respect and encouragement that have given us the certainty of being on the right path.

Anyone who wishes to vilify our policy of détente and peace and denounce the Federal Republic of Germany as a state lusting after revenge and hostile to peace would be pursuing a policy that was neither convincing nor promising for the future. Such forces run the danger of playing the role themselves that they are imputing to others. Anyone who disregards a hand stretched out in all honesty must be prepared to have it said that he is not promoting a détente but hindering it. At the same time we remain clear in our minds—as was said before—that Germany, even two decades after the end of the war, still has to bear the heavy burden that was imposed on it by unrestrained obfuscation and unscrupulous arrogance.

The obstacles of an apolitical capriciousness and of a

juridical substitute for politics can be eliminated only slowly. Nothing can be achieved with mere polemics and with merely replying in kind to vilification. We have resolved to put an end to all overoptimism and to take the people into our confidence. We do not wish to speak at home in a way that is different from the way we speak abroad—different in London than in Paris, different with Russians than with Americans. Some people were displeased at our setting about making our policy of détente and the ensuring of peace consistently credible, but many in our own country and throughout the world have seen how serious we are about this goal and how active we have become within the framework of our possibilities. I was and am certain that we can achieve progress—in the policy of détente, our European policy, our Eastern policy, and finally, also, our German policy.

Honesty requires the point to be made that what has been achieved in many fields lags behind the unextravagant expectations of December 1966. The relationship between Washington and Moscow vacillated between contact and collision. Crippling influences flowed out of the Vietnam war. The controversy between Washington and Paris was more difficult than had been feared. The prospects for Great Britain's reception in the Common Market were far worse than we had hoped. And the counterpositions that were built up and fortified in East Berlin, Moscow, and Warsaw as a reaction to the initial successes of our peace policy were bound to dampen our optimism. Nevertheless, there was no reason to give our course a new definition. On the contrary, our conviction that in the long run we would be successful with a creative and dynamic peace policy has only been strengthened by the obstacles.

In my work as Foreign Minister I was able to find a link in what I had thought and said in the years before—as a young man in exile in Scandinavia, as the mayor of Berlin, and as the chairman of the Social Democratic Party of Germany. Before the Federal elections of 1965 I was invited by the Evangelical Academy of Tutzing to give an account of my aims. At that time I described foreign policy in our time as consisting of general staffwork for peace. Today, too, I say: Anyone carrying on foreign policy as a function of military strategy remains a captive of the vicious circle of atomic armament. War is no longer an alternative to peace. Foreign policy, as a means of a worldwide security policy, must protect the peace, promote the forces of evolution, and strengthen communication between the peoples in the East and West and between the power blocs.

The West still requires military strength for its self-defense, this was true in 1965 and is true today. But it was and is also true that the West must be ready to risk peace. Military détente is desirable; the elimination of the causes of political tension is better. Only if we succeed in dovetailing the two will decisive progress on the path toward a secure peace be possible. In the long run peace cannot rest on the balance of terror. It must be propped up on common interests that are recognized and desired as such. There is a long road stretching ahead of us toward that goal, and only tentative steps forward have been attempted. The pillars that can support a new edifice are not yet strong enough. For a long time to come peace will remain dependent on the relative balance of destructive forces. But, as John F. Kennedy once said, peace is not a static but a dynamic process.

The nuclear stalemate between the United States and the Soviet Union has not led to an abdication of politics. The opposite is true: since the end of 1962, when the two world powers saw themselves confronted in earnest in the Cuban crisis, world peace has been somewhat more secure, but at the same time world politics has become more complicated. The United States and the Soviet Union have remained very largely decisive powers because of their military and economic potential. Nevertheless, the last third of the twentieth century started off under the sign of neither a Pax Americana nor a Pax Sovietica.

The general concern—that there must be no third world war—has become, explicitly or implicitly, an important element—probably the decisive one—in the relations between the two superpowers. The terrible war in Southeast Asia, which has been going on for years, as well as the dangerous crises in the Middle East have been restricted fundamentally because the responsible men at the levers of power are familiar with the monstrous force of destruction at their disposal. To that extent the nuclear stalemate has a function and can ensure relative security. Up to now, however, there has been no real accommodation of interests between the United States and the Soviet Union. There are regional conflicts, which for the nations affected are portentous enough and which also cannot always be restricted with absolute security. The development of China and the confrontations with it are additional potential sources of peril.

This condition of political tension has given rise, in European and German eyes, to a particular, also "national," interest in peace. A country that would become a wilderness in case of war—regardless of what laws of strategy the inferno would be ruled by—can have no higher goal than to work for the peace of the world: first, because this corresponds to a common interest; and secondly, because now as before there is a prevalent fear of military dangers that might have their start in Germany. We really must not allow ourselves to succumb to any illusions. Some speeches made in Germany have given the impression that we are thinking too much of war and too little of a future of peace that is worth winning. The peaceful and just future that our peoples wish for will not come of itself.

Our foreign policy is in fact directed against no one. We are not concerned with playing a superfluous and exaggerated role in the forefront of the stage. We do not wish to sow discord anywhere. The Federal Republic of Germany has no military ambitions, least of all an atomic ambition. It does not aspire morbidly toward a "place in the sun" that can only too easily turn into a place in the fire. What we are concerned with is this: to contribute to the détente and to ensure peace in the world. But of course we shall represent our own interests with peaceful means wherever it proves necessary.

Many hopes were disappointed after both world wars. Today we know better than before that seeking peace requires the courage not to be deflected by setbacks or disappointments. Such courage and tenacity are demanded by any foreign policy with a hope for the future. As a European and as the German Foreign Minister I see no alternative to a policy that makes the securing of peace the topmost criterion.

The renunciation of force is a logical consequence of our policy of peace. Agreements designed to secure this end can substantially improve the atmosphere in Europe and bring about a lessening of tension. They can improve the prerequisites for the attainment of a peace order in Europe and can also be milestones in drawing both parts of Germany into the process of détente, rapprochement, and collaboration in Europe, instead of shutting them outside. There is no people and no neighboring state that would not benefit from a pacified center of Europe.

Our foreign policy rests on firm principles. As things are, it must be rooted in the Western alliance. It seeks peaceful accommodation and constructive cooperation in Europe, corresponding to the behest of the age and the desires of the nations. It is a policy based on reason; it seeks the proper measure. Germany is an indispensable element in any European accommodation. I say this in what I hope is the correct evaluation of our weight and of our capabilities. We are fitting ourselves into the elemental endeavor to preserve the peace, indeed, to bring it about in other parts of the world, too, and to consolidate it on a worldwide scale. That is our meaning when we say that the will to peace and to the reconciliation of nations is the paramount theme and the foundation of our foreign policy.

4

FIRST
PRIORITY:
EUROPE

───────────

There can be no doubt that the European peoples must assume a greater joint responsibility for peace and progress in the world than they have in the past. To do so, they must unite their limited forces; there must be a closer European accord.

In other words, we cannot remain satisfied with what has already been achieved. But we do not wish to underestimate it, either. What has been accomplished during the first two decades since World War II will quite surely not be underestimated historically, particularly the Council of Europe in Strasbourg, which with its Consultative Assembly has performed an important service in the exchange and formation of opinion.

The real political breakthrough is represented by the Community of The Six, which has been encompassed in the Coal and Steel Community since 1952 and in the European Economic Community and Euratom since 1957. The convincing economic success of the EEC and its build-up as a substantial factor in international relations have become a significant Western triumph. In spite of all doubts and risks, progress was made along the path taken by The Six, and its success produced an effect of attraction. Through its progress toward a customs and economic union, the EEC has presented itself as the core of European union.

German policy since the establishment of the Federal Republic and even before has aimed at the economic and political unification of Europe. In spite of the discussion of means and contents, the promotion of the European communities, their elaboration, and their expansion must be considered as a constant of German policy. We strive for the unification of Europe along all the paths that present themselves. That unification, as we see it, lies first of all in the interest of the European peoples that take a direct part in it. Further, it lies in the interest of the partnership with the United States and the cooperation with other parts of the world, not last the emerging countries. One day, we hope, the Soviet Union, too, and the rest of the East will recognize that a Europe unified in this way can be of decisive importance for peace in the world.

The new administration of the Federal Republic of Germany, as I said to the Council of Ministers of the EEC in April 1967, intends to make all possible efforts to attain the goals of the EEC treaty and regards the accord agreed on in the Rome treaty as a fitting form of European unification. In this endeavor it has the complete support of the German parliament. Thus, the administration's position corresponds to public opinion in our country, which, with practically no exceptions, has favored the economic unification of Europe.

In the last few years the EEC has gone such a long way that no member state can reverse it without harming itself. At the same time, this progress means success on the road to the political unification of Europe, for the more the EEC is strengthened and perfected, the more it will effect, through its existence and its dynamism, unification in other fields as well. The balanced development of the Community is so important because the Common Market constitutes a closed-off whole in which each sector affects other sectors. The EEC must not bog down in the status of a customs and agrarian union but should be developed into an economic union and at the same time its external relations should be built up.

In Brussels in April 1967, I made the point—and even today no change need be made—that the three European communities had grown up historically but that their separate continuation was no longer in tune with the times. As I said, they ought to coalesce into a single European community. The fusion of the executive, one had a right to expect, would be the signal for the fusion of the communities, thus facilitating the solution of many of the questions affecting all three communities. The union in administration and the stronger spatial concentration would also be understood and welcomed by the public. Further, I referred to the fact that with the merger of the organs of the communities the decisive phase for the elaboration of a common energy policy for Europe could be introduced, together with the harmonizing of the rights of taxation and the development of a common trade policy, which are indispensable for the construction of the economic union.

The coalescence of the organs of the EEC, the Coal and Steel Community, and Euratom took place in the summer of 1967, following the decision at the end of May by the so-called summit conference in Rome, on the tenth anniversary of the existence of the Rome treaties. In Brussels, accordingly, a joint European commission was formed under the chairmanship of Jean Rey, auguring the departure, after long and valuable service, of Professor Walter Hallstein.

The year 1967 was encouraging in some ways but disappointing in others for the EEC. It witnessed the successful termination of the Kennedy Round, difficult negotiations concerning the lowering of customs tariffs. Of comparable significance were the joint emergence of The Six in the solution of international currency problems and their solidarity vis-à-vis each other and Great Britain in November 1967, when it came to devaluating the pound.

The attempt to expand the EEC, however, as provided for in the Rome treaty and proposed by Great Britain and other European states, was not successful. Franco-German cooperation, also, which had been revived, failed at first in the face of this task, which we shall speak of shortly.

In the beginning of 1967 I stated, in the name of the German Federal government, in Bonn and Paris, in Strasbourg and Brussels, in Rome and London, in the Hague and Copenhagen, that the EEC treaty is open to the entry of all European states. States that wish to enter must, to be sure, agree with the common fundamental concept of the economic and political union of Europe, as well as with the decisions that have since been taken on the basis of the Rome treaty. On the other hand, the accession of new member states will make transition regulations unavoidable. The entry of Great Britain and other European Free Trade Area (EFTA) states would fill in the gap between the two European economic groupings. We cannot take it for granted that such opportunities will be repeated at will. Hence we all bear the responsibility for exploiting the possibility now being offered. The division of Western Europe into two economic groupings must not be allowed to continue. Europe's stance in the world would be substantially stronger if the community were expanded—not only economically and technologically but politically as well.

We had come to the conviction that Great Britain and other EFTA states were earnest in their desire to join the community. Similarly we were of the opinion that the questions of British entry into the community, while surely far from simple, could be solved in an objective way.

An interim balance sheet as of the beginning of 1968 yielded some disappointing results. We still had made no progress in the sought-after expansion of the communities. It is just in this area, however, that I am not one of the pessimists. In any case, I take it as significant that on December 19, 1967, the Council of Ministers established that no one was against expansion in principle and that everyone agreed that the applications for entry were to remain on the agenda.

Nor was any progress achieved in 1967 on behalf of the sought-after political unity. Even the attempt, prompted by the summit conference in Rome, to discuss the possibilities of political collaboration within the circle of foreign ministers remained fruitless. Among other factors, this difficulty is linked to the fact that the French state executive is cool to the idea of any sovereignty above the state. Even independently of that, it has been demonstrated that all those who thought that political integration would evolve more or less automatically out of economic integration were in error. Experience has taught that it is sensible for us to base ourselves on a perspective of intergovernmental cooperation. Qualified political cooperation between governments will not be easy either. But it might mean a great deal. And it would not have to mean that the democratic corrective of parliamentary controls and collaboration would be waived.

In all this the great goal of a United States of Europe should not slip away from us.

Summit conferences—as was shown by the experience of May 1967—are no panacea. Those who take the summits by storm require good form for the ascent, and without appropriate preparations the air of the heights can be dangerous; today Europe is not in its best form for bold mountaineering. I am for a policy that is oriented to imaginative goals and that strives forward but that at the same time remains sober and realistic. We must recognize that a political federation with supranational institutions will not become a reality in the immediate future. As things are, it would not at present be given a shape even among the six countries of the Common Market. In our planning for the future of Europe we ought to cross every traversable stretch of the road in a realistic way. This does not detract at all from the idea of integration, which is just as grandiose a conception today as it was years ago. Nor, for that matter, is it a mere conception any longer, because the EEC already contains, looking beyond the economic factors, partial aspects of political integration that must not be destroyed but further developed.

There is one vexatious burden on the debate concerning Europe that I should like to refer to here. The magnificent debut that remains bound up with the names of Schuman, de Gasperi, and Adenauer was on occasion ideologized in a harmful way. Overzealous interpreters attempted to lend it a partly Carolingian and partly Christian Democratic interpretation. Later there was a question of whether or not this might be counterposed by a Social Democratic ideology of Europe.

Everyone knows where I stand. I am a Social Democrat, but I am against any hard and fast formula which for that reason alone is harmful. What is at issue in reality is for European cooperation to take in all democratic forces. It must not be dependent, in its functioning, on a change of government in one country or another. Leading figures from related political camps can do various things in order to promote European development. They should, however, withstand all forms of ideologization that will weaken instead of strengthen Europe.

In spite of the unsatisfactory state of Western European cooperation I regard it as vital to take a clear look at the overcoming of barriers between the East and the West. I have never conceived of the Western European community as a citadel for us to burrow into and entrench ourselves against the world around us. The Europe of The Six and an expanded Western Europe as well must not stand against its neighbors; it must attract, not repel, them. It must be open, not shut off. Without allowing ourselves to be inhibited by a theoretical dispute over aims, we must move forward to our goal through economic collaboration with the countries of Eastern Europe.

Constructive relations between Western and Eastern Europe are a commandment of our times. For many years I have come out for objective communication with the peoples and governments of the Eastern European states and for the coordination of a policy with respect to Eastern Europe, and I cling to this point in spite of the obvious difficulties.

In May 1964 I said in New York that we must propose joint enterprises to the nations of Eastern Europe and make it clear to them that we are not afraid of the approximation of their standard of living to our own but are willing to help them achieve this goal, a position that corresponds to the original idea behind the Marshall Plan. Independently of political solutions the West should move on to practical projects that are capable of linking Eastern and Western Europe together over and beyond the Iron Curtain.

A few months later I attempted to concretize this proposed goal in a memorandum initially intended for Secretary of State Dean Rusk. In this memorandum I referred among other things to the possibility of activating the

Geneva United Nations Commission for Europe for these tasks, an idea that was also considered on the Yugoslav and Polish side. At the time questions were raised in Bonn as to whether a Berlin mayor was authorized at all to discuss such questions with the foreign ministers of friendly governments —a favorite method of evading the substance of something by quarreling over jurisdictions.

I am eager to emphasize this too: European unification has never appeared to me a way of setting up a front against the United States. My opinion was and remains that wherever we Europeans can progress without the United States we should do so. During the past few years Europe could have made a beginning in a variety of things without waiting for the Americans to go ahead. The Americans would not have been unhappy had there been greater European initiative. We Germans, too, might have done with more initiative and a wholesome self-interest. But there are problems for us in Europe that cannot be solved without the cooperation of the United States and without its support.

The paramount issue is the preservation of peace. Europe alone cannot defend itself in a worldwide conflict, and I do not foresee a time when it could. I therefore believe that there must remain a possibility of acting independently without committing suicide. My further thought is what a catastrophe it would be if the idea of a constructive Atlantic partnership, which John F. Kennedy, with his mixture of realism and vision, flung into the debate, might not still become actuality.

For myself, in any case, it remains incontestable that the peoples of Europe must unite their limited forces in order to assume a greater joint responsibility for peace and progress in the world. It is because of this that a closer European accord is necessary.

5

FRANCE-GERMANY: THE PRIMACY OF PROXIMITY

The development of Franco-German relations is of decisive importance for the future of Europe. Without an intimate and trusting relationship between Germany and France no European peace order is thinkable. Europe cannot be built outside France and Germany.

The reconciliation of the French and German peoples is one of the most important realities of the postwar world. It cannot be shaken, nor can anyone in the world maintain that the phenomenon runs counter to anyone's interests. The reconciliation of these two peoples, who have been hostile to each other for centuries, is anchored in the hearts of the younger generation of both countries and therefore is only conditionally dependent on the relationship between the governments. My conviction of this has been strengthened in many ways during the past few years, whenever I have had occasion to express myself on this theme. People have a feeling that an intimate collaboration between the French and Germans in the Europe of the future will be an abiding element in the consolidation of peace. They realize that friendship with our French neighbors must be one of the primary goals, one of the initial tasks, of German foreign policy in the wholesome spirit of German democracy. After everything we have been through, we must, on both sides, take as our starting point the union of our resources. Both here and there everyone knows that such a union is in our own self-interest, as it is in the interest of the preservation of peace and the welfare of other nations.

In the government statement of December 1966 we put forward these considerations with respect to the Franco-German relationship:

1   The facts of European geography and the sum total of the history of our continent have given rise, in the conditions of the present, to a particularly high degree of accord between the interests of our two nations and countries.

2   Together with France, the oldest American ally in Europe, we regard an alliance between the free nations of Europe, now coming together, and the United States of America as indispensable, whatever shape may be taken in the future by the structure of that alliance because of a changing world.

3   Together with France we have come out for the restoration of the historically evolved European family of nations, a goal that encompasses the counterhistorical and unnatural sundering of our own nation.

4   The Franco-German cooperation that we desire is not directed against any other nation or country. It is rather the crystallization point of a policy that has set itself the goal of a unification of Europe. It is indispensable if Europe is to become a jointly responsible partner. That Europe that speaks "with a single voice," as has been demanded by American statesmen, has as a prerequisite a constantly growing concord in German and French

policy. Europe can be built only with France and Germany together, not without and still less against one of the two countries. What is at issue are practical steps on the road to unification, not the unyielding pursuit of ideal conceptions. What is desirable must not hinder what is possible.

5 For the improvement of relations with the Eastern European neighbors Franco-German cooperation in as many areas as possible is of the greatest value.

6 For all these reasons the Federal government wishes to utilize as concretely as possible the opportunities for the coordination of the policies of both countries that are contained in the Franco-German treaty of January 22, 1963.

At the same time reference was made to the fact that the special circumstances of both nations would cast up differences of interests and opinions in a variety of questions in the future, too. Friendship does not mean the neglect of one's own interests or the mere mimicking of what others say. We have often told our French neighbors openly that we have a different view of the question of extending the EEC. We said that in our opinion the time had come to enlarge the community to include Great Britain and other countries that were ready for it and competent. We tried to convince Paris that the enlargement would mean not only an economic but also a political strengthening of Europe. It may be that we have not yet said this distinctly enough. It may be that it has not become clear enough what our own interests make imperative and how anachronistic we consider it to approach questions of European unity by speculating which of the old national states is capable of gaining hegemony.

We have explained that in our opinion a secure alliance

with the United States is necessary for the achievement of European security and its guarantee. We said that Europe, in the midst of organizing itself, could not go on existing back to back with America, but only with a readiness for open cooperation across the Atlantic Ocean. General de Gaulle, like others, foresees a time in which the United States neither would nor could remain militarily present in Europe as it was during the first two postwar decades. But whereas French policy is bound to appear as though it were consciously striving for a decisive diminishing of the American presence in Europe, we interpret our own interests differently.

It is our view that Europe cannot renounce an association with the United States. This position would persist—as far as we can see at present—even if a satisfactory European security system were to be developed. Meanwhile, it may become important to strengthen the European component within the Atlantic alliance. Here our hope is that French cooperation within the alliance will be maintained as far as is possible, for a total withdrawal of France would raise very serious questions. Furthermore, a scrutiny of the data of changing world politics would be in the common interest. The joint studies of the world situation and European security in the 1970s, as agreed upon and initiated between Bonn and Paris, may be helpful in that respect.

Recently it was my misfortune to become involved in a distasteful altercation. On February 3, 1968, in Ravensburg I said to my party colleagues from Baden-Württemberg:

Franco-German reconciliation and friendship are deeply rooted in the hearts of people on both sides, and that is a good thing. This holds precisely for the younger generation.

I hope that the anchoring is already so strong that even unreasonable regimes will no longer be in the position of
changing it. The impression must never arise that the motto
"Cowardice vis-à-vis one's friend" could ever apply to
German policy.

What holds good for Franco-German cooperation is the
primacy of neighborliness. Friendly, trustful cooperation does
not at all mean that one follows the lead of the other, but
rather that one objectively, clearly, and manfully represents
what one considers and what one's interests make imperative.

Set off by a false report, to the effect that this aimed a
personal attack against President de Gaulle, reactions took
place in France that I could scarcely understand. If I had
had any false illusions, they would have been emphatically
dissipated. Thus, I could do no more than reaffirm my conviction that only if both countries, in spite of some differences of opinion, stand together, only if they constantly try
to find a common approach to the great questions, will this
Europe, which General de Gaulle is fond of referring to as
the cradle of civilization, be anything more than a geographical concept.

I had met the French President many times, beginning
when I was the mayor of Berlin. I paid no attention to the
black and white images of him that many people had
formed. To the annoyance of some people I said as much
publicly in New York on May 15, 1964:

> If we recall President Kennedy's vision, which brought so
> much hope not to my own city alone, it will become clear
> to us how remote we still are from the great goals. We still
> do not have a constructive Atlantic partnership. Instead of
> that we are undergoing signs of crisis in the NATO. And

instead of a free Europe speaking with a single voice, we hear over and over the cacophonies of a strength-dissipating rivalry.

In my opinion it is neither sensible nor fair to make General de Gaulle responsible for all the difficulties we confront in the West. Some of the decisions made by the President of France are not easy to understand, but I have not come to the United States to complain about him. Rather there is cause for us to become aware of the fact that de Gaulle in his own way is thinking of the unthinkable with boldness and independence and has begun to draw conclusions from it.

The equilibrium of terror held in balance by the two superpowers, creates enough free ground to set the congealed fronts in motion. The President of France is making use of this in his own way. And sometimes I ask myself, as a German: "Why, really, should it be he alone?" If we build bridges from the past to the future, it is not obligatory for us to forget the present.

In June 1964 I spoke at the German Society for Foreign Affairs on the interesting experience I had had as a result of the above-mentioned passage in my speech in New York and recalled the truism that in political realities there are positions that cannot be summed up by a simple pro or a simple con. For me, I said, there were three aspects involved when the President of France came up for discussion:

The first is that of immense esteem. Statesmanlike greatness cannot be taken away from this man even by someone who does not agree with many of his decisions. And I believe our people can bear the openness of the considered judgment, which is a good medicine against all thinking in clichés.

The second element concerning de Gaulle lies in the fact

that, from the point of view of the Western community, I regret some of his basic decisions. This holds true for questions of European unification, of the Atlantic partnership, and also of NATO and of nuclear defense. The security of Western Europe is indivisible. It rests ultimately on the trustworthiness of the American commitment. The cement of the alliance is confidence. And anything that might loosen the attachments of the United States to Europe or its interest is bad.

The third element is the fact that de Gaulle in his own way is utilizing the political freedom of movement that has been won by the nuclear stalemate of the world powers. At home in Germany it has often been said: Movement is not good by itself alone. This is of course true. But it is after all no more than one of those catchwords that get one no further. For motionlessness by itself alone is also not a good thing. Especially not when a hard-frozen ice cover breaks up and the ice floes start moving. The name one uses for this event is at bottom not what is decisive. What is decisive is the event itself.

I said that de Gaulle makes use of this situation in his own way. And the question of why he alone should do this is to be understood exactly as it was asked. The Americans and the British make use of the relative freedom of movement in their own way. Other states react similarly. And what do we do? The Federal Republic cannot, of course, play possum. Put less colloquially, it cannot give the appearance of having no interest and no will of its own. Hence the question concerning the use to be made of the possibility of movement can be asked by the Federal Republic, too. But it is, obviously, not a question and not a problem for the Federal Republic only. This is where the sense of the respectful or friendly warning comes out behind the question: Why, really, should it be de Gaulle alone?

For me it was no surprise that after the formation of the new Federal administration there was no difficulty in finding a thoroughly close accord in those questions touching on Eastern policy. Here there was not a question of who had to suit whom but the fact that German as well as French policy desired a détente and consequently was bound to be interested in improved relations with the nations and states of Eastern Europe. Both of us, Paris and Bonn, envisage a joint European future; in this respect German and French interests run parallel. Thus, a trustful and productive exchange of opinion in precisely this area was natural.

But the question has also been raised, understandably, as to why the Franco-German treaty of January 1963 was unable to lead to far more extensive joint political action. Here I must say first of all that I was one of those who was not convinced then that the timing and the form of the treaty had been pondered well enough. Since then I have come to the additional insight that the effectiveness of the subsequent consultations has been uneven. A point will have to be made of not allowing a grandiose task to turn into mere routine.

At the beginning of 1963 the German side regarded as necessary a statement of the Federal parliament to make clear that the Franco-German treaty must not diminish or even bring into question the other obligations and political aims of the Federal Republic. This measure of the Federal parliament secured the assent of the then Social Democratic opposition to the projected treaty. In fact, such clarification was also in the interest of France—even though official Paris took a different view of it—especially because France has always recognized the special situation of the Federal Republic with respect to its need for security and to the division of the country. It was this clarification that excluded any mistaken interpretation of the treaty as being a special alliance at the expense of other vital interests.

The German Social Democrats have committed themselves as formerly, and especially in the Weimar Republic, to friendship with France. After the last war the German Social Democratic Party did everything in its power, when in the parliamentary opposition as well as when a government party, to promote the reconciliation of the two peoples and to strengthen their collaboration. In the great questions of reconciliation and peace it is precisely in this area that there is no party monopoly grounded in the accident of governmental responsibility. Governmental authority has given my political friends and myself abundant opportunity to prove that we are not merely proffering lip service to the unification of Europe and to cooperation with France.

In January 1968, when the Franco-German treaty was five years old, its purpose was bound to be brought into question. We realized quite clearly that the treaty had three different designations. The official title is "Treaty Concerning Franco-German Cooperation." In political usage the designations "friendship treaty" and "consultation pact" have also become common. These wordings undoubtedly merely reflect different aspects of the same political subject. The practical cooperation that is specifically regulated in the treaty is a visible sign of the reconciliation of the two peoples. In accordance with the will of the signers, the treaty sets the seal on their solidarity. To be sure, there would have been no need for this treaty to bring about the historic fact of Franco-German reconciliation and solidarity. For, as I have already tried to indicate, the population and especially the youth of both nations had already directed its gaze to the future. At bottom the governments were merely realizing what people were feeling and thinking.

On the occasion of the signing of the treaty, President de Gaulle and Chancellor Adenauer issued a joint statement, in which they called the cooperation that had been decided upon an indispensable stage on the road to a united Europe. This formulation forestalled the misunderstanding to the effect that behind such cooperation there lay the intention of forming a separate union. The talk of such a union as the kernel of a political community has only done harm to the cause and otherwise not advanced matters.

Nevertheless, the institutionalized cooperation of Germany and France has been anything but a failure. Here I am thinking primarily of the exchange of youth and of cultural links. The picture is not so positive, to be sure, if one takes as a standard the grandiose aims of the signers that, taken together, were to culminate in the formation of a joint policy. But joint action cannot be forced via a mechanism for consultation; it must be achieved through work.

Both governments are committed by the treaty to joint periodical cabinet consultations at relatively brief intervals. The meetings of the heads of the government, of the foreign ministers and departmental ministers, together with subsequent plenary sessions—as a whole all have been fruitful and useful. To be sure, if it had been thought that as a result of such meetings alone a joint policy might come into being, experience has proved this hope to be unwarranted.

The useful instrument of a treaty cannot be made responsible for the blunders and unfortunate developments that have come about during past years, the value of consultation is not thereby lessened. In any case it is important between two neighbors that are so dependent on each other;

but that does not mean that governments must make themselves captives of procedures in the sense that their mere practice becomes the criterion of their relations.

At the first meetings that the Chancellor and I had with President de Gaulle, Prime Minister Pompidou, and Foreign Minister Couve de Murville, a readiness was shown on both sides to fill the treaty of January 1963 with new life. We resolved to intensify our collaboration. Indeed, the economic cooperation between our two countries, including the voting on monetary matters, has made heartening progress. We are striving for further progress in the domains of technology, science, and research and such initial results can be seen, as the joint projects of the Grenoble reactor and the television satellite. Others will follow. There has also been progress in joint plans and in political consultation in the area of developmental aid. In all this it is only natural for us to be also concerned with securing an appropriate economic share for our achievements.

We stand behind the goals of the Franco-German treaty and remain resolved to use this instrument of cooperation and consultation for the good of both countries and for the good of Europe in order to serve peace in the world. As far as we are concerned, the bitter remark General de Gaulle made a few years ago—to the effect that treaties, like young girls and roses, quickly fade—will not come true. We know that a decisive role for the future of Europe is going to devolve on the development of relations between Germany and France.

6

THE
SIX—AND THE
OTHER RELATIVES

Great Britain and the other states that are willing to join must find their place in the Common Market and in the European community. The abyss between the EEC and the EFTA must be filled in.

In December 1966, when forming a new Federal administration, we jointly stated that the Community of The Six ought to stay open to all European states that accepted its aims; we were merely recalling what was already contained in the Rome treaty. We did not offer mere expressions of sympathy for the participation of Great Britain and other EFTA countries but emphasized that we were going to apply ourselves energetically to the extension of the European communities. I have kept to that.

The extension of the EEC is, for us, a common European interest that also corresponds to our own interests in Germany. No one can remain unclear as to what we consider desirable and what we consider possible. But at the same time we have to be clear in our minds that we must not outwit others but have to convince them. Our posture, accordingly, is not one of deviousness but of frank objectivity. We have not proposed ourselves as mere go-betweens but have tried to be honest brokers. It is a question not of whether we want to give offense in Paris or London but of putting through what is possible. As to how far our ability will reach, time will have to tell.

The entry applications of Great Britain, Ireland, Denmark, and Norway, as well as the Swedish note of the early summer of 1967, afforded one of the grand options in European politics. They posed certain questions: Should and must the abyss between the Western European countries go on existing? Should and must European states with a democratic tradition and economic maturity be excluded from the work of unification? In both cases the answer was bound to be only no. On the German side we carefully scrutinized all the related problems, and we concluded that these problems would be solved through that same good will without which the establishment in its time of the EEC would have been impossible.

The procedure for the entry applications was initiated by requesting the European Commission to report to the Council of Ministers. By the end of September 1967 it presented a comprehensive picture of the problems that would crop up during the negotiations with respect to entry. From the very outset we endorsed the principle that newly entering states must accept the treaty itself and all the decisions that had already been based on it. They would also have to be prepared to adopt as their own all the general aims of the EEC for the future. Together with the commission we were of the opinion that the economic problems bound up with entry would be soluble if a positive political decision on the part of the member states led first to negotiations. The problems analyzed in the commission's document, including such complicated ones as agrarian and currency questions, should, in our opinion, soon be clarified by conversations with Great Britain and the other countries prepared to enter.

We have made clear our attitude within the community, in consultations and discussions with the interested parties, and in public statements. We have emphasized that this historic opportunity must not be missed. We have not been light-minded about doubts and objections. To be sure, of course, it also had to be asked what situation would arise if the extension of the European community did *not* come about. We said in advance that there was no question here of a simple situation. Nor could it be denied that the economic drifting apart in Western Europe had already created grave problems for a number of countries. Denmark, which is very close to us, was hit particularly hard.

The economic motives that argued and still argue for the inclusion of Great Britain and the other states in the Common Market are obvious: A broader division of labor makes more rational production and a better distribution system possible; intensive competition strengthens the dynamic forces. Because Great Britain alone is a market of 55 million consumers (compared with 180 million in the EEC and 60 million in the Federal Republic) with a gross national product in order of magnitude between that of the Federal Republic and that of France, Great Britain's entry would raise the production and the economic capabilities of the EEC by a third. If the other EFTA countries were to unite with the EEC, the economic potential of the community would increase by more than a half.

Great Britain can demonstrate significant technical achievements in many areas; for instance, in space and air travel, rocket and atom technique, and computers. This know-how within the Common Market would lead to a rapid heightening of productivity, and Europe would be in a better position to maintain itself vis-à-vis the technology of the super-powers. It is just in this domain that Prime Minister Wilson has made some notable suggestions.

The general economic advantages of entry would be counterweighted by transitional difficulties. In individual areas—for instance, coal and textiles—the competition would become more acute. But we were and are convinced that sensible regulations can be found.

In our opinion there would be no excessive encumbrances arising out of Great Britain's political position either. During the period of the dismantling of their position as a world power the British attempted at first to make use of the historically and culturally evolved relations with the United States—their "special relationship"—in such a way that positions that had been lost might be compensated for as far as possible. But the shift of power in favor of the superpowers detracted a great deal from the significance of Great Britain's special relationship to the United States. England found itself embarking, though rather reluctantly, on a course toward a more intimate connection with the Continent. Even before the entry application Harold Wilson declared that Great Britain would as member of the EEC participate to the fullest extent in all political discussions within the community. The identification of British policy with the growing political unity of the Continent would, he said, have two important consequences: The endeavors on behalf of a détente between East and West could be better coordinated, and a Europe that had been increased by Great Britain would be able to play a bigger role in the world. From our point of view this could only be agreed with.

At a press conference in November 1967 President de Gaulle announced that France would not agree to the acceptance of negotiations with respect to entry. Earlier, to be sure, he had not wanted to exclude the possibility of Great Britain's ultimately mooring its ship alongside the Continental quai. Until then there might be, as he said, some "arrangement" possible.

On the German side we did not at all rule out the settling of commercial or other questions prior to negotiations on entry. But this did not in any way alter our conviction that the problems bound up with the entry of Great Britain and the other countries could be solved. We continued to maintain that the desire to bridge over the chasm between the EEC and the EFTA and the idea of an economic union through the extension of the European communities would finally be effectuated.

We never regarded the entry of Great Britain and the other states as an event that could be accomplished in a very brief period of time. We knew that the requisite negotiations would take time, but we thought it a mistake to delay or indeed to block the acceptance of negotiations. It was our view that the extension of the communities could no longer be dismissed from European discussion. We were bound to take as our initial position that the communities themselves would assume their final form only after the solution of this question too. This position did not imply that we wanted to block the further progress of the communities. On December 15, 1967, immediately prior to the interim decision made by the Council of Ministers of the EEC, the Federal parliament appealed to the cabinet to seek to obtain a decision on the opening of negotiations with respect to entry. I expressed my own view in reporting on the state of the negotiations and added:

The commission recommends that negotiations be entered into. This decision must be made on December 19. This view is also shared by my colleagues from Italy and from the Benelux countries. I myself am prepared for a long night on December 19 so that we know where we are and how things are to proceed. We want to end up on December 19 with a clear conclusion to be put on record by its chairman. We shall resolutely advocate the opening of governmental negotiations.

If the first step, in the sense of official governmental negotiations, is not taken now, then all participants will have to examine the situation that will have come about—each government for itself and the governments with one another, all, or some with each other and in relation to others inside and outside the community. In this connection, in addition to Franco-German and Anglo-German conversations, efforts might also be made by The Five, in the interest but not in lieu of the European community.

I also referred to the fundamental rule of the community, that the formation of opinion had to take place on the basis of the opinions of all parties. A few days before, I had met in Chequers with Harold Wilson and George Brown and with the Social Democratic leaders from other countries. This encounter was not particularly useful, but nevertheless I was able to ascertain that in the given situation the British government—wholly justifiably—wanted to know only whether negotiations would be accepted or not. There was no room for considerations that were aimed at interim solutions. What was to be feared in case of a failure to come to an agreement was obvious. On this point I said the following to the Federal parliament:

The danger that cannot be mistaken lies in this, that the thinking in terms of the community might be harmed, indeed, would with some certainty be harmed, if the impression were to arise that the one-sided conclusion of a *single* government, if it led to a negative result, could determine the rule of action. It is to be feared that the élan needed to take the great decisions lying before the community might fail. Even now it is unmistakable that other extensions will be affected by blocking the entry of Great Britain. There is a threat of stagnation of what has come into being as the achievement of the European community. We would like the extension without endangering what has already been created. It will be difficult to come to any agreement concerning the transition to the final phase of the community as long as the questions of entry are not clarified. It would be wrong for me not to emphasize the seriousness of the situation expressly and vigorously. The government of this Federal Republic of ours does not have its being in the categories of power claims, demonstrations, and least of all threats. But our own interest, which it is up to us to represent, and our understanding of the state of European interests obliges us to speak a clear language and urge our French neighbors not to make things too difficult for themselves and others.

Before it became clear on December 19 in the Council of Ministers in Brussels that because of the French attitude there was not going to be any unanimity with respect to the acceptance of negotiations on entry, I said the following there:

There can be no doubt that we are at a portentous stage in the European community and with respect to European cooperation in general. It remains to be ascertained whether and in what form the work of European unification can be extended and perfected.

The German delegation left no doubt that it considered it right to enter into negotiations with Great Britain, Ireland,

Denmark, and Norway and also to deliberate on the letter from the Swedish government. In spite of a number of unmistakable difficulties we shall regard it as a major step forward if during the next few years we are in the position of strengthening our Europe economically and also of allowing it to become more effective than before in the organization of peace.

For more than half a year the applications for entry have been lying on the table. In Item Number 194 of its report of September 29 the commission recommended that negotiations be begun for the further clarification of the questions cast into relief by the applications. Problems related to the applications have been of deep concern to the European governments, the community, and European public opinion. I believe that both the importance of the subject and the dignity of the community, its member states, and the governments making application warrant that a clear answer now be given as to whether negotiations are to be initiated or not. At the same time I should like to emphasize that the Rome treaty does not allow us to shelve the applications for entry without negotiations with those applying. Nor has this been suggested by any party. I have rather gained the impression that the extension of the community has been affirmed *in principle* by all six of the member governments.

In its deliberations during the past few months the German government has taken those points of view that favor extension, as well as the objections that have been made, as seriously as the subject warrants. The repeated discussion in the EEC Council of Ministers, as well as the conversations that the governments have conducted with one another, have permitted the problems that must be solved in the negotiations to emerge clearly. The comprehensive and painstaking report of the commission has proven particularly helpful.

In assessing all the difficult problems—politicoeconomic, commercial, agrarian, currency—that are thrown up by the extension of the community, I should like to say flatly that in our view not one of these problems is insoluble. To be sure, there must be present that degree of resolution for cooperation that ought to characterize the European policy of our times. Like all the other partners within the community, we, too, know that the individual problems that are to be solved touch on significant economic interests of the individual countries. The German delegation has now arrived at the same point as the commission. Any further clarification cannot, in our opinion, be found by way of studies and conversations between The Six but only by initiating negotiations with the applicants. Only in such negotiations will it be possible to ascertain if the states wishing to enter are ready and in a position to take over the rules of the treaty and the regulations that have been passed since then in such a way that the healthy development of the community is vouchsafed and all dangers of any enduring economic disadvantage for all participants avoided. I should like to emphasize that we have reached agreement on the general obligations that every new member state must assume, that is, the acceptance of the treaties and of their political goals, as well as acceptance of the decisions since the acceptance of the treaties.

We are familiar with the problems that will constitute the primary object of the discussions between the community and its member states on the one hand and the applicant states on the other. We are also familiar with the points of view of the six member governments. We are not, however, cognizant of how the British government and the other governments conceive the solution of these questions in detail. In this connection I am thinking, for instance, of the position of the pound sterling and the regulations for a number of Commonwealth countries, as well as of the rhythm and the determination of the requisite transitional periods. On the other hand, the applicant governments will probably be interested to get to know our opinion on important questions. Here I am thinking of the duration and the shaping up of the transitional measures, and the modalities of adaptation provided for in the treaty, as well as the future formation of joint agrarian financing. It is only on the basis of such negotiations that The Six will be able to arrive at a unitary point of view concerning rights and duties, advantages, and performances of the states wishing to enter.

I think there is a common conviction, shared by the British government, that as long as Great Britain's economy is still not really consolidated, the economic development of the community will also suffer diminution. An important prerequisite for such a consolidation is, however, for Great Britain to base its future economic orientation on solid assumptions. Only in negotiations can trustworthy perspectives for Great Britain's further economic policy be established. For this reason, too, the community must offer a clear answer, which cannot be given by way of indefinite promises and optional procedures. A positive acceptance of the application for negotiation ought to entail the effective and enduring revival of the British economy that we all wish for.

For the inner development of the community, too, which we are all striving for, as well as for a continuing and secure economic development in our countries, such a step forward will create the requisite climate of confidence. We cannot permit ourselves, either politically or economically, to let uncertainty concerning the fate of the entry applications prevail within the community for any length of time.

As we know from experience, negotiations require a certain lapse of time. Our British partners have told us that they wish to enter the community only with a healthy economy; restoring the economy will also take a certain length of time. Decisive reasons support the view that both—the process of consolidation and the negotiations—should be allowed to run parallel to each other. If we can make up our minds now to the acceptance of negotiations, a chronologically optimum solution could be found for both sides—Great Britain and the community—quite independent of the psychologically favorable effect that the acceptance of negotiations wil exercise on the process of consolidation, in which we, too, have an interest. Great Britain's latest currency and economic measures are an important step forward. Our community, which during the past few years has consolidated itself economically to such an astounding degree, should not now for its own part fail in courage and vision.

Understandably, the Foreign Minister of the Federal Republic of Germany would much regret casting a vote on this important question that was different from that of his French colleague. We—France and Germany—are close to each other in other areas of European politics, and we remain dependent on each other. In this connection, however, I must also be allowed to refer to Article 5 of the Rome treaty, which enjoins every member state to desist from any measures that might jeopardize the realization of the aims of the treaty. The treaty mentions the enlargement of the community as one of its goals. The treaty prescribes negotiations to this end. Every member is free with respect to the final, material decision. But no one may block the road that according to the treaty leads to a decision concerning the acceptance of new members.

The German government regards it as necessary that negotiations, in the sense of Article 237 of the Rome treaty, be initiated with Great Britain, as well as Ireland, Denmark, and Norway. The application of the Swedish government for conversations concerning a cooperation that is to be as comprehensive as possible should also be decided affirmatively. What is at stake now is whether or not we wish to and can speak out jointly for negotiations on entry. If that is not yet possible, the applicant governments must be informed nevertheless of the interim result.

But even in the event that the delegations do not vote unanimously, I take as my starting point that the entry applications will remain on the agenda of the Council of Ministers. They will remain, in any case, on the agenda of Europe.

This was the vote of the Federal Republic in December 1967. It met with a French rejection, as was to be foreseen. But three concordant statements were made that we regard as important points of linkage: First, it was emphasized that no fundamental objection to the extension of the community was validated. Second, there was a general agreement, especially with respect to Great Britain, that there was a connection between economic stability and entry. The French speaker, to be sure, somewhat expanded this point, for practically speaking he made total consolidation of the British economy a precondition for any negotiations on entry. Third, it was unanimously observed that the question of entry would remain on the agenda of the Council of Ministers. And it was this last decision that is crucial.

7

FOR

A GREATER

EUROPE

The theme of the extension of the EEC remains on the agenda of European policy making. The British government did not withdraw its entry application; nor did the other countries. Nevertheless, there was nothing surprising about the fact that the Brussels interim response was widely interpreted as a veto and was commented on in correspondingly bitter terms. It could only be hoped that the proverbial British composure would prove itself in this situation, too.

I was surely not the only one who remembered the role that Great Britain had played on behalf of the freedom of Europe. On January 18, 1968, at a dinner in honor of the leading representatives of the Luxemburg resistance I said:

> When Europe was lying in ruins after this tragic war, it was Winston Churchill, in his great speech in Zurich in 1946, who demanded European unity and appealed for a reconciliation between Germany and France.
>
> Much of this has become reality since. It was not in vain that, in addition to Robert Schuman, de Gasperi, and Adenauer, Spaak, Luns and Bech, two Englishmen were awarded the Charles Prize in Aix-la-Chapelle.

And now Great Britain is knocking on the gate of the European Economic Community. As a European I ask myself, somewhat bewildered, why Great Britain must knock. Did it not prove, in Europe's darkest hours, that it belonged to it? I was in Scandinavia at that time, others were in London, still others were listening in to London—but at that time we all knew that Great Britain stood for and suffered for and was consuming itself for freedom. Gratitude may not be a political category, but forgetfulness can scarcely agree with us either.

The transition from its historical attitude toward the world to a new role in Europe is not, of course, so easy for the British as some think. Even in authoritative British circles it was possible very recently to encounter quite divergent conceptions of the character of the Common Market and of the political possibilities of the EEC. Needless vexations were caused by an occasional announcement coming from London of some overemphatic claim to leadership. But in a growing Europe it is not a question of who is leading the parade: it is a question of dismantling old conceptions of hegemony, not of cultivating new ones. We ourselves have disaccustomed ourselves to claims of leadership and do not wish to be confronted by a choice between French and British leadership. In the European community we are, despite all difficulties, about to develop new forms of joint decision making. I should not like to be a party to any old-fashioned triangular relationships between Paris, London, and Bonn. Aside from anything else, this would constitute a disregard of our other neighbors.

In spite of the indicated difficulties of the British in adapting themselves to the new European facts and necessities, there has never been any doubt that Great Britain, once the prerequisites are laid down, will be a loyal member of the community and especially observant of the treaty. Its experience will prove of value to the libertarian content and the democratic structure of the community.

For some time now this has been, independently of the theme of entry, an area full of cares. It would be premature to pursue here the far-ranging ideas dealing with a European parliament based on direct elections, but the terms of reference of the European parliament formed of delegates from national representative bodies are too narrow. The elaboration of the EEC will withdraw more and more substantive decisions from the sphere of the national parliaments without an appropriate shifting of parliamentary controls and cooperation onto the European level. This will only be remedied by extending the spheres of competence of the European parliament.

The Scandinavian countries, too, would contribute forces of freedom to the European union. Our continental thinking has made us far too inclined to underestimate the importance of the countries of the European north, but Europe derives its strength from the diversity of its nations and states. Europe would make itself needlessly poorer if the Scandinavian countries were to remain on the outside; in their flourishing culture and in their economic capabilities they are able to do much that is exemplary. Its countries have a strong tradition of international cooperation, have been involved in projects of peace and humanity, and have spiritual and material reserves of significance for the development of European cooperation. I therefore say that Europe requires the creative energies of its Scandinavian members; the north has an important task in Europe.

At this time it is still impossible to foresee how the questions that have arisen as a result of the deferred entry applications will be dealt with. To be sure, there seemed to be clear signs during the first few months of 1968 that all parties were concerned with not allowing what had been achieved in the EEC to be endangered, still less destroyed. At the same time, it is true, our warning that a lack of unity concerning the questions of entry would make more difficult any progress within the EEC was confirmed.

On the German side we have been obliged to put up with the fact that our policy of accommodation has not been understood and approved by everyone. If one is carrying on an independent policy, one must not be afraid of the reproach of falling between two stools; we sat down not between two stools but on our own stool. It was not that we lacked resolution but that we were guided by the endeavor to avoid any unnecessary harm to European cooperation while at the same time coming closer to the goal recognized to be the correct one.

We have therefore concentrated our efforts on measures and agreements that do not replace the entry of Great Britain but prepare the way for it as effectively as possible. This endeavor has entailed considerations, including those of an institutional nature, as to how the gulf between the EEC and the states wishing to enter it might be bridged over. Further, we have attempted to clear up the question of whether a commercial-political "arrangement" could be contrived that would have a genuine effect from the point of view of entry, that is, in the sense of a gradual growing together of the national economies so that not only would duties arise but also rights would be established. We also raised the question whether adherence to Euratom should be settled first, because the economic and political problems related to the enlargement of the EEC do not apply to Euratom.

The British government has remained very skeptical of

all references to "interim solutions" or "phasing plans." It has seemed to count more on those suggestions made by the Benelux foreign ministers that—with France or without—envisage cooperation in areas that are not taken in by the community treaties. Nor have we excluded the study of such possibilities. When Federal Chancellor Kiesinger and I were in Rome at the beginning of February 1968 we found ourselves in agreement with Italian statesmen—President Saragat, Premier Moro, Vice-Premier Nenni, Foreign Minister Fanfani—that serious efforts must be undertaken to avoid a setback for the segment of public opinion in Great Britain that is sympathetic to the idea of Europe. When we were in Paris in the middle of February, we were obliged to perceive that it was not going to be easy to develop a unanimously supported policy of a step-by-step rapprochement.

But on February 16, 1968, both governments established as a joint conviction their wish for the extension of the communities. Also, an "arrangement" was outlined—in the perspective of the entry of Great Britain and the others—including a progressive reduction of customs for industrial goods and agreements for agricultural products. We were also in agreement about the wisdom of extending technological cooperation beyond the circle of The Six. The British government had already devoted particular attention to this category of problems in the preceding months.

In the given circumstances no substantive progress can be expected, at least in the short run, to bring about a meeting of minds on political cooperation. I find it also difficult to imagine that additional political consultations could change anything now. There has never been any shortage of opportunities for exchanges of opinion in Western European and Atlantic institutions. It is quite another matter that one must clear up in one's own mind the problems that will confront the European community—independent of the relationship to Eastern Europe—both economically and potically during the coming years.

Here it is a question, after all, not only of the extension of the EEC through the entry, sooner or later, of Great Britain, Ireland, and the Scandinavian states but of an appropriate association between the community and our neighbors immediately to the south, that is, Austria and Switzerland, in keeping with their neutral status. Our special economic and neighborly interest in this extension is understandable and should not be assessed by the Soviet Union with any hostility. If in the north, Sweden finds its place in an extended community, an objective settlement for Finland will be facilitated. Like Austria, or even more so, Finland is dependent on good relations with the Soviet Union but at the same time must be concerned with preventing any harm to its export interests in the markets of the West.

Also at issue is what might be called the future Mediterranean policy of the community. In the East there are the associational treaties with Greece and Turkey, but in the West suitable forms will have to be developed for economic cooperation with Spain and Portugal. Other questions arise out of the treaties with the North African states, Israel, and Yugoslavia.

I have mentioned Greece. I must add the oppressive effect on many of us in Germany of the political crisis in this friendly country. On October 13, 1967, I said to the Federal parliament that it would not be hypocritical or imply any meddling in the affairs of another state to say:

> The events in Greece, the abolition of basic rights, and the turning aside from democracy have given us great concern. In the Committee of Ministers of the Council of

Europe the Federal government will join in deciding on the results of the inquiries and the recommendation of the committee pursuant to the complaint under Article 24 of the European Convention for the Protection of Human Rights. Our sole concern in this will be humanity, legality, and democracy, and also the kindred question of the reliability of organizations we are part of.

We do not feel ourselves to be political moralists. I know, moreover, that the interests of one's own country cannot be adequately represented by means of an ideologically constricted foreign policy. However, the destruction of parliamentary democracy, the cancellation of human rights, the fate of political prisoners cannot leave us indifferent, especially when this touches the European community indirectly or indeed directly. In Germany, to be sure, we know from our own experience how little one people can be helped from outside in finding its own way anew to a democratic state based on laws or, for that matter, in constituting it for the first time.

No one should be surprised if we say that dictatorships do not suit the European community; they lead to encumbrances for Western cooperation. And no one should presume anything but this: the sympathies of European democrats are for freedom and justice and for those who must suffer on behalf of freedom and justice. But we must also grasp the complexities of a contemporary situation—which we cannot discuss at this point—and not neglect our own interests or make any improvement of relations more difficult.

8

THE
COURAGE
TO SAY YES—THE
WEAKNESS OF SAYING NO

Our policy on Europe must not stand against something; it must stand for something. And it must link itself vigorously to the requirements of the scientific and technical revolutions.

The beginnings of the policy of European unification after 1945 were in point of time and in their political logic partially—yet surely not only—parallel to the growing threat from the East. The initial unification in the West was conceived by many as a consequence of the Cold War. Some people thought that integration was the political rounding off of what had been the military assignment of NATO, with the sole aim of setting up a dam against communism. In this way the policy on Europe was given a defensive, all-too-narrow or even negative content.

The Cold War of the postwar years lies behind us but difficult confrontations continue that cannot be overcome by illusions, or by becoming prisoners of outmoded formulations of questions. I consider the policy on Europe to be stronger if it is not explained by mere anticommunism.

Rather, Europe should be unified for the good of the European peoples and for their constructive role in the world, and the policy of European statesmen must be harmonized with the long-range goal of a European peace order.

Not only the West but also the East is becoming aware of the importance of all-European cooperation. Slowly, and it is to be hoped not too late, it will become clear that the cooperation and unification of Europe is not directed against anyone. In a dangerous epoch and in a strife-divided world it could, rather, be an example of how nations and states, regardless of different kinds of governmental and social systems, can achieve prosperity and security by peacefully working together.

Reconciliation and cooperation, which we are striving for between West and East, have already become a fact in Western Europe and will succeed in spite of the above-described difficulties. The economic and political unification of Europe is a substantive element of a worldwide peace.

It is true that Europe can no longer consider itself the center of spiritual and economic progress in the world. In disunion our continent would only sink still further, but in cooperation it will have a great deal to offer mankind. If that is what we want, we not only must overcome political obstacles, but also must be prepared to participate in the explosive scientific and technical developments that, in the future, will determine the face of the world.

Europe must not slide into a peripheral position in relationship to the world powers. Steam engines could be built by individuals; airplanes were much more difficult; in space travel, orders of magnitude have been attained that transcend the powers of individual European states. Thus, in our modern world, politics can no longer be thought of as independent of the effects of technological progress. These effects to a great extent will determine the future international significance of states and their coexistence. The scientific-technical, the economic, and the political potential of the individual states is governed today by direct interdependence. The viability of states in the future will depend more and more strongly on their participation in and their contribution to technological progress. The necessity of living up to the effects of technological development touches all the key areas of foreign policy. This factor is as relevant to our efforts on behalf of a peaceful and satisfactory future for Europe as it is to the relationships between industrial countries and underdeveloped countries.

Although the population of the earth is now growing by 70 million people a year, 25 million people starve to death every year. The developed countries in the West and East, in spite of their well-known conflict, are confronted by the question of whether or not they are capable of making a joint effort against hunger and poverty; only if such a joint effort is successful, presumably will they be able to avoid explosive developments in the relationship between North and South.

The population explosion and the scientific revolution are the two great moving forces of our time. The major developments in the future will no longer be derived only from power-political or ideological constellations but also to a large measure from economic and technological capabilities. If the atomic war of destruction is avoided, which every reasonable person must wish for with every fiber of his being, and if it is true that peaceful nuclear science, space travel, cybernetics, and modern biology transgress all ideologies and lead up to a community of thinking, then the political difficulties of our backward present will become transitional difficulties—difficulties that will be soluable.

An economic community during the coming decade is

thinkable only if it is at the same time a closely knit community of scientific and technological progress, a community for the coordinated, peaceful exertion of strength. When we learn to think in categories like these it will be easier to link together enduringly the West of our continent with its East. This progress, which is the only thing that can ensure our common future, must now be reflected on and initiated. For this the preconditions must be created within the individual states.

It is precisely ourselves, in the Federal Republic of Germany, who must not succumb to any soothing dreams of the future. It is precisely ourselves who must be clear in our minds that a phase has been introduced into the history of mankind in which the importance, the weight, and the influence of a state will depend on whether or not it is capable of mobilizing the capital of its talents. We shall have to realize that we still have a research deficit and also an underdeveloped interaction between scientific and political practice. In former years our means and capabilities were linked up far too much, to the detriment of our research, with short-range defensive thinking. I consider that we must now demonstrate an ambition for scientific and technical expansion, that our society must be put in the position of radically modernizing itself.

It is old-fashioned to think that we are giving ourselves the luxury of too much expensive educational training. It is more accurate to say that we cannot afford to let even one person fail to take advantage of a vocational or college education if he is capable of it. It is a question here of the potential inherent in many families of the broad strata of our people. The percentage of workers' children among students, in comparison with Western industrial states, is still frighteningly low. We have an untapped reservoir that is to be explained by the peculiarities of a slowly changing and excessively heterogeneous school system in different parts of our Federal Republic. Finally, there is also a female reservoir that must be tapped if a mockery is not to be made of all the talk about modernity and equality of rights.

It is also the point of European unification that our continent must be able to link itself swiftly and purposefully to the dimensions of the twenty-first century. If the European communities extend and develop themselves, Europe's role in the world, economically and politically, will be greater. European unification is meant, after all, to serve that consistent policy of peace by means of which the political tensions between East and West can be overcome. We are convinced that the cooperation that the Western European countries have already found themselves ready for will also be of decisive importance for the relations between Eastern and Western Europe. Western European unification not only is no obstacle for the accommodation of interests but will prove itself to be a factor that promotes and stabilizes that accommodation.

The Soviet Union and the other Eastern European countries are well advised to view the European communities realistically. The economic capabilities of an expanding European Economic Community will make commerce between East and West even more profitable and attractive. Here I am thinking of an intensified exchange of technological knowledge, an area for cooperation between East and West that is of vital consequence for the peace and welfare of the European nations.

For us there is no contradiction between the unification of the Western European countries and cooperation with Eastern Europe. The Western countries, magnified by unification, should encourage the dialogue with Eastern Europe, beginning a collaboration based on mutual interests over and beyond the differences of systems. The cooperation and the unification of Europe correspond to the logic of our times, one that in the long run can elude no one. It is only through the fusion of the limited forces of the individual nations that we can create a fitting importance for the voice of Europe. Only in this way shall we Europeans be self-conscious and strong enough to assume a full responsibility for the preservation of world peace and the welfare of nations.

European relations with the United States have proved themselves viable in the domain of commercial policy in the Kennedy Round; such cooperation will be extended to other domains as well. The vision of an independent Europe that will speak with a *single* voice and will stand beside the United States as an equal can then become a reality. Even now the cooperation between the two, although not very spectacular, is effective. We are struggling to intensify that cooperation. And I think that in this age of scientific-technical revolution we Europeans no longer must remain preponderantly those who take; here, too, we can arrive at a harmonious partnership.

9

AMERICA
A PARTNER

———

Friendship with the United States—by now a matter of course—is an important element of our foreign policy, as is the alliance that the United States and we belong to.

Because its decisions affect the fate of the entire world, our relations with the United States are different and more complex than our relations with states that are farther away from this position of power and responsibility. Our relations with the United States are not merely based on the calculation of interests.

If the Federal Republic is following a line of greater independence in its foreign policy today, no estrangement from America can be deduced from this. No German statesman aware of his responsibilities—and for that matter no German at all in the Federal Republic whose memory is still intact—would wish or be able to forget that our ascension to economical prosperity and our evolution in Western Europe is due in special measure to the postwar policy of our American partner. How could a former Mayor of Berlin forget that! Did he not witness his city being saved from Stalin and its citizens from starvation?

When Germany—and together with it a large portion of Europe, because of German culpability—was lying in ruins and political reform was hampered by drab material need, the United States voluntarily assumed a responsibility that has been more than a matter of course. It was the United States that, through the open-handed help given by the Marshall Plan, made it possible for our part of Europe to gather together the requisite strength for its reconstruction, and at the same time it provided a military shield for that helpless Europe.

The result of this situation was the North Atlantic Treaty Organization, in which the responsibility borne by America found an equivalent in the united responsibilities of the European partners. It was no small matter for Germany, the instigator and loser of World War II, to be accepted in this alliance as a fully equal member. This must be admitted even by those who in the early 1950s might have wished for a more flexible Western policy and who were harassed by the doubt as to whether all possibilities in foreign policy had really been put to the test.

In any case we Germans have found a first-rate ally in the United States not only for Western security but also as a reliable representative of our own vital interests, as is quite visible to everyone even today in West Berlin.

In the Federal government statement of December 13, 1966, it was said that in relation to the United States we had during the preceding years sometimes overemphasized our own cares and needs and overlooked the fact that even a great power like the United States has its cares and problems—problems for which it expected some understanding and support from its allies.

Almost against its will, since the last war this powerful nation has gotten itself into commitments on all continents. We shall not forget this, and we should consider—as the government statement was worded—how we for our part and how Europeans as a whole might be able to assume joint responsibility for the preservation of world peace and for the welfare of all nations more decisively than before.

The American commitment in Europe cannot be depreciated by maintaining that the United States was only serving its own security: the consolidation of a strategic outpost, industrial expansion, and the conquest of markets for the sale of its goods. Views like these, which are occasionally heard from the extreme right and the extreme left, merely challenge positive contradiction. Nevertheless, there is a problem of "Americanization" in the economic and technological domain, as many Americans are also aware. The American President's admonitions and the measures he has taken for safeguarding the dollar are an impressive indication of America's intentions. We must realize clearly that the problems involved cannot be solved by emotions but only by work and by a partnership based on mutual confidence.

The partnership between America and Europe is not a grocers' union but is based on ideas of freedom that have been fought for and realized in different ways and with varying success in both continents. Western Europe has become stronger and more self-aware under the shield of America. Its economy already partially integrated, it is having a powerful effect throughout the world and is in competition with all the great industrial nations. Europe is becoming aware of its own strength and of the tasks that will fall to it.

Under such conditions it is only natural for the European states to reconsider their relationship to the premier power of the West. To be sure, the first basic question to be asked is: Can Europe dispense with the protection and the partnership of America?

The commitment of the United States is indispensable for the creation of a solid European peace order. The United States guarantee is of decisive importance for the security of the Federal Republic of Germany. The common desire to maintain the peace in Europe and to make it more secure remains an excellent foundation for the deepening of our friendly and intimate relations.

Franco-German cooperation does not conflict in any way with our relationship to the United States but has a quality of its own. We wish to build our European house together with our neighbors and to settle ourselves in it livably. Most of us know how crucial the role of the United States is in ensuring that this house not be destroyed by tempests.

The American presence in Europe is not a goal in and for itself. It serves our joint security. To be sure, the further development of the military and communications techniques, the accords between East and West, and the successes of the policy of détente might make possible a reduction of the troop strength without endangering mutual security. We ought to speak of this sensibly and not allow decisions to be imposed on us either by wishful thinking or by the temporary difficulties of the balance of payments.

At the same time it should never be forgotten that the North Atlantic alliance and the sought-after European-American partnership must go far beyond the realm of military security. The economic and political unification of Europe lies in the interest of the European nations just as much as in that of the United States. Our American friends have told us that Europe must learn to speak with a *single* voice. That means that it will have to be *European* voice.

John F. Kennedy, in his brief period, did a great deal not only to give Western policy a persuasive slant but also to redefine the relationship between Europe and America, thus developing a clear view of the relations between East and West. My assessment has not varied since 1964:

The strategy of peace proclaimed by President Kennedy is to be assessed as a comprehensive attempt to change the relationship between East and West without illusions. It is the attempt to blunt the atomic balance of terror and to work toward the peaceful solution of problems.

This strategy is aimed at not allowing the status quo to become congealed, but to transform it step by step and to overcome it.

At the same time we must make it clear beyond all doubt that Germany has an interest in détente and not in the maintenance of tension. But for any détente worthy of the name what is required are just those measures that will help to overcome the political causes of the tension. And here the German question cannot be by-passed.

We learned from Kennedy to stand on the groundwork of the facts with both feet, but not to become the prisoners of the moment—to see the world as it is, but to think beyond mere defense; to do everything necessary for freedom, but to think ourselves into a world of better cooperation. In the long run a state cannot be stronger externally than it is internally. This means that creative forces must be awakened within. They have a value all their own. And for our relations abroad they are not to be eschewed.

I stand behind the strategy of peace that John F. Kennedy developed and that President Johnson has vigorously continued.

The conception developed by Kennedy on June 26, 1963, at the Free University of Berlin is still embodied in the policy of the United States. This means that the struggle for piecemeal changes for the better remains the policy of the leading Western power. For some time now I have come to the conclusion that that is the only way possible. With the formula of "all or nothing" it may be possible to satisfy emotional impulses but not to carry on a sensible foreign policy.

I did not wait to become Foreign Minister to point out—in Germany and in America—that there is really no need for anyone to be concerned if Europe shows a growing independence and self-awareness, but only if we allow no doubt to remain about the impossibility of any security for Europe in the foreseeable future without the military commitment of the United States. We must say just as distinctly that America could not itself feel secure without the firmness of its friends in Europe. A strong Europe is the precondition for a partnership on a footing of equality on both sides of the Atlantic.

Achieving such equality is not made impossible by America's atomic superiority, which Europe cannot catch up with. Europeans, however, must have their say in the realm of deterrence and securing peace, as well as in strategic planning and decisions. I said as a German active in politics, and I repeat, that I do not wish my country to dispose of nuclear weapons. The majority of my people feel the same; we do not need such weapons. But Europe must never be defenseless. In one way or another the risk involved in attacking Europe must remain sufficiently great.

The alliance with the United States and the other partners of the North Atlantic pact is vitally important for the future we are capable of foreseeing. It is a fundamental element of our foreign policy.

Though this book deals with European politics and a European peace order, honesty—as well as respect for our American ally—demands that Vietnam not be ignored.

Let me express for myself, first and foremost, a profound compassion for the suffering Vietnamese people. What they have had to endure, in both parts of the country, is a Thirty Years' War transferred into this century. This implies a humanitarian duty. It also implies the urgent desire for a peaceful settlement of the conflict and the willingness to contribute to such a settlement leading up to political consolidation.

The present administration of the Federal Republic has not considered it appropriate to undertake an undischargeable commitment or put itself into an ambiguous light by means of statements of "moral support." Nor has it considered it appropriate to impart public suggestions to the Americans.

In the Federal Republic the escalation of the war has given increasing rise to doubts and concern. It is no surprise that such doubts, particularly with respect to the bombings in the north, were uttered in my own party. In a press report— largely distorted—it was indicated, after a meeting of the Board at the beginning of January 1968, that sympathy had been declared for the suggestions of UN Secretary General U Thant and that reference had been made to the resolutions of the Socialist International. But it was also stated that a readiness for peace on *both* sides was needed in order to arrive at a sensible outcome.

In Vietnam—as I said as chairman of my party in October 1967 in Zurich—we have witnessed an increase in the volume of combat equipment, and at the same time in the United States a monumental debate whether this escalation could bring about a military decision. In North Vietnam, on the other hand, there has been an increased determination to hold out and not give in on any of the points listed as preconditions for the acceptance of peace negotiations. In observing a situation in which obviously no one can win or be beaten in a traditional way, the world has been a witness to the agony of a people making immense sacrifices, regardless of whether it is living in the north or in the south.

In 1965, during a brief trip to America, I realized clearly that in the Federal Republic we had a completely inadequate conception of what the war in Vietnam meant for the United States, materially and spiritually. It had unleashed a public discussion whose depth and passion are unparalleled during the last twenty years. This war is a milestone in the awareness of the American people of the burdens, responsibilities, capacities, and limits of a world power. It cannot help but influence the future international sense of direction of the strongest Western power.

These interconnections and developments cannot remain a matter of indifference to us. Previous Federal administrations had been unable to explain the scope of these problems to the population. What is incontestable was the determination of the United States to live up to its word and to the consequences of its word. It was also clear that President Johnson in all his decisions had the quite solid support of his own people. This is not contradicted by the fact that his administration evidenced a powerful desire to reach peace in Vietnam and to help in working out positive programs of development in Southeast Asia. Behind this attempt lay the grandiose task of making the peace of the world more secure; there was no turning away of America from Europe and no weakening of its interest in our own part of the world. Although the Vietnam debate in the United States was far more bitter than comparable discussions in Europe, many Americans felt such debate to be a sign of strength. The American discussion showed that openness can make a nation conscious of what in the long run strengthens rather than weakens it.

In February 1966 I went to New York as one of the recipients of the Freedom Award. I wrote as follows to a man who—in an idealistic way—had been offended by this, Norman Thomas, the veteran American socialist:

> My friends in America represent very various attitudes concerning the appropriateness, sense, boundaries, and responsibility of the present Vietnam policy of the United States. We Germans are no schoolmasters in world politics. But we should surely not be mere followers either, no satellite that considers everything good and fine that the leading Western power considers correct.
>
> I oppose most particularly any simplifying, objectively unfounded comparisons between Vietnam and Berlin.
>
> Precisely someone like myself, who hopes for a full-bodied détente between East and West, cannot lose sight of the fact that in Vietnam a decision is also being reached as to whether the thesis of the American paper tiger and of the possibility of restricted, surrogate wars against an atomic power, helpless against them, will gain the upper hand. It may be that it is only now that the people of the United States will become fully conscious of and frightened by what a burden it is to be a world power, and how often, unfortunately, the decision for a lesser evil is bound up with it. My impression that President Johnson is striving toward a peace under acceptable conditions has not changed. I am advising my friends in Germany to avoid superficial and extremist utterances.
>
> The war in Vietnam has now been escalated for two years. It has become more cruel, tough and embittered. During that time one argument which two years earlier played an essential part, has lost its significance—the credibility and reliability of the United States. If the United States were to

renounce a military solution, this would not affect the trust-worthiness of the United States guarantee vital to the security of Europe, the Federal Republic, and Berlin. The undeclared war in South East Asia hampers a further relaxation of tension between East and West. It implies the risk of widening. That is why peace in Vietnam is also of direct interest to Europe and Germany.

The tragedy of a small people that for more than two decades has not seen peace and is seriously in danger of being decimated cannot be a matter of indifference to anyone. We cannot look on with indifference as a whole people grinds itself to pieces on behalf of a cause that could have been won by peaceful means and still must be. For reasons of humanity this tragedy cannot put up with disinterested spectators—it summons to the stage the party of mankind. Those who would like to consecrate the idea of a total national war are on the wrong warpath. The goal of a total victory of one side or the other, a victory that has as a precondition military annihilation, is in reality the renunciation of any peace that is worthy of the name.

10

A
CHANGING
ALLIANCE

We wish for the consolidation and the further development of the Atlantic alliance in tune with the times. What this calls for is the adaptation of the alliance to the changes in world politics.

For some years Europe has not been shaken by great international crises. In our hemisphere politics is no longer solely, or even primarily, determined by the confrontation of two military blocs. The frozen political fronts are beginning to break up. A gradual reduction of the military confrontation now appears conceivable.

This development would not have come about if the Western allies had not stood together in the great crises of the most recent past and been jointly prepared to repulse all attacks. But has NATO become outdated now that the threat has subsided? Has it made itself superfluous? I do not think so. It will have performed its military task only when its political task has been completed. What is at issue now is to secure what has been achieved and to arrive at an enduring just peace order in Europe.

We are in the decisive years between two eras in which the course is being laid down for a long time to come. Such a thing happens only rarely at spectacular conferences or in momentous political decisions of principle. It is not always wars, crises, and revolutionary movements that determine the course of history. One is reminded of the saying about the ideas that come on the feet of doves and nevertheless lead the world. This saying may apply to the development of Europe during the last few years, for it came about almost unnoticed.

We cannot speak of cooperation in Western Europe or of securing the peace for all Europe without including the North Atlantic alliance in our considerations. Because of the necessary and desired participation of the United States and of Canada the alliance stretches out beyond Europe, yet its center of gravity and its principal mission lie in Europe. This defense alliance is and remains necessary even though a changing world constantly obliges us to reconsider its goals and its methods and to adapt it to developments. Essentially there is nothing new in this. It applies to all unions.

It is well known that a number of members of the alliance would like to improve and strengthen the organs for political consultation and coordination within NATO. This is to be welcomed. We have often made the point ourselves that the East-West policy has as a precondition a certain measure of canvassing of opinion and of communication between the Western partners. This approach remains correct and is worth striving for.

On the other hand, the idea of a "joint policy" within NATO has been turned down, primarily by the French government. It is true that this idea does not involve a joint policy in the literal sense, but there is a divergence of opinion even about the necessity and appropriateness of up-to-date forms of consultation and cooperation. In such circumstances any insistence on far-reaching claims can scarcely be successful. At the same time, however, all the allies seem to be in agreement that the goal of our policy must be an enduring and just peace order throughout Europe, by which I mean an order that will eliminate the causes of tension and overcome the division of Europe.

Moving from an alliance that was concluded in a period of intense international tensions and for the purposes of defense against a very specific danger to a policy of détente very naturally raises a number of new questions that must be answered. A reduction of the tensions between East and West is useful and desirable, yet our policy aims at something further. It regards as its task the elimination of the causes of tension during a phase of the détente and the creation of a situation that as far as human provision can reach will offer no grounds for new and dangerous tensions. The period of détente, which we hope will be enduring, is to be used in order to give European security a solid foundation and to bring about an enduring peace order.

The revolutionary objectives of Soviet policy in Europe have receded; nevertheless the influence of ideology on the Communist leaderships in future must not be underestimated, for it will often distort their analysis of the policies of non-Communist states and societies. More than one conference and publication have even in the most recent period sketched a completely warped image of the West and of its political intentions. Such ideological prejudices restrict the readiness for a detente and for cooperation. They are deeply embedded, and it will not be easy to overcome them.

We have built up our state successfully in the hope that a new, free, and united Europe would be created, in the hope of a European community in which our nation, with equal rights and finally, also, united again, would be able to live side by side with the other nations of our hemisphere. It was toward such a Europe that the Germans in the Federal Republic have directed their policy; it is what they are working for. Our participation in Atlantic cooperation has always been related to our European objectives.

The very constitution of the Federal Republic of Germany permits the transfer of sovereign rights to supranational organizations. The Federal Republic has subordinated all its combat forces to the Supreme Command of NATO. With respect to its allies it has renounced the production of atomic, biological, and chemical weapons, subjected itself to restrictions on the production of other weapons, and accepted controls. In order to avoid any misunderstanding, it was unambiguously laid down in the Federal government statement of December 13, 1966, that we do not aspire to national control over nor national ownership of nuclear weapons.

In short, we have sought a firm anchoring of the Federal Republic of Germany in the Western alliance. We have closely linked our destinies to the alliance and to the Western European union that is being formed under its protection. This affiliation was all the easier for us because our allies accepted our legitimate national objective: the right of self-determination for our nation and a peace treaty that would enable the Germans to live under the roof of a single state.

The North Atlantic Treaty Organization is first and foremost an effective defense alliance. It prevents potential opponents from being tempted to exert political pressure on any one of the allies through military force. But constant effort is required to maintain this defensive strength in the face of constantly advancing technical development. We realize that the commitment in Europe is a great burden on the United States and that some of its citizens feel it is too heavy. It is understandable to ask why a reduction of the burden should not be possible. It will become possible only when the East-West situation permits it. But I am afraid that the time for any significant lightening of the United States burdens has not yet come.

The Atlantic alliance, for the reasons already pointed out, is not summed up by a military assignment. NATO was supposed to be simultaneously an instrument of political cooperation and of an understanding between governments that shared the same fundamental convictions. This goal does not prevent different governments from having different views of different problems, for tensions are characteristic of an alliance of free states during changing international constellations. What is at issue is a constant and at times painful process of adaptation.

The Federal Republic, I said as early as December 1966 before the Council of NATO in Paris, will not evade discussions, based on mutual confidence, of a reform of NATO during the coming years. It wishes to contribute toward a policy of détente between the states of the Warsaw pact and those of the North Atlantic pact, while opposing any danger to the security of any country. The Federal Republic of Germany is no obstacle to the peaceful, secure future that is to the interest of us all. Nor in this respect shall we let ourselves be led astray by the aggressive speeches made against us by Communist leaders in their own countries, in neutral states, and in the countries of our allies.

The North Atlantic pact and its organization may be imperfect; it may not suffice for many of the demands we should be bound to make on any alliance. But that should not seduce us into seeking false alternatives or alternatives that suit ourselves alone, for it must, rather, be a reason for us to improve the alliance in such a way that it can fulfill all the tasks of our own time and of the future.

Bilateral steps are useful for gradually leading East and West together in Europe. Bilateral steps are bound, however, to remain a patchwork and can even lead to great upheavals if they are not linked to the prospect of a European solution. An enduring detente will not prosper against the background of a process of decay in the Western camp. Moreover, any accord at the expense of an ally would be not only short-sighted but dangerous as well.

I know that very little would be solved by a mere call for a return to the unity of a defensive alliance. I am sure that a joint political sense of direction is needed, for a policy of détente requires concrete objectives for negotiation that point beyond the confrontation of military alliances.

It goes without saying that the relationship of the NATO states to the Soviet Union and its allies will never be uniform, nor would that even be desirable. At the Luxemburg NATO conference (June 1967) and on other occasions I have made the point that our policy vis-à-vis the East should be agreed on but must remain elastic. What will be decisive for its success is for each NATO member to keep the alliance in his mind, to defend his allies, and to make their political path easier. The decisions of the members of the Warsaw pact have shown that their initiators hope to split NATO and thus bring about its demise. This hope obviously must be removed before they can begin sympathizing with a policy of détente in more than a merely tactical way.

NATO and a policy of détente are not mutually exclusive. On the contrary, the existence of NATO—that is, its political weight and its readiness to defend our territory against all attacks—has shown that a policy of tensions and crises is of no avail. The weakening of NATO would reduce the possibility of a détente and lessen its effectiveness. The military deterrent has ensured the peace in Europe. It would be light-minded to encroach upon it and to risk losing what has been achieved.

There are various indications that the Soviet leadership and some of its allies have their gaze riveted on the year 1969 in the hope that the alliance will fall to pieces and that the East might influence this process for its own purposes. Anyone who cherishes this hope must be made to see that he is pursuing a will-o'-the-wisp. The alliance has been concluded for an unlimited duration, and I am assuming that it—together with France—will go on existing and that even a change in the Warsaw pact would under no circumstances impel the Western allies to give up their alliance. As long as there is no enduring, just peace order in Europe, it is not decisive whether the Warsaw pact organization remains in existence or is replaced by some system of bilateral mutual aid pacts. In other words, a peace order in Europe will also not eliminate the problem of bilateral pacts.

Our policy of detente is not to be understood in the sense of underestimating and neglecting the vital importance of the Western alliance. On the contrary, we have warned against allowing the bilateral attitude in East-West relations to grow out of hand. In place of that we have worked toward having the alliance as a whole take up a stand with respect to new tasks.

In 1967 NATO, at the instigation of Belgian Foreign Minister Harmel, took up the future tasks of the alliance and the procedural methods of fulfilling them, "in order to strengthen the alliance"—as the Council of Ministers put it—"as a factor in an enduring peace." These studies were participated in by the NATO partners, including France; we took an active part and made a number of contributions. In spite of all the pessimistic prognoses the broadly based discussion proved that now as before NATO is capable of elaborating fundamental guidelines of policy.

On December 14, 1967, the fifteen foreign ministers put together the result of the studies in the "Report on the Future Tasks of the Alliance." By way of introduction they stated that "the alliance is a dynamic and potent organization that constantly adapts itself to the changing conditions" and by way of conclusion "that the study underlines the importance of the role that the alliance can play during the coming years in the promotion of détente and in the strengthening of peace."

NATO came into being as a defense alliance, in order to preserve peace, freedom, and security in the territory of the allies. This task has remained, but something has been added to it. The comprehensive report makes the following point: "The Atlantic alliance has two principal functions. One is to maintain adequate military strength and political solidarity, in order to deter aggression and other forms of pressure, and to defend the territory of the member countries, in case any aggression should take place." For "As long as the focal questions under dispute in Europe, first and foremost the German question, remain unsolved, the possibility of a crisis cannot be excluded." The second principal function "consists in striving for further progress toward a more stable relationship in which the fundamental questions under dispute can be solved." The allies declare that "it is the foremost objective of the alliance to bring about a just and enduring peace order in Europe in conjunction with appropriate guarantees of security." They have resolved "to direct their energies toward this goal by means of realistic measures of détente in the East-West relationship."

Accordingly, we agree with our allies that military security and a policy of détente do not contradict but supplement each other. Without the firm support of the alliance we cannot carry on any policy of détente. Similarly the political objective of the alliance will not be realized without an East-West détente.

The foreign ministers did not content themselves with laying down these guidelines for the future role of the alliance. In order to give expression to the wishes of their governments, they charged the Permanent Council of NATO to elaborate, on the basis of the unpublished individual results of the study, proposals for a policy "aiming at a just and enduring order in Europe, an overcoming of the division of Germany, and a strengthening of European security. This will become part of a process of active, constant preparedness for the time when fruitful bilateral or multilateral discussions of complex questions will become possible between Eastern and Western nations."

The starting point of the alliance is the conviction that our future security must rest on two pillars: on the deterrent effect of the alliance, that is, on one-sided precautions in any given situation; and on realistic measures of mutual control of armaments, limitation of armaments, and of disarmament. The comprehensive report of the Council of Ministers asserts by way of logical conclusion: "The allies are studying measures of disarmament and limitation of armaments, including the possibility of balanced force reductions. These studies are being intensified. Their active pursuit reflects the desire of the allies to work for an effective détente with the East."

11

GERMANY AND THE SOVIET UNION: BEGINNING OF A DIALOGUE

In addition to economic and cultural relations between Germany and the Soviet Union we hope for an improvement of the political relationship between the two of us. Because it would not be realistic to expect an abrupt and fundamental change, we are exerting ourselves to attain an understanding step by step.

The special importance of the Soviet Union—it is obvious —is rooted in its position as a world power and for us, to be sure, also in its position as one of the four powers that are still responsible for the problem of Germany. It was no accident that in December 1966 the Soviet Union was mentioned first in the foreign affairs part of the government statement. It is no contradition to acknowledge the Soviet Union as the leading Communist and East European power and at the same time to take cognizance of the differentiations in the Communist world. But we are going a long way in order to be fair to the role of the Soviet Union and not to give it the impression that we are speculating on differences of opinion in the Communist camp.

Thus we have rejected taking any initiative as far as the relations with the People's Republic of China are concerned.

Nor have we pursued the possibility of formalizing our far-from-insignificant trade relations with China.

This does not necessarily mean it might not be in the interest of a peace policy if China collaborated with the family of nations. A possible later settlement of our relations with the People's Republic of China will, however, have to avoid any disturbance of our relationship with friendly Asian governments, primarily Japan, and with the United States, as well as avoid arousing Moscow's suspicion that we might wish to exploit the Soviet's difficulties with China.

The Union of Soviet Socialist Republics has grown to be a world power, but the Soviet world power remains at the same time a European power. In the international situation of rivalry with the United States, of the potential conflict with China, of the incipient unification of Europe, and of the insecurity in other parts of the world that constitutes a challenge to political intervention, the Soviet leadership has shown little or no inclination to give up power positions, even if in doing so it could secure new, better, and safer relationships. This rigidity is what in essence has characterized the Soviet policy in Europe since the first postwar years. European developments have seemed acceptable to the Soviet leadership only insofar as they consolidate its power position. But détente without the reexamination of power positions is a dubious undertaking.

For us Germans the rigid clinging to the status quo is particularly difficult because it does not open up any prospect of overcoming the division of Germany. For Europe as a whole the present state of division cannot be final either. It is difficult to harmonize the rigid Soviet positions with the properly understood interests of Europe, which has a right to its own, peacefully secured existence, as Europeans are becoming increasingly aware. An accommodation of

interests will not be easy, but it must be sought most tenaciously.

There will be no swift transformation of the European
situation. Every sensible foreign policy in this connection
must take into account a time factor. But it would be a grave
mistake for anyone to regard Europe as the petrified excres-
cence of two spheres of power. It is a living community of
peoples and states. And the transformation that some wish
for and others would like to stop is already making itself
manifest.

It is making itself manifest in the West. It is also mani-
festing itself in the East, where the Warsaw pact has long
since ceased to be the conspiratorial community of ideolo-
gists that wrongly advised propagandists still insist on seeing.
This reference is not to be construed as a way of setting up
artificial contradictions between the Soviet Union and the
Eastern European states allied with it. It would be foolish
and short-sighted, and, for that matter futile, for our foreign
policy to speculate on such contradictions; we are not going
to try to play one off against the other. We must accept the
fact that there is a far-reaching identity of interests between
the Soviet Union and its allies in Eastern Europe. But the
uniformity of the Stalin era belongs to the past; ideology has
failed to extinguish national identities. In fact, ideology is
increasingly influenced by national requirements.

In November 1967 the Union of Soviet Socialist Republics celebrated with unmistakable pride the fiftieth anniversary of its revolutionary birth. I said at the time that it
was not our concern to sit in judgment as to whether or not
the great successes that the ruling party won in and for the
country might have been attainable with lesser sacrifices as
well. The chairman of the Social Democratic Party of Germany, who knows some history, also knows that it would be

senseless to try to put history back on the drawing board for revision. Thus I am of the opinion that we had good cause to congratulate the peoples of the Soviet Union and their government for their impressive achievements. Above all we had good cause to condemn once again the agony inflicted on the peoples of the Soviet Union as a result of Hitler's criminal adventurism. We also had good cause to recall those days when Germany and the Soviet Union gave each other mutual help. The Soviet Union of today will have forgotten the one no more than the other.

In this age of transition—and against the background of the division of Germany—it is a difficult enterprise to bring about good relations with the Soviet Union; a great deal of patience is required. We do not wish either our patience or our good will to fail. We owe that to Europe and to our own country. Our democratic Germany must and will oppose the Soviet Union if and for as long as it tries, by pressure or by other methods, to make its own ideas of state and social order an article of export and thus involve itself in other people's internal affairs. But our democratic Germany can be and the German people would like to be a sincere friend of the Soviet Union. To this it might be added that greatness is also capable of showing greatheartedness. It is not that we are begging for this, but a Soviet Union that would respect the vital rights of the German people would not have to be afraid—and not only because it is powerful— of the German people. And we, those Germans of good will—that is, the great majority—want to see to it with equal concern that no danger of war can ever arise again on German territory.

The face of the Soviet Union has been transformed during these past fifty years; the face of Germany, too. What has remained unchanged is the geography that has made the peoples of the Soviet Union and of Germany indirect but close neighbors and keeps them neighbors (always also taking into consideration the vital rights of the Polish people, who want and ought to live within secure frontiers).

A German foreign minister is not in a position to threaten, nor would this be suitable to my disposition. I am merely making a statement, based on experience, when I say that it is not good, it is not wise, to allow a great people in the center of Europe to continue under the tension of its unnatural fragmentation. I am realistic enough to know that the national unity of the German people—the isolated realization of its right to self-determination—is not today on the agenda of practical politics. Only through the unfolding of a historic process will both portions of Germany be brought closer to each other and linked together; and that process revolves around Europe. But one must desire this process, envisage it, and start in. That process is in the German interest, but it is also just as much—I am deeply convinced of this—in the interest of the Soviet Union, in the interest of all our neighbors, to envisage a peace that is secure beyond all need for precautions, beyond any desire for disturbing changes.

The Soviet Union ought to realize that friendship with Germany, as intended by geography, is an important question that will be formulated in a renewed form if not today then tomorrow. For the interest of both peoples demands that a secure peace be created, an accommodation that no one will have to be afraid of.

The situation has become increasingly complex and entails new problems. Nevertheless, we should remember that only a few years ago the situation now prevailing in Europe seemed to many people to be worth striving for. It is, in fact, a great advance over the time of the Cold War and the political freeze. We have gained not much more but a little more freedom of movement. There are many contacts today between the states of Western and of Eastern Europe. Though for a variety of reasons Germany's starting point was more difficult than that of others, the German government is vigorously striving to promote such relations. Meanwhile, we have emphasized again and again that we do not wish to isolate any state—including the other part of Germany.

Our assertion that relations to the Soviet Union occupy a special priority in our considerations corresponds to the realities and to history. We have said to the Soviet Union that we are prepared at any time to initiate a discussion of all the substantive questions in our relations. We are well aware that such a phase of serious talking takes time. We have also declared ourselves ready to deal with the questions that are more swiftly soluble first—for instance; the resumption of negotiations for the conclusion of a trade agreement, the promotion of cultural relations, accords concerning technical and scientific cooperation (including the application of atomic energy to peaceful ends), and the establishment of a direct air connection between Frankfurt and Moscow.

The government of the Soviet Union knows that we are ready to exchange statements banning the use of force. It goes without saying that we do not wish to evade any question whose discussion is of concern to the Soviet Union. Talks have begun in some questions of mutual interest, but it is still impossible to know how far they will lead. At the moment there is no indication that a substantial improvement in relations is in the offing.

I know that the government of the Soviet Union does not wish to speak of German unity for the time being, but I think it does wish to speak about peace in Europe. We too want that. In details our opinions may still differ considerably, but no one who takes the trouble to have a discussion with us will be able to maintain that we are militaristic and revanchist. In reality everyone knows that we include the German Democratic Republic and the problematic question of the division of Germany in our offer to renounce force.

The moment the possibility of any discussions—however difficult—with the Soviet Union looms up, problems will show themselves in the West, too. The atmosphere, pregnant with secrecy, that made the word "Rapallo" a symbol and a nightmare for Western statesmen was and is obviously hard to eradicate today. In that 1922 treaty we ended the state of war with Russia. It united an economic cooperation with a most-favored-nation clause and formulated a mutual renunciation of war indemnities. Many of those who speak about Rapallo do not know this. Its essence, that is, the restoration of a normal and—if possible—friendly relationship between Germany and the Soviet Union, remains a task that cannot be performed by a single-handed feat. It demands tenacity and intense and quiet labor, but also the readiness of the Soviet Union to investigate together with us the possibilities of such a course.

I am well aware of the encumbrances of the past. But I cannot accept attempts made to force the Federal Republic into a corner where it does not belong. The German people and the Federal government want peace. I think that the governmental responsibility of the German Social Democrats offers an additional guarantee. This party has never agitated for war, and it has never trampled the rights of man under foot. Of course the Social Democrat Party of Germany has not always been right. But it has never given up its political and ethical principles and will never do so in future, either within the government or outside.

In the spring of 1967 Leonid Brezhnev made the remark, during a visit to East Berlin, that the Federal government had hidden a great stone in its outstretched hand. This was a vivid but false image. We are, happily, well out of the political Stone Age. Nor are there any other treacherous weapons in our hand. The party head of the Soviet Union did not say concretely just how or with what the Federal Republic was threatening its neighbors.

In 1967 the government of the Soviet Union made numerous other allusions to the danger of militarism and neo-Nazism allegedly bound up with German policy. On December 22, the Federal Republic responded to such a Soviet statement of December 8, 1967, saying it took the view that it was no service to the efforts for understanding and détente to initiate a reciprocal polemic:

> In June 1967 the Federal government saw fit to suggest to the Soviet government conversations dealing with questions of interest to both sides. To be sure, this also included the support that the Federal government had requested the Soviet government to give it in the prosecution of Nazi criminals.
>
> The German Federal government had hoped that the Soviet government would respond to this initiative by declaring its readiness to engage in constructive talks. Consequently the Federal government deplores the new Soviet government statement, whose threatening tone is unusual in international exchanges.
>
> More particularly, the statement gives a wholly distorted picture of German domestic politics as well as the policy of the Federal government, known throughout the world, of pursuing its aims by exclusively peaceful means. The openly expressed readiness of the Federal government to exchange statements with the Soviet Union and its allies concerning

the renunciation of force is a proof of this attitude. The government of the Federal Republic of Germany firmly rejects the statement of the Soviet Union as an interference in its internal affairs and as a distortion of its foreign policy.

The accusations of the Soviet statement are all the more incomprehensible since in the same statement it is accurately maintained that the views and feeling of the majority of the Germans living in the Federal Republic of Germany are by no means to be identified with those of "hard-core revanchists and neo-Nazis." It is this immense majority that is represented by the parties of the German Federal parliament. It is this majority whose will it is that bears aloft the peace policy of the Federal government.

The German people and its constitutional organs will be able to protect the fundamental order of society based on liberty and democracy. The Federal government hopes that the Soviet Union will contribute its share so that the German people can regain its unity by peaceful means and be able to make its own contribution to a European peace order.

The question still remains, to be sure, whether the difficulties that the Soviet Union made for the Federal government surprised us or whether we had foreseen them. I have never for a moment believed in any rapid improvement of our relationship with Moscow. It is true that I also did not expect the government of the Soviet Union to identify itself, to the extent to which this has happened, with the hostile attitude of East Berlin toward the government of the Great Coalition. In December 1966, for instance, there was still no indication that Moscow would set up as many obstacles to the establishment of diplomatic relations with the Eastern European states as proved to be the case. There is some reason to think that the exaggerated polemic had to serve

as an instrument for holding the Warsaw pact together—
and not, for that matter, with complete success. Its connection with events in other parts of the world, primarily in
Vietnam, is also bound to come to mind.

We have not let ourselves be deflected, either by cross-
fire from abroad or by a lack of understanding in our own
country, from seeking an objective dialogue with the Soviet
Union. I will not be made to deviate from this goal, nor shall
I let myself be deflected from energetically continuing a conversation, initiated with so much difficulty, as purposefully
and as intensively as possible. It is well known that big advances cannot be achieved swiftly. The terrain must be prepared, and for that there must be favorable circumstances and
necessary intervals of time.

It remains our sincere desire to bring about an understanding with the Soviet Union by means of practical cooperation and an exchange of political opinions.

12

THE POLICY
OF DÉTENTE:
MENDING THE BRIDGE
BETWEEN EASTERN
AND WESTERN EUROPE

Accommodation with our Eastern neighbors is a high-priority aim of German foreign policy. We wish to improve our economic and cultural relations and also to initiate diplomatic relations with them wherever circumstances make this possible.

At the same time, we know that a comprehensive accommodation will be reached only after West and East come to an understanding about the foundations of an enduring peace order. We can approach this goal only step by step, in a long-drawn-out process of détente, that is, by means of mutual rapprochement, understanding, and cooperation in all areas of interstate relations. The establishment of diplomatic relations is a means to the attainment of this goal, not an end in itself.

Our policy with respect to Eastern Europe—this must be emphasized again and again—cannot be separated from the shaping of our relationship to the Soviet Union.

The development of our relations with the other countries of Eastern Europe should supplement the development of our relationship to the Soviet Union, not run counter to it. The internal German accommodation is also closely related to our policy on Eastern Europe. We have made it clear that our readiness for a détente includes the German Democratic Republic. This has nothing to do with the surrender of vital interests.

The primary goal of our policy on Eastern Europe is to arouse confidence and eliminate distrust. As we once had to do in the West, we must now, under more difficult preconditions, pay off the mortgages of the past in the East. Our Eastern policy, starting from the given circumstances of today, is intended to help to overcome the division of Europe. Consequently we are particularly concerned with demonstrating the peaceable nature of our means and ends. Statements renouncing the use of force can contribute to this.

In January 1967 we established diplomatic relations with Rumania on the occasion of Foreign Minister Manescu's visit. About the same time, East Berlin and Warsaw, supported by Moscow, succeeded in hampering our conversations concerning the establishment of diplomatic relations with other Eastern European states. The conclusion of the friendship treaties of East Berlin with Poland, Czechoslovakia, Hungary, and Bulgaria does not, to be sure, bar the initiation of diplomatic relations with us, but it means a postponement of the course of normalization.

German policy with respect to Eastern Europe nevertheless showed a positive balance at the beginning of 1968. After the exchange of trade representations with Czechoslovakia, we now figure in all Eastern European states except Albania. We are the most important Western trading partner there; nor are all possibilities of economic cooperation exhausted.

Furthermore, cultural exchange with most of our neighboring Eastern states is growing; for example, the Federal Republic publishes by far more Eastern European literature than any other Western country.

In a number of capitals there is, as we know, a deep-lying desire for political talks and the readiness to normalize relations and to improve their content, but in East Berlin, Warsaw, and Moscow, especially, attempts are being made to block further progress toward improved relations. The influence of East Berlin and its capacities for working against our policy are obvious. The trend in certain European states toward greater freedom of movement vis-à-vis the West, including the Federal Republic of Germany, conflicts with certain economic and military bonds. The common ideology and the will to self-preservation of the Communist regimes are links that are still further strengthened by the friendship treaties of the German Democratic Republic with Poland, Czechoslovakia, Hungary, and Bulgaria. East Berlin also seems to have achieved a certain success with the argument that our policy on Eastern Europe is intended to isolate East Berlin.

In speaking of a positive interim balance at the beginning of 1968, nevertheless, I have in mind the following: First, we have found a great deal of agreement with our policy in the West and in the Third World. Second, some de facto advances have been made. Third, it can be said without hesitation that although there may be setbacks the development as a whole will proceed in the direction of multiplied contacts and improved relations.

It can be stated that an important result of our endeavors and of the support of our friends is that no one can be believed any longer who maintains that the Federal Republic of Germany is a mischief-maker or an obstacle to détente.

Here we are in the midst of a genuine change of climate. The accusations that the Federal government is preparing an act of aggression, that it is imperialistic, that it is jeopardizing the peace, and similar remarks—all such charges go into a vacuum. Anyone who puts them forward only becomes unbelievable.

We have never thought we could carry on an active policy on the East and a successful policy of détente at the price of an alienation from the West. Anyone who in foreign policy thinks in terms of the pendulum stroke misunderstands both its own laws and—in our case—the position of Germany. It was also erroneous to interpret the decision of the Federal Republic in favor of Western democracy as a decision against Central and Eastern Europe. I said in this connection that in foreign policy there were for me no spoiled darlings, no favorite children, and no stepchildren, but only the vital interests of the state and the nation, especially, however, the interest of securing the peace. Our Western allies have been urging us—rightly—over and over again to contribute to this détente during the past years.

At this point I would like to thank those of my European colleagues who in their conversations with Eastern European governments have shown so much understanding in their support of our endeavors to improve our relationship to these countries. I am thinking here of the foreign ministers of the Scandinavian countries and of the Benelux states and equally of the support of the French, the British, the Italian, and the Turkish foreign ministers. We are confident that the explanation of our policy of peace and détente by representatives of countries friendly to us will contribute to a deepening of the understanding of our sincere efforts in the Eastern European capitals.

The initiation of diplomatic relations with Rumania was

an important step, but both sides were obliged to put up with a good deal of criticism. In Germany some people asked why this step had not been taken sooner. Others spoke of a blunder on the part of Germany's Eastern policy because Rumania has remained an individual case. Mistaking the real state of affairs, such critics seem to have been expecting a chain reaction and were baffled when it failed to come about. Because it would be a mistake to let the understanding of our long-term policy be distorted by the ebb and flow of day-to-day political obstacles, my answer to those critics was that anyone who has waited years will be able to be patient a little while longer. From the very outset our calculations were founded on lengthy intervals of time. We are not putting any pressure on anyone, and we shall not let pressure be applied to ourselves. We have patience and confidence, an ability to act, and a long breath.

After ambassadors were exchanged with Rumania in the summer of 1967, a German-Rumanian accord was signed at the beginning of August for cooperation in technical and scientific domains. This accord was followed by negotiations for deepening economic relations. The conversations I conducted in August 1967 in Bucharest and at the Black Sea—the latter with the party head, Nicolae Ceaucescu, who has since become President—initiated an untrammeled political dialogue that can be of service to other countries as well. This is an example of a realistic kind of cooperation that pushes solid bridges far beyond the differences of political conceptions.

The agreement on goods and payments exchange and on the exchange of trade delegations between Czechoslovakia and the Federal Republic of Germany in the summer of 1967 was also an interim result of more than ephemeral importance. The initiation of these official relations was particularly important because Czechoslovakia and the Federal Republic of Germany are direct neighbors.

In February 1968 the gap in the network of trade missions between the states of Eastern Europe and the Federal Republic of Germany was closed by the exchange with Czechoslovakia of missions provided with consular capacities. The agreement was the beginning of longer-range accords that will surely lead to normalization of the relationship between the two states.

Diplomatic relations between the Federal Republic of Germany and Yugoslavia were broken off at the end of 1957 because Belgrade recognized the German Democratic Republic. The present Federal administration declared that it was concerned with the restoration of diplomatic relations. We were quite clear in our minds about the special, uncommitted attitude of Communist-ruled Yugoslavia. We thought we were aware of the conditions under which its relationship to the Soviet Union, which for years had been so tense, had again been normalized. But above all we were concerned with being able to work together with this important member of the European community of states in a policy of détente and in the perspective of a European peace order.

During the period in which there were no ambassadors the de facto links—economic, cultural, touristic—suffered surprisingly little damage, but both sides had an interest in improving what was already on hand. Because neither side set up any preconditions, by the beginning of 1968 there were no real difficulties in resuming diplomatic relations between Bonn and Belgrade. The exchange of ambassadors was no reason for either side to feel triumphant, but it was more than a merely encouraging sign. The domestic reaction in

Germany showed that our population does not hold much with dogmas and formulas that motivated a policy of limited duration, that were mere accessories unable to withstand the course of evolution.

We had the impression that the governments of Hungary and Bulgaria—as well as that of Czechoslovakia—were concerned with normalization, that is, with the resumption of diplomatic relations. However, these governments thought it correct, or timely, to take into account the demands of East Berlin and of others. We respected their position and made it clear that in the interim we would work together to improve de facto relations within the framework of what was possible.

Official Poland assumed an attitude toward our policy of détente that seemed to be irreconcilable. Although the Federal government gave vigorous emphasis to its desire for reconciliation, the Warsaw regime seemed uninterested in any talks. I find it regrettable that it still remains impossible to improve German-Polish relations. Our stated understanding for the Polish people's desire to live within secure boundaries has been dictated by our wish for reconciliation. We have said with honesty that, in view of our position, border questions can be decided only in a peace treaty. In our opinion, however, there is no sensible reason not to improve bilateral relations and begin a serious German-Polish conversation. I should like to reaffirm here my clear conviction that the reconciliation of Poles and Germans will someday have the same historical importance as the friendship between Germany and France.

The interest of the Eastern European states in cooperating with us rests to a large extent on a desire to make economic progress and to participate in Western technology. Economics, therefore, remains for the foreseeable future an especially important element of our policy on Eastern Europe. We should like to expand the economic exchange with the Eastern European states and as far as possible bring about a balancing of exports and imports. Such an exchange would demand a liberal trade policy vis-à-vis the East on the part of the European Economic Community. Wherever for structural reasons no leveling off of trade balances is possible, even when the liberalization is expanded, the granting of long-term credits should be considered. Even though we may take a soberer view of the prospects of "cooperation" than a number of Eastern European governments that have exaggerated expectations of it, nevertheless we ought to examine such projects without prejudice and to evolve constructive solutions.

The cultural exchange, especially where it leads to human and scientific encounters, is of use to all the states participating. We must realize, to be sure, that the possibilities of spreading and receiving information are not the same in Germany and in Eastern Europe. Cultural projects of our own, by means of which we can have an enlightening effect in Eastern Europe, are important and desirable.

We do not try to force political contacts, but we make use of them wherever the occasion offers. The inclination toward such contacts will increase in Eastern Europe insofar as there is an acceptance of the fact that the Federal Republic of Germany cannot be eliminated from the process of détente in Europe. We must, accordingly, work toward objective progress with tact and sobriety.

Détente is not possible if only one side is prepared to get rid of tensions, and we have made practical, concrete suggestions, supported by the Atlantic alliance, for normalizing our relationship to the Soviet Union and the Eastern European states. The present Federal administration is carrying on an unmistakable, consistent policy:

> It has said clearly and concisely that it well understands the Polish demand to live on its own state territory with secure boundaries and regards the reconciliation with Poland as an important part of the European peace order.
>
> This administration has also said distinctly that the Munich agreement came into being under the threat of force; it is no longer valid.
>
> This government has convincingly indicated that the Federal Republic of Germany is not aiming at the possession of atomic weapons or at the power to dispose of such weapons.
>
> This government is not two-tongued: it speaks the same language everywhere.

Among our people it is known with great certainty that we shall not attain a real accommodation until peace, understanding, cooperation, reconciliation, and—yes, I hope, one day—friendship as well prevail, not only in the West but also between Germany and its neighbors in the East.

I know how painful the road will be, but I am firmly convinced that we shall make progress along it. Our Eastern policy has not frozen, nor does it suffer from what has been so frighteningly referred to as the compulsion to success. The nations and the governments of Eastern Europe ought to realize that the German government would be behaving irresponsibly if it agreed to and promised more than it could stand for in the eyes of its own people and hold to in the future. As it is sometimes said in Eastern Europe that such new ideas were those of the Federal Foreign Minister only, I want to stress that they are the joint opinion of the Chancellor and the Vice Chancellor who is also the Foreign

Minister; they are the policy of the German Federal Government.

In the government statement of December 13, 1966, we stated that we were offering to each of the states in Eastern Europe, including the Soviet Union, an exchange of solemn statements renouncing the use of force. With respect to the German Democratic Republic and to the Warsaw pact, we added that we were ready to encompass, also, the thorny question of divided Germany.

The rulers in the other part of Germany have allowed themselves a deplorable step backward since the first months of 1966. At that time it was thought to be possible to achieve for the citizens of the German Democratic Republic, in their connection with us, at least some humanitarian relief. As mayor of Berlin I had to struggle for the modest passes to cross the borders, not only with the Communists in the East but also against the lack of understanding in the West. There was no longer any need for this dissipation of energies, but meanwhile the East Berlin authorities had decided on an isolation that was to be as thoroughgoing as possible. I am certain, however, that Walter Ulbricht and his people will not be able to sustain their policy of cantankerousness, sabotage, and general querulousness. In the Eastern European states and in the other part of Germany the pressure for exchange will become greater and greater in the years before us—in science, in economics, in technology. Anyone who seals himself off, who isolates himself, is setting himself against the mainstream of our times.

Although there are encouraging signs, on the other hand there is the persistent effort of some leaders—primarily, though not only in East Berlin—to fix their allies on a policy whose goal is to stop or at least to hamper a détente with the Federal Republic of Germany. These circles have far-reaching aims. They want NATO to be dissolved and the Americans to vanish from Europe. The possibility is not to be excluded that this political orientation will prevail in the Communist-ruled part of Europe—though, to be sure, for how long remains open.

From the very outset we were bound to reckon with opposition to any activation of our policy on Eastern Europe. The fact that such opposition came primarily from East Berlin was also not surprising. We weathered lively diplomatic and propagandistic activity. Attempts were made to bridge over differences of opinion among the Communist states with respect to the German policy of détente. Sanction was given to the Rumanian interpretation of the Bucharest statement of July 1966, according to which "formalizing" was not yet synonymous with "normalizing" of relations. At the same time friendship treaties were concluded between East Berlin and Prague, Warsaw, Budapest, and Sofia whose essential goal seemed to be to prove solidarity between them and the Communist-ruled part of Germany. In this way the German Democratic Republic was included in the bilateral network of treaties of the Warsaw pact. To what extent the Eastern European states allow themselves to be bound by these treaties vis-à-vis the Federal Republic of Germany remains subject to be sure, to their interpretation, hence to their political decision.

The Federal Republic will not be stopped in its efforts to go on striving for regulated, normal relations with the states of Eastern Europe. I do not see the negative reactions we have had to encounter as final. In the Eastern bloc, as well as in the Soviet Union itself, there are enough authoritative persons who know that the problems touching us both cannot be dismissed from the world by gruff statements. In February 1967, in the Deutschland hall in Berlin, I spoke of the day when no one would be surprised any longer at the emergence of cooperation, confidence, and even friendship not only between direct neighbors but also between Germany and the Soviet Union. At that time some people thought this remark was wholly novel. In reality what was and is at issue is nothing but the fact that the Federal government—and together with it the overwhelming majority of our people—simply want good and friendly relations with all nations. It is useful and necessary to repeat this from time to time.

We shall reach the stage in which it will be even more obvious than it is today that whether the détente in Europe can be promoted by practical progress, agreements, or accords will depend on the good will of the leaders of the Eastern European powers—and not on the attitude of the Federal Republic. What is a reality is that the Federal government is ready for this détente, that it is ready to be taken at its word.

I will not allow myself to be deflected from a path I regard as the right one, either by setbacks or by disappointments. We must cling to the goal of a reconciliation with our neighbors in the East, for otherwise there can be no enduring peace. In all this internal German relations, the relationship to East Berlin, must not be viewed in isolation. In reality there is a threefold aim in our policy on the East: improved relations with the Soviet Union, normal relations with the Eastern European states, and a *modus vivendi* between the two parts of Germany. And that aim will be realized or not be realized, will be promoted or jeopardized, by the developments in Europe as a whole and in the world at large.

The question of the future of Germany and of the position of Germans in Europe is the question of an enduring

European peace order. Only in a peacefully ordered Europe, which has succeeded in building a bridge between East and West and in which nations as equals among equals will vie with each other for peace, justice, and prosperity, will the past be overcome in a positive way.

The policy of the German government rests on the expectation and the hope that we can create a basis for common interests in Europe while mutually respecting differing social orders. The geographical situation of the German people gives us a special responsibility for this. For centuries Germany was a bridge between East and West. We are striving to build anew the shattered bridge, better, sturdier, and more reliable. Such a task can be performed only in an intimate and trusting collaboration with our friends and neighbors.

During the years prior to the formation of the present administration Bonn was encouraged by its allies to take up a less doctrinaire and a more self-confident attitude. Today I can say that we shall not let ourselves be shaken on our course of a consistent policy of détente, free of illusions,

13

THE
STATUS QUO,
OR THE DIFFICULTY
OF THE "REALITIES"

The Federal Republic of Germany has no territorial demands. What it wants is that the status quo of an insecure peace become a secure peace order. The present situation in Europe is the result of World War II. It is a reality that has been consolidated by postwar development and has remained unchanged for two decades. Hardly anyone can refuse to acknowledge this.

If, however, we are requested to recognize *all* the realities that have been created by World War II as the first step toward a détente, something else is being demanded. What is then at issue is the renunciation of every attempt to overcome by peaceful means the unnatural condition of the division of Germany and of the split within Europe. But that would mean a renunciation of common sense.

I never forget in all this that it was Hitler's "Greater Germany" that brought about such unspeakable misery, above all to Eastern Europe. And when present-day Germans let it be understood that they are contemplating the overcoming of the status quo they easily lay themselves open to a malicious misunderstanding. We must be unyielding in our efforts to clear up that misunderstanding.

What is at issue in this peaceful overcoming of the status quo? First of all, the overcoming of the military confrontation. What is at issue is a compatible Europe that will work together in as friendly a way as possible. What is at issue is the keeping open of a path on which the Germans— if it is their freely expressed will—can find a way to each other and live with each other.

It therefore is not a question of Germans putting forward territorial claims. The borders of 1937, prior to the annexations by Hitler, must be regarded as a legal starting point for negotiations aimed at a peace treaty and also as a sequel to the Potsdam Conference.

There is just as little question of the "incorporation" of the other part of Germany in the Federal Republic. Such ideas are outmoded even for those who once clung to them.

The transformation of the present status quo toward European cooperation and a just solution of the German question will take time. No advance can be made merely through impatient insistence. To that extent we have a clear view of the realities. And it is also a reality that we are striving toward this goal by exclusively peaceful means.

One cannot wish to force into a fixed form a process that to human reckoning must last a long time. Aside from that no one would be running a risk if he renounced any maximalist claims. It is true that the East Berlin government may take a different view of this. For it a policy of détente may be the greatest challenge conceivable. But it is very certain that this does not hold true for our Eastern European neighbors. Nor do I believe that for reasons of a false solidarity they will allow themselves to be barred by East Berlin from the path toward a European peace order. They have no need to fear a rapprochement of both parts of Germany.

Moreover, in more than one place during the past few years the question has been raised as to why it is not enough for Poland to have its boundaries recognized by the German Democratic Republic. In the official opinion of Warsaw the two German states are meant to continue. But in that case there is no border between the Federal Republic and Poland. Yet there seems to be a feeling that there may be changes in "the German question."

If the Federal Republic were to speak bindingly on behalf of all Germany, then Poland would still have no need to fear any forcible change of its boundaries. We do not feel legitimated to anticipate decisions of a future all-German Government and the settlement in a peace treaty, but we can respect and recognize the Oder-Neisse-line until such a peace settlement is concluded.

Such an attitude is inspired by the German desire for reconciliation with Poland even before a peace treaty is signed. Nobody thinks in terms of a new expulsion. It is a fact that 40 per cent of the people living in those areas have been born there.

Statements of this kind do not imply renunciation of legal titles. They simply take into account that legal titles do not in themselves constitute a claim to their realization. We know that the Oder-Neisse-line will continue to exist as long as there is a Federal Republic of Germany. It may sound surprising, but the Federal Republic has never claimed for herself the areas beyond the Oder-Neisse-line. It has never demanded that a strip of Federal territory be inserted between Poland and the German Democratic Republic. That is why it can respect and recognize the present Western frontier of Poland without, in doing so, taking anything away from the expellees or robbing the future Germany.

It would be hypocritical to pass in silence over a fact of which everybody is aware: If, in the course of a comprehensive peace settlement, the present situation were to be modified, such modification could never be agreed upon without the consent of the Polish people. Once the mutual renunciation of force which we have offered were declared, Poland could feel safe in its present frontiers. That is the clear and unequivocal meaning of our policy. That is the implication of the relevant wording of our government statement of December 13, 1966.

This stand illustrates a principle of our foreign policy that some people in the East tenaciously mask: What we hope for from the process of détente and rapprochement, the peaceful overcoming of the status quo and an honorable accommodation of interests, is not meant to be accomplished against the will of the nations participating but with their assent. And when I speak of the nations participating I also mean, of course, those countrymen of ours who are separated from us and who also have a will that must not be disregarded.

It is strange that so sober a word as "realities" can be so misunderstood and so wrangled over. What we are experiencing nowadays is the determination of certain Communists to turn all dialectic topsy-turvy and to conduct themselves as though world history would allow itself at some given point simply to be laid down in a fixed form in writing. We see still others sticking their heads into the sand.

In foreign policy a realist without imagination is a simpleton. But anyone involved in foreign policy who is not a realist is a dreamer. Not a day goes by that does not give rise to new realities, and anyone who believes that all present-day realities can be frozen for all eternity is a reactionary fool petrified to the point of utter rigidity.

In August 1967, during my visit to Rumania, I had some instructive experiences—I became acquainted with a beautiful country and encountered agreeable people. Moreover the comments made in Germany on the occasion of a table talk in Bucharest were illuminating. On the evening of August 3 I said in Bucharest:

> As for the great questions of our time, we agree that the maintenance and consolidation of world peace unequivocally deserve top priority. You have spoken, with a frankness we are able to appreciate, of the ties of your country. Well, the Federal Republic of Germany has its own self-chosen commitments in the Atlantic alliance and in the European communities. But our country, like your own, wants manifold collaboration and strives toward a comprehensive cooperation, in Europe especially.
>
> We also agree that in the problem of European security we must take as a starting point the prevailing realities, and that all states, regardless of size, have tasks of uniform importance in the realization of a European peace order. This also holds for both political societies that are in existence at present on German soil.
>
> For all of us the issue must be: to take away from people the feeling of insecurity and the fear of war.

It is true that the phrase "both political societies" was not in my manuscript, but that I consciously, under the impression of my conversation with my hosts, inserted it. That made it no less important. The following evening I made an equally conscious addition:

> Our policy is directed at everyone and against no one. It is aimed at bringing union and not separation. It seeks a just accommodation in Europe and it is also prepared to make

sacrifices. The sole means it makes use of is the power of persuasion; it has renounced force.

My government would like to work toward an improvement of the present situation in Europe, together with all the states concerned. There can, after all, be nothing reprehensible in trying to shape the world in a more sensible and a more just way! And there can, after all, be nothing sensible in taking the condition of the division of Europe and of my own country, and the military confrontation of heavily armed blocs, as history's final word!

We have no illusions. We are completely aware of the real facts of the situation. It is only that we regard it as the task, indeed the duty, of our policy to contribute with all our strength to overcoming the division of Europe and of Germany. For this we look into the future and endeavor to learn from the past. We are no fantasts, but we would like to help Europe to grow together again instead of drifting further apart.

We must start from the status quo. What else is there to start from? But it would be against nature and against reason to renounce any desire for future development. We must see the given circumstances without any blinders and without any wishful ideas alien to reality. And we must wish to change and improve the present-day facts in such a way that tension will give way to peace. This can only be done without force, that is, only in agreement with all those concerned.

We wish to eliminate the source of mischief—the division of Germany—by means of peaceful understanding and once again to give to our own people their peace with themselves and with the world. We wish—to quote my friend Herbert Wehner, the Federal Minister for all-German Affairs—to make things looser, not harder; to bridge over trenches, not deepen them.

Nothing would be more false than the assumption that we have lately come to believe in an isolated solution of the German questions. What is actually at issue is that perspective that leads beyond the reduction of tensions and beyond the banning of the danger of war, beyond a system of security to an enduring and just peace order. At the same time, we realize that the German problem can be solved only in connection with a general European settlement and can be advanced only in a situation of accommodation between East and West. We are not making our policy of détente dependent on any progress with respect to the question of Germany.

In the other part of our country, in the German Democratic Republic, a political system rules that does not meet with our approval, that we reject; but it exists and rules. We want the common substance of a common nation to persist not only in the memory of man. We want to stand by each other, we want the barriers to be lowered—not least of all out of a feeling of responsibility for peace in Europe.

Our point of view regarding the territory that calls itself the German Democratic Republic has been determined by two basic factors. The first factor is that in this area there live 17 million Germans who are our countrymen and who have undeservedly suffered a more difficult fate; who have not lost the war any *more* than those of us in the Federal Republic; for whose fate we feel and assume an obligation and a responsibility; with whom we wish to maintain contacts or create new ones; whose lives we wish to make easier, as far as that is in our power.

The second factor is based on our resolve not to allow

any recognition under international law to be given to the regime that has been set up in this territory—because it does not represent the will of the people, because without Soviet troops it could not have maintained itself, because it prevents the exercise of the right of self-determination, because it is hampering the solution of the German question.

Nevertheless, what is at issue is not the question of who recognizes and who does not recognize whom. What is at issue are the people and peace. We have good grounds for not letting the present-day situation be sanctioned under international law and for not recognizing the other part of Germany as a foreign country. We have made positive suggestions as to how a great deal might be improved if one put aside those points on which no agreement can be reached and if one concentrated on areas of common interest. I think that responsible leaders on the other side, too, under the other political system, will in the long run have to recognize what is expected from Germans in both parts of Germany— that is, to begin living next to each other within our nation in a peaceful way, to have compatible relations with each other, not to impose needless burdens on people, and not to jeopardize the peace in Europe, but to make it more secure.

If the leadership in East Berlin is afraid of finding itself isolated, its fear must be ascribed to its own policy, which by its dogmatic, didactic manner and attempts to speak for its allies in the Warsaw pact and to forbid or make difficult their establishing diplomatic relations with us, ultimately isolates only itself.

We do not desire any such isolation; on the contrary, we are striving to have this area take part in the process of European détente. In a surrounding world that is seeking to overcome the barriers between states, our countrymen in the other part of Germany should not be forced to live as the only ones who are sealed off. Because of this we submitted to East Berlin, in April 1966, sixteen suggestions for an extension of intra-German contacts that can be implemented without either side demanding that the other give up its political standpoint. For we are of the opinion that there are many problems that might be solved within Germany, too, regardless of the great differences of our political systems and points of view.

There was a tempestuous discussion when the Federal Chancellor took cognizance of a letter from Prime Minister Stoph in East Berlin. I could find nothing sensational in this. After the Federal government had made its statement on Germany and the chairman of the Social Democratic Party of Germany had submitted this document, together with a supplementary statement, to the seventh party convention of the Socialist Unity Party (of the German Democratic Republic) such a step was bound to be taken into account. If one undertakes a political sally one must realize that it will have consequences. In any case it is reasonable to read the letters that come in and to answer them. Once upon a time this might not have been so; now it is. What was and is at stake is the serious attempt to make some progress in the German question in the interest of people and of peace. The Federal government is not setting forth its ideas as propagandistic theses with the preconceived intention of eluding the expected consequences. We mean what we say.

An exchange of opinions is not, to be sure, an independent goal. One must know what is worth talking about. Putting up one's maximal demands does not lead far. The opposite side also knows that, and they ought to ponder on the preconditions of intra-German progress. Over there they speak of a desirable cementing of the status quo. What serves to overcome the status quo is called revanchism;

what leaves it untouched is called a love of peace. Such primitive clichés do not fit into the realities of today. Politics must endeavor to make life easier for people in a divided country instead of needlessly making it more difficult for them.

We are not giving away anything when we answer letters from East Berlin. And if deputies of both political orders were to speak with each other, no shrines would be surrendered. We know what we are, what we represent, where we have our mandate from, and what constitutes our obligation to the other part of the German people.

This has absolutely nothing whatever to do with any arrogant claim to speak for all Germany. It is precisely our political and ethical obligation that gives rise to a broad arena for discussions of how the coexistence of Germans in East and West can be normalized. The Federal government has suggested a whole catalog of themes that will allow itself to be expanded and transmuted. Anyone who merely counterposes maximal demands is swimming against the mainstream of the times. He will be able to convince no one, in Germany or abroad.

Vis-à-vis the chairman of the Council of Ministers, Mr. Stoph, Federal Chancellor Kiesinger emphasized that as long as fundamental differences of opinion make any solution of the German question impossible, it is necessary, in the interest of the nation, of peace, and of détente, to come to some intra-German agreements that will facilitate the human, economic, and cultural bonds between Germans in both parts of our country. We champion the welfare of countrymen who are living under a regime they never sought. However much the administrators of political power on the other side bar themselves off they will not, in the long run, be able to avoid taking the only path on which respect and esteem are to be won. To say it clearly and in one sentence, the more freedom the East Berlin regime can let people have, the more recognition and approval it can find in the world at large.

Regardless of the still negative attitude of the authorities in East Berlin, the Federal government will continue its endeavors to loosen up the intra-German situation. The détente in Europe must, we are convinced, encompass the détente in Germany.

It cannot be my intention to draw a propagandistic caricature of the Communist-ruled part of my fatherland. There can be no doubt that substantial advances have been made there, for example, in economic reconstruction. This was no easy matter for our countrymen there.

They are understandably proud of what has been achieved. Nevertheless, it cannot be denied that the wall is standing in Berlin, the death strip stretches from the Baltic Sea to the border of Czechoslovakia, and we cannot cut off our gaze from the injustice or grow accustomed to it or come to terms with it.

Just because of this we shall attempt to make complete use of the politically possible framework of intra-German contacts so that both parts of our people will not drift further away from each other. We are striving toward a better neighborliness in Germany that will permit increasingly far-reaching solutions of the question of Germany. In the long run the Communist leaders in East Berlin will be less able to evade our stubborn and unillusioned endeavors the more our friends in Europe keep in mind the special situation of Germany and its European effects.

Anyone who speaks of a détente in Europe must not do so as though there were no Communist-ruled part of Germany—there is. And what we must accept—not as superfluous polemics but as a fact—is that East Berlin hitherto has evaded all efforts on behalf of a détente by means of either pretexts or unfulfillable demands. In this connection one should recall how they evaded our offer to exchange speakers between the two parts of Germany. I am also thinking of the monstrous difficulties that the East Berlin regime made in the conversations about passes, a matter that is inconsequential in comparison with the questions that must be settled and yet is nevertheless so important for the people affected. There are three decisive points at issue:

First, the continued responsibility under international law of the four powers to solve the German question. This is an important position when it is not made a mere screen behind which to hide one's own inactivity or to deny the political responsibility of the Germans. Moreover, it must be soberly recognized that the Soviet Union shows little inclination to live up to this responsibility, with the sole exception of what is called in Moscow the questions of European security. To be sure, one must realize that the three Western powers have not always been able to achieve any genuine agreement, either, with respect to the German questions. One must recognize these facts in speaking of the responsibility of the four powers.

The second point has to do with the "right to speak for all Germany." Here it is correct, of course, to say that the Federal Republic of Germany is the state in which Germans can freely express their will and in which a government at work for the state has been legitimized by the will of the population. In accordance with the constitution this gives rise to the duty of speaking up for those Germans who are forbidden to give free expression to their will. This political and ethical obligation cannot be exercised in a rigid way. It must take into account the real situation in Germany as well as changes in world affairs. The representatives of Communist Germany must not indirectly determine, either, where the Federal Republic of Germany has to pull down its flag.

The third point concerns nonrecognition. It is completely clear that the Federal Republic cannot regard the regime in the other part of Germany as democratically and legally legitimized. But we ought not spin, or let someone else spin, a cord out of this that can also bind ourselves. What we primarily refuse to recognize is that the other part of Germany is a foreign country for us. Intra-German settlements are not an object for politics with respect to foreign states. Otherwise the de facto split would be cemented as a matter of international law and thus made very nearly irreparable.

The Federal government does not claim the exercise of any sovereignty for German territories outside the area of validity of its constitution. It grants the authorities in the other part of Germany those functions inherent in the power that has been transferred to them. It does not constitute part of our policy to exclude that part of the German people that is ruled by East Berlin from international exchanges in the areas of trade, culture, and other aspects of life. Under international law, however, recognition must not be granted to the regime in East Berlin because for us the German Democratic Republic is not a foreign country.

It remains a fact that the government in the other part of Germany was never legitimized by the people. It is also a fact that the Geneva four-power conferences in 1955 and 1959 foundered on the intransigence of the Soviets. Yet, in the course of twenty years, facts have developed that cannot be denied. They do not vanish through the mere repetition of old demands. The political byplay of the past few years has not brought us the right of self-determination. I have no intention of indulging in speculation as to what might have happened if . . . Most people have long since learned that quarrel about that is fruitless.

During these past two decades it has certainly become increasingly difficult to solve the German question; in this area, too, "prices" have been rising steadily. It may be decisive for the future of democracy in our country that our nation not be left to believe in a miracle-to-come, a belief which one day would be frustrated or even turn into the bitter feeling that our friends have let us down. International dogmatism or sulkiness may be an easy path to tread, but it will not be successful. Whether we like it or loathe it, the world does hardly feel that it owes us something. This is a fact, though not always a pleasant one.

It is obvious, twenty-three years after the war, that German interests cannot be protected if one confines oneself to merely maintaining a legal position. An attitude of mere defensiveness has, rather, facilitated the consolidation of the ruling system in the other part of Germany. The starting point for any attainment of our general German objectives in accordance with the principle of self-determination has not improved during the past few years but has worsened. If we want to change the facts, we must start out from the facts of the present day. In this we are not so conservative as those Communists who pretend to believe they can perpetuate a status quo of division and of the building up of military power in a way that is both undialectical and contrary to history.

On the other hand we can be sure that in the other part of Germany this belief is not shared by everyone even in the leading institutions of the Socialist Unity Party. There, too, there are debates. They are long drawn out and often painful. Nor can they be shortened by our simply deciding, as many in the grip of illusions demand of us, that Ulbricht must become more reasonable.

During 1967 more or less convulsive attempts were repeatedly made in East Berlin to move away from the concept of a single German nation. Positions were taken up that make a mockery of all reason. Some of the Socialist Unity Party leaders seem to have taken it into their heads that the 17 million Germans on the other side no longer have anything in common with us in the Federal Republic —no common past and of course no common future. If a substitute word for "German" had occurred to these over-zealous people, they presumably would have introduced the new word at once. The Socialist Unity Party has meanwhile retreated from this extreme point; it has manifestly recognized it as dangerous for its own position. The people are not letting themselves be talked into the idea that there are two German nations.

Although the wish to construct an enduring European peace order is becoming stronger and more concrete in East and West, further attempts are being made in East Berlin to tear apart permanently a nation that has more than a thousand years of history behind it, an end that is counter not only to the will of the German people but also to the interests of the other European nations. This will be understood precisely in Poland, for there people realize that it has proved to be historically impossible to keep a nation divided over the long run. All nations have the right to live in unity and in a secure national domain. For our people, too, this is not an exaggerated demand, and the Federal government is going to attempt—by exclusively peaceful means—to attain this objective or come close to it. We have renounced force vis-à-vis everyone, as well as vis-à-vis the other part of Germany. We are prepared to prove this in any place and at any time and to proclaim it in a binding way. But no one can impute desires for revenge to us when we say that for us, the people of the state represented by the Federal Republic of Germany—and, I make a point of adding, for us, the Social Democratic Party of Germany— there is *one single* nation, not two. And that is no new reality, but an old one. One day it will be beyond question once again.

Until then we shall have to expend a great deal of effort to make it clear to the nations of Europe and to their governments that our policy aspires to security for all: security in the West and in the East, and security for the Germans, too. For us it goes without saying that this concept must encompass secure boundaries, as was clearly expressed in the government statement and in the policy based on it. In the Federal Republic there is no serious political figure who would want to contest the right of our neighbors to a secure national realm.

There remains in full view on the table of history what the ruling group of the Socialist Unity Party leadership would like to sweep under the carpet. The theme of the consolidation of peace, the theme of better neighborliness in the interest of people, the theme of normalization in the exchange—these themes and others remain on the agenda, even though at the moment they cannot be raised for negotiation.

We must look at the world as it is, not as it might have been, I said in Tutzing in July 1965. German responsibility for the solution of German questions has grown greater. This responsibility can only mobilize the interests of others if the security of peace is its primary goal. The world will have to turn its attention, after it has eliminated the danger in Southeast Asia, to the problem of establishing relations in Europe that are stable, that correspond to the will of the nations, and that thus entail the strongest conceivable consolidation of the peace. The German people can make a decisive contribution to peace. That is our will, and consequently we must attempt to solve the German problem.

A peace plan for Europe is the real target of our desire to implement the right of the German people to self-determination.

The policy of alliances has guaranteed the security of the Federal Republic, including the special Federal territory of West Berlin, and that is a good thing. Our security must not be jeopardized in any place and under any circumstances. But the security of the Federal Republic vis-à-vis an external danger does not automatically bring us any closer to German unity. The so-called politics of strength has proved to be politics based on illusions that are all too strong. Just as deceptive is the widespread hope that the Soviet monolith will collapse, bringing about the unity of Germany all by itself. Nor do defensive, merely anti-Communist magical formulas give any help.

If the Germans do not act, no progress will be made with respect to the German question. The Federal Republic will not evade the task of working toward a comprehensive peace settlement tirelessly and creatively. The preliminary labors for a peace treaty cannot be separated from the theme of the reunification of Germany. They have nothing to do with a surrender of juridical positions.

The rights and duties of the allies with respect to Germany as a whole cannot take the place of the rights and duties of the Germans with respect to Germany. We must not expect more from others than we ourselves are prepared to do and are capable of doing within the framework of what is possible. We need neither tranquilizers from our allies nor Cassandra outcries concerning their fidelity to treaties. We must, rather, be prepared to bear the greatest measure of responsibility for our own fate. We must and we wish to go on acting in concert with our allies, in order to achieve a just and enduring peace for us and for Europe.

I presented this course to the Dortmund party convention of June 1966, when I introduced the notion of neighborliness into the discusion. As Foreign Minister today I have not drawn back from that position. If one were to prefer a foreign word it would be *modus vivendi*—putting aside for the time being those political and juridical positions concerning which no agreement was possible. If Ulbricht and his people prefer isolation, nothing will move in the immediate future, but the cause itself does not thereby lose its rightfulness.

On the other hand, anyone who has been pursuing a policy of his own for many years should neither rejoice at nor be surprised by the fact that everything has become much more difficult.

Our people think more sensibly on many questions than many a person who plays himself up so gladly as the guardian of the holy grail of national interests. Recognizing realities, including disagreeable realities, and taking them into account for purposes of policy does not harm but rather benefit German interests. The German people can expect nothing from people whose whole wisdom is summed up by their seeing that something or other has been "surrendered" today and then the next day giving warnings of "irresponsible concessions." Suggestions of this kind have hampered sensible policies for far too long.

What was meant by the formulation of neighborliness is no longer a sensation today, but is the policy of the government. We have taken pains to see to it that the intra-German

discussion is conducted in a way that is different from before. In the part of Germany for which the Federal government is elected the argumentation is carried on objectively—
and if necessary with objective harshness. The Federal Republic is no longer considered abroad to be a state that is
sleeping through the great political movements of the world.
Our country used to be considered as hampering peaceful
evolution; that image has been changed quite basically. I was
able to observe this during my travels and in my conversations
with political persons from the East and the West. The
Federal Republic of Germany is no such obstacle. It represents its legitimate interests, and it promotes détente wherever and whenever it can. The future will show how important that effort is.

It is not the Federal Republic that runs the risk of ignoring great political developments. This role has been taken
over with immense zeal by the commanders in East Berlin.
To be sure, they always limped somewhat behind developments, but now their reaction occasionally takes on grotesque
forms. They, who have always called on the Federal Republic to think "realistically," will presumably be the last
to take up a stand on the "new realities." This by no means
fills us with joy nor with the slightest tinge of triumph.

For several years Berlin has no longer been the crystallization point of dangerous international crises, and we have
every reason not to complain about that. Yet the situation
of the people in Berlin remains lamentable; they suffer more
than other Germans on account of the division, because those
who bear the responsibility for the German Democratic
Republic are sacrificing all conceivable human relief on the
altar of lifeless principles.

West Berlin is separated from the eastern part of the
city and from its environs by a border that with frightening

cynicism is called "modern." Its fortifications have become
a sad attraction for the whole world. They serve no purpose
other than keeping people from each other. Not even at
Christmas—neither in 1966 nor in 1967—were there any
passes for the Berliners. The attempt to secure agreements
has been shattered by the obduracy of the officials in East
Berlin. Instead of helping the people in divided Berlin, instead of permitting the separated families to reunite at least
on holidays, they launched a malicious campaign against
West Berlin. The leadership of the Socialist Unity Party
raises groundless claims in its desire to alarm the population.
At the same time, the Federal government and the Senate
are accused of wanting to change the status of Berlin unilaterally.

As the German Foreign Minister, and also as a Berlin citi-
zen and for many years the mayor of Berlin, I say that that
attitude and that campaign are the opposite of a détente.
Whoever now threatens to change the Berlin situation unilaterally counteracts all attempts to enhance peace in Europe.

The different views of the status of Berlin are well known.
It is clear that they need be no obstacle to practical solutions
and concrete improvements. The legal basis is the much-
quoted four-power status, which has been frequently used
as an excuse to oppose reasonable solutions and suggestions.
It has been depleted and has petrified during the division, but
it stands.

In West Berlin the occupation powers became protective
powers in the very first postwar years. The relationship to
them changed very quickly. They helped us and as a rule
did not hamper our work. Not only the resistance to the
blockade and the Khrushchev ultimatum, but the reconstruction, too, had the appearance of a splendid common
undertaking. Nevertheless the fact remained that in West

Berlin it is the Three Powers that hold supreme sovereignty. This is, indeed, indispensable for the security of the city. The Federal government has not the smallest intention of experimenting with this situation. This has also always held true for the Berlin Senate and will, I am convinced, hold true for it in the future.

The Western powers did not manage to safeguard the unity of Berlin, that is, to make the four-power status effective, as was its real point, for Berlin as a whole. They and we together were unable to prevent the amputation of the city. But there is no sense in complaining about missed opportunities.

According to our own legal interpretation, which corresponds to the will of the population, West Berlin belongs to the Federal Republic of Germany. The de facto inclusion of West Berlin in our legal, economic, and currency system was not hindered by any allied reserved rights. On the contrary, this inclusion was laid down and brought about with the assent of the Three Powers. This de facto adherence is decisive for the viability of the city. It must not, accordingly, be interfered with.

Politically we used to formulate the interaction between allied and German law as follows: As much adherence and incorporation as possible without diminishing the position of the allies. There is no reason to subtract from this or to change it.

The legal concept of the Three Powers allows for only a conditional union between the Federal Republic and Berlin. It does not prompt the Federal government to raise a claim of sovereignty. This also derives from the reserved rights contained in the Bonn Treaty. It is no contradiction of this treaty—neither legal nor political—that the Federal government is obligated and authorized "to secure the representa-

tion of Berlin and of the population of Berlin externally."
The Federal government, in the external representation of
Berlin, has an obligation that does not diminish the rights of
the Three Powers and that is independent of the differing
interpretations of the legal position. Its obligation corresponds to its will and has always corresponded to the will,
also, of the population of Berlin. Practical agreements on this
basis are possible without touching the differing juridical
views.

These are realities; they are not altogether simple for us,
but we have come to terms with them. They are realities
that the Communists, too, must come to terms with. People
in the East must realize that the political status of Berlin
will not be changed unilaterally. As long as no satisfactory
solution has been found for the question of Germany with
the assent of the German people and of the powers concerned, Berlin cannot give up its status and the powers that
protect it. The Federal government is striving, on behalf of
Germany and thus on behalf of Berlin, for a solution within
the framework of a European peace order. There can be no
negotiations between Bonn and Moscow aimed at changing
the status of Berlin.

The paramount obligations of the Federal government
continue to be to do everything it can to keep alive and to
further the ties between West Germany and West Berlin;
not to weaken but to consolidate the position of Berlin in
the legal system, the financial constitution, and the economic
order of the Federal Republic of Germany; to make the
representation of Berlin in external politics and external
economics as secure as is indicated by the treaty agreements
with the Three Powers; to include Berlin in all attempts to
fortify the human, economic, and intellectual bonds between
both parts of Germany and to loosen up intra-German relations; and to give understanding and trusting support to the

Senate of Berlin without acting as its guardian or crippling its initiative.

For our part, we need not now engage in a full-fledged fight with the East over legal positions the outcome of which would be uncertain and might have consequences dangerous for all concerned. In accordance with our wishes, however, the existing positions must be maintained until the time comes for a comprehensive peace settlement in Europe and in Germany. Until then West Berlin must remain viable and, above all, must be strengthened economically.

There can no longer be any doubt that the Berlin economy is and must remain a part of the Western economy. The economy of Berlin must not be allowed to suffer as a result of its special position. It must, rather, be given the possibility of making use of its geographical situation. It is, for instance, quite unnatural for the rates of growth of the so-called "Eastern" businesses in West Germany to be higher than they are in Berlin. It goes without saying that what goes for the Western part of Germany also goes for Berlin: there is no secure perspective for our people if it does not succeed in bringing about an accommodation with the nations of the East, too.

Berlin can and will work together with us in our peace policy. The policy of détente pursued by the Federal government is a good policy for Berlin, too. The détente must not by-pass Berlin. Berlin must remain the barometer on which not only bad but good weather can be read.

There is no lack of preparedness on our part. It is precisely in Berlin that a first sign must be given as to whether the other side, too, is ready for a genuine understanding. It is the task of German policy to find the path to peace, to European security, and to a just peace order. Berlin has an indispensable role to play in this task, for Berlin holds a promise for the future of our people.

14

PERSPECTIVES
OF OUR EASTERN POLICY

Our foreign policy toward Eastern Europe is being carried out, as has been described, in two closely interconnected realms. It encompasses our relationship to the Soviet Union as well as our relationship to the countries east and southeast of Germany that are linked to the Soviet Union.

If this part of our foreign policy is to be called an Eastern policy, then the relativity of this concept should be pointed out. States like Poland and Czechoslovakia lie to the east of Germany, to be sure, but there are excellent geographical, historical, and cultural reasons for thinking of them as part of Central Europe or, more accurately, Eastern Central Europe.

There is a third realm that cannot be separated from our Eastern policy: the relationship to the other part of Germany. Here it is not a question of foreign policy in the real sense of the word, for in relationship to each other the two German regions are not foreign territory. The regime in East Berlin, however, is so tightly intermeshed with the group of states whose ruling power is the Soviet Union that an Eastern policy formulated without taking German questions into account would be unrealistic.

In all three realms our goals are the same: securing peace, reducing tensions, improving relations, and preparing contributions to a European peace order. While we have been coping with these goals, changes have taken place—especially since the formation of the present Federal government by the two great democratic parties—that are not merely of a gradual or formal nature. In expressing myself on the perspectives of this policy I shall lean on an article that I wrote for the American review *Foreign Affairs.*

It is often said in the East that our policy is a smoke-screen behind which we are clinging all the more implacably to the "negation of realities," to the "politics of power," to the race for atomic weapons, and to the Cold War. This view is wrong. Of course there are some fundamental elements in our policy, as there are in that of every state, that will not let themselves be changed. Germany's policy, too, must be based on facts, the vital requirements of its people and a future stable peace order. We shall of course cling fast to these—and not, indeed, in our own interests alone but also in the interest of our allies and friends and in the interest of the principles of order that we are convinced must achieve recognition in international politics. But that has nothing to do with the above-mentioned reproaches that are cast at us by the propaganda of the East.

One reality is the division of Europe and the integration of its parts into the two heavily armed power blocs. This division runs through the continent and splits Germany. Consequently, one part of Germany has been drawn into the Western camp, the other, into the Eastern. This polarity, too, is a political reality, to be sure a perilous one. It is also artificial and unjust, for it does not permit a people to live as a nation according to its desires. We know, however, that this division will not vanish from one day to the next and that as far as can be foreseen will be overcome only in conjunction with a general improvement of East-West relations in

Europe. We must, accordingly, not only include the factor of time in our policy but also expend more effort on finding rules for the coexistence of both parts.

At the same time, we reject a German policy that would weaken the cohesion of the North Atlantic Treaty Organization or reduce the decisive participation of the United States in safeguarding the freedom of Europe. We are, on the contrary, convinced that we shall be improving our relationship to our allies if, with no illusions, we set our course by the realities and at the same time avoid even a shadow of ambiguity. A solid and enduring détente with the Soviet Union, which together with its allies spreads out over half the European continent, is quite impossible as long as the presence and the active participation of the other world power, America, does not establish a balance of power. A commitment of this sort will be indispensable for a European peace order, too.

Within the framework of these facts, which include a growing convergence within the European communities, there are, however, important changes to be noted. They are to be explained on the basis of the changed world situation and on the basis of the changed political landscape of the Federal Republic of Germany.

An improvement in the relationship between the two world powers has been noticeable for some years now— recognizable, perhaps, since the solution of the Cuban crisis, but above all as applied to Europe. This is certainly not yet synonymous with détente having worldwide effects. Such an assumption would be wishful thinking. We note, however, the American estimate that even with the present-day encumbrances on the American-Soviet relationship, attempts to bring about a détente are necessary, and not only in Southeast Asia. One can take as a starting point the fact that in

Europe we are no longer in a Cold War that might turn into a hot one at any moment. There are, to be sure, no guarantees against setbacks, but it seems justifiable to reckon, at least partially, with a mutual feeling of responsibility on the part of the world powers. Therefore, the fear of Europe to fall victim to a sudden violent clash has receded into the background.

This has brought about certain consequences in the Eastern as well as the Western camp, in the relations of the allies to each other, and between the systems of pacts on a bilateral as well as on a multilateral plane. There is no question at all here of only positive consequences, yet it is possible, nevertheless, to perceive that a process of progressive economic, cultural, political, and human relations has been launched. Neither nationalist thinking nor claims of hegemony that might issue from the world powers, either objectively or subjectively, have been able to stop the expansion of this process. Europe, indeed, Europe *as a whole,* is undergoing a historic transformation in the course of which ancient kinships are being discovered and new ones found. People are talking to each other again. Technical, economic, scientific, and intellectual communications are leading to a fruitful exchange and to a rising understanding for the situation and the interests of others. Political and propagandistic monologues are giving way to more and more dialogue, more and more listening to each other.

We Germans have no desire to constitute an obstacle to this development. Not only do we want to let this process run its course, but we should like to further it. We realize that it is not enough to announce one's peaceable intentions: one must actively strive to set afoot the organization of this peace. For this, what is needed is the renunciation of all forms of use or threat of force in international life. This attitude rests not only on the conviction that a war must never again start from German territory; it is the product of our own vital interests.

The Federal Republic would be drawn into any major military conflict between East and West. It would ineluctably be its first victim. Our people would cease to exist, for the concentration of troops, war equipment, and atomic means of annihilation on German soil is unprecedented throughout the world.

This danger has brought about a special concern on the part of the Federal Republic of Germany and a special obligation to strive tenaciously, even though without illusions, toward the reduction of mistrust and of tensions. This process can make no progress without the active collaboration of the two world powers, of the European states in the East and the West, and of both parts of Germany. And there exists for us a special responsibility toward the other part of Germany.

The German policy of détente must be conducted with resolution and patience. We must maintain our security, our partnership with the West, and our freedom. As part of this, to be sure, there must also be the knowledge that German policy has become more independent.

The Federal Republic has given many proofs of its reliability during the past two decades. It has allied itself so intimately with a group of European states that a process of integration and of the creation of supranational authorities has been set in motion that can no longer be reversed. We have consciously and resolutely chosen this path, not to undo history, which in fact is not possible, but rather to make a new beginning because we are aware of the past and of the responsibility that flows from it. Much of what once was considered essential to a "nation-state" and to a "national" policy—and which to many, seems indispensable even today—has been shed in the process. Thus we have, for instance, renounced national control over our armed forces.

In domestic policy we have shown, at the same time, that a democratic order has grown up among us that is strong enough to deal with extremist political phenomena in a democratic way.

We have learned from the past. We intend to prove ourselves to be a modern, trustworthy state. The conviction has spread even more strongly than before, during the months since the formation of the Great Coalition, that in the present world situation the Federal Republic possesses a special responsibility that parallels the interests of our friends and allies; it corresponds to the often expressed desire of the leading power in the Atlantic alliance, as well as to the thinking of our European allies. A policy of seesawing or balancing back and forth between East and West, by capitalizing on tensions, is now quite out of the question. The political relations, the historic facts, and the forces involved cast such a possibility back into the realm of the frivolous. Our policy implies close consultation with our allies, as well as the knowledge that we do not control interests that concern the Atlantic alliance and the European community as a whole.

On one fundamental issue the political objective has changed: The starting point in the capitals of our allies and in Bonn used to be that an accommodation with the Soviet Union, a bridging over of the power political conflict of interests in Central Europe, was unthinkable unless the problem of the division of Germany was solved first. This position gave rise to the demand that every step of the great powers toward each other, at least insofar as it was related to Europe, be a step that at the same time counteracted the division of Germany. This was to prevent the division, the unsolved paramount problem of Europe, from being sanctioned and petrified. This idea remains correct, but the approach can no longer be to demand top priority for the reunification of Germany.

Our policy today recognizes the connection between European development and the German problem. It is concentrated on changing for the better the present-day status quo of mistrust, of tensions, and of conflicts. If it is to be successful, it must not be burdened with preconditions, neither from one side nor from the other, that constitute an anticipation of what actually has yet to be achieved. Thus, a long and painful road lies before us. In many places it has been piled high with debris that must be cleared away with patience and good will by *both* sides. The less one side is prepared to meet the other side halfway along this path, the more long-drawn-out will be the process of détente, of the real accommodation of interests, and of the establishment of a European peace order.

Our relationship to the leading power in the group of socialist states, the Soviet Union, is of crucial importance. This recognition is due to world political facts, to power relationships and to the interests in Eastern Europe. I therefore make the point that it is no more the goal, or even a collateral intention, of our Eastern policy to isolate East Berlin than it is to bring about or to exploit differences between the Soviet Union and its allies, even if that is asserted in the propaganda of the East.

We shall go on striving to improve our relations with the Soviet Union, which are very far from being as good as we would wish. We are trying, first of all, to get into conversations in those areas in which an understanding might now be possible. There have also been initial prompt-ings for a discussion of more complicated questions. One day we hope—in accord with the United States and our European allies—to be able to have a frank discussion of all the problems between us and thus to take the first steps to-ward mastering them. It is our hope that reason and ob-jectivity will one day triumph. We must demonstrate the requisite patience.

We must recognize the fact that the Soviet Union is linked to a series of other states by manifold ideological and economic bonds and that the German Democratic Re-public has been closely drawn into this field of force.

We should underrate these facts if we were to try to carry on a policy of détente around East Berlin. The struggle for a secure peace in Europe will not allow itself to be parceled out, either regionally or substantially. We can also see this in the political and military events in other parts of the globe where we are not committed ourselves.

The other part of Germany is also a reality. The internal German area, as constituted on the basis of the division, is to a special degree our responsibility and our concern within the framework of a more far-reaching policy of détente. There we Germans have obligations and possibilities that concern us more than other nations. Our policy signifies that we are ready to regulate our relationship to this part of Ger-many differently from the way it has been regulated until now.

We have made it clear, to be sure, that an international recognition of this part of Germany, in which a quarter of the German people lives, is impossible for this very reason. Aside from this, we would in such a case take responsibility for deciding a question whose solution does not depend on ourselves alone. We are convinced that no other people subjected to such a fate would behave any differently. This resolve on the part of the great majority of a people is also a political reality, as is just as well known in East Berlin. We hope that in East Berlin, too, the responsibility for the whole of the German people, so often stated there in a different sociopolitical environment, will never permit such a step that would run counter to history. No one can evade national responsibility. When we raise our voice in the behalf of the German people and give expression—as we know—to the opinion of the overwhelming majority of Germans in the Western as well as in the Eastern part of our country, we do not want to pose as tutor to our countrymen in the East. It is rather that we thereby give expression to the mutual desire to be joined together again.

Our present-day policy on Germany starts out from the fact that the termination of the division of Germany will be a process whose duration no one can predict. What we must do is what is possible now, or we shall succumb to wishful thinking or resignation. Both would be irresponsible, as it would also be, of course, to take the path of least resistance or to certify, against our conviction, democratic legitimation to the regime in the German Democratic Republic.

It is our present-day task to work for better neighborliness between the two parts of Germany. We want to lessen the tragedy of the division, under which many Germans are suffering bitterly. We want to maintain and strengthen the feeling of belonging together.

Hitherto these efforts have remained overwhelmingly one-sided. In practice East Berlin has attempted to evade all collaboration for the reduction of existing tensions. It has, rather, set new demands and made their fulfillment a precondition for any kind of conversation. This conduct may be looked upon as an attempt to create for oneself a better negotiating position, but our experience leads us to assume that the East Berlin leaders are trying to evade all conversation, even when it is sought by us completely unencumbered by any preconditions. The only conclusion possible is that these leaders do not want to hear of any détente and still refuse to recognize the grand conjunctions that are at issue in Europe today and will be still more so tomorrow. In East Berlin ideas are being clung to that belong to the past. This immobility is bringing East Berlin into a situation that is in such contradiction to the realities that more and more difficulties keep cropping up more and more rapidly. East Berlin must constantly conjure up anew the solidarity of its allies. It must strive for the support of a policy that does not always correspond to the interests of the states of the Warsaw pact that are involved.

Such a policy of rigidity is bound to lead to a situation in which East Berlin sets itself against the general trend and turns into an island of outmoded Cold War ideas. One day it will simply become too expensive to maintain in the center of Europe a great people splintered against its will and under unnatural tensions.

The Soviet Union, which must think in its capacity as a world power and as a power with responsibility for Germany, will have to coolly assess its interests in a worldwide context. It cannot evade this task. Perhaps it has already begun such an assessment without admitting it. In any case it has, more than once, during the fifty years of its history, revised important aspects of its foreign policy.

When East Berlin complains that we have been trying to isolate it, all I can do is to reaffirm that that is not our intention. On the contrary, we are of the conviction that if there were to be such an isolation, whether caused by others or through East Berlin's own responsibility, the total process of the reduction of tensions in Europe would suffer and be slowed down. It is our desire to move from opposition toward neighborliness between Germans safeguarded by mutual renunciation of force, without which any future merger within a general European order would be unthinkable. But hitherto East Berlin has been doing nothing but setting up obstacles. Accordingly, the German Democratic Republic is not being isolated by us—it is carrying on its own self-isolation.

Our efforts to resume normal relations with all states of Eastern and Southeastern Europe were disturbed primarily by East Berlin. Nevertheless, progress that should not be underestimated can be noted. We have grounds to hope that the possibilities have not been exhausted.

Three conditions for normal relations with the Federal Republic were laid down by the countries of the Warsaw pact:

1   Bonn had to recognize the German Democratic Republic as a state.
2   Bonn had to recognize the demarcation line between the two parts of Germany and the Oder-Neisse line as state boundaries.
3   Bonn had to give up its alleged ambitions for atomic weapons.

Alongside these, a further demand was made: We had to recognize that West Berlin was an autonomous political unit on the territory of the German Democratic Republic.

The policy of the Federal government is such that all these demands could be answered constructively. With good will and with a realistic assessment of the facts and of the significance of the détente for everyone, there need be no obstacle on the path toward a European security system and to a peace order. To be sure, if such conditions are set up in order to evade all conversations, then they can be put forth as insurmountable preliminaries.

1   East Berlin has long been aware of our readiness to negotiate declarations on mutual renunciation of force. In his "Report on the State of the Nation" of March 1968, the Chancellor expressly extended the subjects he had proposed at an earlier stage to include that of a renunciation of force. Further, it was as clearly stated that, if these negotiations produce satisfactory results, the Chancellor would be prepared to meet the Chairman of the East Berlin Council of Ministers.

Renunciation of force means that both sides assure each other not to violate the integrity of the other part, neither from outside nor from within. This is in accordance with the conviction which the responsible political forces in the Federal Republic have always held that the German question must exclusively be solved in peace and freedom.

Ulbricht has said that renunciation of force must be binding under international law. I say that it must of course be as binding as a renunciation of force which we want to agree upon with all Warsaw Pact states. In the case of the German Democratic Republic, however, the obligation would not be one under international law, because contrary to Poland, the Soviet Union and Czechoslovakia, the German Democratic Republic is not and can never become a foreign country for us.

2   The western border of the Polish state was included in our offer to waive all use of force with respect to everyone. Good relations with Poland are particularly important to us and are a cornerstone of our Eastern policy like good

relations with France in the West. Our attitude toward
Poland, with its proud past in the history of Europe, is also
grounded in the realization that it has suffered much as a
result of aggression. Its resolve to live finally within secure
borders and its refusal to be a "state on wheels" have our
full understanding. A reconciliation with Poland is our
moral and political duty. This reconciliation entails not only
banishing every notion of force but also ensuring that no
seed for a future strife be sown.

A community of interests between the German and the
Polish people is recognizable in many areas, including trade,
technique, and science but also in questions of the limitation
of armaments with the objective of balanced reduction of
armaments in Central Europe. In spite of some polemics we
believe we can sense the great attention being paid to this
question in Warsaw, too. We shall scrutinize very carefully
all Polish ideas within this cluster of themes. The impression
that in preceding years this was not always the case can be
corrected.

The drawing of boundary lines should not stand in the
way of the European peace order. If Europe is determined
to create a security system and ultimately a stable and just
peace order, it cannot be held up by border questions of
the past. Perhaps the statements renouncing the use of force
that we have already offered can be so formulated and
ensured that the present borders of Poland can be recognized for the period for which the Federal Republic can
commit itself, that is, until the peace settlement. If that were
so the border question, in the interest of both nations, would
no longer be an obstacle to a détente or stand in the path of
a European peace system. Also, this question could no longer
be cited as an obstacle by opponents of a German-Polish
accommodation.

3 Since 1954 the Federal Republic has stood alone among the nations with its renunciation of the production of any kind of atomic weapons. In addition, it has subjected itself to international controls over the whole of its atomic industry. We welcome the early conclusion of a universally acceptable non-proliferation treaty which would reduce mankind's fear of an atomic conflict. Such a treaty should be the first step toward the elimination of all atomic weapons and comprehensive disarmament.

The so-called fourth condition can also be overcome. The whole of Berlin—as I have indicated, and as was always respected by the Federal Republic of Germany—has retained a special status ever since 1945, the four-power status, as a consequence of the war and on the basis of international agreements. A special responsibility for West Berlin has grown up on the part of the three Western powers but has not extinguished the four-power status for all Berlin. That means, for instance, that the Soviet Union cannot claim more rights vis-à-vis West Berlin than the three Western powers can vis-à-vis East Berlin.

There has been a variety of points of view revolving around details of this status in the East and the West, as became particularly obvious when the wall was being built in 1961. There is, however, no reason why, if there is good will, it should be impossible to reach practical solutions and improvements. We, in any case, are doing all we can to avoid anything that might lead to the emergence of a dangerous tinder box in Berlin. Consequently we have not touched the status of West Berlin, and so we find ourselves in thoroughgoing accord with the three Western protective powers in the city. The mere fact that the Soviet Union, too, has down to the most recent period repeatedly proclaimed its interest in Berlin and has recognized, at least in principle, a special status for East Berlin, shows that the contradictions here cannot extend so deep that a détente must come to grief on them. If, nevertheless, the specially rigid forces within the leadership of the GDR were to attempt to change the status of Berlin unilaterally, they would jeopardize all endeavors on behalf of the peace in Europe. The Western powers would feel themselves forced to act in harmony with their rights in Berlin and with their obligations vis-à-vis the Berliners. In that case the efforts on behalf of an enduring détente would be destroyed. No one should take such a responsibility on himself.

Our policy in this area, as in the general question of Germany, aims at practical solutions that—without touching the special status of Berlin—would facilitate life in a city, a living organism, that was never before divided, for all those Berliners who had done nothing to bring that division about. Here there exists a special German responsibility vis-à-vis the German city of Berlin. The Soviet Union, too, is aware of this responsibility and at the same time realizes that we have no intention of acting in place of the Western powers.

Summing up, it may be said that in all three domains we have taken the first steps in a new Eastern policy. The way will be laborious. According to our view it leads from the agreed-upon renunciation of force by way of a guaranteed, European security system—in which the two world powers participate—to a solid and just peace order for this continent and with that a solution, also, of all German questions in concert with the Germans themselves and with their neighbors.

The way will also be long. This should not be surprising. Many difficulties have been and are being accumulated. Perhaps too little was done to clear them away. We wish to take this long and difficult road together with all others who are striving for détente and a peace order, especially with the powers that carry the responsibilty for Central Europe and the European states whose future depends on the creation of that peace order.

It is only on this road that Europe will find peace and tranquillity, and the fate of the world cannot be separated from that of Europe. Time is pressing. Even now we sense distinctly the social and economic tensions in broad areas of Asia, Africa, and Latin America that are producing effects in areas not directly affected.

A catastrophe can be avoided only if the full strength of the industrial nations stretching from North America over Europe as far as Japan are concentrated in the service of this grandiose task and are not squandered in a sterile and dangerous conflict. It is here that the truly creative tasks of this epoch lie. In this, the last third of the twentieth century, which we have already entered, it will be decided whether our nations remain so enthralled by the past that they will lose the future altogether or whether they will be able to direct their gaze forward in order to master the future.

15

SAFETY FIRST

Our foreign policy is conceived as a consistent peace policy, a policy by which we mean to eliminate political tensions and curb competitive arming. We are committed to cooperate in proposals for armaments control, reduction and disarmament. On December 6 and 7, 1967, our defense policy was debated in the Federal parliament. In the course of the debate the connection with general foreign policy became apparent and security policy was discussed under its two aspects: defense capability and readiness to cooperate in disarmament. As far as I was concerned, two questions in the debate had priority. First, what has the Federal government done to promote suggestions for the control of armaments and the reduction of armaments? Second, what is it doing in order to come closer to a European peace order and to smooth the path toward it?

As has been seen, the renunciation of force has become the cornerstone of our policy on Europe and the East. We have stated in precise terms our readiness to formulate in a binding way a renunciation of the use of force and of the threat of force vis-à-vis all Eastern European partners.

In the preparatory treatment of this theme we not only have come up against mistrust and polemical imputations, but also have been able to perceive an objective interest in some places. The attitudes of the Soviet government and discussions with it have, it goes without saying, a special weight in all this. Such discussions would have to take place in a confidential manner in accordance with the intent and understanding of both sides. Rapid results cannot be expected. But everyone ought to realize that there will be no lack of good will on our side.

Consultations were held with our allies—within the framework of the Western European Union and NATO—during 1967, concerning the questions of a regional European control of armaments and the reduction of armaments. I have elsewhere referred to the findings of the Council of NATO of December 1967. We wish to collaborate actively in the process of bilateral and multilateral consultations with our allies, with the aim of elaborating specific ideas concerning an offer to the countries of the Warsaw pact.

In order to assume an active role we must carry on our own preliminary study of the problems involved in a balanced reduction of armed forces in East and West, especially of the foreign troops in both parts of Germany. We have such preliminary studies at our disposal, but I am certain that we shall have to give still more weight to these problems—and beyond them to what people have begun to call "peace research"—and that we will have to invest more in them, intellectually and in terms of personnel and organization.

In our policy of détente and of the consolidation of the peace we have been able to count on a high measure of agreement with our allies. That agreement has become clearly apparent in our regular consultations with our French neighbors, as well as with the governments of Great Britain, Italy, and other European countries. It must be made equally clear, to be sure, that the concrete political concert between the Western allies and within the Atlantic alliance still leaves something to be desired. I myself have come out with some vigor for stronger coordination and consultation and was therefore somewhat startled when at the beginning of 1968 it was rumored—with a reference to "Washington circles"—that we were for unilateral actions.

The continued existence of the alliance, its effectiveness, and its further development are necessary from the point of view of a European peace order. There is a good deal of evidence, I am convinced, that an effective European security system could, on a short-range view, be sensibly based only on agreements involving the two alliances, which would go on existing.

The discussions within NATO, in the framework of the so-called Harmel studies, took as their starting point the necessity of a dual foundation for security: appropriate unilateral preventatives for deterrence and defense and realistic measures, free of illusions, to reciprocally control armaments and disarmament. In the so-called negotiations of the three with the United States and Great Britain at the beginning of 1967, we said that we would agree to some cutbacks and troop rotations out of our conviction that our security would not thereby be jeopardized. This is self-evident as nobody would agree to something knowing that his security would be thereby jeopardized. All knowledgeable people realize that, even independent of the focal question of general security, the military presence of each side as well as certain components of it are important factors today. In any case, the reproach that can still be heard in the East to the effect that rearming is going from the West to the East now makes a particularly implausible impression. After all, the Soviet Union, Poland, and the German Democratic Republic have just recently increased their defense budgets considerably. It will be interesting to see whether the de facto though limited changes of the available forces in Western Europe will find

an echo within the Soviet sphere of interests or not. A constructive attitude would create an opportunity to promote
the détente further even though it might be by only a modest
amount. Indifference or deafness shown by the power center
of the East can hamper or halt the endeavors for a détente
and the real though limited chances of détente. That is the
situation.

It is of great importance for our foreign policy that our
contribution to defense (in the form of the Federal army,
the Bundeswehr) correspond to the obligations that have
been assumed.

I think it appropriate to say a word here concerning the
Bundeswehr. I know things are not easy for it. I am familiar
with the objective difficulties of defining a clear defense mission in a constantly changing world situation. The overcoming of this difficulty and of others is not made any easier by
the continuing burden of the past on the position of soldiers
in our present-day society. It may be said that after the
horrors of our recent history this is no cause for wonder.
Nevertheless, I believe that it is time, twenty-four years after
the end of the war, to strive for the right sense of proportion here too.

In the bitter years that followed 1945 there was not only
the allied order to demilitarize Germany; even without that
there were some who had vowed never to bear arms again.
The attitude summed up as "Leave me out" never convinced
me; yet if it was an error, it was an honorable one. Events
have proceeded further, faster, and differently than most
people could have foreseen. It is simply not accurate to go
on speaking now of the dangers of German militarism, but
we know that our country must be capable of standing up
for its own defense in this uncertain world. We also know

that the Bundeswehr is the instrument created for and suited to the purpose. It has put its growing pains behind it, but it has still not rid itself of some other difficulties.

We are faced with many still unsolved tasks. One of these tasks consists of reducing the mistrust of us abroad. Another is to resist energetically the tendency of every army to become a state within the state. A third is to provide the social equivalent, by means of a healthy historical continuity and a just assessment of values, for those demands that developed defense technology imposes on the soldiers. I assign a high priority to this task, for we require an army whose inner strength corresponds to its outer effectiveness. In 1967, there was a debate about the federal armed forces which was brought about by the strained budget and efforts to offset the foreign exchange cost arising out of the stationing of American forces in the Federal Republic. It was no accident that this debate turned into a discussion of the structure of the federal armed forces and the necessity of a reform.

The federal armed forces are not an end in themselves. They are an indispensable instrument of our defense within the Alliance. Talking about a reform of the Alliance necessarily raises the question of what mission the federal armed forces have to fulfill. The Federal government did not yet possess the factual data required to answer that question. These decisions will also have an important political impact.

We can only hope that in the future it will be possible to evenly reduce the strengths of others as well as of ourselves.

The Franco-German talks on the security problems of the 1970s will not, on our side, be conducted on the assumption that because of a threatening collapse of NATO we shall find ourselves in a state of unsecured isolation. We are concerned with an exchange of views between the two sides, between the French and German governments. And we expect to arrive at a long-term view covering all of Europe. We are convinced, however, of the continued existence and development of the Atlantic alliance and its ability to contribute to the process of the consolidation of peace. We also take it for granted that the treaty I signed in December 1966 will also prove effective. We look upon this treaty, involving the status of the French troops in the Federal Republic of Germany, in the context of the agreements between the French chief of the general staff and the commander-in-chief of NATO in Europe.

For the future, it would scarcely be endurable if our allies substantially reduced their military presence on the Continent and then took the view one day that the Bundeswehr was too big. That means that in all future considerations the over-all balance of the Western alliance must be a criterion. In any case we shall strive for this with vigor.

As for the worldwide measures for the limitation on atomic and conventional armaments, the non-proliferation treaty was in the center of international interest in 1967. Other suggestions were not desired. They might have even been looked upon as a hindrance to the efforts on behalf of the non-proliferation treaty, after a resolution of the General Assembly of the United Nations of November 7, 1966, had forbidden such hindrance. I shall have something to say concerning the attitude of the Federal government with respect to a non-proliferation treaty. Here I should like to mention only that in a memorandum of April 7, 1967, we declared ourselves to be for the linking of such a treaty with more extensive measures for the limitation of armaments. In this we brought up once again the idea of a complete cessation of all atomic tests. The previous German suggestion to cut down, in stages and under effective controls, nuclear weapons throughout Europe while preserving the relationship of forces should also be recalled here once again. Though we ourselves are not members of the Geneva Disarmament Conference, we played a not insubstantial role in influencing the draft of a non-proliferation treaty.

With my responsibility as Federal Foreign Minister I must emphasize here the fourfold self-limitation of the Federal Republic of Germany in the nuclear domain:

Renunciation of the production of atomic weapons
Renunciation of control of atomic explosive devices
Recognition of Euratom to control civilian uses of atomic energy
Support of the principle of the nonproliferation of nuclear weapons

A European peace order must be conceived with the awareness that it is not enough to reduce the massing of military power; what is at issue beyond that is the reduction of political tensions, the accommodation of interests, the harmony of nations, and the cooperation of states so that solid foundations may be laid for a healthy European future. But to attain all this one must make a beginning by blunting the military confrontation, and while preserving the security of the European nations and states, one must mutually reduce armaments and come to agree on control measures. Here I should like to recall the German suggestion for the exchange of observers of military maneuvers on the basis of bilateral agreements.

It would not, as we know, be realistic to expect a complete solution of European problems either today or in the immediate future. It therefore is not very useful now to pursue the idea of a European security conference. One day there surely will also be a conference on the questions of

European security and of the consolidation of the peace. But it must of course be prepared. The times must be ripe.

Meanwhile we shall see to it that in the alliance—that is, in an alliance that includes its American pillar—there is discussion as to what European security and a European peace order should be like. This can then no longer be a matter for mere academic discussion. Our people, just like the nations of all Europe, would like to know what the plan for building the joint European edifice is going to look like.

In East Berlin it is considered offensive when we say that a just and enduring solution of the German question must also be found within the framework of a European peace order. This position is said to be a proof that we would like to change existing conditions, a reprehensible goal, it is said, that conflicts with the consolidation of peace. Once again I ask what it means to wish to change. Is it not true that all those who have serious intentions toward peace and toward Europe must be ready to try to change a few things for the better? All those who are striving toward this goal, after all, wish to replace a doubtful security system by a firm one. They want to replace mistrust by cooperation. They want to end the division of Europe. A renunciation of force, including respect for the borders now laid down in Europe, does not, after all, mean that everything can remain exactly as it is today. Not only is the exaggerated military confrontation in the heart of this continent and on German territory unreasonable, but the wall in Berlin and the death strip across Germany are unreasonable, against nature, and against history.

No one for whom the rights recorded in the charter of the United Nations means something and who takes to heart a peaceful and prosperous future for Europe should be confused as to the necessity of changing something by means of agreements, by means of the accommodation of interests. This holds true for the situation in the other part of Germany. It holds true for the relationship between the German territories and the people living in them. It holds true for the goal of a peace order that must allow the German people some hope for achieving national unity by peaceful means. This does not detract from the intra-German renunciation of force but makes it honest. It puts into proper focus the suggestions of the Federal Chancellor in his letters to East Berlin, which are aimed at making the life of our countrymen and the relationship between the two socio-political orders on German soil more acceptable and more peaceful.

In order to help organize the peace we must recognize responsibility for the Western European communities as well as for Europe as a whole. Out of bitter experience and sincere conviction we want to contribute to overcoming fear and mistrust on our continent. We want to do everything so that Europe can grow together in peaceful, constructive cooperation in such a way that it not only does justice to the welfare of its peoples but also can serve the peace of the world.

It must be manifest to our partners that we clearly agree with the policy we have helped to formulate within the Atlantic alliance, and we stick to that policy.

It must be clear to the government of the Soviet Union and to our neighbors in the East that our defense policy does not contradict our striving toward a détente but is subordinated to it.

Our closest European partners must know that we are in earnest when we seek joint replies to the question of the long-term possibilities of European cooperation.

Our own people must know that we do not intend to be the victims of blind chance or a football for the interests of others; on the contrary, we want to safeguard the security of everyone in concert with our friends and allies. We want to work together with them and with complete frankness toward them—as well as with those others without whom there can be no solution—on opening up the path toward the reduction of tensions and armaments and toward an enduring European peace order.

Robert McNamara, a man who organized the defense of the United States in the 1960s (and whose immense abilities, now that he is president of the World Bank, can also serve the underdeveloped countries), once said that in year 22 of the atomic age the world needs no new arms race. What the world needs in this year 22 of the atomic age is—as he said, and I agree with him—a new race of reason. I can think of no better formula for our policy.

16

"DÉTENTE" IS NO CATCHWORD

We are not concerned with general confessions; we are concerned with our own German contributions to détente, disarmament, and the consolidation of the peace.

The idea of general disarmament is no novelty. From being a component of historical utopias it has turned into a postulate of practical politics. Nevertheless, to this day things have scarcely advanced even to the point of beginning a freely agreed-on disarmament. It has become clearer and clearer that the reduction of military strength—beyond some modest measures—cannot be attained independent of a reduction of political tensions and cannot in isolation lead to a secure peace.

Tensions are the expression of conflicts of interest. All peace policies must concentrate on the accommodation of conflicting interests and on the elimination of the tensions bound up with them. Thus, the much-used leitmotiv of the present day is "détente." It is worth making the conception of détente precise so that it does not degenerate into a meaningless or misused magical formula.

Although the confrontation of the world powers in Europe has been lessened, as long as the interests of the United States and of the Soviet Union remain unchanged in Europe,

a détente will not automatically be produced. If the importance of the European arena is temporarily overshadowed
by other global obligations and in consequence the wish for
the maintenance of the equilibrium that has been painfully
reached here comes to the fore, this will not mean that the
specific problems of Europe will be more easily soluble.
That is the dilemma we live in. The milder climate of détente is still deceptive and no more than a forerunner of
what is to come.

Nevertheless, it is surely right to say that an enduring
accommodation of interests between America and the Soviet
Union will be indispensable for a general European détente.
Such an accommodation is feared by many who think it
would be made at the expense of Europe. The two parts of
Europe could hardly enter upon a détente against the will of
their leading powers, but it is nowhere written that the
leading powers, for their part, can, with impunity, disregard
European interests. Such a short-sighted policy would not
lead to any enduring results.

The European détente will become more tangible if the
governments in the East and West learn, from relations
that have been made elastic and freed of mistrust, to give
priority to their own national and collective European interests as against the sterile formulas of thinking based on
blocs. A beginning can very well be made by the reduction
of mistrust and the improvement of relations in Europe before the world powers come any closer to a global accommodation.

It is just such an improvement that we are striving for
and that many others are equally ready to attempt. Communication between different political and social systems has
become possible. We have contributed to a situation in

168   A PEACE POLICY FOR EUROPE

which communications will not be broken off and reason
will not again be overshadowed by the doctrinaire rigidity
of the Cold War.

In January 1967, before the Consultative Assembly of the
Council of Europe in Strasbourg, I made the point that the
European nations and states were scarcely capable of achieving a radical improvement of the East-West relationship if
the United States and the Soviet Union did not also shift
over to this course on a world political scale. Nevertheless,
what the European nations and states undertake toward this
goal does not have a merely complementary effect. On the
scale of world politics it has a quality of its own.

While Western Europe is still preoccupied by the problems of organizing itself, the beginning of a general European community of interests is looming up. It is more than
the joint determination to prevent a suicidal war. It expresses
itself in practical collaboration. In certain areas and between
different partners in Eastern and Western Europe an accommodation of interests is being probed. It is the task of a
European policy of détente to extend this still limited area.
Practical successes can set in motion developments that will
also make possible one day an accommodation of interests in
those domains in which it can still not be attained today.

At the same time, it should be soberly recognized that
the policy of détente is not in itself the goal. In Strasbourg
I explained this as follows:

1   "Détente" is not a magic word. The conception itself
will not bring about the disappearance of the tensions and
contradictions between East and West. The policy of détente is a policy of accommodation of conflicting aims and
interests.

2   Détente is not a goal in itself. It is meant to make

possible an accommodation of interests that will create the foundations of an enduring European peace order. A policy of détente is no capitulation and no flight from reality but is the attempt to gain more and more areas for cooperation.

3 Détente is a comprehensive program. Of course, not all problems can be solved in a single action. One must start where a beginning can be made; one must content oneself with small steps where larger ones are premature. But all this must constantly be in the perspective of wider solutions.

If the government of the Soviet Union and of some of its allies expect us to fulfill unacceptable demands, they speculate on the impossibility of dealing with certain difficulties in the West. That is why it was so important for the Federal government to achieve a constructive clarification of its relations with the Western partners.

What we have in mind is not some nebulous talk about détente, but a realistic program to overcome the East-West confrontation. It includes what we recommended since the formation of the new Federal government, i.e., to consolidate peace through inter-European normalization and conciliation in order to move toward a solution of the German problems within that very framework. This was a starting point for reactivating Franco-German cooperation. It also provided additional common interests with Britain.

The experience and the convictions of my own party, the initiatives and recommendations that the German Social Democrats had been striving for while in opposition, have made their way into official German policy. My efforts for many years as mayor of Berlin, not only against the rigidity of East Berlin but also against some misunderstanding in West Germany, have become an element of German policy. What was still the center of a violent dispute when it was being elaborated at the Social Democratic Party convention in Dortmund at the beginning of June 1966 was absorbed into a joint government program by the end of that year. Our ideas on European security and of a European peace order have become components of official policy. For the first time a government statement asked what contribution Germany can make in order not only to maintain the peace but to make it more secure. It is surely no exaggeration to call this a clear change.

It would be premature to present any plan in detail. Nevertheless, I shall attempt to mention a number of principles that in my opinion might lay the groundwork for a European peace order:

> The peace order would have to take into account the fact that different kinds of political, social, and economic systems exist in European countries and that the individual states have sovereign authority in these areas.
>
> It would have to be ensured that all European states would renounce the use and threat of force, as well as any form of intervention in the internal affairs of other states.
>
> The relations between the European states would have to be guided beyond all this, by the principles of the charter of the United Nations.
>
> The freedom of transit and the free exchange of information in Europe would have to be extended as far as possible.
>
> The NATO states would have to be certain that the peace order would safeguard them what is referred to in the NATO treaty as the "freedom, common heritage and civilization of their peoples, founded on the principles of democracy, individual liberty and the rule of law."

The European states as a whole would have to be able to depend on an effective system for the security of one and all. Such a system of European security would have to be participated in by the United States as well as the Soviet Union. It should result from agreements related to the alliances which, to begin with, would continue to exist. The German question would have to be solved.

The allies will have to strive, with a purposeful, patient, and undramatic policy, to persuade the Soviet and East European governments that the alternative implied by an enduring peace order is more attractive politically and economically for both sides than the present-day status of Europe. It would be unpolitical—because unrealistic—to press for the entire range of the preconditions between East and West for a European peace order at the same time and with the same energy. Priorities must be set up; the most difficult points being at first put aside. They can be brought up for conversation with greater prospects of success when there is a certain fund of joint regulations on hand and a *modus vivendi* that will not oblige either side to surrender its basic positions and that will have relieved the mistrust on both sides.

The road to a European security system and beyond that to a European peace order can, in fact, be made passable only if the military confrontation, as it exists above all within Germany, is reduced and ultimately overcome. To this end what is needed is the East's readiness to seek security more and more in cooperation between West and East and not in the maintenance of a massive confrontation.

Measures for arms limitations and for disarmament have been suggested by both sides. Insofar as they do not upset the balance of forces they might be implemented by express agreements or, first of all, before the agreements are made, by a tacit understanding and by appropriate mutual action.

A beginning should be made with a balanced reduction of the foreign troops stationed in both parts of Germany. In the East's suggestions, too, this seems to be looked upon as a starting point for the indispensable cooperation between both sides. This measure would also make a direct contribution toward an improvement of the general political climate in Central Europe and work against the hardening of the division. The military consequences, especially the demand for evenly balanced reduction, are being scrutinized at present by the Atlantic alliance, so that a realistic offer at a given time can be made to the Soviet Union and its allies.

In a later phase the balanced reduction should affect those combat forces within their own national borders in Central Europe. With this a reduction of the Bundeswehr could also be discussed. If ever a substantial reduction of the foreign combat forces in both parts of Germany takes place, these forces on both sides can and must also be involved, in order to maintain the proportions and to make possible further advances.

Similar considerations hold true for atomic weapons. Insofar as, due to their deployment, type, and purpose, they are an integral element of the combat forces in Europe, they will sooner or later have to be drawn into any balanced reduction of those forces. This does not exclude dealing with the atomic weapons stationed in Europe as a special element, in the general framework of a reduction of the military confrontation, as long as the balance of forces is preserved. Suggestions aimed at this have been proposed on both the German and the Polish side.

Of a different nature are such measures that, while not directly eliminating the confrontation, soften it and which facilitate direct measures or make them possible at all. In this domain the Atlantic alliance is studying, among other things, suggestions for the establishment of fixed or mobile posts for the observation of terrain on both sides of the demarcation line, for the formation of special military missions, and for the exchange of observers of maneuvers.

I am well aware that none of these steps toward a European security system can be taken from one day to the next. They require a painstaking canvassing of opinion within the alliance and—quite apart from a more favorable constellation for both world powers—undoubtedly long-drawn-out contacts with the Soviet Union and its allies. But one thing that could be undertaken immediately is the renunciation by all parties of the use or threat of force in mutual relations. Opinions may vary concerning the ways and means in which this renunciation is to be accomplished. What is decisive is that the already existing obligation to a renunciation of force between the partners of the two European alliances be confirmed without reservation and at the same time be applied to the problems of the East-West relationship in Europe without prejudicing the solution of those problems. In this way the renunciation of force would become the starting point and the framework for the gradual construction of a security system and—beyond that—of an enduring European peace order.

17

A FOCAL QUESTION: THE CONTROL OF THE ATOM

The efforts made since the end of World War II to subject atomic energy to international controls have come to nothing. Instead we have seen a nuclear race begun between the United States and the Soviet Union; Great Britain, France, and the People's Republic of China have also produced and tested nuclear weapons. In the disarmament negotiations of the United Nations the conviction prevailed that the spread of nuclear weapons could best be stopped by a treaty of universal prohibition.

Since the unanimously adopted Irish resolution of December 4, 1961, the General Assembly of the United Nations has passed further resolutions calling for the urgent conclusion of a non-proliferation treaty. Of special note in this connection is Resolution 2028 of November 23, 1965, because it set up special principles for the content of the treaty and emphasized more strongly than before the obligations of the atomic powers.

The disarmament conference of the eighteen powers in Geneva, with its efforts on behalf of general and complete disarmament, ended in a blind alley. For years it occupied itself with the problem of nonproliferation, without any sign of a rapprochement between the divergent points of view. The Soviet Union and other Communist states kept bringing up the issue of the collective defense of the Western alliance. Bilateral conversations between the United States and the Soviet Union remained fruitless for years. During the General Assembly of the United Nations in the autumn of 1966, however, representatives of these two world powers arrived at a nonobligatory agreement concerning certain formulations for a treaty of nonproliferation.

For the first time the draft treaty presented us with the problem of coming to grips politically with scientific and technological knowledge that can no longer be eliminated from the world. The aid and counsel of science are indispensable for politics; but the primacy of political decision must now be asserted in a rather new and unfamiliar domain. Politics leans on the auxiliary partnership of science, but the responsibility of the final decision—and also of important decisions on details—cannot be taken away from the political leadership.

When the Federal government had occasion, at the beginning of 1967, to express itself on the initial results of the American-Soviet understanding, it pointed out that the promotion of a non-proliferation treaty was a principle of German policy.

As early as 1954 the Federal Republic of Germany, when it became a member of the Western European Union and the North Atlantic pact, renounced the production of nuclear, biological, and chemical weapons and subjected itself to international controls. We would have welcomed other states entering upon similar restrictions and thus reducing for themselves the dangers arising out of the spread of atomic weapons. The Federal Republic of Germany ratified the treaty of August 5, 1963, banning atomic tests. Beyond that the Federal government has repeatedly renounced national control over nuclear weapons. It takes as its own the content of the resolutions in which the United Nations has come out for the speedy conclusion of a non-proliferation treaty.

The consultations that we have been carrying on since the middle of December 1966, primarily with Washington, made it clear that the partial draft provided for at the time required changes and additions. We attempted to set up standards by which we could assess a universal treaty banning proliferation. There were essentially four clusters of questions involved here:

1 The unimpeded utilization of nuclear energy for peaceful purposes
2 A clear connection with general disarmament
3 The guaranteeing of security
4 No diminution of regional—and in our case European—efforts for unification

These four clusters of questions gave rise to numerous individual questions that were carefully scrutinized, with the assistance, also, of scientists. It turned out that in none of these clusters of questions were there any interests at stake that touched the Federal Republic of Germany alone and no other state. The Federal Republic was and is, as far as its interests are concerned, very largely in harmony with the other civil nuclear states—in some areas, too, with those that do not belong to any defense alliance.

It lies in the nature of things that the civil nuclear states consulted with each other in order to determine what judgment they should arrive at with respect to the effects of such a treaty on their given national and regional interests and to what extent those interests were in harmony with those of others. This is in the nature of things because in this connection the civil nuclear states constitute the genuine counterpart to the nuclear weapon states. In the circle of the civil nuclear states some are secured by alliances, others are not. Some are members of the disarmament conference in Geneva, others are not.

These conversations have made it clear that the Federal Republic of Germany does not stand alone. We were able to find a great degree of accord on the assessment of the essential aspects of the problem of nonproliferation. During the negotiations, which went on for months, we found a great deal of understanding for our views with our American allies. On a number of questions our consultations with the United States were brought to a positive end.

The unimpeded civil utilization of the atom is a vital interest not only for us in the Federal Republic. The development of nuclear industry for peaceful purposes will go on progressing. The provision of the world with atomic energy will increase. Reactors used for such purposes also produce plutonium, which can also be applied to the production of arms. With the spread of nuclear technology not only will the number of civil atomic powers increase, but inevitably, also, the number of states that will dispose of the objective capacity to produce atomic arms. It is a duty of our generation to stop the military abuse of atomic energy and to promote its peaceful utilization.

The Federal Republic of Germany is ready to support anything that will stop such abuse. It is not ready to accept anything that will hamper the peaceful utilization of the atom, on which the future of the Federal Republic of Germany as a modern industrial state is decisively dependent.

Also, what the Federal Republic can accomplish on behalf of the peaceful progress of mankind depends upon the peaceful use of the atom.

German scientists are known to be working on the development of the second generation of reactors, the so-called fast breeders, and our industry has a good prospect of achieving a high level of accomplishment in this area. We have been striving for an optimal protection of the peaceful utilization of atomic energy and the long-term securing of the supply of atomic fuels by means of binding treaty obligations. Such a treaty most obviously also applies to the exchange of atomic materials, nuclear equipment, and scientific information, as well as to the bilateral and multilateral cooperation of the states with each other or with international organizations in the civil sector. It must apply to research, to industrial activity, and hence also to the export of reactors. We have supported the view that the treaty should even expressly promote the peaceful utilization of atomic energy.

The nuclear weapon states have applied immense funds for the military utilization of atomic energy. Their military experience, to be sure, also spins off valuable knowledge for peaceful purposes. The civil "by-products" of military research are becoming scantier and scantier—so the technical people tell us—insofar as new inventions are concerned. Nevertheless, a monopoly position of the nuclear weapon states emerges for special fissionable material because of the magnitude of the installations and the lower costs of production. Together with others we have come out—not without success—for the sharing by the nonnuclear weapon states of the information and discoveries resulting from the military utilization of atomic energy by the nuclear weapon states.

The projected treaty would prohibit the production of "nuclear weapons and other nuclear explosive devices" by the nonnuclear weapon states, and the passing on of such weapons and devices by the nuclear weapon states. This wording is cogently grounded in the fact that to this day it is impossible to distinguish accurately between military and civil nuclear explosives. For the foreseeable future the application of nuclear explosives to civil purposes will scarcely be of any real importance for Germany. We do, however, welcome the declaration made by the United States, whose research work has not yet been concluded, that it is ready for the establishment of a nuclear explosive service under the supervision of an international authority and regardless of the costs of research and development.

The question of safeguards is very important. Controlled disarmament is a traditional Western demand. It is no novelty for the Federal Republic, which has already subjected itself to international security controls. A consequence of the treaty would be to extend such controls to other states as well.

The application of safeguards must not interfere with economic processes or infringe on industrial production secrets but only counteract the dangers of abuse. What will suffice for this is the control of basic and fissionable material and of the flow of fuels at certain strategic points, if possible by means of automated instruments. Such instruments are not yet in existence. The Federal Republic of Germany will exert all its efforts, in conjunction with its allies and in international organizations, to help develop and establish modern instruments of control. Automation could also make it possible to keep down the costs of a security safeguard system.

Throughout this whole period discussion has revolved

around a draft treaty that does not provide any safeguards in the nuclear weapon states. The Soviet Union has opposed such safeguards on its own terrain. Because of this competitive situation it was of importance when the United States and Great Britain stated at the beginning of December 1967 that they would agree to international safeguards in the civil sectors of their atomic industry within the framework of a non-proliferation treaty.

The spread of knowledge concerning the application of atomic energy cannot be impeded by any sort of restrictions. The production of the bomb is today not so much a question of knowledge as of political resolve. The civil nuclear states are unquestionably performing a real service in adhering to the projected treaty because its essential interest lies in universal validity. Most of them are ready in principle for this because of their perception that any increase in the number of states with independent disposition of atomic weapons means an increase in the danger confronting mankind. If only one more nuclear power were to emerge, people would be afraid of a chain reaction that would be difficult to control.

That is why the civil nuclear states are prepared to contribute their share. This contribution would have to be balanced by one which only the nuclear weapon states can make. There is not only the danger of horizontal but also of vertical proliferation. Stopping the horizontal extension of atomic weapons would be an important step forward, but it still would not solve the problem of making the peace any more secure. One must therefore expect that the nuclear weapon states, in the interest of balanced obligations of the treaty, accept it as a first step toward more comprehensive solutions. A limited non-proliferation treaty must be a beginning and not an end. For the nuclear weapon states this would mean a renunciation of any further development of more and more dangerous weapons; no further increases in the installations on hand, including the means of delivery; the beginning of a reduction; the cessation of the production of fissionable material for military purposes; and the implementation of a complete test ban.

If the nuclear weapon states are ready for such a step and capable of it, the treaty banning proliferation would be the beginning of a movement of international cooperation for ensuring the peace in the atomic age, the goal of the above-mentioned, almost unanimously adopted, Resolution 2028 of the General Assembly of the United Nations. The expectations encompassed there are the hope of all nations throughout the world.

The genuine concern of the Federal government is shown by its memorandum of April 7, 1967, addressed to the participants of the Geneva disarmament conference and to France, which deals with the theme of disarmament in the context of the discussions concerning a treaty of non-proliferation. In addition to the powers in Geneva, we also brought it to the attention of a number of other governments concerned, the Vatican, the Secretary General of the United Nations, and all the missions accredited to the United Nations. This memorandum says:

The devastating effects of atomic weapons make it incumbent on the governments of the world not only to put an end to a nuclear arms race; the interest of mankind demands that nuclear disarmament be initiated. It is only in this way that an international peace order can be created that will vouchsafe to all nations, great and small alike, a prosperous evolution in freedom, independence, and dignity. Germany is resolved to go on working toward this goal together with other countries. The disarmament negotiations of the great nuclear powers have, while achieving some partial successes in the control of armaments, still by no means put a stop to the nuclear arms race. The necessity of genuine disarmament remains all the more pressing. An international agreement on the non-proliferation of nuclear weapons might prove to be a preliminary stage in an effective consolidation of the peace if it is followed by measures of disarmament.

It would have been unrealistic to suggest a special agreement for a general prohibition of the production of atomic weapons and a step-by-step destruction of the atomic arsenal already in existence. It was and remains impossible to disregard the problems constituted by the nuclear arming of the People's Republic of China. The positive reactions to our memorandum, however, encouraged us to give great emphasis to the connection between non-proliferation and disarmament. And this was also given a certain consideration in the subsequent work on the treaty.

The treaty as submitted to the United Nations General Assembly formulates only what is prohibited: everything else is and remains permitted. Questions of the Western defensive alliance are not dealt with in the text of the treaty, but there are connections, so interpretation plays an important role. We had to be concerned with procuring a maximum of certainty with respect to content and form. On the basis of what we and our other partners in the alliance were assured of on the American side, the non-proliferation treaty will not hamper the internal regulations of the Atlantic alliance. There is a certain difficulty in keeping the door open to future defense possibilities in the Atlantic area as well as in the European area, a matter of concern to the alliance as a whole. We understand our renunciation of national control over nuclear weapons, which is an integral part of our policy, as a German contribution to a détente in Europe, and not as discrimination. The arrangements within NATO, through which the Federal Republic participates politically and militarily in nuclear planning, are not affected by the nonproliferation treaty.

On the Soviet side it was said that the Federal Republic of Germany *must* sign such a treaty. This was neither helpful nor evocative of confidence. We made it clear that, as soon as we possess clear data, we shall decide to the best of our knowledge and conscience. It was just these Soviet reproaches and suspicions that showed the special weight ascribed to the decision of the Federal Republic of Germany and how much store the Soviet Union set by the German signature. Here, in spite of the universal character of the treaty on nonproliferation, we were confronted by a special political problem as between a nuclear weapon state and a nonnuclear weapon state.

The Federal Republic does not carry on a policy of political extortion. We reject any policy of nuclear extortion. The Federal government does not talk with two tongues; what it wants to do is to make a contribution to the détente and to an improvement of relations with the Soviet Union and with the countries of Eastern Europe. If in the final study of the treaty on nonproliferation it comes to a positive conclusion, it will be committed to the same restrictions as all the other signatory states. One might really expect the Soviet Union to be able to assess the positive significance of such a step on the part of the Federal Republic.

A balanced non-proliferation treaty can become a factor that will help to weaken and overcome the conflict between East and West. It is unusual but unavoidable for such constructions between East and West to criss-cross, overlap, or supplement elements of the policy of alliances in East and West. This may be confusing, or at least seem so. There is a good reason to think that we shall witness such developments still more frequently in the future. And we shall see that in both camps, with all the caution nourished by the mistrust that has grown up over the years, there will be an attempt to preserve the balance of power that security is grounded on.

The Federal Republic of Germany will be able to defend its interests in such a development all the better the more actively and positively it participates in it. In this world of ours, which has grown so small, with all its perils, its growing global problems, its challenges to mankind, and the international progress in technology and science, there is no longer the possibility of splendid isolation for any nation or any country. The fate of the nation can no longer be determined within the national framework. Security and progress for the nation require cooperation. Not even the Soviet Union or the United States can cope with isolation. In judging the treaty of nonproliferation one must take these considerations into account, too. What must be decisive is whether or not the treaty promotes détente, the consolidation of peace, and the progress of mankind. The excited reactions of individual German politicians have done no service to objective study but have given rise to mistaken assessments of German policy.

On August 24, 1967, the two copresidents of the Geneva disarmament conference presented identical drafts of a treaty in which, to be sure, a clause on controls was still missing. These drafts contained several regulations that were along the lines of our own considerations. Thus, in a binding regulation of the operative section the right of unhampered development and utilization of atomic energy for peaceful purposes and an exchange of information are guaranteed. In the preamble the principle of the instrumental control of the flow of fissionable material at specific strategic points of the fueling cycle is laid down, a clause that corresponds to a desire expressed primarily by the highly industrialized states. The hitherto customary controls through inspectors are to be replaced as broadly and as quickly as possible by automatic instruments, so that unnecessary controls of the techniques of the nuclear installations become superfluous. The expanded preamble also contains a declaration of intent on the part of the nuclear weapon states to place nuclear explosive devices at the disposal of other states on a non-discriminatory basis and at the lowest cost possible. The idea of the participation in the so-called "by-products" of military research is also expressed in the preamble.

On January 18, 1968, these identical draft treaties—including a clause on safeguards—were presented to the Geneva disarmament conference by the American and Soviet copresidents. The Federal government welcomed their presentation and appreciated the improvements that had been achieved. In the operative section, too, the joint draft now provided that all signatories of the treaty bind themselves to negotiate in good faith concerning measures for nuclear and general limitation of armaments and for disarmament.

Amendments of March 11, 1968, underline the connection between the treaty and disarmament obligations of the nuclear weapon states. The safeguards clause was of special importance for us. It allows for the negotiation of a verification arrangement btween Euratom and the International Atomic Energy Agency (IAEA). The European community would be harmed if that negotiation failed, even more so as France does not intend to join the non-proliferation treaty. Moreover, American interpretations made it clear that the treaty would not hinder a development through which the nuclear defense potential of France or Great Britain or both could one day be integrated into a European Federation.

Some wishes remained open. Thus there is no clause banning nuclear blackmail.

We shall see whether further improvements will be achieved during the discussions in the United Nations General Assembly. We cooperate in these efforts, but there must be no doubt about the spirit of any of our criticism. We are in favor of a non-proliferation of nuclear weapons. We shall not have nor do we want any such weapons. And we do not need any such weapons for the policy for which I stand. Otherwise, our efforts to secure peace and reject force would be incredible. This is the very substance of our policy. If the danger of a nuclear war can be substantially reduced, one must be in favor of it provided that the vital interests of one's nation are safeguarded.

18

MISSION:
SECURITY IN EUROPE

We are for a European security system and for a European peace order built up on it. Both together should put behind them not only the Cold War but also the division of Europe.

Mistrust cannot be suddenly replaced by trust. The first step on the way to a comprehensive understanding between the peoples of Europe must consist of taking away their fear of attacks. Only when the security of all is guaranteed can confidence be consolidated and grow beyond cooperation to friendship. Thus, a security system could provide the atmosphere of understanding in which, as we hope, East and West will one day be able to act in concert.

The hostile confrontation of the two power blocs along the Iron Curtain in the center of Germany cannot be overcome from one day to the next. In the area of security, too, therefore, it is necessary to work stubbornly and patiently toward a change in relationships and to build bridges wherever possible.

When we offered the Soviet Union and the Eastern European states an exchange of bilateral statements renouncing the use of force, not the last thing we wanted was to show that the Federal Republic was striving toward its goals only through the peaceful collaboration of all the European nations involved. For this reason we did not insist on a specific form for the exchange of these declarations. This is to be clarified in the course of negotiations..

Once such a renunciation of force has contributed to an improvement of the atmosphere, then the possibility of further agreements that—at first without any change in both alliances—would promote a rapprochement could be probed. Thus, for instance, the exchange of observers at military maneuvers or of permanent observation posts would communicate a greater feeling of security vis-à-vis surprise attacks. Later, more comprehensive agreements would be conceivable between East and West that could entail a change in the alliances and even one day lead to their replacement.

In the preliminary work for a European security system a starting point might be that the present alliances continue, to begin with, and be interrelated. It is also possible to dissolve the pacts and replace them by something new. There are overwhelming grounds for the idea of starting out from the first "model" whenever this theme becomes a matter of practical politics.

It is a good thing for these questions to be reflected on and debated within the alliance. We have a vital interest in these labors, and we are busy with our own constructive contributions. In order to forestall any misinterpretations I hasten to add that the measures and changes being considered must not imply any sacrifice of security. Further, a European security system cannot be divorced from the rights and duties of the world powers. Again and again since the end of the war the East and West have, in the numerous negotiations concerning the future of Germany, presented suggestions for European security, even though very often with tactical aims and not always in touch with reality.

These have become almost limitless in number and content. They have dealt primarily with the following:

The spatial area encompassed by the security system
The stationing or withdrawal of foreign troops
Limitations on armaments
Replacement of the alliances by security regulations based on treaties
Inspections and guarantees

But agreements between East and West in the area of security will come into being only if they are balanced, that is, if neither side is favored. Here what will primarily have to be taken into consideration is that the reductions of armaments and troop strengths in Europe would give the Soviet Union, because of its geographical proximity, a relative advantage. To compensate for this the West must retain a nuclear and conventional defense posture that excludes any miscalculation as to the readiness of the United States militarily to guarantee the maintenance of the security system.

The Federal government has declared its readiness, not only vis-à-vis France, to discuss without prejudice the security problems of the 1970s. To the Federal Republic of Germany, and not to it alone, it is, however, indispensable for the United States to become the bearer and the coguarantor of any future security system. There can be no functioning security system for Europe without the participation of the United States and the Soviet Union.

After the conclusion of the sought-for rapprochement, an agreement will have to be made for a just European peace order in which the division of Germany can also be overcome. It is to be hoped that the governments of the Soviet Union and of the Eastern European states, taking as their starting point the real interests of their peoples, will collaborate with us in the establishment of that peace order. Only in this way can the consequences of the last war be enduringly eliminated and the European nations find their way to fruitful cooperation.

Even though the Soviet leadership is manifestly seeking to avoid international crises in Central Europe, it would still like to limit the détente in such a way that the status quo is congealed, the United States is forced out of European politics, and NATO is dissolved; in that way the Soviet Union would achieve the position of the premier power in Europe. Till now the Soviet government seems to have shown little interest in any détente with the goal of "an enduring and just peace order in Europe."

It is unlikely that the Soviet Union will attempt to expand its power to Western Europe by military means as long as NATO can carry out its defense mission. Nevertheless, there is a noteworthy discrepancy between Soviet military policy and the declared peace aims of Soviet foreign policy. At the conferences of Bucharest (July 1966) and Karlsbad (April 1967) the Soviet Union succeeded in formulating a general line. Nevertheless, within the Warsaw pact divergent opinions concerning the policy vis-à-vis the West manifested themselves. The conflict between Moscow and Peking furthered the "polycentric" movement in the Communist camp. The Soviet Union had to sue for the support of its Eastern European allies in the clash with China and found itself obliged to loosen its curb on them. Meanwhile, the situation has changed again.

The success of the liberal tendencies within the Eastern European states will also depend on whether they can be persuaded by a patient, undramatic policy of the advantages of cooperation between East and West, without their having to fear any jeopardy to the system they have developed. It will be particularly important to convince the Soviet Union itself of the advantages of the sought-for European peace order.

Direct negotiations between NATO and the organization of the Warsaw pact seem for the time being to be pointless. Instead, preference will have to be shown to the bilateral exchange of opinions of the NATO partners with the states of the East. However, a multiplicity of conversational contacts must not give rise to the impression that the Western partners can be played off against each other. We therefore support the view within the alliance that a canvassing of views must take place concerning important matters that affect all or a number of partners before they are discussed bilaterally with the states of the East.

The Soviet Union is giving very strong support to the suggestion of convoking a "European security conference." We think the time for such a conference has not yet come; nevertheless, we shall give painstaking scrutiny to all the suggestions made on this point. An East-West conference will be sensible only if it can discuss more than the sanctioning of the status quo. It would have to take up the goal of overcoming the division of Europe and seek first of all a *modus vivendi* between all parties. It must at the very least give the assurance that it will promote the process of détente. Furthermore, its failure might mean a serious drawback.

A militarily balanced, phased reduction of the armed forces on both sides would contribute substantially to the détente and facilitate the solution of the political problems of Europe. We ourselves have made it quite clear that we are for troop reductions if they are undertaken as measures for the control of armaments on both sides and can be made use of for an active policy of détente and for establishing the peace in Europe. Parity in the reduction of troops would improve the political climate in Central Europe and loosen up the status quo, as well as improve the psychological situation of the population in the other part of Germany.

As already indicated, the unilateral troop reductions of the West projected for 1968 have, until now, not moved Moscow to take the path of a reciprocal action. As an advance concession toward the Soviet standard offer of a parallel, equally phased withdrawal of foreign troops from both parts of Germany, this Western action is quite unambiguous. The Soviet Union, by an "appropriate counterconcession," would open the road to more far-reaching troop reductions that would, indeed, then be evenly balanced. A negative reaction of the Soviet Union would have to be assessed as an indication that it desires to gain strategic advantages from any overtures on the part of the West.

In any further stages of a parallel reduction on a reciprocal basis thought must also be taken of the withdrawal of a mixture of combat forces that on the Western side would contain more of an atomic nature and on the Eastern side, to make up for it, more conventionally armed troops. A connection might be made with the suggestion made in the German "peace note" of May 1966 "not to increase any further the number of atomic weapons in Europe but to reduce them in stages." Here there are concrete points of departure for initial steps toward a system of European security. If the Soviet Union wants the Cold War to recede once and for all into history, if it, like ourselves, desires peace and security for all Europe, then concrete results will not be difficult to arrive at.

In an interview with the Polish newspaper *Trybuna Ludu* published on January 7, 1968, Foreign Minister Rapacki cast a glance back at one year of Polish diplomatic activity. Among other things he said that it could be seen that the endeavors on behalf of a genuine, enduring détente, of security and cooperation in Europe were growing in strength. More and more people in the East and West were in accord that what should be striven for as a foundation for European security was the creation of a collective security system that would make possible the elimination of the present-day division of Europe into hostile military groupings.

These realizations and considerations belong to the solid substance of Federal Republic policy. They have found expression not only in government statements, speeches, and interviews but also in practical politics. Within the circle of the allies, as well as in the measures and suggestions touching on the relationship of the Federal Republic of Germany to the East of Europe, the Federal Republic is working toward an enduring and just peace order in Europe by means of the dissolution of the tensions between East and West. There is, to be sure, a decisive difference to be noted: Polish Foreign Minister Rapacki has loaded many preconditions into his suggestions. We do not set any preconditions. We are convinced that objective cooperation and the removal of mistrust, will enable the creation of the prerequisites to make soluble the problems that now still seem insoluble.

At the same time, I should like to keep in view the fact that there are points of contact between the suggestions of the Polish Foreign Minister and our own suggestions. Like the Federal Republic, the Polish government says that it regards the renunciation of the use and threat of force in reciprocal relations and of nonintervention in the internal affairs of others as a foundation—or, as Rapacki said, as a suitable framework—for a gradual construction of general European security. There may be differing views as to the manner in which that renunciation is to be realized, but what is important is—and on this point there do not seem to be any differences of principle between the Polish government and ourselves—that the general renunciation of force to which all concerned are already committed be reiterated and thus brought to bear specifically on the East-West relationship.

Like the Federal government, the Polish government, judging by the remarks of its Foreign Minister, sees in a worldwide treaty banning the proliferation of atomic weapons a means of consolidating the peace in Europe and of facilitating further steps toward a détente.

Similar to the plans that bear his and Gomulka's name, Rapacki has during the past year repeatedly suggested regional agreements for a freezing and subsequent removal of nuclear armament in as large a zone of Europe as possible. The German government has submitted a similar suggestion, that is, the suggestion that atomic weapons, under effective controls, be cut down in stages throughout Europe while the correlation of forces is preserved.

The Polish Foreign Minister reaffirms the necessity of a safeguards system for the supervision of regional accords. In his opinion such supervision would prevent surprise attacks. We share that opinion.

Foreign Minister Rapacki has also suggested that conventional armaments in Europe be lowered parallel with measures in the nuclear field. This suggestion coincides with the endeavors of the Federal Republic to reduce the massive military confrontation in Central Europe by means of a phased and balanced reduction of forces on both sides of the line of demarcation.

The Federal government regards it as realistic to give the theme of the renunciation of force a topical significance. It goes without saying that this need not prevent embarking on considerations that go beyond that on the road to the improvement of European security. I regard it as sensible—here, too, like the Polish Foreign Minister—to recognize the fact that NATO and the Warsaw pact are both reliable instruments of our security today and in the foreseeable future. Their existence need not stop the reduction of armaments.

There is no lack of subjects for an objective conversation. There is, to be sure, an obstacle to it, an artificial obstacle, when maximalist standpoints are adopted. This holds for all parties. Maximalism is an obstacle that should be recognized as such everywhere.

19

PATHS
TO SOLIDARITY

The present-day world is determined quite decisively by the United States and the Soviet Union, the two superpowers. Europe has largely become an object of world politics. There is a line of division running through its center, a symbol of the extent to which the creative energies of this Continent mutually hinder and consume each other.

On the path to a Europe that will once again draw strength, in security and peaceful order, for its own viability, there will be many obstacles to overcome. We shall have to make our way forward step by step with patience if we wish to further reduce the mutual fear of people and of nations.

Although this progress will be possible only very slowly in the field of political relations, of security, and of the differing systems and views of life, there are other areas in which the people of Europe can even now take steps to meet and work together, including economics, science, technology, and culture.

In the industrial societies of our world, in which distances are shrinking and the possibilities of communication are growing, the human being finds himself placed in a sort of international solidarity from which he can remove himself only at the expense of his own welfare, progress, and common sense. In many areas tasks are set for the scientist, technician, and organizer whose solution goes beyond or unendurably burdens the material, financial, and human resources of a nation. The need for cooperation imposed by things on people and vice-versa gives Europe the possibility of finding itself once again.

Even now cooperation across the still existing line of division is possible; up to now it has existed only in fits and starts. Joint projects do not necessarily have to start with space travel, the atomic industry, and electronics, even though they too are on the agenda. The time is not yet ripe for these as long as mistrust and a concern for one's own safety go on existing.

There are, however, areas in which one can imagine joint projects that will not lessen the military equilibrium but instead strengthen reciprocal security. Here I am thinking of a comprehensive general European infrastructure, a system of providing and distributing energy, the joint building up of a modern transport network, and the telecommunications technology. Such an infrastructure extending beyond boundaries would, after all, necessarily facilitate communication and substantially increase commercial exchange, which no one can deny are in the interest of Europe.

The advantages offered by an exchange of the results of scientific research and technical and industrial developments are so obvious that they do not have to be especially emphasized. But for this type of exchange what is needed is a minimal amount of confidence, which is only just beginning to be gradually built up. Here the first task of the policy of peace and detente will be to open the way to progress. Then cooperation will be able to take on many forms, from basic research to the international use of the structural and geographical advantages in locating industries, with the ultimate goal of the complete freedom of movement for people throughout the whole of Europe.

In order to come closer to such developments new organizations would not necessarily have to be created. There are institutions already capable of development, such as the World Trade Council, the United Nations Economic Commission for Europe (ECE), and the General Agreement on Tariffs and Trade (GATT). Also bilateral contacts on both a state and nonstate level can lead further, as has already been shown in individual cases.

The Federal Republic is ready to take this path, which will benefit everyone, in cooperation with its friends. It is existentially dependent on a peaceful development, because of its geographical position and because of the dense intermeshing of its problems with the surrounding world. Even hints of a parallel attitude in East and West would be hailed by us as a preliminary stage for conversations and agreements.

In this connection we should not forget the cultural exchange that could smooth the way for some positive development. All previous experience confirms this. I am of the opinion that cultural policy ought to be one of the supporting pillars of foreign policy, because modern foreign policy must be understood as a unity consisting of all its elements. No one ought to balk at the phrase "cultural policy," for it does not imply any desire to manipulate cultural values for political purposes. This would be a far too narrow interpretation of what policy is. Doubts of this kind must be patiently cleared up precisely in Eastern Europe, although here they exist in some circles primarily because people project conclusions from themselves onto others.

Such misunderstandings have prevented our cultural exchange from meeting with a like response from the countries of Eastern Europe. It is not we who are unreceptive; our efforts in this area are comparable to those of any Western country. Whenever there is a need for cultural accords in order to achieve a greater liberalization we are ready to discuss them at any time. Luckily there still exists a certain fund of common European cultural values, which might become still richer and receive many new impulses if communication were free and untrammeled.

General European cooperation is not an end in itself. The last third of the twentieth century will be determined by new fronts. The opulent "north of the cities" is contrasted increasingly by the impoverished "south of the peasants." The consumer states, for which the management of surplus has become a problem, stand out against the still-unindustrialized part of the world whose efforts, in view of the population explosion and of famine, do not even extend far enough to maintain their low standards.

Dealing with this dichotomy is the great task of mankind and especially of the highly industrialized nations. It can be solved only if great portions of the energies of the nations are not, as they have been hitherto, eaten up in conflict, in the menacing competition of armaments. The scientific, technical, and economic means for the conquest of need are on hand or can be created.

It is here that a historic opportunity presents itself. It is impossible to see what might stop us or others from cooperating closer in this regard with Eastern Europe and the Soviet Union. Joint projects do not merely bring objective advantages but also reduce mistrust and can give rise to demonstrations of good will.

Europe has no time to lose. It should take over a portion of the tasks facing the world. This not only would contribute to the lessening of present-day tensions in a worldwide framework but it would make a decisive contribution to deflecting onto the orderly path of progress the upheavals that otherwise would have tragic consequences for everyone.

20

...AND
THE THIRD WORLD

Anyone who mentions the Third World today instantly evokes the idea of aid for development, which is not popular. The story of the golden bed and other stories have not been forgotten. Anyone who equates the concept of the Third World to the concept of developmental aid—more particularly of its distortion—is thinking incorrectly.

As mayor of Berlin and as the chairman of my party I had occasion to meet with numerous statesmen from Asia and Africa before becoming Foreign Minister. At times I would feel a little ashamed to discover how little I knew of the concerns of those countries and youthful peoples and how much interest for our own problems I was expecting from just these countries.

Every one of these countries has a vote in the United Nations, and its vote is counted there just as carefully as that of the United States or the Soviet Union. We sometimes smile at the throng of young nations and their lack of economic strength, of power, of international weight, and often forget that we are smiling somewhat at ourselves, too. To be sure, it is true that strategic bombers, divisions, and technology count, but the world we want for ourselves must also heed and take seriously countries and nations that are not great powers in the classical sense and that have no prospect of ever becoming that—just like, for example, Germany.

The growing contradictions between the developed and the underdeveloped nations—that is, the contradiction between north and south on our planet—will prevent any frontal collision between the numerous small countries and the few great countries. Nevertheless, it is unmistakable that the nongreat powers to an increasing extent are aware of and, today very largely independent of each other, represent similar interests. The Federal Republic can journey for a considerable stretch of the same road in tandem with a good many of these countries.

Understood precisely, this means that the Federal Republic must develop a world policy, though of course not in the sense of a world power policy; but the natural interests of every state demand that it make its weight effective. The political arena has grown bigger. The Federal Republic, too, must become familiar with the fact that, as Professor von Weizsäcker has expressed it, we are approaching the era of *internal world politics.*

Germany does not have much world political experience. The not always felicitous and never systematic excursions outside the Continent before World War 1 cannot be described as genuine world politics. In the period between the two wars some people, to be sure, dreamed of reviving the colonial idea, but that remained no more than a dream— luckily for us. Vanquished and divided Germany found itself for the first time confronted by the question of how it intended to determine its position in the concert of a rapidly increasing family of nations: what interests it had to represent as an equal among equals in Asia and Africa, and from what points of view the traditional relations with South America, which at bottom had been determined by culture and economics, had to be reviewed.

It is no reproach, merely a statement of fact, that hitherto this has rarely happened, as is quite natural, because the Federal government was always being confronted by novel decisions that were more urgent or seemed to be. In addition, we also needed time in order to become aware of the breakneck development that, with the birth of the youthful states in Africa and Asia, in its turn diminished the relative weight of Europe—that would have diminished its relative weight even if the two superpowers had not emerged at the same time.

I was thoroughly aware of this need to "catch up" when I took over my present office. A conference in Tokyo of our ambassadors to Asia in April 1967 helped me greatly in understanding the new necessities in detail. By the time this book appears a similar ambassadorial conference will have taken place for Africa in Abidjan, Ivory Coast, and a conference for Latin America will have followed in the autumn of 1968. It will be possible after that to sum up the results.

Independent of such conferences, a number of elements of the world political situation can be tabulated for the Federal Republic:

We are not pursuing a power political role of our own in any continent.

We have an interest in the termination of existing conflicts and in the nonemergence, so far as is possible, of any new conflicts.

Wherever we can work together toward a détente we intend to be ready to cooperate.

We are not delivering any weapons to areas of tension.

In these principles the negative formulations, too, have a positive significance. One of the few good aspects of our legacy from the past is that we do not have to pay off any of the mortgages of being a former colonial power. None of the youthful nations has had to wrest its freedom from Germany. To that extent we do not run into any prejudices but meet a readiness for trust and friendship. That is a fund of capital that the Federal Republic must preserve and can preserve only if it applies its policy of peace and détente also and visibly with respect to other continents.

The world has grown so small today that every conflict, even though it does not attain the scope and the cruelty of the Vietnam war and even if the two superpowers are not directly committed, weighs on the situation in Europe. Every conflict conceals within itself the tendency to maintain or to petrify tension and divisions. Thus, every conflict works against the interests of Europe and of Germany. To that extent we are the natural allies of all those who wish for détente, disarmament, and consolidation of the peace. The more active we are in such questions, the more our voice will find a hearing beyond Europe, too.

Our relationship to the individual states is guided by the principle of nonintervention in their domestic and foreign affairs and by the principle of reciprocity and equality of rights.

It is in the nature of principles to sound general, to find agreement, but not always to be easily carried out. The principles just mentioned above have two effects that in detail do not seem so much a matter of course. Reciprocal respect and nonintervention mean that we must not make our relations with a country dependent on whether its form of government suits us. In most Third World countries there is no parliamentary democracy or anything resembling what we mean by that. The stage of development of these countries very often requires other forms of government. We do not have any political models for export.

What we can do, to the extent that we are asked, is to make our experience available. And that we do gladly. In many countries our social order—despite all the shortcomings we are familiar with—arouses great interest. Our trade unions are sought-after helpmates for the development of many countries.

Every continent and every one of its peoples have a tradition of their own, a history of their own, an experience of their own. For this reason alone it is impossible, or it leads only to unrest, if one wishes to transport automatically anything that has been proved among us here in Germany or elsewhere. All we can do is to transmit our own experience, and we must say to every country in all frankness that it must do the chief part of the work itself; every country, in accordance with its own situation and its own interests, must develop, test out, and fill with life the form peculiar to it with the possibilities at hand. In this there will come about new social forms from which the European or indeed the developed countries in general will be able to benefit later on, for we have no grounds for arrogance. The high state of development of our technique is still no proof, as far as human worth and the coexistence of human beings are concerned, that we cannot learn from other cultures. At the same time we realize that these cultures are ineluctably exposed to the process of technicalization and in this will be obliged to demonstrate the strength of their creative substance.

A further consequence of these principles is that we have no fundamental objection if these countries also develop their commerce and their cultural exchange with the other part of Germany, too—not only out of respect for these countries but also because of our view that more contacts with the outside world and a rising standard of living are in the interests of our countrymen between the Elbe and the Oder. Furthermore, it is not compatible with our national dignity to carry abroad to other continents our internal German disputes and problems, to put it mildly, or to vent them there bureaucratically. Reciprocity and equality of rights do not mean, of course, that the Federal Republic surrenders its own interests. We shall not run after anyone who does not accept our policy of détente, including internal German détente. We are no petitioners. Nor must the Federal Republic allow itself to be blackmailed, either. If a government is of the opinion that it will get a better commodity or better credits in East Berlin, it should do so.

Every country is free to select its own friends. This also applies to the Federal Republic. There is no threat in such an attitude, nor can I see any misfortune if a team of machinists from Madgeburg sets up a well-functioning German installation somewhere in the world.

If we cultivate the friendship of many countries and develop our common interests, the Federal Republic will then find political and moral support whenever it needs it.

There is a third manner by which we can document our friendship with the nations of the Third World. We know today that in a relatively short time we shall be confronted by the problem of combating naked hunger throughout the world. The curve of growth of the areas opened up for cultivation is substantially flatter than the curve designating the growth of population. The "have-nots" against the "haves" was the situation in many European countries during the first industrial revolution, and such tensions, on a world scale, now await us. It makes no difference whether we think of ourselves as the Christian Occident, as a libertarian democracy, or as humanist socialists—the challenge facing us all will put our common ideals to the test.

The tasks arising out of it are titanic. They transcend the forces of every individual nation. This does not mean, to be sure, that the Federal Republic could not make its own contribution to development aid. I see this contribution primarily in an area that will enable these countries to gird themselves against the perils of overpopulation and hunger.

It is not opportunism but the simple truth to say that these tasks of the future can be coped with better by a united Germany, a united Europe, than by a divided one. Europe itself has fallen back and must catch up. There has been as yet no success in convincing the peoples of Asia, Africa, and Latin America that European unification lies in their own direct interest because that is what will release powerful forces.

A Europe grounded in peace and security would be a powerful element of stability. And it is stability that the youthful nations need, that the world needs, so that humanity, which increases daily by the number of inhabitants of a middle-size city, can exist with human dignity. This may sound as though it were a question of some remote prospect, but the lapse of time between the day the first atomic explosion mushroomed up to the skies and the beginning of this year of 1969 is much longer than the lapse of time left to us if we are to save literally many millions of people from death by starvation.

At the beginning of this chapter I recalled that most people think of development aid when the Third World is talked about. As far as the problems of the Third World and the position of the Federal Republic are concerned, development aid is only a single point among many, and not even the essential one.

Perhaps what is necessary is a negative line of demarcation of what development aid is not, or should not be: it should not be charity, not a purchase price for countries or people, not the indispensable fertilizer for mere show-case projects meant to satisfy a desire for prestige. It ought to be aimed at economic utility, as help for the purpose of self-help, with eyes directed at the problems of the next ten to fifteen years. As such it is help for us, too—for our economy, for our exports, for the establishment of markets, for the ensuring of jobs. There is no need for us to be ashamed of speaking these truths aloud.

We should see to it that projects really are of mutual interest. Here the industrial countries have sinned no less than the underdeveloped countries. Every country would like to be independent, but our world—even the most powerful countries—is moving into a situation of constantly growing mutual dependences. Dependence that is not oppressive, in which each individual can develop fully is the goal for the position of the individual in society and of the states in the family of nations.

In the countries of Asia our peace policy has found a positive echo, and many unused possibilities offer themselves for economic cooperation. Strengthened contacts between the economies of Germany and Japan would also benefit regional cooperation in Southeast Asia. For our development policy India, Pakistan, and Indonesia are of special interest because of their size and political importance.

In Asia—though not there alone—there is an impression that export trade is being damaged by the EEC. The dynamics of the Common Market, which lead to increased imports, is overlooked. This factor adds all the greater importance to the demonstration that we champion a liberal course for the EEC, open to the world.

Everywhere in Asia, though with varying intensity, there is interest in cultural relations with Germany, and there have been excellent beginnings toward cooperation in the areas of science and technology. However, we shall be able to perform the numerous economic, cultural, and political tasks lying ahead of us only if our citizens show a clearer recognition of the meaning of Asia for their own interests. We laid all this down at the ambassador's conference in Tokyo and made the additional point that the Federal Republic must lend support where traditional friendship and existing good will come halfway to meet our striving for cooperation, détente, and stabilization.

Of the 122 votes in the United Nations (and in the other international organizations) 39 belong to African states, yet Africa has no more than 10 percent of the world's population. This disproportionate voting strength, but above all, too, our commercial interests, have made it seem necessary for us to be represented almost everywhere by resident ambassadors. Apart from the United Nations, Bonn is the greatest center for ambassadors from black Africa.

Our relations with most of the African states are good; with some of them, very good. For their development they need close cooperation with the industrial nations. The Federal Republic is a sought-after partner, because Germans have a reputation for efficiency and stand less under the suspicion of wishing to meddle than do the former colonial rulers or the Communist countries. An additional link to the eighteen associates of the EEC is taking shape.

Although our policy strives for good partnership, this does not prevent Communist propaganda, especially out of East Berlin, from denigrating us as "neocolonialists" because of our normal relations with South Africa, the Portuguese possessions, and Rhodesia. This relationship has nothing whatever to do with sympathy for racial inequality.

The process of decolonization has been accomplished only in the most recent past and is not yet quite finished. We must expect major convulsions to lie ahead of the continent. It is our task to take care of German interests on the spot even in difficult circumstances, to contribute within the framework of our potentialities to the development and consolidation of the new states, and to further the contact between Africa and Europe, which in the future will be very important for both sides.

In the Middle East, too, we are bound to be concerned with the protection of our economic interests. We likewise have an interest in preventing the security of Europe from being jeopardized by the "southeast flank."

During the Middle East conflict that in June 1967 culminated in an armed clash, we followed a policy of noninterference. This position—propped up on the recommendations of the United Nations—is bound up with the desire for an enduring, just, peaceful solution.

Noninterference does not mean that we could accept a policy aimed at the destruction of the state of Israel; that would be morally reprehensible and would run counter to the properly understood interests of all parties. The restitution payments that were agreed on against the macabre background of the annihilation of millions of Jewish lives have been settled. Today Israel receives economic aid as part of our normal, worldwide programs.

The Arab states have also participated in the German programs, and we are ready for more comprehensive cooperation. Our readiness to give humanitarian aid has been announced, and the Federal government has declared itself ready to make special efforts on behalf of the refugees in the coming years.

In 1965, after the establishment of relations with Israel, nine Arab states broke off diplomatic relations with the Federal Republic. Morocco, Tunisia, and Libya did not join in this measure; Jordan resumed relations in 1967, as did the Republic of South Yemen, established at the beginning of 1968. We have remained present in all capitals and have been able to make various contacts that will serve normalization. This is also to be desired because the cultural bonds that have always existed between the Arab world and Germany can be elaborated and amplified on a friendly basis.

Latin America does not appreciate being drawn into the unnuanced collective concept of "undeveloped countries." And in fact there is a fundamental element in our relationship to most of the countries of Central and South America that arises out of common principles of freedom and human dignity. The Latin American peoples feel themselves to be wholly part of the West. This relationship goes beyond spiritual and cultural connections.

Yet it is precisely on this subcontinent that the question arises as to whether or not the democracies are capable of renovating old structures, of linking together economic growth and social security, and of keeping the banner of progress from falling into the wrong hands.

A number of Latin American governments have begun to tackle the solution of the great economic, sociopolitical, and population problems. German and European policy with respect to Latin America must be aimed at establishing a partnership for progress that will rest on common interests.

German aid beyond the traditionally well-anchored economic and cultural relations can only be modest. It must be embedded in the deepening of political conversations and in the sharing of each other's problems. The feeling of reciprocal dependence, of attachment, and of a common world political responsibility must be strengthened and must prove itself in the chilly air of this era.

21

LESSONS
OF YESTERDAY—
SIGNALS FOR THE FUTURE

In all the ages of human history the idea of eternal peace has been the goal and content of utopias and philosophical systems. The practical results have been rather depressing. But the spiritual energies that were devoted to this ideal have nevertheless not been squandered futilely. Without them there would not be some of the moral principles that in spite of all the tensions in the world have remained alive.

A peace policy in our time must apply itself to the host of problems in the sequence of the realizability of their solutions. It must move on from the simple to the difficult.

This decision in favor of what is realizable is no novelty in the history of peace efforts but comes to light in plans for European unification that can display a history of some six centuries. In spite of all differences they had one objective in common: to set up in Europe an enduring peace order. But they all shared the fate of either remaining no more than drafts or else collapsing in the very first attempt at realization.

Beyond or instead of an immediate regional solution, these efforts tended toward a global peace organization. The League of Nations—with its reasonable and still relevant objectives—was a great hope for many people after World War I. But it was that, unfortunately, only in the preparatory stage. When it came to life, it was incapacitated, by the abstention of America and Soviet Russia and by the exclusion of Germany, from really mastering the problems of Europe and of the world. The idea of international solidarity could not be established. National antagonisms were too strong, and frictions did not allow any space for the beginnings of integration.

The United Nations, too, which was founded at the end of World War II in San Francisco as an optimistic scheme of the victorious powers, is not a full-fledged or perfect representative organ of the nations. Germany is not represented in it, nor the People's Republic of China—Germany because it is divided, China because it is isolated. Nevertheless, the United Nations has a different structure and quality than the League of Nations. It, too, is incapable of eliminating weighty conflicts of interests, and in any "crisis management" success and failure are wholly dependent on whether or not the world powers work together and are capable of uniting from one case to another. But the United Nations has nevertheless established peace in numerous regional conflicts and accomplished a great deal, not only in a humanitarian way but also in concrete international cooperation. This speaks for its usefulness. Beyond that the General Assembly of the United Nations is a mirror of the opinions, hopes and interests, tensions, and conflicts in this world and thus a source of information and inspiration for the foreign policy of many states.

The Federal Republic of Germany does not stand outside the United Nations, though it is not a full member. It belongs to the European Regional Economic Commission of the Economic and Social Council and to all its special and auxiliary organizations. It is making substantial contributions to all the important aid and development funds and is invited to collaborate on specific occasions by the member states and by the Secretariat. Its permanent presence in New York and Geneva offers interesting possibilities for diplomatic and political contacts. The assembly halls and corridors are a place for encounters not easily duplicated elsewhere.

The United Nations is important for us, too. We must not, to be sure, expect too much from it in the way of a cure for the European division and for the establishment of a general European peace order. This task has been set for the Europeans and cannot, in any case, be solved by majority resolutions in the New York palace of glass.

The perniciousness of the European division really does not need to be demonstrated any further. Power blocs that have been formed against one another and are more or less solidly constructed cannot last very long in a narrow space without lapsing into the dreadful danger of a conflict. That is the lesson of history. But the two power blocs on European soil have at the same time organized themselves into two—varying in nature—social orders. In both domains the bilateral possibilities of conflict have been reduced. This state of affairs is to be preferred to a balkanization, with all its incalculable consequences. A collapse of the two alliance systems without their being replaced by a new order would not promise a healthy future.

Social orders are not immutable. We are witnessing an evolution of systems. The gray uniformity of Stalinism belongs to the past. And the very appearance of even a reduced threat has been enough to bring some movement into the Western alliance. It is not simple to distinguish here between causes and effects. Is the incipient détente the consequence or the cause of the evolution? The fact remains that we are living in an age of transition.

Hardly anyone will be able any longer to contest the fact that the loosening up of the cohesiveness within the blocs has allowed national identities to become more obviously visible again. This development, which in principle is surely to be welcomed, also conceals risks. A new order will only be found if the centrifugal forces do not gain the upper hand and if a joint effort is made to find a solution to the disputed questions.

No one would wish to assert that there are no longer any national conflicts of interest in Europe. In the West such conflicts make European unification more difficult, and in the Mediterranean area they lead to a considerable and perilous insecurity. National questions exist in the East, too. Yet we know that the revival of national passions leads to disaster. That, too, is the lesson of history.

We cannot foresee the evolution of the coming decades. We do not know if the present-day powers will really be able to maintain the existing order in the era to come. But one thing is certain: it would not be good for security and for the consolidation of the peace if future German governments had no other choice than to pursue national ends by national means. It is a commandment of historical common sense to solve the German question—the greatest national problem of present-day Europe—within the framework of a general European peace order in such a way that the right to self-determination is satisfied by it just as well as the legitimate interests of the neighboring states.

Taking as its starting point the right of the nations to self-determination, a European peace order must lead to new forms of an orderly and no longer inflamed coexistence of nationalities. That holds true for us, too, but we have learned that for us there is no swift or isolated solution. Together with France and with our other Western neighbors we are setting about the work of overcoming the abyss that separates the nations in the East and the West of our continent and that sunders our own country. Only within the framework of a progressive European peace order is a just solution conceivable for our special problems, too.

Our attempts to bring about a détente in the European situation are still overshadowed by the East-West conflict. But this conflict has been transformed and will be transformed still further. Some previous prophets of world revolution have also begun to perceive that there are more important interests and developments than the triumph of an ideological system. The ideological revolutionary must, in the age of atomic weapons and space flight, become a relic of the past. I am therefore convinced that we—as the result of a process full of contradictions—shall make progress when it is a question of normalizing relations between the nations and states of Eastern and Western Europe.

Europe will ultimately comprehend that the peoples in the East and the West share a common destiny beyond everything that divides them. This destiny can be turned to good only by an enduring peace order. That is the way in which we intend to work on the construction of the European community and on making a bridge across Europe. Anyone who sabotages this policy becomes a disturber of the peace. In the long run disturbers of the peace will prove unable to maintain themselves in Europe and in the world. Anyone who pretends that this policy is neo-Nazi, revanchist, and militaristic is denouncing, with outmoded catchwords, a policy of truthfulness. We have invited statesmen from the West and the East to come to us, to talk with us, and to form their own picture of German life. It is not we who are threatening our neighbors with military aggression. We offer them, rather, a mutual renunciation of force. It is not we who vilify everyone who does not share our opinion in everything. We endeavor to argue in an objective way and to put ourselves on good terms with those, too, who think differently.

It is true that the securing of peace and order in Europe is not difficult only because of the existing power relationships. The ideological division is still a reality. But even the ideology of communism is not a canon cast in iron that could survive unchanged for centuries. Today communism, even in its own realm, is anything but a strictly hierarchized and undisputed world religion. It has been transformed, and it will be transformed still further. Transformation happens to be the destiny of systems in this age of ours.

Our own Western social orders are surely not immutable, either. As far as we can foresee—and in accordance with the will of their peoples—they will cling firmly to the idea of democracy. But they will go on constantly developing further; they will have to be open to change and to the new challenges of the surrounding world in order to extend to the limits of the horizons that keep being set further and further away by technology, by the sciences, and by the new industries. The freedom of the individual will soon no longer be a question of a political constitution but an organizational problem of a technicalized environment.

It is too soon to speak of any rapprochement between the two contradictory worlds of ideas. Yet these are developments that I do not consider illusory but ineluctable and that we must prepare ourselves for. The material future of mankind will be molded still more strongly than now by technique and by the natural sciences. There will be little room for ideological dogmas. The socio-organizational problems of the highly industrialized states will grow steadily more similar to each other in the course of technical-scientific progress. That can facilitate the understanding between them and permit them to become more conscious of the common nature of their interests.

For the time being the present offers only scattered signs that make such a development believable. Nevertheless, there appears to be, here and there, a clearer recognition of the vast demands heralding the advent of the future. The states of Eastern Europe are also subject to the urgent priority of solving economic and social problems as rapidly as possible, and such solutions will be possible only in a stable international situation. Greater economic independence must be secured, while at the same time the requisite stability must be still more extensively guaranteed. This is hardly a question of ideology. In the Eastern bloc a system of unity in diversity is growing up—also a sort of equilibrium of interests, which the leaders of the Communist Party of Rumania have formulated as follows: "Diversity constitutes the ineluctable and irreversible framework for the activity of the Communist parties."

Policy in the Communist countries is almost exclusively determined and controlled by the Communist Party. When changes occur, consequently, they are bound to be internal party changes. Indeed, there are signs of them even now, but that does not imply that they mean any democratization in forms we are familiar with. If the Communist parties intend to carry out their role as leaders of the state, they will require, in view of the challenges of the second industrial revolution, a broader social base than in the past. Endeavors to establish such a broader base are unmistakable everywhere in Eastern Europe. The intellectual and technical elite is strengthening its influence. And the campaign for active collaboration in economic and social life is more intensive than hitherto.

If evolution within the Communist realm keeps being determined more and more strongly by objective necessities and by material interests, this can increase the chances of finding a common language for the assessment and accommodation of interests between East and West in Europe.

These lines had long been written when promising developments took place in Czechoslovakia. They were the exclusive merit of those who, in that country, courageously and with a sense of proportion, did what they thought right. They wanted to make Socialism more attractive and to adjust it to the future. They wanted to prove that Socialism and dictatorship were not necessarily synonymous. The conservative forces then tried to reverse the "1968 Prague Spring" by forcible intervention from outside. The Czechoslovak people has met that attempt with an attitude that commands our whole-hearted admiration. We do not know what the outcome of this struggle will be. And we can but wish that our neighbor nation be spared new sufferings. We do, however, know this: The internal process in the CSSR under the leadership of the changing Czechoslovak Communist Party as of now forms an integral part of European history and like anything that happens on this continent will have its effects on the neighbors, all neighbors, of that country.

In East Berlin little internal progress of communism is to be noted. But the intransigent attitude of the German Communists has less to do with ideology than might often be thought. It is the expression of crude self-interest that sees itself threatened by progress. But if the general European interest in an enduring peace order is what puts its stamp on our future, the East, too, will be unable to ignore the fact that a quarter of the German people is not a pledge worth surrendering security and peace for.

And indeed the recognition is growing that the nations of Europe must and will not simply come to terms with being permanently divided by the conflict between East and West. The insight is growing that Europe belongs together not only through its history but also through its destiny. Even fundamental differences of political conviction and of social structure need not hold back the states of Europe—and will not, as experience has already shown, stop them—from working together in areas of common interest for the consolidation of an enduring peace. Ideological group interest and thinking in terms of blocs will have to retreat behind these "new realities," and it will become obvious how much both the national interest of every people and the interest of Europe require organizing peace.

22

PERSONAL
EXPERIENCES

When I took office I had intended to sit at my desk as much as possible and travel as little as possible. In practice this intention proved to be realizable only to a limited degree. Good will alone does not suffice.

Established practice of consultation makes the foreign minister travel a lot. The amount of time, preparation, and personnel involved is not always proportionate to the results. Yet, even if all concerned were aware of that danger and tried to counteract it, a considerable measure of routine would remain unavoidable.

Wherever one wants to press a point and prompt other governments to some particular course of action or hold them back from certain actions, distant trips are often necessary. Jet flight, which has made even the greatest distance shrink to a few hours, theoretically saves us time. Yet this advance has cost us dearly—just because it seems to take so little time one decides on additional lightning trips. Instead of being made freer because of the modern means of communication—not lazier, but freer for reflection, for reading, and for tranquil conversations—they lead to a highly developed form of slavery.

The teletype sees to it that over and above other information there is a scarcely interrupted torrent of information

coming into the headquarters of the Ministry for Foreign
Affairs. To pick through the abundance, to separate what
is essential from what is otherwise also necessary, and to
study it is once again a question of the economy of energies.
The timetables of government, party, and parliament also
press their rights.

In looking back on the period since the formation of the
present Federal administration in December 1966, I can perceive that the problem of having time for the important
things has become of equal significance alongside all others,
including the most important substantive problem. It is only
a relative consolation to know that one's colleagues are in
the same boat. In any case, it is a sign that governmental
procedure is in urgent need of reform.

In this respect, too, we are living in a period of transition.
The mechanisms of conducting foreign policy in an age of
"world-wide domestic policy" will have to be different from
those that have come down to us. We are working, on occasion painfully, with an outmoded range of instruments today,
when it is a question of assessing the growing drive toward
multilaterality, toward the satisfaction of a hunger for information that scarcely lets up for a single hour, toward the
heeding of the desires of a pluralistic society. The provision
of additional jobs in the budget is occasionally unavoidable,
but it can also mean a postponement of structural decisions.

The word "reform" is—methodologically, in any case—
the answer to this problem. I know that a reform, particularly of the Foreign Office and of the Foreign Service, is a
task that is difficult and not to be realized speedily. One will
have to keep in view the necessary modernization of governmental activity and not pass heedlessly by the experience of
other states. I hope that the basic lines of a reform will be
worked out among us before the next elections.

This Federal administration set about its task in December 1966 with some elan and much good will. If one recalls the very modest and by no means roseate picture of the situation in which the Federal Republic of Germany found itself at that time with respect to foreign policy, one may surely say without exaggeration that the danger of isolation has been banished. We have gained some more latitude, and we have found out at the same time just how limited it is.

It is a question not only of the restrictions arising out of objective factors. Subjective, internal political factors, too, can be a substantial obstacle to the development of an independent and realistic foreign policy. And indeed, not only traditional, nationalistic, and selfish party influences exercise a retarding effect; there are also obstructions that grow up out of illusions, a flight from reality, and political incomprehension.

It was impossible to bring about the extension of the European communities in *one* new swoop, but it seems certain to me that this theme will no longer be dropped. This single, decisive component of our European policy will make a heavy claim on our activities in the field of foreign policy. And we shall have to accustom ourselves to the idea that on occasion we shall have to waive agreement and ready ourselves for a difficult period.

Nor will the other, the East-West, component of our European policy bring more than partial further advances. For a long time now it has been my view that in the condition of German division time cannot be relied on to work for us. The policy of détente meant casting off some ballast; it made our ship ocean-going, to be sure during a period of ebb tide. But unlike the times of ebb and full tide, in politics the times when the waters will rise again cannot be determined or forecast with any certainty.

Only very few observers were aware that 1967 brought us, after tenacious efforts on our part, an offer of talks from the Soviet Union, the first ones since the resumption of diplomatic relations in 1955. Everyone will understand that the thawing out of congealed and iced-over barriers between the Soviet Union and the Federal Republic of Germany is impossible in a few months. It is obvious that the restoration of friendly relations lies in our interest. No one can doubt that this is impossible without dangers and risks. Anyone who is afraid of these should not speak about Eastern policy. Anyone who underestimates them should be kept away from Eastern policy.

There can be no question of selling out. These silly catchwords create the impression partly that those in charge of German policy have nothing else in mind and partly that there is nothing else. The problem is formulated by the facts: both sides must probe their positions if they are to and wish to collaborate fruitfully with each other. And that is indispensable for the interest of security and of détente in Europe. At the same time, it can even be useful to recall Konrad Adenauer's recipe—the one about installment payments—that in its time was applied by him with some success to the West. We shall be able to apply this profitably to our relations with the East only if we maintain our relationship of friendship and trust with our allies.

In this relationship there is no either-or. Foreign policy is the sum of all factors made to bear fruit in the interest of a country. Nevertheless, I should like to emphasize here once again that friendship with the United States is of vital consequence for us. It is all the more important if we are steering toward a Europe that is to play its own role and serve the peace by its own means.

The distance between today and the year 2000 is shorter

than that between the year 1933 and the present. Yet we realize that the policy of the Federal Republic of Germany is still influenced by the year 1933 more strongly than by the year 2000. That burden and inheritance cannot be simply shed from our internal politics nor even our thinking. In foreign policy our opponents take advantage of the general habit of and the capacity for keeping the past in mind better and for imagining the future with greater difficulty and turn these against us. Our friends as well as our enemies, both inside and outside, must be fully aware of the fact that the problems of tomorrow—the population explosion, the north-south conflict, the revolutions in science and technology— need to be solved today. That is impossible as long as we keep looking backward.

We have entered the last third of this century. German foreign policy must be free for it—or make itself free for it. And by doing that we shall set free additional energies for peace in Europe and the world.

About the Author

World-famous mayor of Berlin: 1957–1966 (he left Germany in 1933 and served in the Norwegian Resistance during World War II), Herr WILLY BRANDT is a key figure in the current German coalition government, which took office in December 1966, holding the offices of Foreign Minister and Vice Chancellor. As leader of the Social Democratic Party, he is a strong contender for the chancellorship of Germany when elections are held in the fall of 1969.